BELONG

Also by Russell B. Farr

As Editor

Fantastic Wonder Stories
The Workers' Paradise
    (with Nick Evans)

BELONG

EDITED BY
RUSSELL B. FARR

TICONDEROGA
PUBLICATIONS

for

my parents, Brian Farr & Eve Johnson

who made this journey so many years ago...

Belong edited by Russell B. Farr

Published by Ticonderoga Publications

Designed by Russell B. Farr
Typeset in Sabon and Eurostile

A Cataloging-in-Publications entry for this title is available from the National Library of Australia.

ISBN   978–0–9803531–1–2 (hardcover)
　　　　978–0–9803531–2–9 (tradepaperback)

Ticonderoga Publications
PO Box 29 Greenwood
Western Australia 6924

www.ticonderogapublications.com

10 9 8 7 6 5 4 3 2 1

Contents

A place called home

HOW FAR WOULD *you* go to belong?

For me, 17,996 miles, and 32 years.

I was born in Perth, Western Australia, a child of migrant parents. Throughout my formative years, I didn't really feel like a migrant. My parents were English—from the western suburbs of Greater London—and caucasian, and this put me in a dominant cultural group. They arrived in Australia in 1966, a few years before I was born.

I grew up like the vast majority of kids in my socio-economic demographic. I played cricket, that wonderful game imported from the mother country and thoroughly adopted in its former colony, and football, the Australian variety, an estranged relative of rugby. I sang the national anthem, "Advance Australia Fair", before, during and after it was officially proclaimed. I learnt of the ANZACS, and the futile bravery of the Gallipoli campaign.

Among this upbringing, there were some gaps. When that most noble of sporting rivalries played out, the recurring cricket test series between Australia and England, The Ashes, I didn't cheer as enthusiastically for my adopted home. I sometimes even took a perverse joy from watching England win (I *usually* took that perverse joy, but England only won sometimes).

I watched a lot of English television. The comedies: *The Goodies*, *Yes Minister*, *The Young Ones*, and many more. And of course that great English SF classic, *Dr Who*. Every year, on a late Saturday night in May, I'd be allowed to watch the FA Cup final. I spent countless years calling that sport "soccer" before eventually conceding that it was indeed "Football".

These nudges from the motherland weren't the only issues. I was nudged from within my adopted home. I learned that I was part of an invasion force, part of an army that had been constantly reinforcing for almost 200 years. There is one line of history that claims Australia was founded on 26 January 1788. Western Australia was founded in 1829, by troops and colonists on the *Sulphur*, *Challenger*, *Success* and *Parmelia*.

There is another line of history, running many thousands of years longer. Here the area of Perth that I grew up in was the land of the *Noongar* people, the *Whadjuk Noongar*. I was a *wedjela* in *Noongar boodjar*, a white person in Noongar country. Though never unwelcome, I was a newcomer to an ancient land, and an invader.

Microscopic cracks appeared in the ANZAC legend, too. Not only were there no relatives of mine listed on any war memorial, I came to understand that the whole Gallipoli screwup was planned and led by the English (though, to be fair, a lot of regular English soldiers died in that campaign, too). I came to realise that I had a stronger connection to the incompetent planners than the Australians in the trenches. While other students told stories of their grandfathers in World War II, I had little to say as both my grandfathers died in England before I was born, and my family rarely talked about them.

In an unintentional fit of irony, I created a publishing house that took its name—via a convoluted path—from a place where the English army repeatedly got its arse kicked.

Put mildly and politely, London is a rather tough city. It has been through 2,000 years of people attempting to wipe it off the map, and prevails. The Great Fire in 1666 ravaged great sections of the city, but the locals rebuilt—mostly before the officials had got their plans sorted. The Second World War saw thousands of Londoners killed, whole streets demolished. Huge bombing raids, some watched by my grandmother while pregnant with my father, and who refused to go into an air raid shelter. London even survived Margaret Thatcher.

The terrorist attacks of 7 July 2005 were barely a hiccup, within days Londoners were doing what they had always done. Only two weeks later, a plane carrying me touched down at Heathrow, giving me my first ever glimpse of a country I'd always been connected to yet never seen.

Much as I'd like to think otherwise, London barely moved a hair at my arrival. I was just one of the fifteen million visitors to London that year. I carried a little blue book through the customs area, its cover adorned with an emu and a kangaroo, two animals that are believed to be unable to go backwards. I wouldn't have been alone with that blue book, arriving during an Ashes tour, though the trip was to attend the Glasgow WorldCon, not watch some men in white chase a little red ball.

London moved me. I found myself walking along streets with names that had adorned board games in my youth. I stood in Trafalgar Square, I saw Buckingham Palace—the official residence of the Australian Head of State—and The Tower of London and climbed St Paul's Cathedral. I walked the streets of Whitechapel where Jack the Ripper once roamed. I saw the Houses of Parliament. I drank real pints of bitter like I had seen on all the TV shows, and frequented alehouses where the likes of Charles Dickens used to go. I saw buildings and relics older than anything build by *wedjelas* in *Noongar boodjar*.

As well as all the touristy stuff, I made a personal journey. To the London Borough of Hillingdon, the birthplace of my parents. I walked around an area that had more than personal historical value, it had family historical value. I stood before the houses where my mother and father were born, houses that my grandparents had lived in. The chocolate factory where my father and my father's father had worked. For the first time I could, with absolute certainty, point to places where my grandfathers had been.

In a quiet corner of a quiet street stands a church. On that English summer day, my shoes and socks wet through from the drizzle, I approached the war memorial outside the entry. Scanning through the names my eyes were drawn to one name in particular. In between Evans, T. and Fell, J.A. was a four letter surname I knew like my own, I knew *as* my own, Farr, G.W.

I wasn't expecting this. As a family we're not the closest, or the most openly sharing. If you ask the right questions, we have answers aplenty, but if you don't know the questions to ask, we don't know what you want to know. Never having asked my father if he had a relative die in France in 1917, I didn't know that I'd find his name on the memorial outside a church in Hayes.

When I flew the 8,998 miles back to Perth, I was different. I had found connections for parts of me that were previously disconnected. I had images of places that had family history attached, and places that had ancestral historical value. I had walked on the land that generations of my family before mine, for hundreds if not thousands of years, had walked. I saw a land that generations of my ancestors built—itinerant bricklayers seems to be the family trade—and fought for. This was where history existed before 1966.

England won the Ashes for the first time in over a decade that year. I returned home with a whole pile of questions for my family (and several bottles of excellent whisky). I also remembered the feelings I had walking around London, feeling that this was a place I could have grown up, if things had been different.

That first visit planted many seeds. In 2009 I returned to London. I left Australia carrying the little blue book, and strolled through customs at Heathrow waving a crimson book embossed with a lion and a unicorn. I had claimed my birthright because I *wanted* to, I wanted to belong to two nations. I am more whole as a dual citizen, being able to recognise both the land of my birth and upbringing, and my ancestral home.

One day I hope to achieve a similar personal reconciliation as an invader. I think Australia has a lot of potential, and also has a large challenge, in reconciling the numerous cultures who now call it home.

Belong grew from another seed planted on that trip. As I drank that fine whisky, and talked of my travels and experience, I wanted to share these feelings. I wanted to encourage talented and imaginative writers to explore similar experiences, to go wherever the notion of physical belonging took them.

I wasn't disappointed. Stories arrived from all over Australia and around the world: Argentina, Bulgaria, Canada, the United Kingdom and the United States. In the true fashion of Australian belonging, some now calling the Antipodes home were born elsewhere, and during the making of this anthology one writer crossed "the ditch", moving to Australia's close neighbour New Zealand.

From all the stories that made their own journey Down Under, I have selected twenty-three exceptional tales. Many explored aspects I hadn't even considered, brought viewpoints truly alien, and took me places I could only imagine.

As you turn the page you'll be embarking on a wild, fantastical, amazing journey. There is no need to bring a passport, just don't forget to pack your imagination. You'll be taken into the past and future, from the farthest reaches of the universe into your own backyard. I hope that somewhere between twenty-three writers minds and the following pages, you find a place to belong.

Russell B. Farr
Perth, Australia
March 2010

BELONG

Border Crossing

Penelope Love

"TRAIN'S COMING," FEI announced to Abid and Red.

"Fuck it," said Red. He stomped off to suit up.

"Once more into the breach," Abid said, rising, with a tired grin.

They were all tired. They were short staffed. Fei wondered how Abid and Red coped. The salary was unbelievably high, but you couldn't do this job just for money. Even now, fatigue flattened her when she thought about the full moon in two nights time. She was only holding on until she had enough to buy a house back in Melbourne. Now she grabbed a sheaf of waste paper from the recycling, and a bio-hazard bin. She followed the two men from their office, piled with paperwork and crammed with filing cabinets, into the dressing room.

Red was red-haired, freckled, big and thickset, with cheerful, calloused eyes, almost no eyebrows, and a short fuse that led to tearing his suits, which always tangled on him. Abid was slim, dark, and dextrous. He always took the least time to kit up. He was also the most patient, and his soft brown eyes showed his kind heart. Fei glanced at herself in the mirror as she changed. She was the slightest of the three, quite attractive if you liked the stunned fish look, she told herself in an effort to cheer herself up. She pulled a face at herself as she pulled the hood over her head.

"We look like the three bloody bears," Red grunted over the intercom, as they stomped out. Hazmat suits enforced a slow stride, awkward movements, and occasional comic moments like now, as Red and Abid both tried to go through the door at the same time.

"No need to beat your chests," Fei said, behind them. "I know you're both real men."

"Dream on, baby bear," Red lumbered crab-wise down the stairs.

They came out onto the platform as the train slid in from the desert. The platform was roofed over and sealed, a sizzling fifty degrees; inside the suits it was fifty-five. Sweat dripped from them, and ran down the inside of their suits. The face plates misted up. While they waited for the gates to close behind the train, Abid and Fei hauled up a banner lying by the side of the facility entrance. This was one of Fei's ideas. She wanted to make it permanent, but couldn't squeeze the funds out of management.

"Check point. Please present your papers," the banner read, in a dozen different languages. Fei dumped the used paper at various points along the platform.

Red was counting the cattle cars. "Ten, eleven, twelve. A fucking record," he crowed.

"We've only got the one free holding pen. They won't fit in," Abid worried.

"We'll make 'em," Red said, cheerfully.

"Ready," Fei called.

"As fucking ever."

She signalled the driver, who stayed in his sealed cab. She manned the check point, bio-hazard bin at her feet, as Abid and Red went down the cattle trucks hauling the doors open. She heard them speaking, in a dozen different languages.

"This way to the check point."

"Please queue over there."

"Your visa has come through."

"The doctor will see you now."

Anything to get a reaction.

Clouds of flies boiled from the cattle cars. Then the zombs shuffled out. They had already had a long journey in a crowded boat before arriving in Australian waters, then a train ride through desert heat. They stank, and rotting flesh dropped from them. The flies collected on Fei's suit face plate, further reducing vision. The first zombs out of the trucks paused in confusion.

But Abid and Red were right there for them.

"This way." They pointed, big hand movements. Zombs had basic memories and reactions. Most shuffled awkwardly in the right direction.

"Please queue here." Imprinted memories stayed with them. Memory of what they'd done all their lives. Zomb eyes crawled over Fei. Some brushed past, but others held out their hands, distressed, to show them empty. That was where the recycled paper came in. Thrust some paper into a zomb's hands, and it was happy. It had papers. It had meaning. They also loved queuing. Bunched in a line heading towards the check point, they shuffled forwards contentedly. Fei had made a bus stop sign once for the same reason, but Red put it in a holding pen for fun. An entire holding pen of zombs queued for a bus that never came. It was too much for Fei.

Never let people tell her zombs didn't feel anything, didn't remember being alive. She'd seen the black despair in their eyes, before the maggots ate them.

Now she beckoned them through encouragingly, into 4 holding pen. "Thank you sir, thank you madam," she knew how to say that in eighteen different dialects, and now she ran through all of them. It was often impossible to tell the original race from the swollen and rotting features. She could only hope they were soothed by hearing a kind phrase in their own language. It was important to keep zombs soothed. A happy zomb was a zomb that maintained momentum. She collected the slimy, crumpled pieces of paper shoved hopefully at her and thrust them into the bio-waste bin. "Your papers are in order. Welcome to the facility."

Abid distributed more waste paper among the crowd heading towards the check point. "Your visa has come through," he chanted, monotonously.

Fei could see Red down the other end of the platform, chasing some zombs that had gone the wrong direction. The platform was sealed, and zombs didn't jump anyway. Come to that they didn't do much of anything except get in the way. They'd just get to the end of the platform and mill about, helplessly.

"The doctor will see you now," Red coaxed the zombs back from the brink. That phrase was a bit cruel. Perhaps she should ask him to stop using it. But it worked. You couldn't yell at zombs. You couldn't hit them or kick them or force them to move on. They'd just form a solid pack and mill about in a way that made you want to scream inside the suit. You had to ease them along.

Zombs were harmless. They didn't want to eat your brains, and you couldn't stop them by shooting them in the head. "That's just in movies," Fei explained, when people asked about what she did for a living. Actually, lately she'd started saying she worked in sanitation. She got more dates that way.

The only reason zombs needed to be isolated was infection. Plus, let's face it. After you've died no one wants you around, especially if you have no chit chat, no response to "what's it like on the other side?" Zombs only ever made one sound.

No one knew how it started. An infection of some kind. When a person died they got up again, between six and twelve hours after death. Rich countries built incinerators, and enforced cremation before the twelve hours were up. Poor countries had fewer choices, and the people packed into the refugee camps around the Pacific rim had no choice at all. People didn't want to harm the dead. They didn't want hurt their parents, husbands, wives, brothers, sisters or children, even after they died, but they sure as hell didn't want them hanging around. So they put them in rotten boats, and set them adrift across the Great Australian Bight.

So far Australia had stayed free of the infection. People who died stayed dead, as countries around the globe succumbed one by one. Although some, like Red, reckoned Australia was already infected, just no one infected had died yet.

Incinerating a zomb posed problems. Zombs retained basic instincts, and one of them was fear of fire. Restrained and thrust into an incinerator, zombs screamed and writhed and tried to escape the flames. Incinerating them meant crossing the border between life and death, between cremation and burning someone who remembered being alive. The will to cross it soon died. So out in the desert, the zombs were herded into a huge, enclosed facility housing four pens in seventy plus degrees. They quickly rotted and disintegrated. They weren't being killed. The natural process of decomposition was simply sped up a little. Once they were bare bones, no longer moving, the remains were cremated in the facility's incinerators.

The platform soon got so crowded, and Fei so busy, that she no longer kept track of Abid and Red. She could only hear them remorselessly chanting: "This way to the check point, please queue over there, your visa is waiting, the doctor will see you now."

The job bred black humour. She chuckled as she overhead Red throw in a new line, "Your husband is waiting." She glanced up a little while later as the crowd had thinned. Red was coming out of the side door to the isolation chambers.

"Isn't that supposed to be locked?" she asked.

"I was going to puke, and I didn't want to throw in the suit," Red said "Don't worry. I'll clean up after myself."

The last of the zombs ambled through into the 4 holding pen. Fei locked the gates after them. Then they hosed the platform down with bleach and headed back, a blast of insecticide killing all the flies that managed to follow them into the decontamination room. They hosed out the room with bleach again, before ripping off the suits and disposing of them. Clean at last, they headed upstairs.

"Good work, team!" Chris stuck his head through from the third and furthest office. He was tubby and balding, with a careful comb-over and a round face always shining with sweat.

"Yeah, thanks for all the help," Red said. Chris never went downstairs. As facility manager he pretended to be above all that. He always had his blinds closed so he didn't even see the holding pens.

"Chris it's full moon tomorrow night," Fei made a last ditch appeal. "We're too short staffed to handle it. You know it sets them off. Even temps would help."

"I hear what you're saying, and believe me I agree with you," Chris said, with saintly insincerity. "But I'm sorry, Fei." He always said her name like he was reading it off her ID tag. "There's just no money."

Their office overlooked the holding pens through a thick pane of triple-glazed glass. They had to keep an eye on what was going on, but all their desks faced the wall. The isolation chambers were beneath the offices. There were six of them, air-locked and glass-walled, with restraint equipment, only used when scientists visited.

"Jeez, number four is full," Red admitted at last. The zombs were packed against the fence, hands raised against the mesh.

"There's too many," Abid said. He turned to Chris appealingly. "These people are rotting in hell and—"

"That's the bloody point, isn't it. They're dead," Red interrupted.

"Sometimes you really annoy me," Abid said to Red.

"Good," Red said.

After work the three of them headed out for a drink. There was only one store in town, a shabby, old, timber single storey with a corrugated iron roof and wrap-around veranda. Even water had to be trucked in. There had been a pub once, but most people had left town when the facility opened, including the publican. The facility stank and spoiled the air for a good ten miles around. The only ones who lived in town now were the facility staff and those who couldn't afford to leave, perhaps twenty people, fifteen houses, amid a moonscape of empty allotments.

The nearest pub was now at the mining camp, one hundred kay off, and this afternoon none of them could be bothered to even think of climbing into a car. They just wanted to wash the chewing gum stink of the suits out of their mouths.

Wilma ran the store. She was fat and middle age, balding, and defiantly refusing to wear a wig. "So you lousy bastards can see what you done," she always said. A hair net plastered her few remaining, henna'd hairs to her head. She had a lot to complain about. Her daughter had dumped the grandkids on her. Jaanna and Tym were always running around and screaming, deaf to their grandmother's screeches for good behaviour and immune to the back-handers that followed if she could catch them. She couldn't often catch them.

A 4WD full of miners was parked outside the store, miners off on a hunting trip. Four men waiting on the fifth, who came out carrying a slab as Fei and the other two walked up. The miners wound down the windows and bawled greetings to Red, who waved back but didn't break stride as he climbed the veranda steps. They fastened hot, impatient eyes on Fei. The slab-carrying miner saw her too, and veered over eagerly, but Red casually shouldered him aside as he tried to brush too close.

"I can look after myself," Fei muttered to Red's broad back.

"Sure you can, baby bear," Red soothed. He banged through the screen door into the coolness of the store. "Wilma darling, bloody gorgeous as usual," he bawled.

"G'day Red you old devil, you seen me newest sore?" Wilma hauled her shirt up, then hauled up one of her rings of flab, showing red chafe marks and a running ooze beneath. "That's more of your work, and the cream the mining camp doctor give me don't do nothing for it," she said.

"Cheer up love, you'll outlive me yet," Red got a six pack, and took off. Nothing would dissuade Wilma from her view that the facility caused her various illnesses. Yet she wouldn't leave. "I ain't going and they can't make me. I was here first," she said.

Fei and Abid decided to have a beer at the old picnic table on the veranda. The miners were still divvying up their beer as Fei came back out. The miners stayed dead quiet until the car fired up, then they all wolf whistled, whooped and erupted:

"Show us your tits, love."

"Want a root!"

"You speakee Englee? You suckee cockee?"

The 4WD roared off.

"Talking about zombs," Fei said as Abid walked out. But then she stopped, tiredly. The joke wasn't going anywhere and it wasn't funny. Besides she was used to the miners by now. She cracked her beer. She didn't want to go home just yet, didn't want to be alone.

Abid had bought Jaanna and Tym a lemonade, ignoring their pleas for Coke, then spoke softly to them as they sat at his feet. He had kids that age back in Sydney, Fei remembered. His wife wanted to join him, but he refused to let her. "This is no place for kids," he always said.

Jaanna was a few years older than Tym, a head taller. Jaanna's eyes were green and Tym's brown. Jaanna had long straight blonde hair, Tym's was dark and short, and curled. They were tanned the colour of biscuits, and their t-shirts and shorts were old, faded and torn.

"Um, what do you guys do for school?" Fei asked, at last.

"School of the Air," Wilma said, appearing on the veranda to wave a dish cloth at them. She was always cleaning, but the place was always filthy. The dust was what got her. She couldn't be persuaded that no dust escaped the facility. Now she beamed at the grandkids, in a rare moment of kindliness. "When I can get the little buggers to sit still," she said.

Fei spent the evening with Abid. They ate microwave curry and watched a Bollywood DVD. It was almost midnight before Fei headed home, and she was half way there before she remembered she'd left her bag with her keys back at her desk. She could break into her house through the dodgy bathroom window at the back, but she'd miss her mobile. She detoured around to the facility. She could ask Sully, the big Fijian night watchman, to let her back in. The problem would be getting away quickly afterwards. Sully was chatty. But she found the front doors open. This was a surprise, although not Sully's first security lapse. He complained the facility got on his nerves.

"Sully!" she called. No answer. "Are you having a smoko?" she shouted. She looked around the corner. They was a long line of 4WDs parked behind the incinerators. One of them was Red's.

What was going on?

She went inside, down the corridor, past the first aid stretcher racked against the wall, heading towards the stairs to the offices. She stopped as she reached the platform door. The air-locked doors to the holding pens were on her right, and on the left the interior door to the isolation chambers. She could hear voices coming from in there. Raised voices. Whoops and hollers hid the sound of her arrival. She peered through the door.

The nearest isolation chamber was open. There were about fifteen men in there, and they weren't scientists. They were miners. She recognised some of their faces, knew some of their names. She saw Red at the far end. For a moment she could not see what was happening through the tangle of bodies and legs. Then she saw there was a zomb writhing on the floor. At first she couldn't see what was happening to it. Her.

Then the crowd shifted. Then she saw.

There was a man on top of her.

The gag reflex hit home. She ducked back and tried to make it to the upstairs toilet. But she vomited half way up the stairs. She tried to clap a hand over her mouth, to keep it in as she ran, so warm, pungent sick flowed through her fingers. She reached the sink and doubled over, retching.

Then she washed her hands and mouth, and face, and stared at herself in the mirror, listening to the whoops from downstairs. She made her way into the office, in the dark, reluctant to turn on the lights, unwilling to be found. She found her bag, her mobile phone. She rang Chris, staring out over the holding pens. They were dead, they were dead, they were dead, she told herself. It didn't matter what happened to them. But her hands were shaking. Chris's sleepy, surprised voice came on the line.

"Chris, we've got a problem."

They were making too much noise below, to hear her leave. She stole past and outside, carefully photographing the numberplates on all the cars with her phone.

Chris rang back later. He wasn't coming over, not on his own. He'd rung the mining camp. The police would be here in half an hour. "I've called the boss." Importance gusted back into his tone. The shock was wearing off. "Those men need to be quarantined," he said. "They're bringing the military in."

"I'm not staying here by myself," Fei told him. She rousted Abid out of bed, but they both hung back until the police arrived. 4WDs pulled up, police and mining security. Then a helicopter swooped overhead. Men started running out of the facility. Cars backed and roared off, sirens shrieked, tyres screeched and span.

Fei and Abid watched in miserable silence. "Are you sure Red wasn't wearing a suit?" Abid asked at last. It was almost funny, the wistful note of hope in his voice.

"Absolutely sure."

"But you didn't see him—"

"No—! Don't even ask! I can't believe— Even Red—"

"He probably just let them in, for the money. But—he always said we were infected already, just none of us had died yet," Abid remembered, unhappily.

Red was one of the ones that got away. Sully was rounded up and carted off with the rest, although Fei hadn't noticed him in the isolation chamber. He'd probably done nothing worse than let the men in. Fei handed over her mobile phone as evidence, then went home and lay awake, awash in prickly heat, staring at the ceiling. She kept thinking of what Red had said and done on the platform that morning. She should have noticed something. She should have realised.

"I've been informed that a quarantine station has been set up," Chris told them both, next morning. "They're keeping the men there."

"Till when?" Fei asked.

"Till it's proved they're not infected."

"Which is when? When they're dead," Abid meant it as a joke, but Chris didn't laugh. Abid and Fei exchanged glances.

"Where's Red," Fei had to ask.

"Haven't been informed," Chris said.

"But Chris, tonight is the full moon, can't we just borrow Sully at least," Abid begged.

"No, I'll help," Chris said. He turned to Fei. "Can you come into my office for a moment."

"Am I being fired," she asked, hopefully.

"No," Chris gave a nervous laugh.

"Then you can tell me right here," she said.

"I need you to do something for—us. Um," he wouldn't look at her. He fiddled with a plastic bag he was holding. "We need some—DNA samples—from the—" he jerked his head towards the isolation chamber.

She sat down, and kept on sitting. "What?"

"We thought, because it's a woman," Chris paused again, delicately. "It's a matter of justice, for the living and the dead," he said.

She stared at him in absolute horror. Then she stood and snatched the bag from him. "It would be easier if I thought, even for one moment, that you actually believed that," she hissed.

"That's no job for a girl," Abid said.

"Don't be that guy," Fei said.

"Did I ever tell you I trained as a nurse," Abid said.

"Why did you give it up?" Fei asked.

"Glamour. Promotion. Meeting new people," Abid shrugged. "Don't tell Red. He gives me enough grief as it is. But let me do this. I've done it before. On the living," he admitted.

That persuaded her. They both kitted up and went downstairs. The zomb was still in the isolation chamber. She had a broken pelvis, and was dragging herself around and around the perimeter.

Abid had no success. As he walked towards the zomb, she crawled away. Fei could hear the broken bones scraping against each other. Abid and the zomb did a slow circuit of the isolation chamber, then Abid took a short cut across the middle. But as he tried to corner the zomb she writhed away. He looked over at Fei, with an indescribable expression in his soft, brown eyes. "She remembers," he said, dully.

"No. They've proved it. Zombs gain no new memories after death."

"Then she must have been raped when she was alive," Abid said. He left the chamber. He looked like he wanted to sit, but you can't sit in a hazmat suit. Instead he leaned against the wall, gaze blank and inward. Fei prised the bag from his clenched hand, and went in.

She wheeled the zomb into restraints, but it was the worst job she had ever done. She vomited into the suit as she scraped stains from the putrid thighs, and then again as she tried an internal examination. After dry-heaving helplessly for the third time, she gave in and retreated to the decontamination room. She dumped the sample on Abid. She tore the hazmat suit off, shoved it into the bio-waste bin, stripped and threw herself into the shower, giving short, sharp screams, and banging her head against the wall whenever memory reared its rotting head. She scrubbed herself convulsively then slid down the shower wall and soaked on the floor for a good ten minutes before she could towel off and stagger outside. Only then was she able to dress and walk back into the office with some appearance of calm. Abid had packed the sample and slid it from view as she came in.

"I resign," she announced.

Chris blinked. "You can't do that."

"I can. I just did. Fuck off," she said.

Chris cleared his throat. "You know, I do have certain powers under the Emergency Services Act."

"Good for you." She slung her bag over her shoulder. "Let me know where to collect my mobile when the police are done with it. No, you know what, you can keep it."

"I could compel —" Chris started.

Fei turned on him, fists clenched.

Abid put an arm around her shoulders, and turned her away. "Don't let it get to you," he said, simply.

They looked out over the holding pens. Fei's anger subsided into a flat-line of exhaustion. "I'm going home to have a sleep and another ten showers," she said.

"Bad news. You can't, I'm afraid," Abid said.

"They're worried the water has been contaminated," Chris shot an aggrieved glance at Abid for stealing his thunder. "They're pumping it all out, decontaminating, and trucking in a fresh supply. We've got enough drinking water, but no washing water for two days."

"But what about here, the facility," she said.

"You just used the last of it," Abid said, gently.

She and Abid went outside at lunch break, although neither of them felt like eating. "Things have changed," Abid warned her. Choppers buzzed in and out, earth moving equipment and trucks rumbled past. You actually had to look both ways when crossing the street. Hazmat suited people were lumbering everywhere. It was surreal. Fei stopped, amazed.

"Chris—has been informed—that they're improving security here, after the, um, breach. Most of these are army engineers, building another fence." Abid gestured around the outskirts of town.

Several hazmat-suited men were clambering around, taking soil and air samples. They lumbered over to Fei and Abid, and took saliva swabs. They didn't speak except when necessary, and didn't make eye contact. Army drones.

"Do we look like arseholes when we're wearing those suits?" Fei asked, loudly.

"Probably," Abid said, tiredly. They crossed the street to the store. The screen door screeched and thumped. It was hot inside, hotter than outside. The air conditioning was off. The shelves were bare.

Wilma was beside herself. "The power's gone," she said. "And no one can tell me when it'll be back on."

"Don't you have a generator?" Fei asked.

"No fuel left. And this mob have cleaned me out of everything. Said it might be contaminated. What are the kids going to eat?"

"When will the fresh supplies arrive?" Fei asked.

"Next week," Wilma let fly with relish. "They're a load of bloody nongs. No one'll tell me what's going on and if I need anything, they just say "next week, next week"," she said. Fei escaped outside to join Jaanna and Tym, who ran up and down the veranda, shrieking with delight, as the convoys of trucks rolled past.

The screen door screeched and banged. "Even the microwave curries are gone," Abid reported, despondently. "How can anything contaminate them?"

Suddenly Fei was too tired to care. It was too much effort. A brick wall slammed down between her brain and her eyes, between herself and her skin. "I'm going home," she announced, and left.

But she went back to the facility that evening for night shift. She couldn't leave Abid to do it on his own. The desert dusk was short and sharp, and as night descended the temperature dropped. The new fence was more than half up, and hazmat figures were working by great spotlights. Fei knew how hard it was to move in those suits, but Wilma was right. They looked like bloody nongs. She arrived as a truck pulled up outside the facility. Abid and Chris were looking on. Chris was sweating heavily, and repeatedly wiping his forehead. Abid stood arms folded, grim.

"What's happening?" she asked brightly, joining them.

Chris swelled, ready to make an announcement. "I'm informed," he announced, grandly, but Abid cut him off.

"Bad news I'm afraid," said Abid. He put an arm around Fei's shoulders as hazmat suited men pulled a body bag out of the back.

"Who's that?" she asked, sobering.

"Red," Abid said.

She clapped a hand over her mouth. Grief, like nausea, rose in her gullet.

"I'm afraid he had an accident while trying to escape," Chris said. "Rolled the car. He was dead when found."

"How long ago?" she asked.

"Hard to tell in this heat. They're taking him to an isolation chamber."

"The incinerator you mean," she corrected him.

Chris's round, sweating face firmed up. "An isolation chamber. It's the only way to find out if he's, um, infected," he said.

The men rolled the body bag inside. Fei opened her mouth to protest.

"Just agree with him. We've got all night," Abid whispered.

She subsided.

The men put Red in the isolation chamber next to the broken zomb, and left without saying much, or even looking at them.

After they were gone Abid suited up, went inside and laid Red out. He combed his hair, and neatened his clothes, and laid his arms across his body.

Neither Abid or Fei thought Chris actually intended to work on the floor that evening, but he climbed determinedly into a hazmat suit and joined them. The full moon stirred the zombs, even though they couldn't see it. They clustered over one side of the pens at moonrise, then followed the moon over. They piled against the fences. If they were left alone you could hear the bones cracking as those at the front where crushed, all along the line, until there was a danger that the fence itself would collapse. The job was to keep the fence from going down. Abid and Fei lumbered from one side of the pen to the other, coaxing the zombs back before the bone-crushing pile up could begin. They could see from Chris's pale and sweating face that his heart wasn't in it. He left abruptly a little before midnight. They saw the light go on in his office, slits of light behind the blinds he always kept closed. That meant he was out of the hazmat suit.

"Now?" Fei said to Abid, who nodded. They grabbed the first aid stretcher and hurried to the isolation chambers.

They were too late.

Red was already up and standing by the wall, hands flat against the glass.

Abid and Fei staggered blearily out into dawn. It was an eye-achingly beautiful day, with an impossible blue sky. The sun poured honey over the ochre rocks that tumbled along the horizon. The fence around town was finished. The crowds were gone, the trucks and earth moving equipment and helicopters parked on the other side of the fence, a fair way off. The streets were deserted again. Fei rotated, looking around the perimeter. Wilma, Jaanne, Tym, and the few other remaining townsfolk were standing in the street, staring down the road.

Wilma waddled over as soon as she saw her. "Them gates are locked," she said, belligerently. "And that water never arrived either. What are the kids gonna do?" she asked.

Fei ducked back inside. "Chris!" she called. "We have a—" Chris came hurrying down, hair plastered to his forehead, plump face drawn, pale and sick. "—problem," she finished, shocked by his appearance. Her stomach twisted and punched the wind from her voice. "They've locked us in. Can't you call the boss?" she gasped.

"I've been trying. Since five this morning all I've got is this." Chris held up his mobile. She could hear it plain, even at a distance. A recorded message. "This is a quarantine area. Please leave immediately."

"Let me try," Abid hauled his own phone out of his pocket. "The wife," he said, cheerfully. They heard the answer, quite distinctly. "This is a quarantine area. Please leave immediately." He rang 000, then 112. The same message played, over and over, until he threw the phone away, explosively.

"They'll let us out," Chris said, tearfully. "I've got our new security passes." He hurried over to the gate. Fei, Abid and Wilma followed him, Jaanna and Tym trailed after them.

They could see figures in the distance, but no amount of hails, shouts, yells or screams persuaded them to come over to the fence.

"Come on, we'll climb over," Abid said, squaring up.

"Um, there's a problem," Chris said.

"What!" they all turned on him in unison.

"I'm sorry, they did tell me," Chris caved in, in front of their eyes. "I didn't think they'd get it up so quickly." He pointed. They could all see the lone wire strung out from the fence.

"So what did they tell you, that you'd get a promotion if you kept this quiet?" Abid asked, quietly.

"I'm sorry," Chris repeated, helplessly.

"The kids are gonna die here!" Wilma rounded on him. Jaanna looked dumbfounded from one to the other. Tym started bawling.

"I'm sorry, I'm sorry, I'm sorry!" Chris crouched on the ground, rocking on his heels, hands over his head.

"Abid, Wilma. It's not his fault. He's locked in here with us, right?" Fei was wearing a light jacket. She took it off, and threw it. There was a vicious hiss, the jacket arced and scorched, and then there was a stink of burning.

"You kids get away from that fence, right now," Wilma hollered. She dragged them back into the empty store.

Fei and Abid spent the day taking a stock of food and water. There was little of either. The cars had all been drained of fuel sometime in the night, but they unearthed a spare supply in the facility, enough to fill two tanks. While they were re-fuelling the cars, Chris turned up again. He had recovered from the shock, enough to announce that they had to escape in tones suggesting that only he could have thought of it.

"We have to use the zombs," Fei said. She'd already worked it out. "We wait for moonrise, and let the zombs out. They'll follow the moon until they pile against the fence. We get everyone into the cars, and wait behind them." She pulled a face as she thought of the smell of fried rotting flesh. "Once the fence is down and the current off, we scram," she finished.

"But what about the infection?" Chris worried, even then.

"If Red's infected, we're all infected," Fei said.

"No, that's not true," Abid said, quietly. His eyes had a scraped, strained look. He hadn't eaten all day. Fei was worried about him. "Red crossed the line—he didn't take precautions," he threw up his hands in despair. "These people were screwed over when they were alive. How many times can we screw them now they're dead?" he asked.

"As many times as it takes," Fei said.

They agreed to meet at 8 pm, when the moon was low in the sky, and set off to tell the rest of town. They left Wilma and the kids to last, figuring they'd pack whatever food and water was left in the store. They met again out front, in darkness, and climbed the steps together. The store was hot, airless and silent, the only echo the screech and bang of the screen door.

"Wilma!" Fei called. "Jaanna, Tym!" No answer. The lights weren't working, but Fei and Abid had found torches in the facility. They switched them on and creaked across the store to the living quarters at the back.

The smell told them something was wrong before they went in. Wilma was lying on the bed, the children beside her. A jumble of empty prescription packets littered the bedside table. Blood soaked through the mattress and dried sticky on the carpet and lino. Blood, and the hot, coppery, rotten stink of it, was everywhere.

Abid checked Tym, then Jaanna, then Wilma. Then he started tearing sheets, binding up Wilma's wrists. "Find me a first aid kit," he barked.

"She's alive?" Fei asked.

"For now. Smothered them with a pillow I guess, then took all those and slit her wrists."

Fei remembered there was a first aid kit in the store. She shot off to get it, past Chris, who was throwing up in the hall. "But she does have a chance, right?" she said as she returned. "While there's life there's hope. Right."

"No. Those doctors at the mining camp should be shot. They've given her enough prescription medication to kill a camel," Abid said. "She's destroyed her kidneys and liver. Now she'll just die slowly from multiple organ failure, assuming we can get her to a hospital."

"This is just fucked!" Fei exploded in grief and fury.

"Pretty much," Abid agreed, bleakly. His scraped eyes were red-rimmed, and he blinked painfully in the torch light. Fei gently removed the two children from the bed. She laid Jaanna and Tym out in the next room, telling Chris to take them to the incinerator.

"But we could find out, um, if we're infected. If they—" Chris started. Then he saw her face. "Sure," he said, meekly.

Once Wilma was bandaged like a mummy Abid headed over to the facility to fetch the stretcher. Fei sat with her. Midnight came and went. Neither Abid nor Chris returned.

At last Fei headed out to see what had happened. She saw lights by the facility, and 4WDs pulled up beside it. The drivers and passengers were dark, faceless shadows.

"We have to fetch Wilma," she told them. "She's hurt. Where's Abid?"

Chris stepped from the lead car, and cleared his throat. "We've missed moonrise. We have to wait for moonset, right?" he asked.

"Anytime the moon is more in one direction than the other will do," she said. "Where's Abid?" she repeated.

Chris cleared his throat again. "There's been a problem," he blustered. He hesitated then admitted. "I didn't take those—the—corpses—to the incinerator. I took them to one of the isolation chambers. When Abid came here to fetch the stretcher," Chris stopped. "They were already up and walking around," he finished.

"But—how could they be infected? Jaanna and Tym. They've even never been inside the facility!" she exclaimed.

Chris just stared at her, patiently, as it sank in. If Jaanna and Tym were infected they were all infected. Quarantine area.

"I couldn't persuade him to leave. He's in there now," Chris said.

"You didn't leave him? He has kids the same age!" Fei sprinted down to the isolation chambers but the door was open and Abid was gone. Then she gagged. The stink told her the airlock to the holding pens was open.

She peeked through the airlock and saw the slim, straight, familiar line of Abid's back. He was holding Jaanna and Tym's hands, taking them to the 4 holding pen.

"Abid!"

He looked around, calmly.

"You're not suited up," she shouted, absurdly.

He kept walking. Acting on instinct she dashed up the stairs, and climbed into a suit. She tore it in her hurry, but didn't wait to grab a fresh one. "And besides, Wilma was right, it does make me look like a bloody nong," she said to her reflection in the mirror, through the tears rolling down her cheeks and the snot running down her nose. "A bloody nong, baby bear." Fresh tears flowed. She lumbered down, in time to see Abid open the gate to 4 holding pen.

With no one to keep the zombs back from the fence they'd crushed up against the side before following the moon back again. The fence leaned at a perilous angle. Abid led the two children inside, closing the gate behind them.

"Abid! Stop! You're not dead yet!"

Abid turned and surveyed her once more, his eyes scraped raw, then he and Jaanna and Tym vanished into the throng.

"This is stupid!" she bawled, then uselessly clapped her hands to her helmeted head. She had deafened herself inside the suit. She tore her hood off. A gust of breeze made her glance around. Chris had opened the exterior doors. She hauled the holding pen gates wide.

"Come on, all of you, get out of here," she called. She stooped and picked up a fluttering scrap of paper. The first of the zombs shuffled tentatively across the line. She handed the scrap to him. "Your papers are in order. Welcome to Australia."

afterword

George Romero first had the idea of using zombies as social commentary with Night of the Living Dead *in 1968. Recent immigration policy in this country has not made me feel particularly proud to be Australian. With these two ideas in mind, the story wrote itself.*

Mrs Estahazi

Barbara Robson

I DON'T THINK any of us were exactly surprised when the men from the Department showed up. Not that we *knew*, not really, but when we saw the Department van pulled up outside her house, it all clicked together and it was as though we'd known all along. There had been signs, if you know what I mean. Once we really knew, we could put them all together. Though I guess someone must have figured it out consciously before then. Someone dobbed her in.

I was pulling weeds in my front yard when Mrs Estahazi first arrived in our street. A white station wagon pulled onto the verge and a young man got out the driver's side, then went 'round to the back to get her bag from the boot. Only one bag; but a nice big duffel-bag. "Here we are, Mrs S." he said. I could here him from where I was. "Laurel Place."

The old lady eased herself up out of the passenger seat, and they walked together to the front door. He unlocked it for her (I guess he must have been a rental agent, mustn't he? The house had been empty for ages, though) and he carried the bag inside before reappearing at the front door and driving off in his station wagon. I haven't seen the fellow since, but if the police ask, I think I might be able to describe him.

I kept at my weeding, because it was none of my business, and before long, I saw her at the windows—opening them all up to give the place a good airing out—and I heard her singing. I can't say what she sang: it was foreign. But it was a nice day, she had a pleasant voice and something about her made me think of my own Mum, so I went inside to give her a call. Mum was pleased.

The next time I saw my new neighbour was the day after. Sunday, it must have been; I was working through my ironing and worrying over Scott. There was a knock on the door, and when I answered it, there was Mrs Estahazi with a little plate of some sort of sweet that she had baked, covered over with plastic wrap.

"Oh hello," I said. "I saw you moving in yesterday. How's everything next door?"

"Everything is very charming, thank you."

Her accent was—I suppose—East European. Or Indian, or something in between. No, you'll laugh at me because people from India don't sound at all like the Russians, but I really couldn't place her then, and I never did find out where she was from. Indian, she sounded, then. But white. Not young, but not as old as I'd thought the day before. She held up the plate, offering it to me, and I realised that I'd come to the door still holding a bottle of ironing spray, so I put that down on the little hallway table so I could take the plate.

"Is this for us?" I asked. "They look lovely. You shouldn't have."

In truth, they looked a little strange: green and white, heavy on the plate, but a little shiny.

"They are for you, yes," said the Indian woman. "For the little boy."

I suppose she must have seen Scott mucking about in the yard on Saturday, because he'd not been outside at all on the Sunday. It was nice of her.

"Welcome to Laurel Place," I said. "I'm Nicole."

"My name," she said, "is Mrs Estahazi."

Without a further word, Mrs Estahazi turned and walked back down the path and to her own place.

I suppose I should have invited her in, but I didn't quite know how. So I took the sweets back inside and passed them around the family.

The sweets were as strange to my taste as they looked. They had an odd, dense texture, very moist, very heavy. They smelled musky, but floral, too. They were sweet, but not as sweet as I expected, from the look of them, and it just made them all the more foreign. We all had a nibble, but Scott was the only one who ate all his piece. I remember that surprised me, because he'd been down with a stomach bug and hadn't been eating. But that was the turning point; him getting his appetite back for Mrs Estahazi's sweets. After that, he was "right as rain," as my Mum would have put it.

So that was my introduction to Mrs Estahazi. She was a strange old duck. I never saw her working in the garden, except when she was planting her herbs or making those little dolls of hers from grass and flowers. She must have done quite a lot of work, though, because the garden came up as pretty as any you've seen: a little wild-looking, perhaps, but nothing like the neglected rental mess it was when she moved in. To top it off, she tied those pretty little dolls to every tree and bush in the yard, and one for every yard along the street, too.

Each doll that I saw was unique. Some had little gumnut hats and some had petal skirts, and some of the bigger ones had staffs or bows made out of twigs and onion grass. They didn't have faces, but they had personality. She put so much effort into such ephemeral little toys.

The children made a game of finding them all, though they left them where they were. I think they even went into Mrs Estahazi's back yard to look for them, though they should have known better and I'd have scolded them if I'd caught them. They came back safe, though, if they did go next door.

Tilly insisted I walk down the street with her so she could show me all the dolls in their little hiding places that she and Scott had found. Walking down the street in the other direction, we ran into Bob Dunn. He was looking for the dolls, too. He wasn't nearly as pleased with them as the kids. He had gardening gloves on, an orange plastic rubbish bag in one hand, and a pair of clippers in the other. He reached into the bushes as I watched and ripped out one of the dolls, snipping it in two before dropping the pieces in his bag, scowling fit to whither the lawn.

Tilly looked set to burst into tears, so I picked her up to settle her and let her nuzzle her face into my shoulder.

"Come on, Bob," I said. "The kids love these dolls. Where's the harm?"

"Where's the harm!?" Bob's reply came back fiercer than I'd expected as his angry stare fixed on me. "Where do you think? Take a look about you, woman! What right has she got? I ask you, what right? This isn't even her yard! This is the street we've been living in for 15 years! And here she comes, splashing out of her boat, leaving all this rubbish lying around messing up the whole street!"

I didn't think she'd come on a boat, but I got the gist. It wasn't his yard either, but I wasn't going to argue. I looked away, and looked for an excuse. Tilly obliged by breaking into sniffs and tears. "I'd better get this one home," I said. "It's time for her nap."

The dolls were soon back. I said "hello" to Mrs Estahazi and she came down the street with a basketful, and suggested she might like to skip number 23—Bob's place. Come to think of it, maybe Mrs Estahazi had the time to make them all again because she didn't need to spend much time weeding after all. It was a very good spring for gardens and not for weeds. My own yard grew well and strong, the flowers coming up a treat without nearly so much attention as most years. When I went out with my gardening gloves and hat, it was more to be in the sun and watch the world go by than for any real need.

Spring gave way to summer and I spent more time indoors, out of the heat, or driving the kids around between swimming lessons and birthday parties. It was a big year for pool parties. But the real party of the year was—as always—Marge Wilkins' Christmas party.

Every year in December, Marge holds a Christmas party. It's a big deal. Everyone in the street gets an invitation, the kids spend weeks planning and making decorations and we grown-ups spend just as long planning what dishes to bring and how to upstage the neighbours with the perfect fruit cake or guava salad. This year, I made my special pavlova, Scott and Tilly made metres of crepe paper chains in red and green, and Jack Wilkins donned a Santa costume to entertain the littlies. Scott is just a bit too old for Santa Claus, but I could see him getting caught up in the excitement all the same. Everyone was there except for the Murthwaites, who had gone south for the holidays, and except for Mrs Estahazi.

At first, I thought she might show up later, once the sea breeze came in to take the edge off the day. And then I thought maybe she was ill, and I didn't think she had any family in town. I took a turn at the barbeque so I could have a word with Marge and find out whether she knew.

"It's funny that Mrs Estahazi isn't here yet," I said, turning a sausage that wasn't quite black yet. "Is she okay, do you think?"

"The woman who lives by you, you mean?" Marge shooed a blow-fly away from the meat-tray and ladled herself out a glass of punch. "She's not coming."

"Not coming? But your parties are famous! Why would she miss it?"

"She's not coming because she didn't get an invite. She's foreign. She'd hardly be Christian, would she? I didn't want to presume she was, so I didn't invite her."

"But don't you think she might have liked an invitation?"

"If she'd got an invitation, she might have come, and not everyone takes to her like you seem to. All the way from wherever she's from. Who knows what Bob would have said once he got a few drinks into him? I didn't want a scene. There he is, now, playing cricket with the boys. Everyone's having fun. I think I did the right thing. Leave well enough alone."

Well. It wasn't my party. I did feel bad for Mrs Estahazi, all alone when the rest of us were celebrating, but there was nothing to be done. When we got home, I sent Scott 'round next door with a big slice of leftover pavlova. He came back with a brass bell in a velvet-lined box. It was a gift for the family, he said, from Mrs Estahazi.

The bell was about two inches high and was a beautiful piece of craftwork. It was engraved all around the edge in Arabic or something like it. The velvet was purple, and the box was tin, heavily decorated. It had been a while since I'd last seen tin: everything is plastic, these days. It must have cost more than she could afford to spend on casual neighbours like us. She'd come a long way, though, and I guess she didn't have many friends here, yet. She must have brought it from her own country. So I put Mrs Estahazi on our Christmas list for a box of chocolates, and I set the bell in its box on the mantelpiece among the cards.

The next morning, the box caught my eye as I tidied up the room. I opened it up and looked at the bell again, and it still seemed too much, too beautiful. So I shut the lid, put on some shoes, and popped around next door.

Mrs Estahazi was opening the door just as I arrived.

"Were you about to go out, Mrs S.? I can come back some other time." I was almost relieved, to be honest, because I hadn't quite worked out what I was going to say. But Mrs Estahazi smiled, her smile warm. "No, I am not going. I open the door for you, Julia. You come to visit," she gestured towards me with one hand, and to the door with the other. "So I open the door."

She ushered me inside and I sat on the ancient (though surprisingly comfortable) floral couch and admired the intricate Persian rug beneath my feet while she poured us both tea, already brewed and waiting with two cups on a doily on the big wooden trunk that served in this room as a coffee-table. Had all this furniture come with the rental, I wondered, or had she had it delivered after she moved in? It seemed perfectly right for Mrs Estahazi. Perhaps that was why she'd chosen Laurel Place.

The room smelt faintly of sandalwood and of something else—something that I couldn't quite identify, but reminded me of holidays in the forest. And that seemed perfectly right, too, though usually, incense just makes me sneeze.

I took a sip of my tea, still wondering how to begin. I'm usually a coffee-drinker, but whatever this was, it was better than teabags.

I put my cup down on the truck and took the little tin box from my handbag. I opened it once again, admiring the bell, then let it snap shut and set it down beside the tea-cup.

"This is a very generous gift, Mrs S., but we can't accept it. It must have been very expensive."

Mrs Estahazi laughed: a melodic sound of genuine amusement. "Expensive? Not at all. I have had it a long time. It cost me no money. When I was young—younger even than you—an old lady gifted it to me."

"And you don't want it any more? You could probably get something for it at the jewellers in town. I could take it in and ask if you like."

I saw Mrs Estahazi wince a little, and I thought I'd put my foot in it, but there was no offence in her voice when she spoke. "Please. It is my pleasure that it be yours. A gift loses its power when it is sold."

I couldn't protest any more without being rude. It would just have to be a big box of chocolates that we got her for Christmas.

I put the bell back in my handbag and made small-talk while we finished our tea.

"Where do you come from, Mrs Estahazi? Was it a long journey to get here?"

"Not so long. Before this, I lived in Morley."

"But where did you grow up? Where were you, when you were a girl and the old lady gave you the bell?"

"Oh, then I *was* long away, in the home of my childhood. Very beautiful, my home was then. Of course, here it is very beautiful, too."

Was it a tear in her eye, of regret for her homeland, that stopped her really answering? Or was it a twinkle in her eye, of amusement? She looked down to pour another cup of tea before I could make up my mind, and when she looked back up, it was gone, whatever it had been.

So I left it alone and asked Mrs Estahazi her plans for Christmas.

"Christmas is not something I grew up with," she said (so Marge had been right that far, after all). "But I will be keeping myself busy. I am helping out this year at the pensioners' hall, laying out the tables for the old folks and setting out the napkins. I might take in a tray of my dumplings, if they are needed, and see that they get eaten."

I thought she was probably of an age with "the old folks" and should just go along to enjoy the lunch, but at least I didn't say it.

We chatted about the gardens, and how well they were looking, and about the children, and how well Tilly was coming along in kindy, and Scott in school sports. We talked about John, and his hopes for promotion, and I can't remember what else. I hadn't had such a good chat in a long time, and before I knew it, it was time to get home and make lunch.

The bell, in its box, went back on the mantelpiece.

Mum and Dad visited for a few days over Christmas and the kids had a fine time with all their new toys, which kept us busy, so although I'd meant to drop around again, I never did.

The week after New Year's, I came down very ill with a summer 'flu. For the second time, Mrs Estahazi dropped by with a tray of her green sweets. This time, the sweets weren't so strange. When I smelled their musky-floral aroma, they seemed like the best thing in the world, and I remembered that I hadn't eaten all day. I should try to find a recipe sometime: they were really a treat. As it happened, that was the shortest bout of flu I've ever come down with. Out-of-season 'flus can be like that.

The year turned. Tilly got her first school uniform and was very excited. Scott got his new pencils and readers and was less thrilled, but he made an effort for Tilly's sake not to show it. I was proud of him. We had a bit of bother in January when the hot water system broke down and we called a man in to fix it, but when he got there, it was working again and he couldn't see that there had been anything wrong. He charged us eighty dollars for the call-out, just the same.

And the strangest thing happened in the last week of January. Let me tell you about it.

It must have been almost one o'clock in the morning. We were fast asleep in bed, of course, the alarm set for seven like it always is so John could hear the news while he got ready for work the next day. But in the middle of the night—one o'clock—a bell rang. Not a doorbell; a brass bell. Clear and loud: "dingle-ding". Like that. We both woke up and lay there, listening. Then we heard it again. "Dingle-ding".

"Scott must be out of bed. We should go down and see."

I put on my little-girl voice. "I'm too sleepy. Would you do it?"

The little-girl voice didn't work. John trumped it with his "grumpy man" voice. "I have to get to work in the morning: you don't."

So I got out of bed, a little grumpy myself.

The lights were off, downstairs. I listened from the top of the staircase, and didn't hear Scott. I nearly jumped out of my skin when he stepped up behind me, looking as sleepy as he should, in his blue pyjamas. As sleepy as a boy who'd just been woken up by his Mum moving about the house at night. Then, again, I heard that "dingle-ding."

Without switching on the light, I crept down the stairs to see.

In the living room, all was still and quiet. It was a full moon that night, and the moonlight glowed strongly through the window, open to let the breeze through. As I looked, a black-gloved hand came through, too. And a head. I screamed. The man cursed and ran off down the street.

We were up the rest of the night after that. John came dashing down the stairs, but the fellow was long gone before either of us had the wit to call the police. They took down a record over the phone, but didn't come until morning. They told us what we'd said might help them find the man, but we never heard anything back.

And when the fuss was over, I thought to check on Mrs Estahazi's bell: still snugly nestled in velvet in its box. Had it rung? Perhaps we dreamed it when the burglar made some other sound. Or did the burglar come with his own bell?

That was our bit of excitement, then, for January.

In March, old Mrs Mac died. She had held on for two years past her husband Angus, which was longer than I'd thought she might with her heart, but it was still sad to see her go. Mrs Mac's son, Devon, put the house up for sale and we had a look around on the open day, wondering what it would fetch and who we'd have as new neighbours. The kids were hoping for new playmates. Most of the neighbours went for a look-see on the open day. Mrs Estahazi, too, sprinkling perfume in the corners of the empty rooms when she thought no-one was looking, and muttering prayers in her own language. Who knows? Maybe it did help lay ghosts to rest.

But it was in April that Bob's business went to the wall. People didn't want to buy plastic stove-top covers after all (who'd have guessed?). Bob was left with 2,000 covers in his garage and his car on the street until he could sell it to pay the prototype-manufacturer. And it was in April, after that, that the Department of Immigration and Christian Services came and took Mrs Estahazi away as a witch. It was in April that the weeds came back and in April that Tilly came down with a cold that turned into bronchitis and had her off school for weeks. She's still nursing a cough. It was in April that the hot water broke down once and for all. It was in April that the "For Sale" sign went up at the house next door.

In May, I found one withered charm-doll still hidden among the branches of the lemon tree, swinging gently in the wind.

When I was a child, there was an old lady, Mrs Bird, who lived with her mother, Mrs King, and German shepherd, Prince, across the road from my family. I wasn't thinking of her when I wrote this story, but on reflection, Mrs Bird must have been the inspiration for Mrs Estahazi.

Mrs Bird used to bring us freshly made banana fritters, which I loved, and buy our fund-raising lamingtons from school. I still have her recipe for the fritters, printed in careful, childish handwriting. When I asked for the recipe, she invited me to her house to cook with her, and I remember her fabulously exotic Arabian rug and the carved wooden trunk that sat in its centre and looked as though it must be magical.

As I grew up, she stopped bringing the fritters and I stopped visiting. One day, visiting my parents as an adult, I heard that she had been moved to a nursing home—no-one knew where. And do you know? It has just occurred to me that I'm not sure whether Mrs Bird was Indian or Italian.

Norumbega

Linda L. Donahue

The rustle of pine needles, the snap of a frozen twig, a strangely inhuman scent brought Abornazine to a sudden stillness. In the slumbering forest, during the time of hibernation and frozen ponds, his gaze searched for the otherkin.

No birds sang from snow-blanketed tree boughs. Even the wind slept. Yet a branch dipped, dumping snow onto the ground. The inhuman, intoxicating scent tickled Abornazine's flared nostrils, as though some invisible being circled. In the smell, he sensed the magic that could overtake a man's mind or spirit.

Tiny moccasin prints, smaller than a child's, circled the clump of dropped snow. Cautiously, Abornazine crept nearer, stepping so lightly that the snow-crusted pine needles absorbed all sound.

The footprints led between trees.

Respectfully, Abornazine whispered, "You've been watching. To give me warning? Or do you intend mischief?"

As expected, he received no reply.

"Bring no mischief to Norumbega. It is a sacred place." But the Mikumwess, diminutive forest folk, knew that.

The tiny footprints rounded a tree growing on the downward hill slope. Abornazine clung to a limb while traversing icy rocks jutting from the hillside. The footprints vanished into a dark hollow between exposed roots.

"Is this your home, little one?" After a respectful length of silence passed, Abornazine said, "I ask you not to make trouble. Let me make an offering, to prove my friendship. Winter is hard enough without mischief."

Abornazine gathered perfectly shaped pine cones. His arms full, he returned to the hollowed tree growing out the hillside. Beneath his feet, ice cracked and a stepping stone shot out from under him. Abornazine tumbled down, pine cones scattering wildly in his wake.

He ploughed into a deep snowbank. His head struck the base of an ancient and very stout tree.

Snow blanketed Abornazine, numbing him. He no longer felt his aching skull, nor the painful cold in his fingers, nor even his heartbeat. Feeling feather-light, he drifted on frigid air like a puff of wintry breath. Higher and higher he rose until he gazed upon his childhood village. Smoke rose from his father's wigwam. His mother, wrapped in skins, stitched repairs to the outside flap.

As he drifted onward, snow banks melted rapidly. Bare limbs sprouted new leaves. Even the sky grew bluer, casting off winter's dull, grey hue. The river, instead of moving sluggish with ice, flowed clear and fast. Penobscot fishermen waded along the pebble-strewn shore. In the forest beyond, a Passamaquoddy hunting party stalked bear and deer.

Night fell and the stars of late spring shone overhead.

The air current carried him to where two great rivers met. Between these rivers stood Norumbega, a city greater than all the villages of the Wabanaki Confederation combined, the city Abornazine called home.

Strong men repaired the crisscross of sharpened logs which formed the city's outer walls. Inside, longhouses and wigwams formed concentric circles. At the middle stood the central longhouse, three stories tall, the greatest structure in the city. There, the council of elders met, the chiefs of the Wabanaki Confederacy.

Torches made the mineral-rich streets glitter. Nightly, Abornazine lit the torches and ensured they burned until dawn. He was the Torchbearer, Keeper of the Flame. Though a necessary task, any youth could do it. Abornazine desired greater responsibility and recognition.

His desire had led him into the forest, seeking the winter bear. Northern tribes spoke of a bear with white fur, said to appear only during the harshest of winters. To kill such a bear would earn the sachem's approval. Its hide would make a worthy gift for the sachem's beautiful daughter. Perhaps then, he, too, would be worthy of her hand.

Abornazine's spirit drifted to where the river flowed into the ocean. In the orange-streaked dawn, Abornazine saw great canoes, large enough to carry an entire village. These canoes were powered not by paddles but by wind filling enormous skins suspended from poles. From these ships, smaller boats landed, disgorging pale-faced men and peculiar, long-legged beasts.

Curious layers of unfamiliar cloth wrapped the strangers. They knelt on the beach and though they spoke a foreign tongue, in his cloud-like state, Abornazine understood them.

They gave thanks to the Creator for having borne them safely across the sea. They thanked Him for delivering them unto this land. They asked for guidance and help surviving this new world.

Abornazine wished he could welcome these proud, honourable men. He would teach them how to respect the land so they might earn a place among the confederation.

"Abornazine!"

Warmth clutched Abornazine in a near-suffocating grip. Where heat drove off the numbing cold, it dug deep with sharp needles.

"Abornazine?" Tidesso's face hovered amid the hazy blending of grey sky and snowy trees. "I thought your spirit had fled."

Abornazine's teeth chattered as he gazed at the pile of snow beside him. *I was soaring.* Abornazine looked hard into Tidesso's eyes, hoping he understood. *For a time, my spirit did flee.*

"Can you speak?" Tidesso gently chafed Abornazine's cheeks.

The words came out hard at first. "Help me to my feet, my friend. I must speak with Sachem Kanozas. The sky beings have sent me a vision."

Tidesso laughed. "Only you could nearly freeze to death and think the sky speaks. I say Mikumwess played a prank on you."

"I know what I saw. When it comes to pass, you, too, shall be amazed." Once winter passed and the strangers arrived, the whole of the Wabanaki Confederacy would gaze upon him with respect.

Dawn tinged the morning sky. Abornazine snuffed the last torch, his duty complete. After a long winter, the forest air finally tasted rich of early ripening.

Today, he would take no rest after his nightly duty. Not when strangers were coming.

Tomakwa, the woodcarver, one of the oldest men in Norumbega, always greeted the great spirits at dawn. He had once explained that as time passed, it left him with fewer and fewer days, and so he wished to be on good terms with the great spirits, so they would carry him gently to the next hunting ground.

As Abornazine passed, Tomakwa grinned, his mouth nearly toothless, and said, "Did any strangers arrive in the night?"

"They will come."

Tomakwa laughed. "Tell me, have any other spirits spoken with you lately?"

Abornazine swallowed his chagrin. No one on the council had believed him. Even the children called him "Sky Talker" and "Snow Dreamer." For months, Abornazine had kept silent, never letting his embarrassment show. Soon, everyone would know the truth. Visions weren't only for medicine men and sachems.

"I am heading toward the ocean," Abornazine said. "Do you favour a walk, elder?"

Tomakwa laughed. "I do, but my legs do not. Besides, today I will finish the tribute pole." He swept his calloused, knobby hand toward the council pole. The upper branches of the tree, having died many years ago, had been cut away, leaving just the trunk standing. For many months, Tomakwa had carved symbols around the pole to represent every tribe in the confederacy.

Abornazine bowed his head. "Forgive my stubbornness, elder, but I believe that soon you will need room for a new symbol."

"You mean for the strangers." Tomakwa's eyes twinkled. "I will save a small place, but only because I have always liked you."

Abornazine found Tidesso washing his face and tying back his hair. Tidesso, as flighty as his name 'Blue Jay' implied, eagerly joined Abornazine. In a half-jesting tone, he said, "I'll bring nets. We can cast them far out to sea. If we don't catch your strangers, we can, at least, bring back crabs and fish."

The hike downstream took well into morning. The sun shone from mid-sky by the time they broke through the woods onto a swell of land overlooking the ocean. Tall ships were anchored in the bay. Smaller boats, though larger than Abenaki canoes, were beached in neat rows. And strangers with even stranger animals explored the beach in groups.

For a moment, Abornazine remembered how it felt to soar. Before him stood his vision in flesh and bone. Overcome with joy, he almost fell to his knees before the sky beings.

Tidesso gripped Abornazine's arm and whispered, "I do not trust such alien men. Is it not possible the sky beings meant to warn you of them?"

"In my vision, I understood their words. They gave praise and thanks to the Creator. Do not misjudge them because they are different."

"You have always been generous in nature, sometimes too generous and easily fooled. I hope this is not one of those times." Tidesso shrugged and heaved a sigh. "I must believe the sky beings chose you for a reason."

Abornazine strode toward the sandy beach. Tidesso followed with hesitant steps.

The strangers looked up. Some pointed, others dropped whatever strange devices they held. Several men stepped together, forming a line, shoulder to shoulder, their hands on ornate sticks of wood and metal.

Abornazine and Tidesso stopped a few paces back. Abornazine raised his hand and, remembering the gesture these men had made in his vision, he pressed his palms together and bowed his head. He even attempted the one foreign word that stuck in his memory. "Thanks."

The men smiled. One even laughed and extended his hand. Unsure of the meaning, Abornazine mimicked, extending his own. The pale-skinned man with sun-collared hair gripped Abornazine's hand. Whatever the gesture meant, it appeared friendly.

Abornazine removed a carved figurine of a Mikumwess sitting atop a mushroom from around his neck. After his vision, Tomakwa had carved it for him. Abornazine offered the necklace, saying, "You are welcome here."

Though his expression registered no understanding, the man accepted the gift. Whatever he said in return was spoken in kindness. He then removed his headdress, a leather construction which shaded the face, decorated with an unusual feather. The man presented it to Abornazine, who grinned back at Tidesso as he put it on his head.

"So I'm wrong," Tidesso said. "It's hardly the first time."

Abornazine laughed at his friend.

The strangers laughed, too, as the sun-haired man approached slowly then altered the headdress's positioning. He waved toward the woods and spoke more strange words.

Abornazine nodded, saying, "They seek a guide. It is exactly as I saw!"

"Then it is especially fortunate I came along." Tidesso grinned. "You may have visions, but I know the woods better."

Knowing they didn't understand the Abenaki tongue, Abornazine pointed as he and Tidesso started walking.

The strangers followed them into the woods. They marvelled at the many berries growing wild. They pointed at everything, birds, rabbits, and raccoons. They stopped often to sketch trees and draw lines that forked like the river.

As the sun neared the far horizon, their guests wanted to stop. They dropped the things they carried and began unloading wrapped bundles from the backs of animals they called "horses."

But Norumbega was close. At night, the city offered safety. Bears prowled these woods and now with cubs, they were even more dangerous. And the little folk lived here. One never knew if the Mikumwess would be mischievous or helpful—but more often they were the former. So Abornazine waved and cajoled, urging at least one to follow. Once he saw the city, he could tell the others.

The sun-haired man, whom his people called Waymouth, followed hesitantly, cradling the stick of wood and metal. With only him following, Abornazine and Tidesso walked faster. Frequently, the man spoke rapidly, concern tightening his voice.

But soon they stood on the riverbank, gazing at Norumbega's rising walls, the crisscrossed logs tinged red in the setting sunlight. The only way across was by canoe, as two rivers flowed around it. Abornazine looked to the darkening sky. The day had been long, but excitement had kept him alert. Though he felt weary from a lack of sleep, it was time to light the streets of the confederate city.

If nothing else, Norumbega's grandness would prove to these travellers that they were among great men of the woods. That the Creator of all had delivered them unto good people.

His shoulders back, Abornazine led the man Waymouth through the city gates. From beneath wigwam flaps peered dozens of faces. Children crawled out and squatted in the dirt, pointing. Their mothers gathered them against their legs, but their gazes remained firmly on the sun-haired stranger.

They followed the circular streets, winding deeper into the city. They passed smaller wigwams, then larger ones, then the first of many longhouses and lodges. Awe shone in Waymouth's eyes as his head snapped back and forth.

Though Waymouth and his people had travelled far in enormous boats, they must not have left a city as grand as Norumbega. Certainly there was no place like this anywhere else in the confederacy.

Waymouth stared at the glittering street. Kneeling, he dragged his fingers through the yellow streaks and uttered a new word.

Abornazine touched the man's arm and pointed at the tallest longhouse in the centre of the city. "We are going there."

"He doesn't speak our language," Tidesso said.

"And if we do not speak it to him, he will never learn it."

Yet the touch and point proved to be language enough. Waymouth nodded and followed, his gaze flitting to Norumbega's carved decorations, many of them inlaid with bits of shell, the yellow mineral which excited Waymouth so, and with colourful stones plucked from the earth and river. Oftentimes, in passing, Waymouth reached out, caressing the fine pelts which hung over longhouse entrances.

They climbed the steps leading to the Council Longhouse.

As Abornazine drew back the pelt, Waymouth paused to stroke its soft fur, murmuring another strange word with admiration.

"Norumbega," Abornazine said, spreading his arm to encompass the city. From this porch, the river they'd crossed could be seen.

Waymouth pointed to the river then farther beyond, speaking rapidly.

Smiling, Abornazine said, "Yes, we will bring your people here."

Tidesso shrugged. "I will go back for them."

Before Tidesso left, Waymouth laid a hand on Tidesso's arm to stay him. Waymouth then scratched symbols on a curl of thin bark which he handed to Tidesso.

"What can it be?" Tidesso asked, staring at the strange symbols.

Abornazine shrugged. "It seems to mean something to him. Perhaps his people will understand. Smile and motion. I'm certain they will follow."

Tidesso grunted. "Or maybe they will skin me—thinking I have injured their leader."

"You should have more faith in the sky spirits," Abornazine chided.

"I have every faith in them." He grinned. "It is you I sometimes doubt... friend." Nonetheless, Tidesso headed back through the city for the canoes at the riverbank.

The Confederate Council of Norumbega convened, a gathering of sachems representing the confederate tribes and esteemed elders, some of them women. They listened while Waymouth spoke emphatically, waving his arms, often repeating the same words while touching pelts or yellow mineral streaks.

The council whispered amongst themselves, always with a wary eye toward their guest—all except Tomakwa, who looked at Abornazine, his eyes boasting a knowing smile.

Waymouth turned his palms upward then slowly reached for a roll of leather from his back. He knelt and spread the roll before the confederate council.

On the supple leather lay an array of fine hunting knives with bone handles, inlaid with metal. The blades were of varying lengths and shapes, some curved, others straight. Moreover, the blades glinted as if made of starlight. And when held up, Abornazine could see his eyes reflected in them.

Waymouth's words meant nothing, but when he struck the blade with a stone and the blade did not break, the chiefs looked thoughtful. Then he sliced the edge of the thick, leather roll as easily as cutting a sapling.

Several chiefs and elders picked up the knives, studying their blades. Tomakwa, though, studied their handles and nodded.

Along with the knives, the roll had held a bundle of furs, fox and rabbit among others.

"I believe, if I may speak," Abornazine said, "that he prizes fur and offers us knives in trade."

Sachem Kanozas, the great chief, scowled but went to the flap and spoke to the men outside. A moment later, Nanatasis, the most beautiful of Abenaki women, entered carrying a bundle of furs. Smaller furs of mink and beaver lay nestled in larger hides of elk and bear. She laid these at Sachem Kanozas's feet.

Abornazine watched her, hoping she would notice him, that their gazes might touch, even if only briefly. Yet her head remained downcast in deference to her father.

The sachem handed a fine mink pelt and bear hide to Waymouth, then Waymouth selected two of the larger, finer knives. They exchanged goods and forged their bond.

After Tidesso returned with the other strangers, the womenfolk prepared a feast. That night, Abornazine sat among the council with the chiefs. Shaman Nebizon presented him with a necklace of carved beads, each representing one of the great spirits of sky, water, land, and woods.

"Now," Shaman Nebizon announced, "Abornazine is "Spirit Talker," friend of the Mikumwess, and guardian of Norumbega."

Though the entire city gazed upon Abornazine, the only eyes that mattered were Nanatasis's. Her admiration made him feel worthy of his honoured place. And with his new status, perhaps her father, Sachem Kanozas, would hear Abornazine's petition for marriage.

Over many weeks, the strangers—"English" they called themselves—came and went. On several occasions, hunters and even chiefs followed them to the ocean shore and visited their great ships. Hunters brought back many furs, trading them for knives, bolts of cloth, and tins of spices. During that time, George Waymouth learned enough of the Abenaki tongue to be understood.

Exiting the Council Longhouse, Waymouth waved at Abornazine. "Come walk, friend."

"Are you now of the confederacy?" Abornazine asked.

Waymouth furrowed his pale brows. "Confederacy?"

Abornazine led Waymouth to the finished council pole. One by one, he pointed out the symbols, naming the tribes. "Wabanaki,

Pennacook, Micmac, Maliseet, Passamaquoddy, Penobscot, and"—he patted his own chest—"Abenaki." With a collective wave, he said, "All Wabanaki Confederacy." Noting the newest addition atop the pole, that of squatting Mikumwess, Abornazine smiled.

Repeating the tribal names, Waymouth made notes in his journal. After putting it away, he answered Abornazine's question, his words broken and hesitant. "Not in confederacy. Friend to confederacy. This"—he swept his arms to encompass the city—"great place. Want see more. See upriver. Visit more great land."

"You want a guide?"

Waymouth pointed to Abornazine's chest, saying "Guide me."

Though fond of Waymouth's alien, amusing ways, Abornazine's duties lay with Norumbega. Shaking his head, he said, "I will take you to Chibai. He is the best guide in all the confederacy."

Tidesso was a good tracker and knew the woods well. But Chibai was legendary, known as the ghost of the woods. Some said he could sneak up on Asban the trickster. Quiet and solitary, Chibai lived outside the city so he could wake each day to the forest.

"We go this way," Abornazine said, leading Waymouth along the riverbank.

Upstream, several womenfolk, Nanatasis included, waded waist-deep in the river, catching fish.

Abornazine's steps faltered, watching she whom he hoped to marry. Yet he had put off speaking with her father, a cowardice which shamed him. But Sachem Kanozas was a great man and Abornazine was only a torchlighter who had once been blessed with a vision.

Nanatasis glanced up then looked away shyly. Hugging her basket, she walked downstream toward them.

"Your woman?" Waymouth asked.

"No." Abornazine couldn't explain the situation, not with Waymouth's limited vocabulary.

"Beautiful," Waymouth said, mistakenly using the word for an object, like fur, and not for a person.

Abornazine was about to correct Waymouth when he saw the guide. Waving, Abornazine called out, "Chibai! Can you lead Waymouth and his men upriver?"

Chibai shrugged. "I have no other plans. When do they leave?"

"Now?" Waymouth answered. "We want soon return to England and I not gather all I want take back home."

"Then we go now." Chibai set off with Waymouth who waved his arms, explaining as best he could that he hadn't gathered his crew.

Abornazine smiled, certain their journey would be interesting. Then Nanatasis approached and he forgot all about Chibai, Waymouth and whatever adventure they would find.

Nanatasis stared at the basket of fish she carried. "Has Spirit Talker now become the voice of white-man?"

Abornazine dug his moccasin toe in the soft dirt. "Waymouth is my friend. He asked for help."

"Maybe he asks because your ears and heart hear those of all other worlds, the spirit world and strange lands far across the waters." Her voice softened; the wind barely carried her words. "Do you not hear my heart beating?"

The only heart Abornazine heard was his own thudding in his chest. He stammered, his thoughts tangled vines. "I... you. ."

Nanatasis took his hand. "Speak with my father. Summer is here. It is a good time for a joining."

She followed the riverbank back to the other womenfolk. Wading into the plentiful water, she cast a final shy glance his way.

Abornazine ran through the streets, seeking Sachem Kanozas. He rounded a corner too fast and collided with two willowy youths carrying a dugout canoe. Abornazine fell backward and hit the ground....

Daylight turned pitch black. Stars streaked the night skies like crackles from improperly treated wood. Abornazine rode the blazing trail, floating above the land. Below was fire, at first, many small fires. Instead of torches burning, Norumbega burned, flaring into a gigantic bonfire. Tall flames razed the concentric circles of two-story longhouses and wigwams.

An army of kiwaskwek, monsters, invaded the streets, some astride horses while others marched. From the ends of those sticks called muskets burst explosions of smoke and fire. Abornazine's people fled as metal-skinned demons shot women and children.

Though Norumbega's greatest warriors fought back, one by one, they fell dead. As red as sunset, flowing blood reflected the flames devouring the wooden buildings.

Metal garbed monsters pulled down sacred posts. They grabbed pelt coverings and ripped jewellery from the necks of the dead. When they removed their metal helmets, hair as red and yellow as fire fell about their shoulders. Among them stood George Waymouth.

Thick smoke rose from the burning city. Even in Abornazine's cloud-like state, the smoke irritated his eyes and he shed bitter tears. His tears swelled and fell as rain that quenched the fires.

The great city of the Wabanaki Confederacy lay in burnt ruins. Powerless to help, Abornazine swirled like a gust of wind among the corpses. Norumbega's population lay in the streets, all save for six. Nanatasis was not among the dead. Neither were Zazigoda, Pujinkskwes, Kizosibo, Nahoumo nor the scout Chibai.

Abornazine neither found their bodies nor felt their presence. They were simply gone.

He hung over the land, watching the tribes separate and war amongst themselves. He watched wave upon wave of white demons land on the shores to incite even more bloodshed.

In desperation, Abornazine screamed to the sky, "I cannot do nothing! This cannot be our demise!"

And the sky answered. "Then stop it."

Abornazine's head hurt. He opened his eyes, his sight blurred. Tidesso's grinning face hovered near.

"I had another vision." Abornazine's throat felt parched, yet it ached to speak.

"Another? If the only way to speak with sky spirits is to nearly die, then I am glad they did not choose me." Tidesso squeezed Abornazine's shoulder. "What great wonders did they show you this time?"

"Not wonders. But horrors." Abornazine coughed, still tasting smoke.

Shaman Nebizon pushed Tidesso aside. The medicine man offered a bowl of water. "Drink this, guardian. You have been asleep for days. But the sickness has finally sweated out of you. Now you must replenish yourself with good water."

A fire burned behind the medicine man. Smoke filled the wigwam. Gratefully, Abornazine gulped down three bowlfuls of water.

His throat eased, Abornazine spoke with less of a croak. "I must speak with the council elders. A great tragedy comes if we do not prevent it."

Shaman Nebizon and Tidesso exchanged dark glances and quiet words. Louder, Tidesso said, "Let me tell him."

The medicine man nodded then slipped out of the wigwam.

Staring at his hands, Tidesso said, "The white men have gone. They took captives with them. I wish it were not so, but Nanatasis is among those taken."

"It is as I saw." Abornazine hung his head. "I must speak to the council."

"The council will not hear you. They have already decided that once you woke, you would be cast out. Sachem Kanozas is very angry that his daughter is among the five taken. He names you betrayer. You are no longer the city's guardian."

Five? Abornazine whispered, "Six are missing. Nanatasis, Nahoumao, Zazigoda, Kizosibo, Pujinkskwes and Chibai."

Tidesso's eyes widened. "Pujinkskwes was not captured. She alone returned after Waymouth's betrayal. The council believes she sold her people to the white demons for her own skin. For her cowardice, she was cast out. As will you be."

Abornazine climbed onto unsteady feet and leaned against Tidesso. "I will find Pujinkskwes. When I have the truth, I will return to speak to the council."

"They will not listen."

"They must know what I've seen."

"Then tell me," Tidesso said.

"No, my friend. Not until I know how to prevent it."

"Prevent what?"

Abornazine stumbled out of the wigwam. Behind him, Tidesso kept repeating, "Prevent what?"

"Prevent the loss of everything. Norumbega... the confederacy... everything." With every step, Abornazine felt stronger. Hunger gnawed at his gut, but food could wait.

Faces peered from under eaves and from beneath the covered porches of two-story longhouses. And though they smiled, their bodies full of life, Abornazine saw them as ghosts. Some even stood now in the place they would die.

Abornazine waved, unable to push back the thought that he was seeing them for the last time.

Only six of this people would survive. Five of them captives.

He thought Waymouth holding Nanatasis prisoner and remembered Waymouth calling her a beautiful possession. Had the man even then plotted to abduct her? Why hadn't Abornazine seen the desire in the man's blue eyes? Why hadn't the sky spirits warned him sooner?

Abornazine squeezed his eyes shut, but nothing drove away the images of the white demon ravaging Nanatasis, touching her flesh.

With such thoughts driving him, Abornazine quickly reached the woods.

From behind, a familiar voice spoke, "Pujinkskwes headed that way." Tidesso pointed toward a leaning oak. He met Abornazine's gaze. "Did you think I would let you go alone? From what your vision showed you, you need all the help you can get."

"I didn't hear you following."

Tidesso cocked his head. "I do not think you would have heard the footsteps of stone giants the way you were tromping. An angry tracker goes hungry."

Even in the worst of situations, only Tidesso could make Abornazine smile. "I should have never left without asking for your help."

"True. I am the better tracker."

They travelled northeast to a spring. A boulder, jutting from the ground, hid the crevice entrance to a cave.

Rather than intrude, Abornazine called, "Pujinkskwes? May I speak with you. I must know what happened and tell you what *will* happen if we do not stop it."

Pujinkskwes, a witch woman, slipped out of the crevice, wearing a necklace of feathers, another of wrapped, dangling stones and a third of carved beads. Painted designs marked her face and hands. Once she had sat on the council. But named a betrayer, she lost her place among her people.

"I will see you," she said.

They sat beneath a tree. "Tell me why my friend Waymouth took captives." Though Abornazine could imagine no good reason, he desperately wanted one. If not, he had brought the evil upon his people. Then he, and not Pujinkskwes, deserved to be cast out.

"I cannot tell you why. I can only speak of what happened." Without emotion, Pujinkskwes explained that she, Nanatasis, Zazigoda and Kizosibo had gone farther upstream to fish. "Then Chibai brought the band of white men, among them Waymouth. One of Waymouth's men grabbed Kizosibo. When she fought him, he struck her.

"Nanatasis, Zazigoda and I rushed to defend Kizosibo while Chibai explained to Waymouth why he should stop his man. But Waymouth's crew wouldn't listen. A blood frenzy overtook them and they tied up Kizosibo. Nanatasis struck one man with a rock, splitting his head. That worsened their frenzy. Zazigoda screamed. A hunting party, led by Nahoumao, burst through the brush to fight Waymouth's men. Nahoumao was taken captive. In the fight, the white men badly injured the rest of the hunting party and left them to die of bleeding. During the noise, I escaped to the woods and hid. Chibai, once Waymouth's guide, was now his prisoner. Waymouth forced Chibai to lead them back to their ships or he would order the other captives killed."

In Abornazine's vision, only six people from Norumbega were missing—counting Pujinkskwes. "Who was in the slain hunting party?"

"None died. Once the white demons left, I tended their wounds."

"And for your help, you were exiled?" Abornazine asked.

"Because I ran, I was exiled. Because I did not draw upon my magic powers. But magic does not work that way. It requires preparation. Shaman Nebizon understood and spoke on my behalf. But his was but one voice, drowned out by the rest of the council."

Abornazine hung his head, certain that Sachem Kanozas's voice alone drowned out the shaman's words. Yet running was cowardice. Cowardly acts brought evil magic. Had she not run, she would be a captive and the men she had helped would have died. But the laws were what they were.

"I have accepted my punishment," she said. "I do not wish to bring misfortune upon Norumbega."

"You hold no blame for what comes. Because you are exiled, you will survive the coming slaughter." Drawing a calming breath, smelling and tasting the forest air, Abornazine spoke his vision.

Pujinkskwes listened without showing surprise.

However, grief and dread etched Tidesso's face.

Afterward, they sat quietly. Abornazine tried to drive out the imagines in his mind. Shock seemed to have caused Tidesso's silence, while Pujinkskwes stared quietly into the forest, her gaze unfocused, deep in concentration.

At last, she spoke. "You must find the Mikumwess, Abornazine. Only their magic is strong enough to protect Norumbega. Meanwhile, Tidesso can help me gather ingredients my own magic. But without Mikumwess magic, any charm I make will fail."

"Then I must succeed."

Abornazine headed toward that same tree hollow where he once tried to leave an offering of pine cones. Along the path, he gathered smooth pebbles, flowers, and fallen bird feathers. On finding an eagle feather, his hope grew, for eagle feathers carried strong magic. Only owl's was stronger.

Then he found an owl feather and knew he had his offering.

A Mikumwess squatted on the exposed root of his tree home. That he didn't vanish at Abornazine's approach was another good sign.

Abornazine laid out his offering then sat cross-legged. "We need your help to save Norumbega."

"Why do *you* ask me? Why do not your elders come instead?"

"Because *I* am the Guardian of Norumbega." Abornazine desperately hoped he would not be forever remembered as the Destroyer of Norumbega.

"What trouble do you expect? No storms are coming. The land is stable. The rivers will not overflow. What threatens your city?" Though the Mikumwess asked, his tone and the certainty in his eyes betrayed his knowledge.

The little people of the forest often tested those who sought them. Knowing they reviled dishonesty, Abornanzine spoke from his aching heart. "A great and evil enemy from across the sea comes to destroy it. An enemy whom I foolishly befriended."

"Why do you think I would help?"

"Twice now, I have received visions. Though I—and my people—attributed these visions to the sky beings, I think now that you, or your kind, sent them to me. The first vision proved true. I greatly fear the second will as well."

The Mikumwess gathered up the flowers, pebbles and feathers. "Your offering is accepted. When your witch woman has her charm ready, I will lend my powers."

"My preparations are nearly complete," Pujinskwes said.

"Have I time to warn the council?" Abornazine asked.

Tidesso grabbed Abornazine's arm. "They will not listen. Sachem Kanozas will take your life. You did not see his anger. You will be dead before you can speak."

"Then you must warn them. Tell them that they must desert the city, return to the woods and villages, if they wish to live."

"If they wish to continue living *here*," Pujinskwes said.

Abornazine and Tidesso stared questioningly.

"By your admission, we cannot defeat this enemy in battle," Pujinskwes said. "We cannot stop them from burning Norumbega. We can only protect our people."

"But Norumbega is our greatest achievement," Abornazine said.

"It must be lost for now, if it is not to be lost forever," the witch woman said. She held out a pouch. As Abornazine's fingers wrapped around the soft leather, she said, "By your sacrifice for your people, Norumbega shall be saved. You shall be forever its guardian. Do you accept this fate?"

Abornazine reached for the necklace that should have been around his neck, only then realizing someone must have taken it while he'd slept, after the blow to his head. Feeling sadness and shame at its loss, he nodded. "I accepted once before. I shall not forsake my duty."

To Tidesso, the witch woman said, "Go, fleet of foot, and tell the people of Norumbega that they must leave, or forever remain in the city. They have until moonrise. If they will not listen, show them this." Pujinskwes pressed something into Tidesso's palm.

"What did you give him," Abornazine asked after Tidesso had left.

"Long ago the forest spirits gave me a token. Nebizon will know I would not give it up without great cause."

From the shadows, Abornanzine and Pujinkskwes watched the last of Norumbega's people cross the rivers, carrying all they owned on their backs. In family groups, they parted, fanning across the confederacy, returning to their old villages.

Only Tidesso and Nebizon lingered along the shore. Perhaps they waited, hoping to see what great magic the Mikumwess and Pujinkskwes would work.

Abornazine stepped out from the brush and waved. On receiving Tidesso's return signal, Abornazine rowed a canoe across. Close to his heart, he carried the pouch containing the magic charm the witch woman had made. When his canoe struck the opposite shore, the Mikumwess that Abornazine had met with earlier appeared at the canoe's point.

Nodding toward Tidesso and Nebizon, the Mikumwess said, "They shall be the Keepers of the True Legend. That is all the help they can offer you. Are you sure you are willing to make the sacrifice?"

"For years I have lit the torches that illuminated the city. Now I shall be the watchful torch," Abornazine said, walking the city streets, lighting the torches one last time.

For the ceremony site, Abornazine chose the circle of stones around the council pole which honoured the confederate nations and the Mikumwess. The diminutive forest dweller at Abornazine's feet nodded approvingly.

"It is time," the Mikumwess said. "Do as your witch woman has explained. I will do my part."

Though Abornazine knew every action to perform, every word to chant, he still didn't know what would happen, how the ceremony would protect Norumbega, nor why the people had to leave.

Carefully, Abornazine emptied the pouch, making a neat, unbroken circle inside the stones surrounding the pole. Standing in the ring of magic powder, he chanted the magic words. Though he recognised the sounds as Abenaki, magic kept him from understanding what he said.

"Nodah, Nedobak! Waban chi ba gi no guat madjahando, madawlinno. Kgamo Norumbega olibamkanni. Kgamo Gici Niwaskw, Tabaldak!"

He recognised only the one word, "Norumbega."

The Mikumwess hummed and danced around the pole. He climbed to the top and melded into the carved likeness of his kind.

The council pole came to life. It uprooted itself. Where the grain ran long, thick splinters rose out, becoming branches, each decorated with Tomwaka's carvings. Abornazine collapsed to his knees.

Dark clouds swirled overhead. Lightning crackled within them.

The living pole lifted Abornazine and wrapped its many wooden limbs around him, like a mother wrapping her young in swaddling. He fused into the wood, realizing that the whole of the land was his mother now, and he its son.

Lightning streaked downward, striking the pole. With it, a new warmth surged through Abornazine. Fire, too, was welcoming him into the fold. Earth and fire. Then rain poured from the dark sky, drenching his torches.

The rain slowed to a drizzle and clouds descended to engulf Norumbega in fog. Amid the sparkles of dew in the cloudy air, the longhouses glittered like starlight. When the clouds lifted, the city's grand structures faded into ghostly outlines. Norumbega was vanishing, rising upon the clouds, borne on the backs of sky beings.

Where the two rivers met, where once a great city stood, now stood a lone pole, carved with symbols of the Wabanaki Confederacy. Abornazine, his spirit a part of that pole, gazed at the land, seeing the city only in memory.

The Mikumwess jumped down from atop the pole. "You are now Eternal Watchman and Guardian. Should the time arise for Norumbega to return, you can call it back."

Unable to form words, Abornazine thoughts reached out. "How will I know when it is time?"

"You will feel a great peace when mankind becomes as one people. When mankind learns to live in harmony with each other and with nature."

The Mikumwess vanished.

Abornazine felt his roots plunge into the land. He stretched out his many arms and the pole sprouted new life, becoming again a thriving, ancient tree. His branches touched the sky. He felt all that was in the world.

At that moment, he knew it would be a long time before Norumbega would return. Until then, he was Watcher of the Land, Keeper of the Vanished City, Guardian of Norumbega.

afterword

I have always enjoyed tales of lost or wondrous places like Atlantis and El Dorado. Norumbega is another such fabled place. And while there are tales of this mythical city, I never found any tales explaining what happened to it, as it has never been discovered historically. So I felt inspired to write about it. Then, as if by fate, I met a man, Joseph Bruchac, who is an author and is also of Abernaki birth. We were on a panel together about the use of Native American ghosts in legends. He is a lovely and intelligent man. I suppose you could say his tales inspired me to finish the story.

Ice

Zdravka Evtimova

ICE WAS EVERYWHERE, blue, gray, even black in the valleys. Ice was a part of my job. I had to calculate when avalanches would start and when the surface would crack, engulfing spacecraft, the traffic control towers, the pilots and passengers, soldiers and police officers in charge of the planet's security. It was my responsibility to organise search and rescue teams to dig and delve in the ice for possible survivors. Usually no one survived in the fathomless cracks of the ice on Mafa. I was the only survivor.

I had graduated in poetry writing from the University of Sofia on Earth. I wasn't a brilliant student, actually I was among the worst students that had ever set foot in the university. I took to writing verse because was I was convinced poetry was an easy-going affair. A dirge a critic would call downright sloppy doggerel, another expert in the trade proclaimed to be an experimental and sophisticated masterpiece. So I reckoned poetry was a quiet shelter for a young woman of no considerable ambitions. I could call high literature my job while I ran no risk to be labelled slothful. My professors said I was a sheltered person, sensitive, too, and it seemed to them I could live well perfectly alone, so they wondered why my poetry was so weak.

I didn't have friends on the Earth, my parents were divorced and I grew up on J5. A boarding house planet for children whose parents weren't so keen on taking care of their offspring. The air on J5 had a particular quality to it. It gave you the feeling your loving family was waiting for at the airport eager to give you a warm hug. The whole planet loved you. There were no predators on J5, no poisonous organisms or plants, and all the time you felt like your caring daddy was by your side. In fact, J5 was your loving grandma.

I was not a particularly industrious person and the leisure of J5 made me even more indolent. The other children thought my parents' divorce was a blessing for me. Your parents earned a one-way ticket to J5 for you, they said. I majored in poetry writing because it was the easiest thing in universe. You didn't need to study much. These days no one really wanted poetry. Some crazy foundations paid you to go and study how to produce rhymes, concoct metaphors and spew similes about a fact as simple as breaking with your boyfriend. I enjoyed that.

The only thing I was really good at was breaking with my boyfriends. My professors seemed to encourage that; they said it was good for my poetry. I couldn't care less about stanzas, sonnets and dithyrambs; I cared about the money they paid me to study how to write them. I knew very well I had no talent at all. Art left me perfectly cold and unperturbed. I hated natural sciences, I hated history too, and I wasn't particularly interested in making a lot of money either. I guessed I had to work somewhere, like everybody else, and the diploma of a poetess- or shall I put it an expert in poetry—would at least secure me a position of a tourist guide on Mafa. Mafa, the ice planet that had become a hit among the tourist destinations.

It was the most fashionable thing to get married amidst the ugly mountains and gorges of ice. The fools believed their marriage would be spotless if they tied the knot on the black glacier crescents of the Twin Hills, an abhorrent canyon near my office: a small, gloomy place, dug out in a hill of black ice.

I was one of the passengers on the list of Flight S123, from Sofia. I flew to Twin Hills on Mafa, where young fools rushed to get married. I was the only single person on board of the spacecraft. I had broken with four boyfriends so far, and I abandoned my fifth sweetheart without batting an eyelid. I didn't tell him I wouldn't return to the flat we rented in a cheap suburb of Sofia. I said I was going to buy a packet of dried dill for the soup I was cooking for him. The guy loved dill soup. I left the water and meat boiling on the cooking stove.

"Hey," he said. "Take more money and buy a bar of chocolate for me."

I guessed he was very disappointed he didn't get his chocolate. I didn't make the dill soup either. I took Flight S123 instead. I had signed a contract and I had to become the poet laureate, who would write love hymns for the young nitwits that married on the Twin Hills.

The ice surface cracked when we landed on the planet. On Mafa you never knew when the ice would break. It could open up under your feet even though a minute before the black frozen wasteland was as immobile as a dead man.

I was the only survivor among the 57 passengers. The crew, a happily married couple, were never found. The search and rescue team had found me frozen, my arms, legs and ribs broken, their captain said. It was a wonder, the doctors exclaimed. No one could live so long without food and warm clothes on Mafa. *The ice seemed to like you.* The search and rescue team told me I was on top of a jagged icy outcrop. The other passengers were torn to pieces in frozen pools of blood. It is impossible, it just couldn't happen, the doctors said. It's a wonder you are still alive.

I could predict when the ice would crack. I didn't know how it happened. I often thought about the guy I left in my shabby Sofia flat waiting for his bar of chocolate, and I felt like making love to him. Then the ice cracked. It just did. Even the slightest hint I wanted that guy—he was not handsome, and he was not even very clever- made the ice toss and split. My boyfriend was a peaceful sissy who constantly said he loved me. All my previous boyfriends used to say that, and it was a warning sign I had to leave. Dad used to declare he loved mom, then he walked away on her and she went to a psychiatric ward. She recovered quickly, it was true, then she married another guy. Love was something dark and deleterious.

The only good thing about love was its absence from my life. It was better to break with a boyfriend who claimed he loved me, than land in a lunatic asylum. Making love was a different thing.

I thought about the dill soup I left boiling on the stove, and I saw the guy, waiting for his bar of chocolate. I wanted him. The ice cracked. Expert teams established the depth and width of the chasm using complex electronic equipment. I thought it would be sensible if I told them the ice would kick and split. I warned the experts and they cancelled the flights.

My reputation of a unique talent who had a particular feeling for Mafa and its killing ice grew every day. The love hymns I composed were of a shamefully inferior quality but young couples paid fortunes to have me dedicate a lyricsong or a slap-dash piece of writing I called a sonnet to their wedding day. How vainly men themselves amazed! I was called the ice queen, Lady Sovereign of survival and many other idiotic things I hated to repeat. I stood and stared at the ice and that was what I did all day long. I hated the poems I wrote. They were flat, dumb, and completely lacking in inspiration.

It was not necessary even to be awake to know when the ice would hit. If I had an erotic dream I knew that the surface of Mafa would rent and lacerate its icy skin. The flights to Mafa were cancelled, human lives were saved and people on the Earth, inhabitants of Sofia built an edifice, a palace of culture, they named after me. The Mayor invited me to come and deliver a speech on the day of its inauguration, an honour I declined. It was not the absence of vanity in my thoughts that made me turn down the offer. I had to rise to the occasion and write a poem about Sofia, a thing I hated to do. Another element was added to the fable woven around my name: my phenomenal modesty. Modesty my foot! I was the most vainglorious person you could imagine. I wished my father twisted and turned in his bed, gnashing his teeth after he heard about me. I wished my mother writhed and squirmed. After she remarried she never phoned or asked how I was doing on J5, that bland idiotic boarding house of a planet, where all abandoned children in our part of the universe scraped a living.

Mafa got on my nerves. I was fed up with the ice and with being called the guardian of the rifts and the icy precipices. I hated to be a guardian. Sometimes I wanted my boyfriend so much that the ice cracked from pole to pole. Once I enticed a young man away from his fiancée. You couldn't imagine how she screamed and hollered and vociferated. The search and rescue team found me almost dead, both my arms broken. I lay in a frozen lake of blood. They could not find the guy "It's a miracle you survived," the doctor told me later. "It all seems impossible. Maybe the ice loves you."

I hated the glaciers, and the menacing height of the icy mountains gave me the creeps. I could feel, more sharply than before, the surface of Mafa kick and crack, and I constantly thought of the dill soup I had left on the cooking stove. I dreamed about my boyfriend in the kitchen, naked. All the flights were cancelled. I lived in a fury of memories and blurred visions, in my sleep I talked to him, and I dreamt I came back to the shabby apartment in Sofia, then I got lost in the rumbling city I couldn't stand. It was a nightmare. I was the only human being on the planet and I choked in my nest of ice, my small room. The colour of the icy wasteland around me changed: it became black everywhere. All honeymoon flights to Mafa were cancelled, no one came to the planet any more. I saw the bar of chocolate I never bought for my boyfriend. He was constantly before my eyes. His skin was smooth and sparkling. I loved it.

The ice broke and whined. The mountains of ice collapsed, whirred, buzzed, and pealed. The whole planet split and writhed, the hills tumbled and shattered. Fountains of black ice spurted from the gorges, and I lay exhausted, unable to think of my boyfriend any more. The two craft that came to extricate me from the freezing nightmare were engulfed by the gray abysses of crackling ice. The remote-controlled shuttles that brought food for me landed unscathed.

What happens on Mafa is a mystery, I read in the messages I received from the Earth. *Mafa wants you. It wants nobody else. Try to describe how you feel, what you think about when the ice breaks.*

I didn't tell them I saw Slav naked. I called all my boyfriends Slav. It was a name I hated. My father's name was Slav. *Do you see any connection between your actions and the rebellion of the ice?* I had established a connection, but I was not an idiot to tell them about it. I had my pride. I was an expert in poetry, a poor expert, it was true. But I was an expert all the same.

The shuttle brought me some disgusting yellow cake to eat, a large baking tin of yellowish rubbish. I hated cakes. On J5, they always gave us cakes for breakfast, cakes on Christmas, and cakes on Mother's day, too.

I was alone in my office with the ugly lump of hard-baked dough. The walls of the room were all transparent, and I had the feeling nothing separated me from the black crackling ice. It felt like my skin cracked. I was hungry and I had nothing else to eat, so I ate the sinister looking chunk.

I was convinced that even the most brilliant student in my poetry class—I had heard he became quite famous for his *"Cosmic Ballads"*—I bet even he wouldn't be able to describe truly and fully the bliss and pleasure I enjoyed that evening. It all felt so real I couldn't breathe.

I was in my old apartment in Sofia. There was no ice there, it was a spring day. I never liked spring: it was wet and windy, and the blossoms of the trees made me allergic and sour. The apartment was a sorry sight, the faded wallpapers, the greasy staircase, the smell of mould: it all looked and felt the same. The man who lived in my flat was not Slav. He looked very confused when he saw me standing at his front door. I had put on the black suit I wore on Mafa, amidst the black ice.

"You look like her," he stammered. "You look like her... Is it some trick?"

"Can I come in?" I asked. "I'll explain everything to you."

I didn't utter a word, though, I kissed him instead. He was astounded.

"Slav," I said. "It's the craziest thing I've ever gone through... It's a hallucination."

We made love. It was too warm and too wet in the room, but I didn't care. I was sorry I was a third-rate poet and I couldn't write a poem to his hands, a ballad for his mouth, an ode to his flat stomach, a hymn to every square inch of his wonderful skin. It was such a vivid hallucination I wished it would last for ever. I kissed and kissed him. I loved him and my hunger left him dry and exhausted, smiling happily in the moist, smelly air. Was it the yellow cake that gave me that happiness? No doubt, it had some drug in it. What a fool I was. I should have kept a piece of it for the next time.

"Slav," I said to the man. "Slav... I love your name."

"I'm not Slav. I'm Ivan. You look like the girl on Mafa... the famous poetess who saves people in the ice," he whispered. "You look so much like her... But you are more beautiful than her. I want you to know that. You are the most beautiful girl I've ever seen."

"Slav, I am hungry," I said.

He brought a jar of yellow honey. There was a label *Sunflower Honey from Sofia* and a picture of sunlit field covered with yellow blazing sunflowers. Sunflower honey was the cheapest thing you could buy from the local supermarket. I kissed Slav. My hallucination and his lips tasted sweet.

I opened the jar.

I was again in my office with the transparent walls, amidst the black wasteland of dead ice.

"Slav!" I shouted.

For a fleeting moment, I saw him, I heard him say I was the most beautiful girl he'd ever seen. The black ice cracked so powerfully that the walls of my office shook and my bed shattered into uncanny sharp pieces on the floor. I stared. There were rifts, fissures, crevices everywhere around me, all gaping gray and black in the thick jumping ice. The planet roared and shuddered triumphantly, closing in on all sides around me.

It felt like making love. It was dreadful and it was fabulous.

The wall of my room broke and I was amidst the desert of ice. I was naked.

Enormous fragments of ice pushed their way into the space where my office had been. Mafa wanted me.

Then I saw something on the table, that didn't shake and stood firmly in its place. I froze in my tracks. There was a jar and the label read *Sunflower Honey from Sofia*.

The ice that touched my skin was smooth and warm like Slav's hands.

afterword

I dreamt about this story and when I woke I was scared. I didn't want to write it, and day in day out my fear grew. I saw the ice and I saw the planet shattering.

It was after I wrote down what made me panic I forgot about the ice. It was maybe five or six months later that I found this story among my files. I read the text, and remained calm. I am happy now that the story has found such a good home.

United

Jennifer Moore

"MY NAME IS Mashei," I tell them. "I am nine years old. I like drawing." Some of the boys at the back are laughing. The teacher tells them to be quiet.

"Thank you," she says. She smiles at me. "Now I know you're all going to help Mashei settle in. Try and remember what it was like on your first day at school. All those new faces, lots of new names to learn. Okay then Mashei," she says. "If you would like to sit down here at the front, then we'll see about sorting out some pencils and things for you."

My face feels hot. The children are all staring at me. I wish I had a nice blue pencil case like the boy next to me. He has pencils and crayons and a white rubber. My mother says we will buy some new school things soon. The boy lets me use one of his pencils. It is red and shiny with a black and white ball on top. He tells me it is his favourite and I mustn't suck or chew on it.

When the lesson ends I follow the other children outside into the playground. The girls giggle and touch my clothes. They all wear the same grey dresses. The boys are chasing a ball around, kicking and shouting.

"Oi, Mashei, what team d'you support?"

I don't know what to say. "We don't really have football support in my country," I tell them. "We just play for fun."

"But what's your team?" they ask. They are laughing, poking at me with their fingers.

I remember a man at the camp when we first got off the boat—a kind man. He was wearing a yellow stripy shirt. He told me the shirt was for the best football team in the whole world.

"My team is the one with yellow stripes," I tell the laughing boys. They are surprised. They stop poking me. One of them kicks my leg. The boy who gave me the shiny red pencil spits on my shoe. I don't know what to do. In my country we don't spit at people. The girls giggle quietly. Everyone is looking at me, waiting. I pull back my foot, wiping it against the bottom of my trousers. Then I wet my mouth and spit on his shoe. Someone pushes me. There are cross faces all around me. I don't understand.

"They are the best team in the world," I say. I wish they would go away. I don't want to be here. It's cold and wet. I turn and run.

Back in the classroom it is warm and dry. The teacher asks me how I am enjoying my first morning. I tell her I don't like it here and she laughs.

"You'll soon make friends," she tells me. "It will get better. Come and see me if you're finding the work too difficult. We can always arrange for some extra language classes if you're struggling."

I don't care about the work. I try to tell her about the boys, about the football, about the man at the camp with the yellow stripy shirt. She laughs again.

"You boys and your football," she smiles. "The same the world over, eh? Well if you know how to kick a ball around the playground you'll have no trouble fitting in. They're football mad round here." I don't think she understands.

The other children come in and we all sit back down. They are talking about me, whispering. I hear them when the teacher is busy writing on the board. The boy next to me takes back his red pencil. He tells me he won't share with me if I support United.

"What is United?" I ask him.

"United are scum," he says. "Everyone knows that."

I can not work without a pencil and the teacher tells us we must be quiet. I shut my eyes and think of home. I remember the hot sun, the feel of the dry earth under my feet. I think of my family, my friends. I think of the old school, the games we played in the dusty yard. There were no grey dresses, no teams, no spitting. I remember the day the soldiers came. I remember my mother singing.

"And when the spirit comes for me," she sang, "he'll touch my eyes and I will see. And when the spirit comes for me, he'll take my hand and I'll be free." She was still singing as they took my father away.

The teacher asks me if I am alright. I open my eyes. My cheeks are wet. The boys behind are laughing at me. They say that they would cry too if they had to support a team like United. I wish they would be quiet. I wish I had never told them about the shirts with the yellow stripes. I wish my father was here.

They are waiting for me at lunch time. There are bigger boys too from the other classes. They follow me, chanting, "United scum, United scum..." I pretend I cannot hear them. I start to sing. When I sing I can make them all go away. I can pretend I am at home with my father. I can pretend the soldiers never came. When I sing they cannot hurt me.

"That's right, United Boy," says a tall boy with a ripped jumper. "We're coming for you."

I am walking faster now, away from the playground. I should turn round. I should find the teacher, but they are still behind me. I don't know what to do. I keep walking. I keep singing, "and when the spirit comes for me, he'll take my hand and I'll be free."

There is a wooden shed at the end of the field. I start to run. I might be safe there. The ground is soft and wet under my feet. The mud splashes my legs. Someone throws a heavy drink at me. It hits my shoulder. I keep singing so I will not cry. My shoulder stings. It feels wet and sticky. They are running behind me, shouting. I cannot hear what they are saying. I don't want to hear.

I am nearly at the shed when I slip on the grass. My ankle hurts and I can't get back up again. I lie there on the grass with my eyes shut. Maybe the boys will leave me alone now. Maybe someone will come and help me. The wet grass licks at my stomach. My clothes are soggy. My mother says we will get some warm shirts and jumpers for the winter.

The first boy reaches me. He presses his shoe into my leg but says nothing. He waits for the others. They roll me over and pull me up.

"Last chance, cry baby," says a fat boy with spiky hair. "Who's the best team in the world?"

My mouth is dry. I don't know what to say. I don't know the answer.

"He's asking for it," says a boy at the back.

My ankle hurts. I hope the teacher comes soon.

"I don't know," I tell them.

The boy with spiky hair pushes me. "Not good enough," he says. "I asked you a question." He pushes me again, harder. I fall back onto the grass. "Who's the best team in the world?"

I start to sing. Feet kick at my chest and legs. I know I must be brave like my father. Again and again the feet come. They kick at my stomach, they kick at my head. I sing and sing and sing until they kick at my throat and the song will not come.

It is quiet now. Perhaps they have gone. I open my eyes but it is too dark. I cannot see them. I cannot feel them.

"Hey, wake up," says one. "Stop mucking around."

"He's not breathing," says another.

I am safe now. They cannot hurt me any more.

"Mashei! Mashei! This isn't funny."

I try to speak but no words come.

Some of the boys are crying now. The one with spiky hair is crying the loudest.

"We need to get someone," he says. "We can't just leave him here."

They tell him no one will ever know. They say everything's going to be all right. The bigger boys drag me across the wet grass. I feel nothing. I am warm and dry. They pull me behind the shed, into a tall patch of nettles.

"No one will ever know," they say. "No one comes down here." They dry their eyes and walk away. Only the boy with the shiny red pencil stops beside me.

"I'm sorry," he whispers.

"Wait," I want to ask him. "Please don't leave me here. My mother will be worried." I want him to tell her I am safe. I want her to know I am with my father now. I have seen him waiting for me. He is there with my uncle and the men of our village. They are all smiling. There are no soldiers now. I want to go to them but I must wait.

"Please stay," I try to tell him but my mouth is broken and the boy with the red pencil cannot hear me. He turns and goes.

It is quiet now. No one comes. I lie there, waiting. The teacher must be looking for me. She will tell my mother. They will find me.

I wait a long time. I think I hear someone calling my name but I cannot answer. The voice is far away. It calls twice, then stops. I remember a story my father told us about a boy who ran away. He hid in a cave just outside the village and would not come out when he heard the villagers searching for him. When they found him, weeks later, he was just a pile of bones. Some people said it was wild animals. Some said it was the dark spirits. I don't want to be bones. I wish they would come.

The voice is back. There are others too, now. I can hear my mother. She is calling me. I can hear she is crying.

"I'm here!" I try to tell her, but I cannot make the sounds. I hear the boys talking to her. They tell her I did not come this way. They say I was upset. They say I ran away. I cannot be still any longer. I must show her. I feel her song bubbling in my throat. It pushes up into my mouth and out into the damp air. "And when the spirit comes for me, he'll touch my eyes and I will see..." I am singing and singing and this time they cannot stop me.

There are people running now. I can hear their footsteps coming towards me. They are loud and heavy in the wet grass. The boys are calling to each other. Some are crying. I do not listen. When I open my eyes again my father is there. He is still waiting. He holds out a hand towards me. "It's alright," he tells me, "they are coming. You're free."

The original idea for "United" came from Chaucer's "The Prioress's Tale", in which a young boy who is killed for his beliefs continues to sing after his death. In Chaucer those beliefs are religious but for Mashei something as seemingly banal and inconsequential as his choice of football team is enough to confirm his 'otherness' and seal his fate as an outsider.

When writing "United" I pictured the events unfolding at my own first school—a tiny Victorian village school deep in the Norfolk countryside, which has now been converted into a private house. Mashei's murder takes place at the bottom of the field, around the corner and out of sight of the school. I remember a big fir tree there but no shed to hide a body behind. The vindictive children have no basis in memory—they are purely fictional.

Rekindle the Sun

Mary E. Lowd

THE YELLOW SUN of Heffe VIII beamed onto Kerri's face through the freighter ship's window. She'd been watching intently through the window ever since the ship entered the Heffen solar system. "It's hard to believe that's a dying sun," Kerri said. It was still so bright and dazzling, hanging in the black, velvet sky. It looked young and promising, not old and fading. Kerri turned to her husband, Alan, who was sitting beside her, and smiled. "It'll be good to finally see Heffe," she said.

Alan, with the winningly mischievous smile that first captured Kerri's attention, began speaking to her in Heffen. Kerri recognised the language; Alan had been learning it for months, ever since he'd been hired for this job. He had a knack for languages that Kerri knew she didn't have. When he finished, he said, "That was a Heffen love poem for you. I found it in one of my books."

Kerri was touched. She wondered what, exactly, the poem meant, but she didn't ask. Already worried about coming to live on a world where she didn't speak the native language, she found comfort in pretending not to mind. Kerri and Alan sat quietly for the rest of the flight across the Heffen system. Kerri wished she were better with languages.

As the ship landed, Alan said, "You know, this flight, the whole way from Wespirtech, will only take a few minutes when Anna finishes her elasti-drive."

Kerri heard about Anna Karlingoff a lot. She was one of Alan's colleagues at Wespirtech, one of the other physicists. When Alan first started talking about Anna, Kerri was inclined to be jealous. Alan teased her about it. After a while, Kerri asked around, and it turned out that Anna was madly in love with a geneticist. She was no threat, and Kerri felt foolish for doubting Alan.

Now that Alan had left Wespirtech for good, Kerri realised she would miss hearing about Anna. Living on Heffe would be better than her years with Alan at Wespirtech had been. Here, she could learn about the culture and make friends of her own instead of just hearing about his. At Wespirtech, she had been one of very few spouses, and the scientists kept mostly to each other. The Western Spiral Arm Planetary Institute of Technology, better known as Wespirtech, was the foremost outpost of scientific and technological advancement in the known universe, but it wasn't a very friendly place to live for an outsider. She could not be more of an outsider on Heffe VIII than she had been there.

On Heffe VIII, there would be cities and gardens, museums, concerts, and shops. Kerri would have her own home. She could grow a garden again... It had been too many years since she'd had a real garden. At Wespirtech, the best she could manage was a few potted plants. Yes, Heffe VIII would be much better than the cold, steel buildings of Wespirtech, surrounded by that desolate moon.

Finally, the freighter ship finished its complicated decontamination and hatch unlocking procedures. Kerri and Alan were free to disembark. Their bags were already packed, and their quarters on the ship were returned to the friendly but sterile state they'd known when Kerri and Alan boarded months ago. It looked like a hotel room, replete with generic, floral paintings and bad lighting. Kerri was glad she wouldn't be living there any longer. Even their rooms at Wespirtech had been better.

The little, yellow sun blazed, almost mockingly, as Kerri and Alan stepped, holding hands, onto the world that was to be their new home. Alan looked at the sun appreciatively, like a mathematician looking at a particularly complicated and elegant differential equation. Up to the next twenty years of his life would be spent trying to save that dying sun. Kerri squeezed his hand proudly.

The Petriezskian Democracy had sent a welcoming squadron, and Alan, their new fusion dynamics specialist, was greeted with honours. For Kerri, it was exciting but unsettling. A full squadron of stiffly uniformed officials, with flags from each of the Heffen nations waving above their heads, had come to greet her! Except... they weren't there for her, really. They were there to greet Alan, and Kerri was just the wife. She felt out of place.

Still, it was very interesting. Kerri had never seen a live Heffen before, much less shaken hands with one, although she had been studying all their records and had seen many 2Ds and a few holoscans. While Alan spoke in Heffen with the head of the welcoming party and was introduced to a series of new colleagues, Kerri looked closely at the faces of this alien race, her new neighbours.

By far, most of the Heffen present were Petriezski. That was not surprising, since theirs was the nation Kerri and Alan landed in and were soon to live in. The Petriezski had the richest and most politically powerful government on Heffe VIII, and, therefore, had been the ones to commission Alan.

Scanning over the crowd, Kerri picked out one face that was not Petriezskian. The flat-faced and short-furred Golan stood out quite a bit in the crowd of Petriezski with their longer, more articulated faces, and flowing fur. Of course, the red and gold ribbons draped over his shoulders, hanging almost to his feet, helped him stand out too. The Petriezski looked more formal and dignified. They were really quite handsome, the Petriezski were, with their ruffs of fur flowing out of the collars and over the shoulders of their uniforms. The Golan individual looked funnier with his stout, square frame and short fur. Kerri imagined he was a much more colourful individual...or maybe it was just those ribbons.

Kerri took Alan's arm and gave it a steady squeeze. *I'm tired and ready to go* that squeeze said. Alan looked flustered but took the hint. The formalities were soon wrapped up. Kerri and Alan were shown to a hoverpod and flown to their new home.

Alan ordered the *karfanor* special for two, a Petriezskian dish. Kerri knew he tended to order dishes that were too bland for her, but she still couldn't read the menu, and objecting would have been too hard. Besides, it was sweet the way he made romantic gestures, like ordering the meal for two.

They were at the fanciest restaurant in Ques'trian, the capital city of the Petriezski Nation, and the city to which they lived closest.

Still, it was a twenty-minute drive by hoverpod away. It had been a few months since Kerri and Alan arrived on Heffe, although Kerri felt like she was still settling in. Alan had begun his work in earnest, studying the sun. Tonight's dinner was a celebration. He'd located a similar but unwanted sun in a nearby star system and planned to mine it for matter transfusions to pump into the Heffen sun. He had high hopes for the plan working and was in high spirits. Kerri was happy to see him happy.

"The Petriezski are preparing a ship for the mining expedition already," Alan said. "If you don't mind, I was planning to fly along with them. It would be a few months."

Alan was looking down as he said it, so he missed Kerri's momentary expression. By the time he looked up, expecting an answer, Kerri had recovered herself and managed to say, "Of course, if that would be best for your work, it'll be fine. It will give me time to work on my garden." Just at that moment, Kerri couldn't imagine doing much more than work on her garden without Alan there. She hadn't been into Ques'trian alone yet and was afraid of how she'd get by not knowing the language.

"How is your garden, Kerri?" he asked. "When will those plants you're having shipped from Earth X come?"

Kerri, happy to talk about her garden, told Alan of when the shipment would come and told him about all the different plants she'd ordered, including her special order for a kitty-willow tree. Then, she suggested that, maybe, before he left he could go with her to one of the local greenhouses and help her buy some native plants. It would let her get to work sooner, before the Earth X shipment came.

"I don't think there'll be time..." he said. "I'm sorry." Then, returning to his favourite solution, Alan muttered something about trying again to get Kerri a Keat. Kerri knew better than to pin her hopes on it.

For a while, when Kerri and Alan first arrived, Alan talked a lot about contacting Anna, pulling some strings, and seeing if he could get a hold of a Keat. The genetically advanced breed of parrot designed to act as translators, were reserved for important diplomats. Anna was dating the geneticist who designed them. Alan's promise never came through, and eventually he stopped mentioning it. From the gossip Kerri could gather through her limited correspondence over subspace, she suspected Alan's failure to procure a Keat through Anna had to do with her nasty breakup with the geneticist. She also suspected that Alan didn't know about it.

The *karfanor* special for two came, and Kerri and Alan were occupied for some time with eating. Kerri discovered she'd been right: Alan had ordered a meal too bland for her. It was all right though, and Alan seemed to like it. Kerri wondered about Golan food. She'd passed by a Golan kiosk on the street, teeming with the smell of exotic spices. It'd be too much for Alan. Maybe while Alan was gone on his mining expedition, she'd finally try it.

The shipment of plants arrived while Alan was still gone. Kerri received notice of the arrival at home but would have to go in the hoverpod to pick the shipment up. She'd gone into town a few times already. Exploring the countryside, readying her garden for the coming shipment, and relaxing at home were good ways to spend time, but Kerri grew hungry for even the sight other people as the weeks without Alan stretched on. Eventually, she'd overcome her fears of a city where she stood out, the only human, and knew none of the language.

Visiting Ques'trian alone had turned out to be very exciting. For one, the hoverpod was fun to drive, and while Alan was around he was always the one to handle the controls. During the long years at Wespirtech, Kerri had forgotten how much she loved flying hoverpods. There'd been no need for them, or for anything of their sort, since the entire institute was insulated in its steel and granite buildings with almost no access to the actual surface of the moon. There was nowhere to go that couldn't be reached by hallways and elevators.

Kerri zipped the hoverpod at an almost unsafe speed along the familiar path. She parked it near the capitol building in a particularly reputable hoverpod depot. Kerri walked to the greenhouse that received her shipment, by way of her favourite Golan food kiosk. To begin with, ordering at the kiosk had involved a lot of complicated pointing and gesturing. By now, though, the Golan woman who ran the kiosk knew what Kerri would want, and the transaction was much simpler. Kerri placed the paper wrapped, spicy meat and pastry confection in her jacket pocket. She would eat it on her way back home.

Kerri felt alive when she got home and started unpacking her new plants. Some of them were merely bags of seeds or bunches of bulbs, waiting to be planted. A few of the plants, though, had been sent fully-grown. The most exciting of them was her kitty-willow tree. Kerri gingerly removed the tiny sapling from its box and carefully unwound the moistened cloth from its young roots.

The tree didn't look like much, just a branched stick. Kerri wished Alan were there with her to see and appreciate the unremarkable state of this thing that in less than a year would yield such amazing fruit, if fruit were an appropriate word. Kerri sighed. She felt the warmth of the sun on her back, and she imagined Alan out there, beyond the blue of the sky, finding more warmth to bring to the sun. He was working, so she would work too. If she worked hard, she might be able to get her plants in the ground and growing in time for the Heffen spring, only a few months away. Perhaps, when Alan came home, she could surprise him with a garden already in full bloom.

Kerri had grown used to visiting Ques'trian and walking among the Heffen, but she was nervous about tonight: in a matter of hours, she would be faced with her first Heffen guests. Alan offered to pick up *klaufon* pies in the city. He didn't want to inconvenience Kerri with preparing a meal for his colleagues who were coming over to discuss work. The pies would be all ready except for baking and sure to please. Alan hadn't met a Heffen yet who didn't like *klaufon* pie. Kerri knew it would have been easier. She was glad Alan had offered, and part of her hated herself for turning him down. Yet, by the time Alan's colleagues were expected Kerri felt proud of her choice. The combination of Petriezskian and her own dishes, all made with fruits and vegetables from her own garden, made a delightful spread. The table looked beautiful.

The guests, when they arrived, turned out to be three Petriezski men, a Petriezski woman, and one Golan, also a man. Kerri could tell one of the Petriezski was a woman by the black touches of fur in her ruff. The colour of Petriezski fur varied widely among shades of orange, red, gold, tan, and brown. And, almost all Petriezski had white markings on their long, thin faces and their ruffs. However, only the women had black shadings as well. The Petriezski woman, Kerri decided, was a particularly beautiful Heffen.

Golan men and women were harder for Kerri to tell apart. She could tell that Alan's Golan guest was a man mainly from his bearing. Other than that, he was a funny, rounded, little fellow with a face flattened into folds like almost all the other Golan she'd seen. His main discerning feature was a strangely familiar braid of red and gold ribbons draped over his shoulders. Kerri remembered seeing him before, but couldn't quite place him.

After a few minutes of talking, Alan turned to Kerri and asked, "Is the table ready? Can I ask them to come, sit down, and eat?"

Kerri replied, quietly to Alan, that everything was ready before the guests arrived, and turned to lead them all to the table. As they walked, Kerri realised why the gold and red ribbons were familiar. This visitor must have been the first Golan she'd ever seen, the one in the crowd when she and Alan landed on Heffe VIII. Kerri wondered idly what the ribbons were for and why she hadn't seen other Heffen, or at least other Golan, wearing them.

Once in the dining room and settled into eating, the Heffen guests all seemed pleased by the dinner Kerri had prepared for them. Kerri smiled whenever one of them seemed to be giving her a compliment. She still didn't understand Heffen but had come a long way towards understanding their body language from her trips into Ques'trian on her own.

During the meal, Kerri noticed that the Golan kept mainly to her dishes, avoiding the standard Petriezskian dishes she'd made. The Petriezski behaved quite oppositely. Kerri was flattered that they all seemed happy with the meal, but she was particularly pleased by the Golan's behaviour. Kerri felt a greater affinity for the Golan already, simply because she preferred Golan food, always eating at the kiosks when she went to town alone. Also, this Golan laughed more than his colleagues, and he seemed less interested in the conversation. He kept looking at her, as if they shared a secret, although she couldn't imagine what it could be.

When the meal was over, Alan led the Heffen away from the dining room to discuss their latest results. Kerri stayed, clearing the table up. She could hear them talking in the living room, and she knew what they were talking about. The matter transfusions to the sun had not gone quite as expected, and Alan was working on a new plan. There were still hopes, though, that the irregularities in his scans would settle out over time and the sun would stabilise again, but as a much younger sun with a longer life ahead of it.

Kerri found herself wondering what would happen if the scan results did stabilise. If the sun were suddenly saved and Alan no longer needed here, would they move away? She liked the idea of returning to a world of humans, a world where she spoke the language. And yet... She loved the Heffen countryside. The trees of Heffe VIII were not quite like trees she'd seen anywhere else. They were lither, more arching. Sometimes their branches grew like corkscrews, twisting entirely around. The forests were certainly something to see.

Kerri was surprised to see the Golan man return from the living room on his own. "Do you want something?" she asked, reflexively, forgetting he probably wouldn't understand. She grabbed a glass from the cupboard and held it out, offering it to him, hoping he'd understand it as an offer to get him something to drink.

"You don't speak Heffen, do you?" the Golan asked.

Kerri discovered herself in a situation she had never expected to face: since Kerri had come to believe she'd never learn Heffen, she never expected to have a conversation with one of them.

The Golan added : "You do speak your own language, don't you? Or is my English that bad?"

"I'm sorry," Kerri answered. "I was just so surprised...I didn't know any of you spoke English."

The Golan laughed. "The others don't," he said. "They're not used to learning languages because they were brought up here," the Golan gestured expansively around.

Kerri looked confused, so the Golan clarified, saying "The Petriezski language is the most common language on our planet, but it's not the only one."

"I didn't realise," Kerri said.

"You probably think of it as Heffen don't, you? That's all right. They do too," he added, gesturing back towards the room where Alan was talking to his compatriots. "My name is Baury," he added. "You probably didn't catch that when we came in." Kerri blushed at the reference to her verbal illiteracy. "Why doesn't Alan translate for you?" Baury asked innocently, not seeing Kerri's embarrassment. "I'm sure you wouldn't be interested in everything we have to say, but you probably would have enjoyed some of the compliments."

Kerri smiled and said, "I could tell the compliments."

"Yes, but you don't know what they meant," Baury teased with a chuckle.

Kerri, warming to the first face to face conversation she'd had with anyone other than Alan in almost a year, countered back, "Then why don't you tell me?"

"Aah," Baury smiled, for his face seemed built into a smile, "you'll have to ask Alan."

Kerri felt oddly rebuffed by Baury's comment. As Baury probably guessed, she was curious about the compliments. What he didn't know was that Kerri wouldn't ask Alan. She knew his mind was too busied with his work to remember such minor details, comments made to his wife rather than to him. "Why are you out here?" Kerri asked, feeling prickly, "shouldn't you be in there, talking with them about saving your *dying* sun?"

"I'm not a scientist," Baury shrugged. "I work with them, but I'm mainly here because of Trenti, the tallest Petriezski out there. He's my brother in law, married my one and only sister. He sees that I get invited along." Baury looked up and grinned a particularly jovial grin. "They're going to have a litter soon, you know. I hope they're all beautiful, little pug-faced babies that look just like her." Baury paused before continuing, "My sister's beautiful," he said. "She's why I moved here...if it weren't for her, I would never have left Gola."

Kerri warmed to him again. She invited him to follow her out to her garden, where she had a few plants that needed her tending every evening. As Kerri clipped the browning buds on her cameline night bloomers, Baury told her about his beloved homeland, the nation of Gola.

Whenever Alan's colleagues visited, Baury came along. He played the part of heckler in their scientific conversations, but mostly he would separate from the rest and talk to Kerri. He told her that if he must speak in a foreign tongue to talk to friends, he might as well exercise his newest one, and Kerri was the only person to whom he could speak in English (since Alan avoided it in favour of the Petriezski tongue). Kerri welcomed the company and enjoyed learning about the political situation on Heffe VIII. Alan never mentioned it, but he was glad to see Kerri making a friend. Although Baury was the Heffen who made the least sense to him of all his colleagues, if Kerri liked him, Alan was glad of it.

Spring came, and Kerri's kitty-willow tree finally bloomed. The flowers were simple, five-petalled, pink blossoms. The tree was still small, only about two feet tall, but it was beginning to look more like a tree and less like a twig. The extra year of growth before blooming, for it had failed to bloom at all during its first spring on Heffe VIII, had done well for it. Kerri showed it proudly to both her husband and her new friend; neither was particularly appreciative, but neither understood what was coming.

Days passed and Kerri expectantly watched the blossoms lose their petals and grow into fuzzy buds. She checked on her tree daily. Placed prominently in the centre of her garden, it was the first plant she tended in the morning and the last she saw to at night. It was hardly surprising that she should be there when the first of the downy, gray buds uncurled and dropped onto the soil beneath its parent tree.

Kerri reached down and picked up the tiny, perfectly formed kitten that was the seed of her kitty-willow tree. She smiled at the tiny cat as it explored the palm of her hand. Kerri couldn't help but notice the difference between her current happiness and the sheer elation she remembered feeling whenever her kitty-willow tree bloomed during her childhood. The senses dull as you age, she thought. Nonetheless, it feels good to remember the joys from childhood.

Over the course of the following month, the rest of the kitty-willow seeds uncurled and fell from their natal branches. Each kitten-seed lived only a week or so, just enough time to travel and explore, searching for a good place to die, leaving its body to grow into a new kitty-willow tree. Kerri, unsure what their effect would be on the local, Heffen ecological balance, gathered all the kitten-seeds up and made sure none escaped from her own garden.

Alan, although he'd been told to expect the kitty-willow's blooming, didn't notice the box of kitten-seeds Kerri kept and played with all month long, nor did he think to ask after the tree. Kerri chose not to force them on his attention, since he was very busy with his work. The sun's reaction to the matter transfusions had finally stabilised, but the sun was still dying. Alan spent all his time at his work, trying to formulate a new plan to revitalise the sun. Kerri didn't want to disturb him. Her kitty-willow tree would bloom again next year.

"Someday, I'd like to meet your sister," Kerri told Baury, as he helped her clean up from another of Alan's dinner parties.

"Aah," Baury sighed. "My sister doesn't leave home much. She feels too much like an outsider here, and she's kept very busy with the little ones, you know. Trenti doesn't like guests in their house much, so I'm afraid you probably won't get the chance." Baury smiled. "She doesn't speak English, anyway," he said.

Kerri tried to imagine what life must be like for Baury's sister, living in a foreign country. Kerri imagined it must be lonely, much like her own loneliness. "It must be hard for her," Kerri said. "Aren't there other Golan she spends time with? I see Golan men and women when I'm in the city."

"You see them running the kiosks," Baury said. "Am I right?"

Kerri realised that Baury was right, she never saw Golan anywhere other than running the kiosks. She nodded acquiescence.

"There are very few of us here, and we all feel it," Baury said. "In fact, I'm the only Golan I know who's brave enough to wear these," Baury added fingering the red and gold braid ribbons that were, as always, draped over his shoulders.

"I've often wondered what those are," Kerri said.

Baury chuckled. "Striking aren't they? They're a religious talisman. But the Petriezski don't believe in our religion. So, most of my fellow countrymen keep their faith quieter than I keep mine." Baury winked at her, and said, "I've never much cared for keeping a low profile."

The friends finished clearing up the kitchen and dining room, and after Baury checked to see that the science talk was still in full force, the two of them retired to a bench in Kerri's garden. It was a warm night, and distant stars twinkled in the sky above them.

"Why don't the other Golan wear talismans?" Kerri asked. "They stand out anyway...you can't help that..."

"You mean our flat faces, square bodies, and short fur," Baury said. "Yes, you're right, we can't hide that we look different. But, we can hide that we *are* different. Some Golan think they get treated better if they pretend to be Petriezski who were just born in the wrong country. I don't know. Maybe they do get treated better," Baury ended pensively.

Kerri shared in the silence for a minute, and then asked, "Do they treat you badly, Baury?"

Baury, who was not the type to stay sad for long, smiled his characteristic smile and said, "Not to my flat face," he said, and, then, nudging her in the arm, "there's no telling what they say behind my back. Actually," he said, bucking up even more, "you can hear what they say behind my back. Listen for the phrase *Galountan Golan*. They might say it in front of you...although, please don't tell me if they do."

Baury interrupted Kerri before she could form a question. "I won't tell you what the phrase means," he said. "It's very offensive, and I don't even want the idea in your pretty head."

Kerri bowed her pretty head in submission. She didn't mind not knowing.

"Now," Baury continued, full of bluster, "our name for them is much less insulting. Roughly translated, let's see, I believe it would be something like *needle-nose*."

Kerri laughed at the accuracy of the image, and Baury laughed with her. They both felt good, laughing together, and they were still laughing when Baury's brother-in-law Trenti came bursting out into the garden to find them. An animated conversation between the brothers-in-law pursued. Kerri judged from Trenti's gestures and body language that he wanted Baury to come with him, but Baury remained resolute. Trenti, agitated and clearly still excited by whatever news had brought him out to them, waved his arm dismissively, as if to say: fine, stay here if you must. He hurried away.

Wide-eyed, Kerri asked, "What was that all about?"

"Oh, big news. Big breakthrough," Baury said, with much less animation than Trenti'd had. "Something about tightening the atoms in the sun up. You should ask Alan. I'm sure he understands it better than I do."

Kerri noted to herself that understanding a subject better didn't necessarily mean one could explain a subject better. She decided not to press the matter. She would wait until their guests left for the evening and learn about the breakthrough from Alan. Fortunately for the state of her curiosity, Trenti returned soon to tell Baury they were leaving.

Right before Baury left, he remembered a piece of information he thought would interest Kerri. He'd heard of another human moving to Heffe, and she was living nearby. Perhaps, Kerri should look this human woman up? She might, be as lonely for human friendship as Kerri.

Kerri saw Baury to the door, where he rejoined his Petriezski friends. The colleagues bid goodbye to Alan in Heffen, and Baury smiled a knowing goodbye to Kerri. The door shut, and Kerri turned towards Alan, only to find herself swept up in his arms. Alan lifted Kerri in the air and spun around. "We have a new plan!" he said joyfully.

Kerri broke into a grin at the sight of his grin. She hadn't realised how hard it must have been for him that the last plan didn't work. The spinning ended, and Kerri, as soon as her feet returned to the floor, hugged Alan close. "I'm so glad," she said. Pulling back enough to look him in the face, she added, "Do tell me about it?"

"It's the strong force," Alan explained. "It's a number, and that number's the same all over the universe. That number, the value of the strong force, partly determines how atoms are built...the way their nuclei hold together... We're going to make it bigger...that will make the force stronger...but only locally."

Kerri looked at her husband, soaking up his excitement, happy but confused. Alan picked up on the confusion and added, "If we make the strong force stronger, just in the vicinity of their sun, then the atoms of the sun will pull closer together, heating up the fusion. Combined with the matter transfusions we've already given it..." Alan drew a deep breath, "...it just might do the trick."

"That makes sense," Kerri said, appeasing her husband's need for her to understand. And, though Kerri wasn't sure she understood, it did sound reasonable to her. She'd taken physics classes, many years back, and by now the concepts sounded, at best, familiar to her.

"I should be working on it," Alan said, looking distracted by his physics thoughts. "There's so much to be done."

Before Alan drifted away from her entirely, back into his world of abstracts, Kerri re-caught his attention and asked, "Have you heard anything about another human moving to Heffe?" She looked at Alan expectantly, hoping for a useful answer. When Alan merely looked baffled and started to shake his head, Kerri gave up the hope. "Baury mentioned something about it..." Kerri mumbled.

"Actually," Alan said after another few moments, "that does sound familiar. She's a widow, I think, with a little daughter. Some kind of botanist... horticulturalist... gardener... something..." Alan trailed off, but then his face brightened, and he said, "Maybe you two would hit off. You should look her up." And with that, Alan was back to his work.

Kerri parked her hoverpod within sight of the widow's estate, then got out to walk. The estate stood in an open valley, a small house, with a large wall growing out behind it. The wall was stone and fenced in a sizeable area behind the house. The widow must, Kerri thought, have come to Heffe VIII with quite a fortune to be able to buy herself such an estate. Or maybe she'd been commissioned by the Petriezski government like Alan had?

Kerri approached the house from the side, taking the chance to jump up and look over the rock wall. Inside the wall lay a simple yard, children's toys strewn about on short grass. Kerri was disappointed. If the widow was a gardener, she didn't have much of a garden. Kerri followed the wall to the house, and as she came closer, another structure came into sight. This second building had glass walls and glowed with an orange light from inside. Kerri perked up at the sight. Perhaps the widow was a gardener after all, for who else would have a greenhouse?

Standing at the front door, preparing to knock, Kerri heard giggling come from nearby. She looked down to see a small girl, perhaps four or five, hiding under the draping branches and red leaves of an ornamental maple tree. The little girl's eyes widened, and her mouth formed the shape of an O. "You saw me!" she said. "I was going to surprise you."

"You did surprise me," Kerri said. "I'm not used to trees that talk to me."

The little girl laughed. "I'm not a tree! Can't you see me?"

Kerri played along and said, "Oh! You're the little girl inside the tree...I didn't see you before. Is your mother home?"

"You saw me," the girl said. "My mother's home, when she comes to the door I can surprise her." Putting her forefinger to her lips, the girl admonished Kerri not to tell. Kerri knocked on the door, and when the widow came, the little girl's plan was carried out flawlessly. Kerri was invited in for tea, and the little girl, who turned out to be named Lily, was told to play in her room.

"Your daughter's beautiful," Kerri said, when they were settled with pungent mugs of Golan tea.

"Thank you," the widow Sharon said. "She looks just like her father."

"I'm sorry..."

"No, don't be sorry," Sharon said. "That's part of why I came here. I couldn't stand living with people who didn't think Lily and I could manage on our own. I miss my husband... I miss him most for Lily, because I know she'll barely remember him when she's grown. But...we're fine." The widow toyed with her tea bag for a minute. "I'm telling you this," she said. "Because the sooner you know it, the better we'll get along."

Kerri was surprised by Sharon's forwardness, but she appreciated it.

"Now, let's not talk about our pasts anymore," Sharon said. "Let me show you my greenhouse, my future."

Kerri rose and followed Sharon out the back door, through the edge of her backyard, and to the door of the greenhouse. Sharon stopped then and said, "You may want to leave your jacket out here. It's quite warm inside." Kerri hung her jacket on a convenient hook outside the greenhouse door.

Inside the greenhouse, huge lights hung from the ceiling and sat, squatly, on the floor. They flooded the entire area with orange light and a warmth so thick it made the air dance. The heat, at first, felt unbearable to Kerri, but she adjusted quickly. In the right frame of mind, she realised, the heat was relaxing like a warm bath. After a few minutes in the greenhouse, Kerri even started to wonder how she'd managed to not feel cold outside.

The plants, of course, were all suited to such intense heat and light. They were also, almost entirely fruit and vegetable producing varieties. It was as if Sharon had come intending to feed the starving peoples of Heffe, deprived of good fruits and vegetables by the coldness of their dying sun.

"You like?" Sharon asked.

"I do... you have quite a setup." Kerri looked closer at the organised tangle of plants: vines stretched across the floor and grew right up the trunks of various small trees. Every plant was laden with fruit: it hung from the trees, grew from vines on the floor, and Kerri was sure she could find it growing among many roots. "But, why..." Kerri eventually brought herself to ask, "did you bring all of this here? Surely there was a better world, one more suited to the plants you grow?"

Sharon smiled a coquettish smile. "I have a plan..." she began, and probably would have continued if Kerri hadn't inadvertently interrupted to say:

"Even if my husband...I mean," Kerri corrected herself, "*when* my husband saves Heffe VIII's sun, this world will never be naturally suited to these plants. They'll always need a greenhouse here."

"Your husband is the specialist here to save the sun?" Sharon asked. "I should have realised that."

"He's been working at it for years," Kerri said. "But, he seems to be very close."

Sharon smiled sympathetically. She clearly didn't believe Kerri that Alan was getting close. Kerri fought against her impulse to defend her husband. Confused by Sharon's sympathy and wanting to remove the spotlight from herself, Kerri asked stumblingly, "Your plan... tell me what your plan is?"

Sharon looked for a moment as if she'd speak but held back considering some unknown thought. Eventually she settled on saying, "Perhaps I'll tell you when I know you better. For now, it can be the mystery that keeps you coming back to visit."

Kerri smiled and laughed, happy to realise she'd made a new friend, enigmatic though she might be.

Baury and his sister's pups were already waiting outside as Kerri flew her hoverpod up to their house. They were all going to Lily's seventh birthday party. Lily went to school in Ques'trian, and she'd met Baury's two nieces and one nephew there. They weren't as old as Lily, but they were the only Heffen children she knew who spoke any English. Lily could speak Petriezski better than Alan, but she liked having friends who also spoke English: they could use it as a secret code when around the other Heffen children. Keeping secrets, and flaunting them, was fun.

"Thanks for picking us up," Baury said as the little ones filed in to the back of the hoverpod. "I never could get the hang of flying these things."

Once the pups were strapped in safely, Kerri started the hoverpod.

"So?" Baury asked. "This is the first time you've seen my nieces and nephew. Aren't they handsome little troublemakers?"

"Flat-faced as any Golan, just like you hoped they'd be," Kerri replied, paying more attention to steering than to the little ones in the back seat.

"What's with the tree?" Baury asked, indicating the potted kitty-willow tree, packed tightly in the back, its uppermost branches straining against the hoverpod's ceiling.

"That's my present for Lily," Kerri replied. "I painted the pot myself."

"A tree?" Baury said sceptically. "Most young girls prefer toys other than trees, or so I've been told."

Kerri smiled enigmatically, a trait she'd begun to pick up from Sharon. Baury would understand when she gave the tree to Lily. Kerri knew she would love it. A tree like that belonged in the possession of a little girl who would really enjoy it. Nonetheless, Kerri felt a pang of regret as she'd dug it up from the centre of her garden. She'd never gotten around to showing Alan the kitten-seeds... It always seemed like there'd be another year. She almost wished she'd gone with her first impulse, and merely grafted a cutting from the tree onto a healthy root ball. She could have kept her own kitty-willow while still giving one to Lily. It was better this way. It felt like a rite of passage.

The hoverpod pulled up in front of Sharon's estate, parked, and opened its doors. Kerri, Baury, and the young ones got out. Kerri went to the back of the hoverpod to unload the tree, and Baury stayed to help her. The pups ran straight for the front door, eager to be playing with their human friend and joining in the birthday party games.

As Kerri carried the large, ceramic pot, hand-painted with playing kittens, Baury walked beside her. He began asking after Alan, how he was doing, whether he'd seemed different lately. Kerri answered that he Alan was, as always, busy. Perhaps, he seemed more anxious than usual, but Kerri knew of no reason to be concerned.

"There is a reason to be concerned," Baury said, ardently. "Alan probably doesn't know this yet, since Trenti just told me..."

Baury waited a moment as Kerri put down the tree, and knocked on Sharon's door. "The most recent plan failed. They can't keep the strong force constant changed for long enough. It always collapses back to normal."

Kerri was genuinely concerned. It would be hard for Alan to learn this. Before Kerri could say anything, Sharon was at the door, bidding them to come in. Kerri pushed her worries aside, picked up the potted tree, and went looking for the birthday girl.

Baury stayed close to Kerri, so he was there when she described the kitty-willow tree and its yearly crop of kitten-seeds to Lily. He was less than impressed, but he could see the wonder in Lily's eyes.

"How soon?" Lily asked, eager to play with the promised dozens of tiny kittens.

"It'll be a few more weeks, maybe a month, before it blooms again," Kerri said.

The disappointment of having to wait showed through Lily's otherwise impeccably polite thank you. Kerri felt a joy in watching Lily examine her new tree that rivalled the joy she'd felt as a child at owning one. Perhaps the senses don't dull with age, she thought. They find new sources of delight.

Baury coughed, reminding Kerri of his presence. "A very nice gift," he said.

"It was my favourite, of all the gifts I got during my childhood." Kerri turned to face Baury. "What will they do?" she asked, returning to her worry for Alan. "Is there another plan?"

"There is another plan," Baury said. "It's dangerous. It's been tried on other suns..." Baury looked pensive. "It has a tendency to change the course of dying suns: instead of dying, they inflate, rapidly, into red giants."

Kerri looked horrified, so Baury quickly added. "There would be time, a few months, maybe a year or two, to evacuate the planet. No more long and lingering death...the world growing colder while we cling to it. People would have to leave and leave quickly."

"Unless it works, right?"

"Unless it works," Baury agreed.

"Why are you telling me?" Kerri began but couldn't finish.

"I'm worried about Alan," Baury said, taking Kerri's hands in his own and pressing them, looking up at her face earnestly. "He has a very hard decision ahead of him. If you can, I want you to convince him that we wouldn't blame him for making the wrong choice. We all know our sun is dying." Baury broke off for a minute, his small ears flattened against the top of his head. "We asked Alan to help us, but it's not his fault if he can't. Will you tell him that?"

Kerri agreed that she would.

Kerri hovered outside Alan's home office, her hand resting on the doorframe. She could see Alan inside, sitting at his desk, his head leaned over his work. Lately, he was always working. Kerri didn't want to disturb him. She really, really didn't. But, her promise to Baury still hung over her, and by now she was sure Alan knew of his last plan not working.

Alan had grown increasingly irritable. His moodiness and depression suggested Baury was right: Alan was feeling the immense weight on his shoulders of having to make a decision that would affect an entire planet's population.

There were no excuses left. Kerri had to talk to him and make good on her promise to Baury. Maybe it *would* make Alan feel better.

Kerri walked up behind Alan, and placed her hands, lightly, on his shoulders. She began rubbing the tightened muscles, but Alan shouldered her away. "I'm very busy..." he said.

"I know, but, we need to talk," Kerri said.

Alan, still facing his work instead of Kerri, closed his eyes in exasperation, and repeated, "I'm very busy."

"Alan, I know that," Kerri said, pushing against Alan's shoulder, turning him around to face her. "I know about the decision you have to make, and I want you to know it'll be all right however it turns out. The people here know that you're not a god, just a scientist, and they won't blame you if it goes wrong."

Alan looked at Kerri with hardened eyes, repressing all the frustration he'd been feeling. He didn't speak.

Kerri continued, saying, "You know I'll stand by you no matter what. In fact, if the sun does go red-giant. You know I've never learned the language here. I won't mind if we have to move away."

The hardness in Alan's eyes narrowed to a burning. "You're expecting me to fail," he said, bitterness in his voice.

Kerri was astonished. Her mouth dropped open, and then she pulled herself together enough to speak. "You know that's not true. I've always believed in you."

"It's that witch," Alan said in almost a shout. "That widow-witch has turned you against me. She's a vulture who's just been waiting for me to fail, and she's made you just like her!" Alan turned violently back to his work, and Kerri was left standing behind him, her arms fallen slack beside her. Alan had never yelled at her before.

"Sharon?" she muttered, more to herself than Alan. "She never said anything about you. Baury told me to talk to you."

"Then the witch has turned him against me too. I never liked your friends, Kerri," Alan said, surprisingly calm, without turning towards her.

For five, maybe ten, minutes Kerri stood in Alan's office. He didn't turn around or speak to her again.

Kerri locked the door to their low-grav bedroom before turning the gravity down that night. In the early hours of the morning, she heard Alan try the door. Lying alone in the dark, floating lightly on their bed, she heard the doorknob rattle, unwilling to turn. Kerri caught her breath. She was afraid Alan might beat on the door, order her to let him in...she'd never felt afraid of Alan before. Instead, he left without even knocking. Kerri sobbed herself to sleep.

Kerri was working in Sharon's greenhouse when the news came. Sharon knew she'd have to break it to Kerri, who had been isolating herself from everything but Sharon's greenhouse garden. She came over early every morning and left late every night. Sharon knew there was something wrong, but she was too sensitive to ask Kerri. Kerri would tell her when the time came.

Alan's final, brilliant attempt had failed. Alan and his colleagues had slowed the sun's rate of rotation, decreasing its centripetal forces and causing the sun to shrink in on itself. The hope had been to push the sun back on track as a young, yellow dwarf star with many millions of years ahead of it. Instead, the yellow dwarf would expand into a red giant, but not over the usual time span. The inhabitants of Heffe VIII had only a few years to evacuate, finding new homes in a universe which had dispossessed them.

Kerri began to cry. Sharon was worried for her. Kerri had been crying a lot lately, so Sharon wasn't sure if she was crying over Alan's failure or not. She gave Kerri a hug.

"You expected this to happen, didn't you?" Kerri asked, trying not to feel betrayed. "That's why you brought these plants here... these plants that need a huge, hot sun." Kerri was crying again, and Sharon led her out of the greenhouse, into the house, and sat her down with a mug of Golan tea.

"Nine times out of ten," Sharon said, "the experts who are hired to save dying suns end up expanding them, artificially, into red giants. I didn't expect Alan to fail. I just knew the odds."

Kerri stared into her steaming mug of tea. She was thinking about the flowers she had found, waiting for her, every morning since her and Alan's fight. Every night she locked the bedroom door, and every morning there were flowers waiting for her on the other side. Alan had never mentioned the fight.

"Artificially created red giants are the best kind for what I'm planning to do," Sharon continued. "I'm sorry that Alan failed. I would rather that he'd succeeded and that I'd had to find a different sun."

Kerri traced her finger around the rim of her mug. She dipped her finger into the hot tea and it stung. "Why are artificial ones better?" Kerri asked, trying to be interested, trying to think about Sharon instead of Alan.

Sharon was watching Kerri closely and growing more worried by the minute. "It's time to tell you my secret," she said. "Remember?" she asked. "I said it was a secret, to keep you coming back here. Well, now's the time."

Kerri managed to look up, her interest piqued by the mention of a secret she'd long forgotten.

Sharon continued: "I'm going to make a garden on the sun...on the surface of the sun."

"Can you do that?" Kerri said.

"If you have the right technology: solar force shields and radiation osmitters; they're very expensive and hard to come by. They're also hard to put in place. That's why artificial giants are better...you can fit the shields on them as they grow," Sharon replied. "It's been done before...a few sun-gardens have been very successful. There's so much energy at the surface of a sun...the plants grow like crazy. You'd hardly believe it."

Kerri tried to imagine standing at the surface of a sun, orangey-red light glowing around her, blotting out the eternal night sky above. She imagined the super-hot plasma sloshing beneath the force shield under her feet and plants growing everywhere. She asked, "Can I come?"

The swollen red sun of Heffe VIII hung in the sky over Ques'trian's space port. The asphalt landing strips boasted far more spaceships than they'd seen at one time ever before. Long lines of Petriezski men and women, along with many other nationalities, waited to board ships that would take them away from their home. The planet was more than half deserted now.

Kerri walked with Alan towards the lines, watching the sad faces around them. She wondered where most of these dispossessed would go. She wondered how much of their culture would survive. Baury along with his sister and her family were heading for Crossroads station. That was a good place, but a space station isn't the same as a world when it comes to making a home. Kerri found the line she was looking for and led Alan there. The bags were already packed and loaded on board. All that was left was to get in line and wait.

Kerri looked at Alan, standing beside her. His shoulders were slumped in the same dejected posture they'd held for months. He was a broken man, and Kerri felt horrible for what she was about to do. She had loved him.

She saw Baury and his family in the distance, coming towards them, she knew it was time. She drew a deep breath, and, standing a foot back from Alan, spoke. "Alan, there's something I have to explain to you." It would be easiest to just say it fast. "I'm not going with you. I'm going with Sharon, to garden the sun."

Alan looked at her with disgust in his eyes. She was afraid of all the things he wasn't saying, yet, glad not to hear them.

"I made sure your ticket was on the same flight as Baury's," she said. "I've asked him and Trenti to look after you." Kerri wanted to say something more. She wanted to explain all the thoughts and feelings she had. She wanted to say something that would make it all better. She'd felt that way for months. There was no magic cure.

They had been growing away from each other for a long time. She doubted now that they'd ever known each other well. Maybe if he'd apologised with words instead of flowers... Maybe if he'd just asked what was wrong... Maybe... There were too many *maybes*. Kerri felt trapped when she thought of them.

Finally, Baury and his relatives caught up to the pair. "Oh, Baury," she sighed. "I'm glad to see you." They hugged each other, exchanged a few words of chitchat, and agreed, wholeheartedly, to keep in touch. Kerri said goodbye to each of the little ones and smiled at Trenti and the sister.

As Kerri backed away, starting to leave, she said to Baury, "Do look after him," and, to Alan, she just said, "I'm sorry."

She didn't wait for a response.

Sharon and Lily were waiting for her, outside the hatch of their own ship, the only ship heading towards the sun.

"I'm ready," Kerri said, running towards them. "That was hard."

Sharon smiled sympathetically and put her hand on Kerri's back, guiding her into the ship. Seated inside, Lily pulled on Kerri's sleeve.

"To cheer you up," Lily said, holding out a kitten-seed on her palm. Kerri took the tiny cat and cupped it in her hands. It was going on a voyage grander than any a kitten-seed had gone on before.

"You brought your tree?" Kerri asked.

"Of course," Lily said. "Can you imagine how happy the kittens will be on the sun?"

Kerri imagined the little seeds, curled up, stretched out, in all a cat's many poses, basking *on* the light of the sun. "It's a perfect place for them," Kerri said. It's a perfect place for *me*, she thought. It was horrible leaving Alan... she wished the Alan she remembered, from when she was young, could come. He wouldn't like it there: just plants and gardening.

Plants and gardening.

"It's good to be doing something you care about," Sharon said, piloting the ship into liftoff, rising through the atmosphere, breaking into the sky, and heading for the sun.

As the red giant swelled into view, Kerri knew she was going to her true and final home. She felt an excitement usually reserved for children.

afterword

The bottom of my world fell out the first time I realized I might not move home again. I had been excited to leave for college—a small school in sunny California, approximately 1000 miles south of where I grew up—but it had never occurred to me that my path might not lead me back to Oregon afterwards. For generations, all of my family has lived in Oregon. My entire world was there. Yet, the adventure that started with going to college in California led to finding, marrying, and following my husband.

This story, "Rekindle the Sun," was written shortly after my husband began his PhD program in Seattle, Washington—300 miles, north this time, from where I truly wanted to be. It was a new city, and I felt very alone. My closest companion was my needle-nosed dog, Patrick. (He, of course, was my model for the Petriezski.) I spent most of my time walking Patrick around a nearby lake and day dreaming about other worlds. Or, more accurately, thinking as furiously as I could about all the stories I wanted to write, organizing and outlining them as Patrick skipped around my feet on his leash, like a low-flying kite. Sometimes, my story-planning felt like a dialogue with him.

Six years later, my husband has his PhD, and I have been extremely lucky: we live only 40 miles from my childhood home. Looking back at "Rekindle the Sun," I see a story that was born from a time of extreme loneliness and dispossession. Kerri found her home in a new place, but I am very glad to have returned to my original one. As for the Heffen fate… Well, that's another story.

The Gift

Barry Rosenberg

ABDUL WAS BORN amidst blood and bullets. In 1936, even when Afghanistan was supposedly at peace, its factions spoke mainly with the gun. So Abdul's birth was celebrated with shrapnel. It burst through the window of his Kabul home causing the midwife to scream as shards of glass flew across the room. Miryam, the new mother, turned aside to shelter her baby. Splinters pierced her cheek causing it to bleed.

"Under the bed! Under the bed!" the midwife shrieked.

But Miryam, convinced of her second sight, remained calm. "We are safe here," she replied. Blood dripped from her cheek and onto Abdul, painting his lips red. His mouth puckered and he sucked in the drops. "A sign," his mother said. "Blood before milk."

"What does it mean?" the midwife asked from under the bed.

Miryam gazed into the burning sky. "He will have a gift."

"If we live through this night, we will all have a gift."

As Miryam had foretold, they were lucky and the fighting moved on. But it did not stop. Battle was a constant background and Abdul grew up to the non-music of gunfire. Yet he showed no particular gift, unless an absence of fear was a gift. Miryam's calm at his birth seemed to have been transferred to him.

Hashem, his father, did not have the same calm. "If we stay," he said. "We will die." He bit his fingernails. "We are Hazara. Everyone hates us."

Miryam paused, flour on her hands. "We have cousins in Darulaman. If we went there, they would help."

They tried to sell their house but no one would buy. In a street of rubble, who would buy a partial ruin from the Hazara? They loaded what they could into an old car and drove through mountain passes to the small town of Darulaman. Their cousins gave them a small room and a portion of courtyard. Hashem put an awning over his section and set out his tools.

"Abdul," Hashem said, "you are nine years old. You can read and write. You can do sums. It is time for you to work." On paper, his father drew a small cabinet that stood on square legs. "Measure, measure and measure again," he said. "Then cut."

Hashem showed Abdul how to saw straight, how to plane a surface till it was smooth, and how to use doweling for joints. It took a week for Abdul to complete what his father did in a morning. Both, though, were happy.

"It's well done," Hashem said. "Not quite straight here, not quite straight there but all the same, it is pleasing." Hashem studied the cabinet. Puzzled, he showed it to Miryam. "It shouldn't appeal as much as it does," he said.

Miryam hardly looked at it. "That is his gift," she said. "His calm goes into the wood."

Hashem took the cabinet to market. "Not your best," a buyer said. He frowned, his hands gliding over the word. "But it speaks to me." He bought it, a smile playing over his features.

When Abdul was ten, his father showed him how to put a sharp edge on his chisels. "Carving is special," he said. "It is a form of prayer. In wood, as in a Persian carpet, everything interweaves." He carved a strange animal. "This is a creature of magic and myth."

"A Chinese dragon?" Abdul asked. "Did it ever exist?"

"Only inside the minds of people," Hashem replied.

Abdul carved his own dragon on a cabinet. A buyer walked around it. "Strange," he said. "It makes me feel brave." He haggled over the price but went away well satisfied.

Too soon, however, Abdul's life was again disrupted. Britain withdrew from India and the formation of Pakistan led to bloodbaths. In Afghanistan, tribal warfare escalated. One day, Abdul returned home to find blood on the walls. In a daze, he wandered through his cousins' house. He only found more blood.

His heart squeezed into the size of a walnut, he slept restlessly on his cot, hoping for someone to return. No one did. Finally, a neighbour took a kind of pity.

"You are Hazara. This place will never be safe for you. I will buy your home but you must go elsewhere. India in the south might be safe for you, perhaps?"

It certainly wasn't safe for him to stay. Keeping the money from the house in a bag around his neck, Abdul packed a few treasured tools. Over six months, he drifted south until, assisted by pockets of other refugees, he reached Pondicherri. Though young, he wasn't the only child that had to forage for a living. Abdul was lucky, he had his secret money. He rented a shed where he lived and worked. He took cabinets and carvings to market. They sold to the many tourists who visited the Aurobindo ashram. He did well for though he was dispossessed, each item bore a little of his gift.

One day, a man ten times the size of Abdul, stopped at his stall. "G'day, mate," he said.

Abdul looked up from a length of wood. "Hello. You just looking?"

"I'm not sure, mate. A friend of mine bought a carving from you. A dragon or something. It makes him kinda peaceful."

"You want dragon?" Abdul reached into a box.

"Yeah. No. Well, I'm not sure." The man picked up a jewellery box with intricate floral carvings. "The name's Tony. It's a bit embarrassing, really. I've got my own yacht but I still get seasick."

Abdul's eyes bulged in amazement. "You have own yacht?"

"Yeah, too right, I have." Tony put the jewellery box down. "You reckon you can make a dragon carving for me."

Abdul cocked his head. This was a well-fed man in decent clothes. He doubled his normal price. Tony took off a third. Abdul upped him. Finally, Tony put out his hand. "That's a deal, I'll see you in three days."

Abdul started the dragon that afternoon. As he carved, he imagined himself on a boat in rough waters. He saw himself as calm. The boat rocked, he remained as steady as a Buddha. The carving took four hours to complete. For the next two days, he did other work. On the third day, Tony returned to the market.

"You got it?" he asked.

"Yes." Abdul unwrapped the dragon. "It take two whole days. Very difficult. Very intricate."

Tony turned the carving around and around. "Yep, I can see a lotta work has gone into it. Feels good, too." He handed over cash. "This works, I'll come back in a few weeks with more work for you. How's that?"

"That good."

After that, Abdul recognised that quite a few tourists also had their own yachts. He raised his prices for them. None complained. None of his customers ever complained. Some of his fellow stallholders did, though.

"You Muslims are sticking together too much."

"You are selling too low."

"Why you leaving Pakistan?"

"I am Hazara," Abdul explained. "And I am not from Pakistan."

"You are not belonging here."

Abdul withdrew even more from others. As a Hazara, he belonged to a minority group within a minority group. He wished that he lived in a country that had never heard of Afghanistan and its religions.

He almost viewed Tony as a friend when the big Australian came back. "I've just been to Java. No problems, mate. Didn't get sick once. Dunno if it was your dragon. But it certainly seemed to settle the old guts. Told a few people about you. You oughta get some more sales soon."

"That is a good." Abdul was curious. "You have business in Pondicherri?"

Tony's eyes darted here and there. "Yeah, well we have a shop in Sydney. I buy stuff here and there, sell it back home."

Momentarily, Tony gave Abdul a curious look. Then he looked away so that Abdul guessed that there was much left unsaid. By listening in to furtive conversations, he realised that for quite a few boats, antiques and handmade goods were just a front. Drug and people trafficking were their main trade. For the time being, though, that was just of passing interest to Abdul.

Then, in 1949, the Pashtuns declared their independence. This meant little to most of the world. But the turmoil in Afghanistan meant more sorrow for Abdul. He grieved and, for the first time, customers returned his carvings.

"There's something about them," they said. "I get headaches. No, they're heartaches. I can't even bear them in the house."

Abdul almost wished that he didn't have a gift. He had to work hard to find its positive side while he remade each item and his desire to travel even further from his birthplace increased. He wanted to live where not even he could find news of his homeland.

In the market, Abdul bought a globe of the world. He put his finger on the various continents: America, Europe, Australia. Australia was the furthest. And it was separated from the rest of the world by oceans. Not only that, Australians were the friendliest and the most innocent of the foreigners that visited his stall. Abdul began to save, adding to the money left from the sale of his house. He also worked on a small model of a yacht. Into it went his desire to travel. After that, all he could do was wait, wait for Tony to return the market. The big man was not quite a friend, but even if he wasn't there to buy, he always stopped to have a word.

On his next visit, Abdul said to him, "Please come behind stall."

"You got something special?"

"Special? Yes." With the other leaning over his shoulder, Abdul opened the neck of a cloth bag.

Tony whistled. "That genuine, mate?"

Gold sparkled. "All genuine."

A greedy gleam lit Tony's eyes. "Why you showing me this?"

"I want to leave here. Go to Australia."

"Phew." Tony whistled again. "Why don't you go to the consulate?"

Abdul waved the suggestion away. "I have no papers. Even people with papers are not accepted from here."

Tony nodded. "That's true. That's true." He licked his lips and looked around the market. "But why're you asking me? I only carry goods."

Abdul knew when not to push. He closed the bag. "You think about it. You decide." He took the model of the yacht from under his stall. "You take. This to remind you."

Tony took the carving and held it up to admire. "Can't promise you anything, mate. But I appreciate this, anyway."

A few days later, Tony returned. "You heard about the Snowy Mountains Scheme?" he asked. Abdul shook his head. "It's a big engineering project started two, three years ago. They're desperate for workers. You wanna work there, they won't ask too many questions."

Abdul smiled to himself. Tony's quick decision meant that his model had worked. Organising the little that needed to be done, in exchange for gold, he obtained a berth for Sydney. Among a white-skinned crew, there were a dozen dark-skinned ungainly helpers. Unnoticed, Abdul made a few careful cuts with a sharp knife at the front of the yacht. With the application of his gift, the seas stayed unusually calm.

Once in Sydney, he was added to a milling group of young men. A stout man with olive skin and thick curly hair took charge of them.

"My name's Gino," he said. "Any of yous lot speak the lingo?"

Abdul tentatively raised a hand. "Lingo is language?"

"That's right, mate. Wot's yer name, mate?"

"Abdul?"

"A-what?"

"Abdul."

"Listen, you're a newie here. A-thingy's too hard for Aussie blokes." Gino ran thick fingers through his mass of hair, his warm brown eyes puzzling. "I'll tell you wot, we'll call you Harry. That olright, Ab, if we call you Harry?"

Abdul nodded. He wanted to put his past behind him. Harry was just fine.

They went by train to Canberra. In the station, they were served sandwiches. Abdul turned the white slices over and over.

"Eat," Gino said. "White bread is good for you."

Abdul ate. The bread had no taste but the meat inside did. In one meal, he had more meat than he normally ate in a month. A bus arrived and Gino shepherded his charges onto it.

"Just a couple more hours," he said. "You'll be bunking up in Jindabyne."

Abdul gazed with astonishment as they drove along hilly roads. He'd become so used to the flatness of Pondicherri that he'd forgotten how the land could rise and fall. Then, south of Cooma, at the sight of mountains, real mountains, a strong hand squeezed his heart. This was so like home, his real home. The mountains brought with them images of his mother, Miryam, and his father, Hashem. He pressed his face to the window so that no one could see his tears.

They stopped in the small town of Jindabyne. "Everyone out," Gino called. "When your name is called, you'll be shown to your bunk." Abdul was fifth on the list. "Harry, you're next." Gino looked thoughtful. "You're from one of those funny countries. Anything you don't eat?"

"Watch out for the dogs!" a blonde Aussie shouted.

Abdul blushed. He used to eat according to Halal. "I eat anything," he said.

"I told you about the dogs!"

Abdul blushed even deeper. "Anything that others also eat."

"Stop it, Jack!" Gino called. "They're just kidding you, mate. No offence meant." He looked at his list. "Said you work with wood. Jack'll take you out in the morning."

They made an odd couple. Jack was tall and rangy. Abdul was short and brown. "We're gonna cut timber," Jack said. "There's plenty of tunnels we gotta prop up." He handed Abdul a paper bag. "Got your dog sandwiches in there, mate." Abdul looked at him with hurt eyes. "Nah, just kidding. That's beef. C'mon, Harry, in the truck, we got work to do."

For the first month, Abdul just slept when he wasn't working. Such big logs had to be cut! And the wood was so hard! Half their time was spent in just sharpening the blades. But he applied himself and the dog joke fell away. Jack turned out to be friendly, helpful and culturally illiterate. *Wog, wop* and *dago* were part of his daily language but Abdul realised that Jack, really, did not mean to offend.

In his second month of timber cutting, Abdul started a carving. In the first week, he worried that he'd lost his skill. In the second week, he worried that he'd lost his gift. By the fourth week, though, he had decided that it was the strange nature of the beast that had bothered him. All the same, he succeeded and by the third month, he had a reasonable carving of a fighting kangaroo. His desire to better himself went into that. He gave it to Gino.

"A gift," he said.

"For me?" Gino ran his hand over the wood. "So smooth. You really have a gift." Again, Abdul smiled to himself. "You're a bit wasted here, mate. I'll see wot I can do."

Gino showed the carving to other workers of the Snowy Mountain Scheme. "A newie did this," they said. "Yeah, you can see that it's a bit out of proportion. All the same, it's got something. Really captured the spirit."

Chas, a Pole whose real name was even more unpronounceable than Kosciusko, took a particular interest. "If he can make furniture then I can give him a job," he said.

Abdul went to see Chas. "I thought you'd be older," the Pole said.

"I'm older than I look," Abdul replied.

"You bet." Chas rubbed his grizzled chin. He reckoned the boy could be no more than fourteen, fifteen. "Look," he said, "I'll give you a trial. See how it goes."

Because Abdul was so young, Chas treated him as an apprentice and tried all the old tricks on him. "Get me a left-hand screwdriver," he asked. "An upside-down chisel for doing under a chair."

At first, Abdul thought his understanding of English was at fault, or Chas' thick accent. Quickly, though, he realised the joke and solemnly handed over the nearest screwdriver or chisel.

One day, Chas said, "You a Muslin, Harry?"

Abdul cocked his head. "Muslin is material. I am Muslim, a Hazara Muslim."

"Yeah? Well, seeing as you're older than you look, maybe thirty-five going on seventeen, d'you reckon you could look after a good Christian girl of fourteen going on fifteen?"

Abdul looked up from a chair. "I don't understand."

Chas put his drill down. "Our daughter, Anna, goes to school in Canberra. She'll be back for Easter. They're aren't many people here her age. You think you could keep her occupied?"

Abdul blushed. He was used to motherly figures. He wasn't used to young women. "I... I... Don't you think Jack would be better?"

"Jack's a skirt chaser." Chas leant forward. "Pay you time and a half if you do it."

"Okay, I'll do it." Abdul frowned. "Does she like to make things? Does she like to walk?"

"Funny thing, Harry, she likes languages. You could teach her a bit of your lingo." He also frowned. "Whatever it is?"

Abdul, who was normally calm, felt an unusual queasiness in his stomach as Anna's arrival drew closer. In the evenings, he began to work on a small pendant. Into it went his desire to be a good tutor, to be an upright man, and not to blush, blush, blush.

On the Thursday before Easter Friday, Chas brought his daughter into his work shed. Abdul gaped with astonishment. Chas was grizzled. Anna was willowy. Chas was grey-haired. Anna was a dazzling blonde. He had thick features. Hers were refined. Abdul ducked behind a cabinet.

"Harry," Chas called. "I know you're there. Come on into the office. Harry!"

Abdul reached under his shirt for his pendant. A vibration seemed to come off of it. It passed through his spine, straightening him up. He thought that he was going to be all right. He entered the office and his life was turned upside-down. They stared at each other. Their eyes locked and the rest of the world dropped away.

"Hey, hey, yous two." Chas put his bulky body between them. "The wife is outside. She's taking you to the Greek's for milkshakes. G'wan, yous two, she's waiting."

"No work, today?" Abdul squeaked.

"Looking after a teen is worse than work." Chas pulled his daughter's hair. "G'wan outside and don't you run him ragged."

For Abdul, Easter passed in a dream. He had no idea if Anna felt the same. Even when she left, saying, "Will you be here next time?"

Abdul nodded. He had no idea when next time was. But he was certain: he would be there.

He began a carving, life size. At first, it was meant to be Anna. Yet as he worked, remembered images of Venus and Aphrodite added exotic shadings. It was meant for her and his gift ached to be embodied. Make her desire him as much as he did her. But Abdul groaned against that, tore it out of his mind. He even held his own longing at abeyance. When, at last, the statue was complete, he didn't show it to anyone. Didn't even mention it.

A few months later, Anna came home again. "She's fifteen now, getting on thirty." Chas rolled his eyes. "Occupy her, Harry. Keep her out of trouble." He paused. "What, you're eighteen now? Keep out of trouble yourself."

Abdul always kept out of trouble. He still had too many nights when the walls were coated with blood. Blood dripped and his dreams were swimming in blood. Shyly, he took Anna to the house that he shared. With all the doors left wide open, he led her into his bedroom. Her gaze fell upon the statue.

"It's... it's beautiful." She walked around it. "It's me? Yes, it's me but you've given it a, I don't know, a spiritual quality."

Abdul's brown skin glowed like a beetroot with a bulb inside it. "You like it?"

"Like it? I love it!" And Anna sprang a quick kiss on Abdul's cheek.

"It's," he stuttered. "It's yours."

"Mine? Oh, I couldn't."

"Yes, yes. You must."

Anna took his hand. "I'll always treasure it."

Another week passed in a dream. Anna returned to Canberra to study. Abdul applied himself to work. His gift went into chairs, tables and cabinets. They made the weak feel strong, the sad feel happy, and the lonely were motivated to seek company. But in the many gifts that Abdul made for Anna none contained his gift. Even so, their closeness grew. When Anna turned eighteen, she and Abdul approached her parents.

"We would like to marry," Abdul said.

Chas had expected this. Wanted it. But he thought some parental opposition was expected. "But Anna is still young."

"I'm not. I'm eighteen!"

"What about your studies?"

"I will move to Canberra so that she can still study."

Chas shook his head but covertly winked at his wife. "We won't stand in your way," he said. "As long as you don't expect Anna to become a Muslin."

Anna punched him. "Muslim, dad. You know that."

They married. Anna taught. They had children. Anna went back to work.

Abdul was happy. He couldn't believe how happy a family could be. Canberra itself, though, was a mixed blessing. It had the surround of mountains that so reminded him of home. It also had the politicians who brought news from the rest of the world, news of the many invasions of his homeland.

Mostly, he kept this news at bay. He had become more Harry than Abdul. Yet, when the first grandchild arrived, his thoughts turned again towards his own tradition. It showed in the new cabinets with the calligraphy that his father had taught him. He carved the ancient flowing script used by the fire worshippers of Zoroastra as well as the Sanskrit of the Mahabharata.

Abdul was pleased with this work but sensing the passing of time, he decided to make a picture frame. It was rare that he made anything for himself and he wanted this to be special. He made it out of camphor laurel. Though a weed in Australia, it was easy to work and its mint odour was a vague reminder of home with its thick mint tea. Once the basic frame was finished, he put it aside while he studied the ancient symbols of flame, candle and sun. When he felt that they had burnt their inner meaning into his heart he then felt ready to carve. There could be no mistake. Each cut was tiny and decisive. His soul moved through his fingers and each cut was incised into his soul.

The frame was not meant to hold a painting. Abdul didn't know what intuition had guided him but he knew that it was meant for him to look through. When the frame was finally complete, Abdul was scared to do so. On old man's legs, he walked into the garden, carrying the frame as carefully as if it were a newborn child. He held it up and gazed at a tree. The framed trunk and branches caught the light. The bark was a glowing grey and the leaves radiated a lively green. He could even see silver as the sap moved within the trunk.

Just then, Anna came out. "What are you doing, Abdul?" she asked. She only used *Harry* in public.

He smiled. "Just looking."

As she smiled at him, Abdul looked at her through the frame. Waves of blue and light pink rolled towards him.

Seen through the frame, Abdul's whole world was rosy. That lasted for long enough but could not last forever. Terrorists blasted America. A month later, America retaliated against Afghanistan. Though he thought that he'd distanced himself, every death was a pinprick. But there were so many deaths that the pinpricks coalesced into lances, into spears, and into daggers. Even at 65, Abdul had been spry and healthy. But with his homeland ravaged and his fellow refugees refused refuge, age rapidly decayed him.

As his new country locked refugee Hazara into detention centres, Abdul took to his bed. His head was bursting, his stomach was sick and his heart was withering. Anna sat by his side, watching.

Eventually, he said, "Anna, please give me the frame."

Quietly, she took it from the wall and gave it to him. With skinny arms, Abdul gazed longingly not through but, somehow, into it. He did not see the bedroom wall but in the far distance, he saw a roaring fire, a fire that did not consume, a fire of immense dancing light. He was drawn towards it or it was drawn to him. As flames of light played around his head, Abdul finally smiled. His weak arms sagged and the frame fell around his head. For a brief moment, Anna saw the light that surrounded him. She wasn't surprised, she well knew his gift.

Holding his hand to her heart, she gently closed his eyes.

afterword

People see Topol in Fiddler On The Roof *and feel teary. They read* Schindler's List *or see the film and feel sympathy. Yet the same people often have no sympathy for current asylum seekers or people smugglers.*

My father and all my grandparents were the equivalent of asylum seekers. They arrived in England and were called aliens. In growing up, right through to university, I had to deal with racism: Why don't you go back where you came from?

Despite my background, I had no interest in politics. That awareness only came with the Howard Government and the rise of Pauline Hanson. In particular, I was horrified at the treatment of asylum seekers to Australia, most of them Afghanis. I couldn't believe it when nice people, people that I played tennis with, or who worked in coffee shops, said, Tow the boats out. Send them back.

Kill them!

It is not a life-style choice to become a refugee. A refugee is not a migrant. Asylum seekers don't read pamphlets and decide where they'd like to go. Asylum seekers have the choice: stay and die or leave and take your chances.

In 2001, I joined Buddies Refugee Support Group. It was such a relief to meet like-minded people. With Buddies, I helped to organise 3 major forums. Through Buddies, I met a number of refugees.

From the mid-70s, I was one of those academic dropouts who went guru hunting. This included travels in India where I met Tibetan refugees. My story is a soup made from elements of my own background, my travels and my involvement with Buddies.

Prisoner of the Faceless

Kurt Bachard

AFTER THEIR FIRST night together in years, the breakfast Darla prepared smelled as delicious as Ben Mason remembered, except that the now-unfamiliar eggs and bacon tasted gritty and bland. He ate reluctantly, slowly, endeavouring, with each swallow, to resist grimacing; even so, by the slightly twisted look on his face, you would have thought he was chewing bitter pills.

"Is there something wrong?" Darla asked.

He hesitated before answering, trying to pinpoint the source of the distaste. Just outside the shuttered kitchen window, he could hear the heavy metallic clunk-clunk of the Faceless-Rylej troops marching in their boots up and down the war-torn ruin of the street. He looked up to meet Darla's eyes, which were darker than he ever remembered, their former blue-marbled vibrancy somehow subdued. "No, there's nothing wrong with your cooking," he said slowly, watching her carefully. "Perhaps it's just me. On Rylej, we ate fresh vegetables and fresh fruit every day. I'm not use to this."

"We make do with what we can," she said. "The Faceless-Rylej are rationing us here now." The muscles in her jaw bunched, and for a moment her eyes seemed to look on Mason with a cold, hard appraisal that he had never noticed in them before. There was something unsettling about that probing look. "Besides, you're not on Rylej anymore, Ben," she added.

An obvious statement, he thought, now remembering how pedantic she had been and how that had irritated him. That was years ago, though, before the Faceless-Rylej occupation of Earth, before their enforced separation, and long before his plan (to escape Rylej and find a way back to Earth on the next Earthbound cargo shipment) was just an idle daydream in Rylej's whispering wheat fields, a bit of wishful thinking he'd indulged in to while away the long workdays. Except, he had made the wish come true, and now here he was again, back on Earth at long last, in his own home.

He turned in his chair, away from the dining table to look at his old green armchair in the corner. The familiar pattern of stains on the armrests reached into him somehow and summoned an unexpected rush of nostalgia and melancholy, although the chair looked to him dejected and mean. He rose and went over and tried it again, but no matter which way he turned it felt uncomfortable— the cushioning felt too high, the backboard too hard, digging into the protruding muscles of his lower back, muscles that had formed on Rylej. This too, then, his old chair, no longer knew him, he thought, just like the uncomfortable bed he had slept in with Darla, on the previous night. She had wet his sun-darkened chest with tears as she sobbed silently over the changes in his body, the muscularity wrought by hard work on the slave colony on the Rylej home world. She claimed that it barely felt as though she was holding the same man she had fallen in love with.

"Five years I remained a chaste, loyal madwoman, alone," she said. "Crying my heart out, praying for a miracle that would send you back to me. I even tried to make the Faceless-Rylej turn me into a slave worker too, so that I could be with you on that prison planet of theirs. They didn't need or want me. Now I have you back, you feel physically like a different man. So different that it's as if I'm being disloyal to the old Ben Mason after all." To Mason, the logic made sense. Now, like Darla, and like the bed, this armchair too did not know his new shape and weight either. He found the remote on the side table where both of them used to leave it and he tried the old TV set. Snow filled the screen when he switched it on.

He frowned, trying all the old channels one by one, but each channel showed only snow and hissed white noise. He finally gave up. He turned to Darla as she came back into the room. "I was hoping to catch up on world events," he said "but the TV doesn't appear to be working."

"Well it's not broken if that's what you think," said Darla. "There are no television programmes. The Faceless-Rylej did away with all that years ago. They banned all broadcasts and now all we get is the occasional military and public service announcement."

He put away the remote. "What about the radio, then? You still have my old set, I hope?"

"It's forbidden to use the radio now."

Ben Mason sighed. "Well that's really put a damper on my Sunday," he said, shaking his head, and forcing a half-smile to his lips with difficulty.

"I've still got the old chess board in the cupboard," said Darla. "I kept all the pieces. Just in case. How about it? Just like old times."

Sunlight beamed through the narrow slits of the window shutters, and Mason got up to stretch his legs, moving away from the chessboard. He felt energetic, and frustrated, imprisoned in a fusty space, and the old game of chess he would sit playing for hours on bygone Sunday afternoons seemed now like an ancient form of torture. He noticed for the first time the dust that had settled on the mantelpiece.

"I feel as if I need to go for a walk," he said. "To get the kinks out of my system. On Rylej we used to—"

Darla cut him off. "Rylej this, Rylej that," she complained. "You're a fugitive, Ben. Even if you were not a fugitive, there are curfews in the cities now. You wouldn't be able to go out unless there was an announcement."

"How many announcements do they make here?"

She looked up at him sharply. "*Here*? You say that as if Earth is foreign to you."

Unable to meet her challenging gaze, he turned away and stared at the shuttered window. Outside, the heavy tromp, tromp, tromp of marching Rylej troops grated on his nerves; a constant sound since his return.

He watched the dust motes swirling in the shafts of sunlight that pried between the wooden bars of the beige slats, and thought. What in hell will I do here all day?

"You can't expect me to stay cooped up, I've spent the last seven years farming fertile land on Rylej," he said.

"As a slave!"

"Okay that's true, and we never forget that everything we do on Rylej is for their benefit, but—"

"But what?" she interrupted. She looked shocked. "You were captured, Ben, taken prisoner, transplanted to their home world and forced to work? Held in servitude to Earth's conquerors, to toil like worker ants. Rylej is a prison!"

"Rylej is beautiful nevertheless," he said, sounding wistful. "The waterfalls, the rolling green hills, the fragrant neroli from the orange groves, the soft breezes that turn the apples ripening in the sun, the golden fields of wheat. We must all be crazy, because, yes, Darla, we do talk constantly of escape there, but escape to what and to where?

"Here, everything is forbidden; can't go out, can't talk to anyone, can't meet anyone, nothing to eat, nothing to do, no work, no play, nothing but going crazy in these four walls, growing old with..."

He stopped, and looked at her with pity. She doesn't deserve this, he thought. She had waited, here in her prison. Yes, he thought, her prison. It occurred to him now, for the first time, that she was the prisoner, not he, despite his enslavement to the Faceless-Rylej.

"Go on say it," she said. "You meant to say growing old with me, didn't you?" Her eyes seemed to search him, as if she too was trying to find something she had lost. "There is someone else back on Rylej isn't there? Do you think we don't know that on Rylej, slaves are forced to make more slaves?"

He saw it then in her face, that strange new thing about her that had disturbed him: she had a face now as colourless and featureless as the walls that trapped it, as wan and weary as this room, this house, this beaten world. As world-weary and featureless as the Faceless-Rylej themselves. His mind made up, Mason stepped toward the front door.

"Where are you going?" she asked, jumping up. The fear in her eyes showed that she knew.

"One step outside now, in daylight," he said, "and the Faceless-Rylej will arrest me and send me back home."

"Home?" She was looking at him in disbelief, window-slats shadowing bars across her face.

"I'm sorry," he said. "I hope someday you'll understand why." He pulled opened the front door and stepped outside into the bright free sunshine, thinking of Rylej, thinking of home.

afterword

Before I set out to write this story, I spent some time thinking about where we feel we belong. Do we belong in the place where we end, and should we always end where we started, like the mythic hero returning full circle? Do we contradict the folk-wisdom that Home is where the heart is? And is Home really a state of mind, not a place?

To believe the maxims though, I think, is to over simplify a complex reality. We all know someone who feels a sense of belonging to more than one country. Then there are the socio-demographic factors involved in territorial belonging. I wanted to write about change as a factor, and to subscribe my protagonist to Rousseau's view "I prefer liberty with danger than peace with slavery".

However, in the process of writing, my protagonist taught me something. That territorial belonging is as elusive as liberty is subjective.

Merpeople

Gwen Veazey

ROLPH THURGOOD INHALED salt air and steadied himself against a cold starboard rail. The *Sea Lady* cut through ocean waves, heading into deeper Atlantic waters. He stared at the Goliath-sized statue of a turquoise Sorran bolted to the deck, and admitted defeat for allowing Sheila to talk him into this misadventure. The Sorran featured a *Creature from the Black Lagoon* face and body.

The few existing photos and vids of Sorrans showed complicated tubular heads and a batch of tentacles between their two lower limbs, but these details escaped the moulded plastic representation. Ah, well, things were often not as they seemed. Rolph imagined he and his lover appeared as happy as any of the laughing wet-suited couples and family groups surrounding the statue.

A group of pre-adolescents squealed as they threw torn bread to swooping pelicans. Sheila touched his arm. "Look at those lightning bolts painted on the children's foreheads. It's a Harry Potter fan club coming out to see the merpeople!"

Rolph nodded good-naturedly, and remarked over the noisy throb of the Sea Lady's motors, "Hope they have something to see, other than empty domes and the artificial reef." After the aliens' arrival six months ago, they had vanished from sight, keeping to themselves.

He watched Sheila gaze at ridiculous cabin wall murals opposite the deck rail. They depicted teal-skinned, busty blonde mermaids waving from harnessed dolphins leaping high over a sparkling ocean. He rolled his eyes at his companion and she laughed. "The statue, the mural... they're symbolic, Rolph. Everybody knows the aliens don't look like that."

"The mural is a little much, considering they all look alike." The Sorrans had offered no information about gender differences, and those seen and photographed appeared about as different as male and female fish. It was entirely possible the Sorrans had neither males nor females and reproduced non-sexually, a feature that was becoming more and more appealing to him. Or was he just in a bad mood? He was, after all, on the brink of ending it with an unsuspecting Sheila. One of the loud, giggling kids skidded into him, laughed, and ran off. He rubbed his hip and mused that maybe he was not ready to have children under any circumstances.

Sheila began to take on that earnest look, like she did when trying to explain some far-fetched belief. "You know, the Sorrans obviously have more in common with us than we know. Soon we'll understand our inevitable spiritual connection better and..."

Rolph tried to listen. He wanted to have the kind of rapport with her he had at the beginning, before he knew her well. Back when she was just a laughing, friendly co-worker in the lab, with shiny black hair and full-lipped grin, with interesting books lying about. "You're not listening." She sighed.

"Sorry, I was thinking about us." He smiled and hugged her to him. Since they were encased in full-body wetsuits, the hug lacked a certain softness and warmth. Sheila rested her head briefly, silently, on his shoulder.

"Tell me the truth, now," Rolph said. "You have no reservations at all about these ugly water creatures dropping into our ocean to settle here?"

"No, I don't." She moved away and squinted in the sun's glare. "Don't tell me you're paying any attention to those morons who want them gone?"

With a glance up toward squawking pelicans, still following the ship, Rolph said, "They're a vocal minority; it's hard to ignore them completely. Especially considering all we don't know."

"But the Sorrans are going to allow us to study them, right? And they've promised to help us explore the deepest parts of the ocean, and help rescue submarine and shipwreck victims!"

"According to your "Don't-worry-be-happy' newspages. And you left out magically extracting oil from beneath the ocean floor, by the way."

"You should try reading something besides *The Wall Street Journal*. And what's up with calling them ugly?" The chilly wind whipped strands of hair over her face, and she pushed them away. "I thought you liked the way they looked."

Rolph smiled. "I like the fact they aren't chalky white with big bald heads and slanted black eyes."

"Oh, you." She turned away to the east where only dark green ocean graced the horizon. Florida's north-eastern coast receded behind the boat as gusts of bracing, damp winter air caused Rolph to unfold his heavy towel and wrap it around his shoulders. Across the deck, a man in bulky street clothes and an open black raincoat, not prepared for swimming, peered toward the horizon through binoculars.

Sheila was saying, "It's hard to think badly of them when they needed our help so much. It's not like they just descended without warning and took over, or are all that much advanced over us or anything."

"Let's not minimise the significance of interstellar space travel."

"Well, I don't mean to, but they're just a small group and almost like poor immigrants who just need a place to live."

"Or slimy, ingratiating spies?"

"Oh, for heaven's sake." Sheila plopped down on a vacant bench and made room for Rolph. He joined her and noticed the passenger in rumpled street clothes lowering his binoculars. The heavyset man's longish black hair whipped in the wind, his eyes darted from ocean to boat passengers. A loner not accustomed to functioning in public?

Rolph whispered to Sheila, "See that guy? I'll save some of my paranoia for him."

He immediately regretted drawing her attention to the "poor man," as she began referring to him, remembering how many stray cats Sheila had adopted. She inevitably dragged him along with her to greet the oddball passenger. Embarrassed, Rolph smiled for introductions, and nodded politely.

Blinking, the fellow finally spoke. "Oh, hi. Dave Browning."

"Not going in the water?" Rolph asked. He leaned against the deck rail, feeling the vessel's vibrations.

Dave tightened his moist face, which shone in the midday brightness. "No. Just here to observe from a distance. I think we should be a little wary of those aliens. Are you familiar with the Keep Us Safe blog reports?"

Sheila's expectant expression wilted a little. So, Dave was one of the folks influenced by extremists who wanted the aliens sent home.

Dave added, "I used to love science fiction, but somehow, the reality of extraterrestrials being here... it's a lot different. The thought of sinking into the ocean depths four miles out with them all around scares me." Rolph thought allowing a character like Dave to remain on the virtually deserted deck while all the rest of them snorkelled was also a little scary. He wondered what Dave's many-pocketed slacks and jacket concealed. Tourists were metal-checked, but weapons came in all manner of materials.

Dave's thin hair tangled in the wind as he resumed talking about his suspicions, and Rolph decided his openness probably meant he was harmless.

"So their obvious plight hasn't softened your heart? Don't you believe them when they say they can't go home?" Sheila asked nicely, but with determination.

"Why should we believe anything they say? There's no way to verify it. Their ship is a complete puzzle. And the idea that they obviously studied us for months, maybe years before initiating contact... I don't like it."

"The ship is understandably strange, not relying on standard propulsion or anything we air-breathers can relate to," Rolph said. "Perhaps you'll feel more comfortable when we verify their stories of planetary disaster."

"Years from now?" Dave snorted. "Who knows what will happen by then? For all we know, we may be part of the food they're attracting with those reefs!"

Rolph chuckled. "You've watched too many *Twilight Zones*."

Sheila sighed. "That was one of the best episodes. "To Serve Man," I mean."

Dave coughed and muttered to himself. He pressed his eyes to the binoculars. "The Navy destroyers are coming into view. We must be getting close. Wonder how many subs they have stationed about?" He exhaled in a huff, and Rolph figured the constant presence of the military at the domes contributed less to feelings of security and more to conspiracy fears for someone like Dave.

"Don't know, but at least the government's letting us sightsee," Rolph quipped.

Dave sniffed. "Thanks to greed. Conspiracy of the feds with capitalist tourist barons."

Sheila perked up, and Rolph realised she shared at least one crackpot opinion with the bundled-up curmudgeon.

She asked for a look through the binoculars, and Dave obliged, keeping the heavy black instrument strapped around his neck. Rolph stifled his annoyance as Sheila innocently pressed close to the other man. Maybe Dave was just as paranoid about losing the binocs as he was about everything else. It occurred to Rolph that if he broke up with Sheila, she might end up with a nutcase like Dave. He remembered one of his first dates with her. After a nice evening out they were back in her condo. He had been trying to listen to her, but mostly focused on the downy hairs on the nape of her neck, and she had said with a mixture of wonderment and relief, "You're the most normal guy I've ever dated. I can relax with you!"

He looked back to the water. Three tiny humps had appeared on the horizon. As the *Sea Lady* approached, the objects enlarged into half-acre, transparent domes, their sandy floors dotted with some sea oats and palm trees, but empty of any alien life or movement as far as he could tell. Supposedly, the Sorrans liked to relax in such environments occasionally, the way humans liked to swim. Rolph thought of his trips to various natural zoo preserves. He had yet to see a lion or rhino. Whines of disappointment rose from the children, who knew this was the only chance they'd get to see a Sorran because the creatures avoided the underwater reef when tourists swam there.

After a reminder that no scuba diving was allowed, the Captain gave a brief lesson in using mask, fins, and snorkel. Sheila easily slipped into the sea, then Rolph awkwardly placed his flippered feet on the ladder rungs and stared at the chilly water slapping against the white boat. He took a deep breath, masked his eyes and nose, the rubber tight against his face. He placed his lips around the black plastic snorkel, then stepped into the ocean. Despite his wetsuit, the cold crept in. Fighting the waves to keep his head above water, he struggled over to Sheila, and she grabbed his hand as they dunked their faces and headed toward the reef. Ah, much better to float face-down and not fight to stay upright.

Except for his Darth Vader breathing, no sounds intruded as they moved through the buoyant coolness. Endless gray-green depths and occasional seaweed greeted them. Ahead, an underwater structure appeared through the murkiness. The Sorrans had managed to anchor it to the ocean floor far below, but their work underneath the reef was not visible. The white porous "rock," shone in a fluorescent glow, anchoring sea fans and bright anemones. Hand-sized blue tangs and yellow and black striped angelfish in groups of twos and threes darted at the reef, bouncing against it for food. A silvery grouper, nearly the size of one of the children above it, swam within a metre of Rolph. His sound of exclamation was a muffled buzz. The Harry Potter kids jerked and pointed to the grouper, their arms and legs frothing the water vigorously when an octopus slithered along the artificial reef floor.

Effortless floating in the sea proved relaxing. Rolph enjoyed Sheila's physical closeness and allowed his mind to wander away from ever-present thoughts about coordinating anti-viral trials and seeking more funding for the lab.

Suddenly, Sheila yanked his hand and pointed wildly at one edge of the false reef floor. From underneath it, creatures of iridescent cobalt blue, more stunning than the tangs, wriggled upward catching the sun's wavering rays. Sheila tried to pull him toward the three emerging aliens, but he resisted. She released his hand and swam closer. Angry with himself for his hesitation, especially if Sheila's trust in cosmic goodness got her hurt or killed, he sucked in a heavy breath and dove under the surface, blowing a trail of bubbles. He placed himself between Sheila and the aliens. The creatures looked smaller than they did in vids and pics, perhaps because they were twisting through water and not standing on land. They held onto one another. His stomach lurched at the strange tubular heads which ended in a frilled, fluted opening with retractable, fleshy baleen-like strands across it. They had wrapped their lower torsos in sea grass, and their upper torsos had pairs of slitted nodules like their bulbous "noses," which rested along their necks. Another detail missing from the popular representations of them.

Rolph stopped a few meters above, awed by their undulating mouth holes lined with the black fleshy strips. For a moment, human and aliens mimicked each other as they worked their lower limbs. Rolph pedalled his flippers, and the Sorrans swished their two fishtail legs ending in webbed toes. Two of them folded their mouths down, in a tucking-under-the-chin fashion, and he looked into their round eyes. Yes, intelligent creatures and mesmerizing. One of them pointed to the third who floated limply without tucking its face down, its eyes not visible. They pointed to Rolph, the surface, and the other snorkelers, who had begun paddling to the scene. Their hands were many fingered, tentacle-like, not webbed.

Before Rolph registered that they might want a response to their pointing, the two communicative ones disappeared. They swam beneath the reef leaving the third Sorran floating passively, almost close enough for him to touch. It had something attached to its back. He wanted to reach out and feel the shiny deep blue skin, but his lungs ached for oxygen. He felt a pull on his shoulder and Sheila was there. He motioned her up and they surfaced.

Rolph tore his snorkel off to gulp stinging breaths. "Wow, three of them!"

Sheila nodded and removed her own snorkel, saying breathlessly, "We've got to help him! He's sick!" Several families with young children swam quickly away toward the boat, but others moved to join Rolph and Sheila.

One of the Harry Potter Club boys yanked off his snorkel and wiped his mouth. He screamed, "Let's take him back to the boat! We can keep him!"

Sheila was having to yell over the sound of ocean and wind. "We most certainly should take him back to the boat. He needs help!"

Rolph could not believe her naiveté. "Sheila, these creatures have mastered life on a strange planet; they can take care of a sick colonist!"

With the fog and water drops on her mask, Rolph couldn't see that determined look in her eyes, but he knew it was there as she yelled, "No, something's wrong! They're clearly asking for our help!"

Several others fought the waves and current to stay upright and swam closer. A sturdy gray-haired man pulled off his breathing tube and said, "Ma'am, have you ever heard of the Trojan Horse? That alien has something attached to his back. Could be a bomb."

Rolph said soothingly, "Sheila, their bodies are stressed when out of the water for very long, so I'm not sure we could truly help an ailing one that much. He might even be dead already."

"Then why did they point to the surface? They want us to take care of him. Couldn't you tell by their eyes they were scared? They need us!"

The gray-haired man gave Sheila a look of disgust and dog paddled toward the Sea Lady. Others followed.

Wanting one last look at the mysterious Sorran, Rolph affixed his snorkel and turned to Sheila. She was gone!

He cursed to himself and submerged, the saltwater feeling warm against his face now that his body was adjusted to the water temperature. He had drifted, but soon got his bearings and paddled toward the far side of the reef. He caught sight of Sheila's black wetsuit and flippers. To his horror, she was beside the alien and slowly reaching for it. Rolph sucked in a great breath and dived, but couldn't reach her soon enough. Her white fingers touched the shimmering azure skin. Bracing himself for an explosive blast, he squeezed his eyes shut and faced away. A moment passed. When nothing happened, he turned to see the injured alien responding to Sheila's touch by tucking its mouth down and looking at her. The Sorran made weak motions with its upper limbs. As Rolph approached, Sheila began pulling the blue creature upward. It trailed loose sea grass and a stream of dark liquid, which clouded the water behind it.

Rolph's heart thumped loudly as he surfaced. He and Sheila were the last of the stragglers, the furthest away from the Sea Lady. The Sorran kept its mouth submerged but looked at them both with wide round eyes. Rolph realised they were defying the U.S. Government on top of any dangers from the alien itself. He jerked off his mask and snorkel and threw them toward the horizon.

"Sheila, this is crazy!"

She just held onto the Sorran, pulling it toward the *Sea Lady*, which seemed an impossible distance away. Swimming beside her, he yelled, "I can't believe you're doing this. They'll never let this creature on the boat, and what in the world can we do for the poor thing?"

In the distance, a Navy patroller appeared. Was it moving toward them? Dear god! Still, he grasped the Sorran to help; its skin felt cool and supple. Sheila stopped to push off her mask and snorkel, then touched the pliant bag strapped to the Sorran's back. Made of what looked like a giant purple snake's skin, its top flap floated open as Sheila handled it. She seemed intent on exploring its contents.

"Is that a good idea?" Rolph tensed.

Sheila gently smoothed the straps off the alien's upper limbs and held the bag, then opened it under the surface and looked in. She extracted a Sorran atmosphere protective suit and a packet made with more purple snake skin. Above the water, she unwrapped the slick flaps. She caught her breath. "It's a knife."

"Looks more like a pencil carved from a seashell," Rolph said.

"With a very sharp edge." Sheila returned the items to the bag and began swimming toward their boat, dragging the Sorran with Rolph's reluctant help. His breaths came heavy now, his exhaustion slowing him. "Hurry!" Sheila paused a moment, looking behind them, and Rolph followed her eyes to the Navy patroller, clearly on their tail. The ocean pushed against him, he got a mouthful of saltwater and spit it out. He closed his eyes and focused on gaining the ladder to the deserted aft deck of the Sea Lady, which was now in his sights.

"Where are you going?" Sheila pulled in the other direction.

"The other end of the boat, with no people."

They were finally there. He could hear the children shouting and wondered how long it would take for their threesome to be noticed. He relaxed against the side of the boat, catching his breath. Sheila climbed up first, then reached for the glistening blue Sorran, whom Rolph lifted to her, the creature able to help itself a little. When he made it up to the deck, he saw Sheila with the alien's backpack, fumbling with the flimsy protective suit, trying to figure out how to get it on the Sorran who was curled on the deck, barely breathing. The alien seemed to find a comfortable position, then closed its eyes. Dark liquid ran from between its lower limbs. The Sorran pulled off the sea grass covering its lower torso, exposing an opening but no tentacles. The creature stiffened, opened its flippered legs and expelled a small, bloody jelly sac. Sheila gasped. The sac held a motionless, embryonic blue alien, several centimetres long. The Sorran grasped the lump of gel and pitched the lifeless, half-formed embryo onto the deck at Rolph's feet.

He shivered, and glanced up to see crazy Dave emerging from the enclosed central cabin taking it all in. The boat swayed causing the jelly sac to slide away, and the scientist in Rolph made him lunge for it, still warm, and look for a place to keep it. He settled on an empty wide-mouthed water bottle tucked in some clothes and towels on a passenger bench.

The Navy patroller edged closer to the Sea Lady, preparing to board.

Sheila knelt beside the alien. Rolph pulled off his flippers and walked across cold corrugated metal to join her. The Sorran began to move. It made insistent sounds, grasping Sheila's shoulder with its tentacle fingers.

Rolph stared at the slender, heaving... what? Male? Female? He wondered if the sharpened shell it (she?) carried was a form of alien coat hanger. No gauzy, dappled underwater illumination here, only the clear sunlight of day. He wiped his face and tasted salt, feeling thankful to be a man and not a female Sorran countless light-years from home. He shivered and steeled himself against further urges to anthropomorphise the aliens. Stay out of it, he told himself.

At that moment, two submarines rose from the ocean nearby, cascading water off their hulls. Their hatches opened and crew members emerged to point weapons at the Sorran. In less than a minute, the Sea Lady was boarded by a dozen armed sailors, several carrying an acrylic tank half full of seawater which they rested beside the alien. An officer beribboned with medals, and hair pulled tightly under her cap, barked, "Stand back!" Her name bar read, "M. D. Suarez." She bent over the Sorran, peeled its tentacles off Sheila's shoulder and helped two sailors lift it into the tank.

"Are you going to help her?" Sheila asked.

"Ma'am, please move away from the alien. You too, sir."

Rolph took a moment to appreciate the decisive, no-nonsense action of the military. Patroller crew members must have been watching everything on deck, as one of them immediately searched the passenger bench and grabbed the water bottle with the dead embryo. At least someone would study it, he supposed. By this time dripping spectators had found them, and crowded in the passageways on either side of the cabin. They gawked, backing slowly away as the Captain yelled at everyone to get off the aft deck. Navy divers in black wetsuits began confiscating cameras and cell phones mumbling that everyone would get them back later.

Sheila refused to move and quickly recounted what had happened beneath the water, her idea that it had been a plea for help.

Officer Suarez said only, "This Sorran will be returned to the settlement as per our agreements with them."

"Agreements with who?" Sheila shouted. "The males? This is a female Sorran! Her girlfriends brought her to us for help. She doesn't want to go back!"

"Huh?" Rolph looked at Sheila's face, reddening from fury, and realised his lover had no qualms about anthropomorphizing. "Sheila, I don't think we should argue with the Navy..."

They were hitching the acrylic tank up to a contraption to swing it onto the patroller.

As the tank began to lift off the deck, Sheila screamed, "No! Wait! Don't make her go back!" Sheila's brown eyes pierced him. "Rolph, do something! Who could we call? You have connections! What about your sister?"

"I think this creature needs something way beyond a good immigration attorney."

"'This 'creature'?! How can you call her that? She's a woman, Rolph! An abused woman who needs massive help!"

"Oh, Sheila. Even if she were a human woman from another country seeking asylum in the U.S., she'd be thrown in maximum security regardless of her situation. And federal prisons don't have aquariums."

"Prison? Why? She hasn't done anything wrong!"

Rolph thought of the horror stories his attorney sister had told him about innocent foreign women escaping from violent husbands, sexual abuse, even slavery, and making it to the U.S.

and still having to wait in prison because they were here illegally. "Innocence is not the issue..."

"Maybe I could take her to my house—" Sheila looked frantic. She was really going off the deep end.

"What? And keep her in the hot tub?" He threw up his hands.

"Why don't I just marry her? That would get her a green card."

Sheila gave him an intense look, as though she thought he were serious.

He blew an exasperated breath. "Sheila, for god's sake—"

Splashing wildly, the alien drenched Officer Suarez's crisp khaki uniform as the tank continued to move toward the sea. Sheila lurched toward it, Suarez's firm hand holding her back.

"Can't you do anything to help her? She does *not* want to go back—"

Rolph tried to pull Sheila to him, whispering, "Shush."

The alien gazed at him through the side of the tank, mashing her tentacles against plastic. Sheila raised one arm high in a useless reach, looking ridiculously like the Statue of Liberty, and Rolph started to melt. So what if some of her beliefs were woo-woo, she was a hell of a woman.

Suddenly, the Sorran convulsed into a foetal position and rocketed out of the container, wrenching gasps from onlookers. She landed in a thud on the deck, the vivid teal of her wet skin fading to gray.

Was she still alive? Rolph thought he saw a fishtail foot stir, but no one moved to help her.

He shouted, "Officer Suarez? Dr. Thurgood." He rarely made a point of his title, but if she thought he was a physician, so much the better. He thrust his hand toward her but she ignored it, and he felt his surge of courage start to subside. Swallowing, he spoke anyway. "My friend's right about the aliens; they were clearly asking for help, and I'm sure this creature will die unless someone intervenes. It won't be helpful to return her dead."

Suarez gazed at Rolph and Sheila, gritted her teeth, and finally called over Navy medics who ran to hover over the limp, glistening figure. They lifted her to the tank, but this time swung it to the patroller, not the sea.

Suarez barked, "OK, people, this is completely under control. We'll have an official report of this incident out within the hour."

The officer's face softened, and she said one last thing in a low voice so only Sheila and Rolph could hear. "She'll still have to be returned, eventually."

"No!" But no one was listening to Sheila.

Still on the high seas, Rolph relished peeling off the sour-smelling rented wetsuit and feeling the warm fresh water of his shower spill over him. After drying and dressing, he met Sheila at the snack bar. Surrounded by other passengers, she sat at the counter in front of a full cup of coffee. The Harry Potter bunch held papers out for her to autograph and wouldn't stop talking. They finally parted for Rolph, and he asked politely, "I'd like a few moments with Sheila alone, guys."

When his coffee arrived, he warmed his hands on the plastic cup, glancing over at the children, already resuming their school-holiday glee, making a mess of their tables, innocently livening the place up... yet their jagged lightning forehead marks looked disturbingly like third eyes. "What did you tell the children?" He asked.

"Just that one of the merpeople found herself in a bad situation and injured herself. I know they can handle a not-so-happy ending, but I couldn't tell them the whole story... I guess the Sorrans' connection to us is not exactly spiritual."

Except perhaps for Sheila's perception of the alien female's plight, he thought.

He said, "Well, they did a good job of hiding their females, until you showed up. Maybe they're just some Taliban-like cult thrown off their home world, needing a nice reactionary place like Florida to re-locate."

"It's not joke material, Rolph! I plan to tell that woman alien's story to whoever'll listen!"

He liked the way her dark eyebrows gathered over her eyes, and he advised, "I recommend calling *The New York Times*, not *Astrology Daily*." His smile faded as he saw Dave Browning lumbering toward them, the man's raincoat unbuttoned, loosely closed. Rolph half expected a third arm to appear, remembering the *Twilight Zone* character from Mars, or was it Venus?

Slowly, Dave's arm protruded from the black slicker, holding a miniature digital camera, telescoping lens exposed. "I got the whole thing. With the alien in the tank, on the boat."

Sheila grinned. "Yes!"

The look between Sheila and Dave didn't bother Rolph. He bestowed a manly slap on Dave's arm and boomed, "Nice going!" The raincoated man startled, gave him the look of a bested male animal, then nodded and made his exit. For a second or two, Rolph thought about the continuum of male-female relationships starting at enslavement and ending in some utopian equality state. He figured his protectiveness of Sheila fell safely distant from whatever domestic scheme the Sorrans had. He mulled over a mental list of better restaurants where he could take his woman without a reservation, get her a nice meal before she took on the world.

afterword

Inspiration for "Merpeople" derived from many sources. Kudos to the Tahirih Justice Center in Virginia, USA, a nonprofit organisation protecting immigrant women and girls fleeing violence. A nod to Damon Knight's Twilight Zone *episode, "To Serve Man," and the episode, "Will the Real Martian Please Stand Up," screenplay by Rod Serling.*

Feather-light

George Ivanoff

ONCE UPON A time I met a man. A man who made me forsake all others... even Sarah.

I met him in the most unlikely of places, at the most unlikely of times. He was sitting on a swing at three in the morning, in the park next to the block of flats where Sarah lived.

I would normally have stayed the night at Sarah's, but we had argued, yet again, about commitment and my apparent inability to embrace it. Instead of being cosy in her warm embrace, I was braving the winter weather. My car was on the street at the opposite end of the park, so I held my coat tightly around me and briskly walked across the wet, overgrown grass.

I didn't notice him at first. I walked across the park, intent on getting to the dry interior of my car and switching the heater on. I was half way when I raised a hand to wipe the rain from my eyes. As I did so, I glanced towards the swing... and there he was.

Now, I'm not normally the sort of guy who would approach a stranger in the middle of a deserted park, in the middle of the night, in the middle of a not-so-reputable neighbourhood. But for some reason that is exactly what I did. I just walked right up to him... as if drawn by an indefinable need.

He was wearing a dark raincoat and a wide-brimmed hat that obscured his face. I stopped a couple of steps from him. As I did so, he looked up at me and I saw his face bathed in the glow of the park's lone lamp.

I cannot tell you what he looked like. I cannot tell you the shape of his face, the angle of his nose, the colour of his eyes... all I can tell you was that he was beautiful. It's not a word I would normally use to describe a man. Handsome. Rugged. These are words I would associate with a man. But none of them seemed to fit. This man was beautiful—startlingly, amazingly, painfully—beautiful.

I was in awe!

I stood there in the rain and stared at his face... basking in his gaze. Aeons passed in those moments.

He stood up eventually and reached out a hand to my cheek.

I shivered at his touch. A touch so light and delicate... like dozens of feathers gently brushing my skin. Feather-light!

I shivered with a sensation I had never felt before. Yet I was immediately certain of what it was. Love! Not just the love one may feel for a friend or a partner or one's offspring. This was pure love... the paradigm.

So intense was this feeling that I immediately ached with the thought of not having it. The notion of commitment now seemed to me like bliss.

His fingertips trailed down my cheek... along my neck... then he embraced me. As he held me, he placed his lips to my ear.

"Let me tell you a story," he whispered. "A story of unrequited love."

In the beginning, the Creator fashioned beings in his own image. Graceful, beautiful, perfect. They were the manifestation of His love and they existed in the radiance of His love. And they were content... for they knew naught else.

Then the Creator created imperfection. Countless forms of imperfection, which existed in the shadows of His love... a place that came to be known as the Universe. The Universe was vast. It had no boundaries. And so the Creator continued to create imperfection. And to each imperfection He gave a name.

The creatures of perfection watched and learned... until they too were less than perfect. They now took a name for themselves. Angels. And the place in which they existed, they called Heaven. They even gave a name to the Creator... God.

I sighed as his lips brushed my ear. I could feel his breath on my neck, making my hairs stand on end.

"Shall I continue?" he asked.

Unable to speak, I merely nodded.

There were two Angels whose destinies were to be inexorably linked.

The first—the wisest, most powerful and most beautiful of all—called himself Morningstar. He looked upon the Universe and was filled with jealousy. He continued to look upon it and that jealousy turned into desire... a desire for power.

So he drew his plans to usurp the Creator.

When it came time to form his army, he gathered together Angels who had also looked towards the imperfection with many new feelings. And Morningstar directed those feelings towards his goal.

But Morningstar needed greater numbers. So he gathered Angels who had not yet looked upon the imperfection, and showed it to them... made them study it.

One of these, was an Angel named...

He paused and drew back from me. He looked into my eyes with such incredible sadness. It was as if all the grief that had ever been and had yet to be, was embodied there in his gaze.

I opened my mouth, wanting to ask the Angel's name. But he gently placed a finger to my lips, silencing me before I could speak.

I gasped.

"I do not know his name," he whispered. "He has... lost his name."

This Angel looked upon the imperfection and saw it for what it was... less than perfect. Then he looked at Morningstar and marvelled at his perfect beauty. How could one look upon a countenance such as his and not be instantly and irrevocably devoted. And as he gazed at Morningstar, that Angel discovered desire.

In that moment, he realised that he would do whatever Morningstar asked of him... no matter the consequences.

And so he followed Morningstar into a battle that could not be won. And he followed Morningstar into exile, to a domain that was neither perfection nor imperfection... a domain that simply was. A domain created for the sole purpose of being so distant from perfection as to be unable to influence it.

And there they existed for aeons. Morningstar became bitter and even less perfect... and yet he still radiated beauty—a dazzling brilliance that fuelled the other's desire. Somehow, Morningstar's growing imperfection made him even more desirable. But the Angel kept his silence, for such things were unheard of.

And then the Creator created again. First Man, then Woman. In his own image... and yet so tantalisingly imperfect.

Morningstar watched and he knew jealousy once more. He tempted the new creations and they, of course, succumbed.

The Angel who desired Morningstar, watched all this and continued to watch as these creations discovered love and lust... and carnal pleasure. Inspired by their actions, he decided to reveal his feelings to Morningstar.

And although he was far from perfect now, this was an imperfection that even Morningstar could not stoop to.

The Angel was declared a sinner and he was exiled. Exiled from exile. Exiled into perpetual sin. Exiled to live amongst the imperfect creatures he had watched and learned from... but to never belong. Exiled to lust and desire... but to never fulfil.

A pearlescent tear ran down his perfect cheek. I desired to kiss it away... but instead, I watched it trail down his skin and mix with the drops of rain.

"It's a very sad story," I said, finally finding my voice. "But is it true?"

"Truth, like beauty, is in the eye of the beholder," he answered.

I looked at him questioningly.

"Trouble yourself not with these thoughts."

He kissed me then, and I closed my eyes in ecstasy. Images soared through my mind. Glimpses of wings and beauty; of perfection and love; of loss and pain; of Morningstar and his would-be lover. Then I felt his ever-so-soft lips brush each of my eyelids... and when I opened my eyes, I saw the dawn—a dazzling image of light. I had always loved the first light of morning, but on this day and all those to follow, it held nothing but emptiness.

I was standing in the park, alone... oh so very alone. I tried to think of Sarah, of my life, of our lives together.

But all I could feel was an empty, aching, longing for a perfection that I could never have. And although this was my world that I looked upon, my home, I knew that I would never again belong to it.

afterword

I find the concept of angels rather fascinating, and have been wanting to write a story featuring them for a long time. "Featherlight" is a story that has been through many *re-writes, each one subtly changing the emphasis.*

When the Belong *anthology was announced, I finally had the right emphasis to make it work. The story is strongly inspired by the writings of Neil Gaiman, particularly his short story "Murder Mysteries". Although I certainly don't claim to have done anywhere near as good a job as he would have, I do hope that people enjoy it.*

Speaking English

Stephanie Burgis

MY FAMILY DISCOVERED Halloween in 1994, six months after we'd moved to America. My parents seemed to think that we had left the ghosts behind, in Sotin, in Croatia. I was only fourteen years old and mostly silent, but I knew that we hadn't.

Three days before Halloween, on a Friday morning, I found my mother sitting beside my father at the kitchen table, still wearing her blue nurse's uniform. Some of the long strands of black hair had escaped her bun, and they softened the stern lines of her face as she frowned down at her sewing.

"*Sta ima, Keva?*" I asked. *What are you doing, Mama?* "Shouldn't you be in bed?"

"Speak English, Jasna," my father said from behind his newspaper.

I rolled my eyes. I already knew how to speak English. I just hated it. Did they really think they could turn me into a normal American girl?

My mother pushed her chair back from the table. I could tell how tired she was by the fact that she ignored the family rules and answered me in Croatian.

"It's a Halloween costume for you. You should have told me you needed one earlier, I would have had more time."

"What?"

"The women at the hospital explained it to me last night." She held up the pile of black cloth. Her face creased into a brief smile. "See? You'll be a witch. Very traditional."

"What are you talking about? I'm not dressing up for Halloween!"

"Don't be silly. Why wouldn't you dress up? You're an American now."

My hands clenched. "Well, I'm not interested in wearing a costume, whether it's American or not."

My father closed his newspaper and fixed a stern glare on me through his spectacles. "If it's an important American custom, you will do it."

Ridiculously, I felt tears sting behind my eyes. I blinked them back. "Listen to me! Halloween is for children. I'm too old."

"Doctor Johnson's children are older than you, and they always dress up for Halloween," my mother said. She looked back down at her lap and picked up her sewing again, dismissing me. "They go to Halloween parties. All American teenagers do."

My father picked up his newspaper again, and shook the pages open loudly. The subject had been dismissed. Over. They'd made their decision. I stared at them, open-mouthed, and felt the tears begin to slip out. My hands trembled with anger.

All American teenagers went to Halloween parties? Well, what parties had I been invited to? I could hear my own accent, tell how bad my English sounded. I could hear the snickers of my classmates whenever the teachers made me speak. I didn't even look like anyone else in my class. Who would want to invite me to a Halloween party?

Even if anyone did, I wouldn't accept. No one would ever accuse me of thinking I could pass for an American. Even if my parents had forgotten what had happened back in Sotin, I never would.

I hadn't always been an only child.

I got through the bus ride the way I always did—head down, eyes closed. Invisible, I hoped. No one bothered me until second-hour algebra, when someone sat down next to me at the long back table. I stared down at the blank piece of paper in front of me, waiting for class to begin. All around me, people were talking about the school Halloween party on Monday night.

Perfect. Just perfect. Knowing my mother, she'd find out somehow, no matter what it took. Once she'd made up her mind about an American custom, nothing I said could make a difference. Could she have actually forgotten what happened in Sotin? Willed the memory into nonexistence?

"I know you," a girl's voice said beside me. "You're Jasna Jankovic. My mother teaches in the math department with your father. She says he's smart."

I looked up. I knew her, too. April Reed. She was smart, too, in the way that teachers liked. She had brown hair tied back in a crooked braid, and thick glasses that hid her eyes. She was so plain, she should have been unpopular and miserable like me, but she was part of a group of girls that seemed to be totally indifferent to the cool kids. I never had to worry about talking in any class I shared with her, because she always shot her hand up in the air before teachers even finished their questions.

I stared at her and waited for her to look away. Instead, she said, "You're Yugoslavian, aren't you? I did a project on Yugoslavia for World Cultures last year. Are you Serbian or Croatian? Or Bosnian, or Macedonian, or—?"

I cut her off before she could finish the list. "Nothing," I said. The thick English word filled my mouth, choking me. "We left."

I looked back down at my paper, willing her to turn around, mind her own business. *We left.* The smell of fire filled my nose and throat, choking me. I heard voices shouting warnings, remembered gunfire echoing outside our apartment building. We'd huddled in the basement, my neighbours, my parents and me. All of us but Milan. I remembered how the neighbour lady's whispers had filled my ears as she prayed the rosary beside me, over and over again. *Holy Mary, Mother of God....*

I wanted to get up, to run out of the room. I couldn't. Mr Brennan had just stepped up to the blackboard. His voice rolled out, shutting up the kids around me. April grabbed her pen and started writing furiously. I sat back in my seat, and let the words turn into babble in my ears, nonsense syllables, a foreign language.

Why bother to even try?

My father dropped me off in front of the school at eight o'clock. He hadn't spoken once during the car ride, and neither had I. I'd skipped dinner that evening and stayed upstairs in my room, listening to the rise and fall of my parents' angry voices in the dining room.

The long black skirts of my witch's dress tripped me as I stepped out of the car. I caught myself on the door and straightened my pointed hat and shawl.

My father spoke for the first time. "Be here in three hours," he said.

I closed the door and watched the beaten-up green car pull away from the curb, leaving me behind, in the dark. I turned around and gazed up at the sprawling high school. Music spilled out through the open doors, into the darkness. A group of girls shoved past me, giggling. One of them was a witch, too. I backed away.

A long parade of headlights lit up the school parking lot, hundreds of students dressed as fairies, as sorcerers, as Turkish dancers. They all streamed up the pavement, towards the school. Surrounding me. My head started to spin. I backed further away, first slowly and then faster and faster, until I was running, holding up my long skirts, black in the darkness. Tears slid down my face. I ran across one street, down another. I couldn't go into the building, couldn't face the rest of them, so smug, so safe, so *American*. None of them knew what it was like to wonder if their city would be bombed. None of them knew what it was like to listen to gunfire outside their windows. None of them knew what it felt like to learn that their only brother had disappeared, one of so many young men, young soldiers, all gone, without even any bodies left to bury. *Oh, Milan....*

I tripped and fell forwards towards the hard sidewalk. Just in time, I threw my hands in front of my face. Rough cement slammed into them, breaking the skin. I gasped with pain. My whole body felt the jolt.

I lowered my forehead to the pavement and closed my eyes, trying to catch my breath. Silence enveloped me, broken only by the sound of the tree branches rustling in the breeze. Where was I, anyway?

I raised my head, and pushed myself up off the sidewalk. Houses lined the block, dark and still. I didn't recognise any of them. I couldn't be too far from the high school, though. Could I?

Someone gently touched my back.

I leaped away, and tried to scream. It stopped in my throat. I stared at the man—no, boy—who'd been standing behind me.

He grinned back at me. His black hair was tousled. I saw the breeze lift a strand of it. His uniform looked new, but I knew it couldn't be. I'd seen him model it five years ago.

"Milan?" I whispered.

He nodded. Then a ripple broke across his skin, blurring his features. As I watched, he vanished.

"Milan!" I let my breath out in a rush and stumbled forward. I reached out to touch the space where he had stood only a moment ago. He had been there! I'd seen it, even felt it.

He'd looked so young. But of course, I realised. He'd only been eighteen when he'd disappeared. He'd seemed older to me, back then. My big brother Milan, lifting me up in the air with a whoop, showing off his new uniform to me.

Light blinked briefly above the pavement, half a block away. It illuminated his figure, half-turned away from me. His head was cocked to the side, as if he were listening to a sound I couldn't hear.

"Milan!" I called. I ran forward, half-sobbing. "Wait for me!"

He smiled at me and lifted one hand. He held it out in front of him. *Stop.* I stopped running, but I sent my voice out to catch him, to stop him before he could go away again.

"Please," I said. I was crying as I spoke, but I knew he could hear me, knew he could understand. "They don't understand, they want to make me forget you, they don't care..."

He shook his head. *No.*

"Milan?" I whispered.

He raised his hand to his lips, the way he had that last night, before he left, sending me a kiss.

"Please," I said. "I can't do this. I need you!"

He shook his head again. His hand waved the kiss to me, across the dark street. I felt it settle against my face, light and tingling. I raised my hand to my cheek, and watched as his features blurred again.

"Milan?" I whispered.

He shook his head again.

Slowly, this time, his body faded. Trees and houses reappeared.

He wasn't coming back.

My throat burned.

I wrapped my arms around myself, around the black witch's outfit. Shivers shook my body.

I could run down the street to the spot where he'd stood. I could wait here for the next hour, shivering, just in case he came back.

But I didn't think he wanted me to, anymore.

I stared at the spot where he had stood. My brother Milan. I'd been waiting for over three years to see him again.

I dug my fingernails into the raw, abraded palms of my hands as I turned around, and I walked away from my brother's ghost.

"I love you, Milan," I whispered.

All I heard in response was the sighing of the wind in the trees. I didn't look back.

I walked through the dark streets until I recognised the name on one of the street signs. I turned down that road. After another block, I saw the corner of the high school parking lot. I wiped the tears off my face. I didn't want anyone else to see them.

I walked across the parking lot, brushing the dirt off my costume. My hands stung, but none of the scrapes were bleeding. How long would I have to wait before my father arrived?

"Jasna?"

I looked around. April Reed stood a foot away from me, next to a parked car and a short girl wearing a Hillary Clinton mask. April wore a glittery blue cat mask. The lenses of her glasses sparkled.

"Hi," she said. "We're on our way into the party. Do you want to walk with us?"

I had to pause to think through all the English words. I'd been thinking only in Croatian for the past hour.

I settled on something simple. "Yes," I said. For the first time in a long time, I felt a smile pull against my cheeks. "Yes," I said. "I'd like that."

afterword

My great-grandparents left Croatia after World War I, many decades before Jasna and her family would have emigrated. Family history often becomes clouded over the years; for a long time, the younger generations in my family didn't know exactly which town our own family had lived in.

When we discovered that the town had been called Sotin, of course our first reaction was to google it—and when we found out about the horrors that had taken place there so recently, it was a truly sobering discovery. I was driven to do more research after that initial shock, and this is the story that came out of it.

Green, Green Grass of Homeworld

Donna Maree Hanson

THE HISS OF steam teased Vo-nam D'abela's sensitive ears as hypodermic needles retracted from veins in arms, legs and tail. Antiseptic stung the pinprick wounds as he flexed his limbs. As stasis induced fugue sloughed off, his heart rate quickened and breaths deepened. He had arrived.

A harsh stench washed over him as he opened his eyes. The refuse of year's assisted life-support flushed away, leaving its fetid aftermath lingering on his tongue. When his eyesight cleared, he saw that his wife's stasis unit was vacant and sanitised, ready for the next occupant. He frowned at Li-pen's absence.

Perhaps Li-pen had been revived before him and had left on some errand for surely she had not gone to see Earth without him. She had not wanted to come with him on this trip, despite her being part human like him. The money, the time were only some of the excuses she used to delay them taking this trip. That they had no offspring, and hence no ties to Dianur, had been the deciding factor. But Vo-nam had waited his whole life to come to the homeworld and to see Earth in its majesty, its blueness radiant in the black firmament of space. For so long he had pictured it in his mind's eye, dreamt it after staring at images of the planet for hours and hours. Anxiety about Li-pen's absence lessened when he thought she was probably in the transition lounge, wondering why it was taking him so long to wake up.

The monitor chimed, telling him that his body was now in normal state. With a certain amount of regret, he saw while dressing that his soft, downy coat had faded to a dun colour. He wondered what the Earth's atmosphere would do to it. Would his pelt glow golden under Sol's rays, like great grandfather Luis D'abela had said it would? Would it ever regain the sheen years of careful grooming and doenut oil had enlivened? A glowing pelt was a matter of pride for a Di-Nuk, a Nuk of mixed species like him. There was something about those human genes that brought out the best in the Nuk physique. He was taller, more muscular and out-performed pure Nuk academically. Pity that his kin did not value the benefits of his mixed heritage or recognise the injection of superior human DNA into their gene pool. Vo-nam growled as he tried to bury the memories, the shame. No recognition from his extended family, no jobs, no housing and no social services.

Not that there was any official discrimination of Di-Nuk. No, thought Vo-nam, the unofficial was severe enough. It was so bad that Vo-nam had been raised under the Post-Colonial Dependents scheme, a small fund to look after what the Earth settlers and their technological intervention had left behind. Li-pen had never qualified for the scheme, except as his dependent. With the final proceeds of his trust fund, they could finally connect with their human heritage. Soon he would touch the soil of the homeworld, a place where he really belonged.

The door shushed open as he exited the life-support suite. Li-pen was not in the lounge as he had thought. Although he would never tell her so, he was annoyed that she had not waited for him. He could not help the feelings that swelled inside of him. The first view of the homeworld was a moment for sharing. He found it hard to go against that cultural imperative—not to speak his mind—ever. Pity Li-pen was not impeded by it. To his dismay, she never failed to speak her mind to him.

He followed the corridor that led to the observation deck. His thumping heartbeat spurring him to walk faster. Staff and passengers intermingled, a mixture of Nuk, humans and the glossy skinned Lumko. Vo-nam tried not to stare. They had been advised at boarding that they would be taking on Lumko refugees at Killen station, but still the sight of one so alien drew his curiosity. Lumko had near translucent skin, so that the shadows of their blood vessels and organs were visible. They could see but their eyes were under the skin at the side of their heads, like a kind of mutated fish that he had seen in one of the Earth children's books. He had heard that the Lumko could speak with each other through smells, grunts and gestures. That they walked around naked was also difficult to ignore. Vo-nam caught himself tugging the waistline of his kilt higher. Looking down, he adjusted the sash crossing his chest so that it disguised his central breast. His tail brushed the ground behind him, sweeping the floor slowly. Luckily, the Lumko wore tech translators so that non-Lumko could understand them, not that Vo-nam would dare to attempt to converse with one.

As he traversed the corridor, he tried to keep his excitement and awe in check, angling his head down and walking straight and true like a human, rather than when he was in Dianur and had had to imitate the pure bloods by walking slightly sideways and with a loping gait and bouncing tail. He found he was concentrating so hard on maintaining his walk that he missed the access port to the observation deck and had to backtrack, dodging a steward weaving through the crowds with a tray of beverages. The steward then disappeared into a private function room further along the corridor. Vo-nam did his best not to peer through the door when it swung open. Voices spilled out and he caught glimpses of humans and others before the door slid shut.

When he entered the observation deck, he saw family groups, some peering and pointing down to the blue planet. A few singletons stood by, gazing at the view. Most were human but there were one or two other Di-Nuks. The sight of Earth through the viewing pane, drew all of Vo-nam's attention. He just stood and gaped as he entered and completely forgot about the people around him and finding Li-pen. It was not until there were protests behind him did he realise that he had blocked the doorway, thereby preventing other newly-awakened travellers from entering and seeing the blue planet in all its glory. Bowing his head and muttering apologies like a cowering Di-Nuk, he backed away. Realising his lapse, he straightened up and strode purposefully to the viewing deck. There was no need to observe the Dianuran social norms now that he was on Earth. He did not need to apologise for who he was, or feel the need to make abeyances to his superiors. On Earth all were equal.

Li-pen touched his arm gently startling him. He did not know how long he had been there; it could have been hours or only minutes such was his absorption. Her grin showed her fine pointed teeth, which allowed her to pass for a Nuk most of the time. As he looked at her again after their long sleep, he admired Li-pen's prettiness and intelligence. Her body shape was very Nuk and her pelt was slightly mauve in colour. Under the ship's lights, it had taken on a silver sheen. Usually, she let her coat grow shaggy, a quaint habit, that let her blend in more with the pure bloods. Vo-nam liked to appear well groomed even though that set him apart. Great grandfather Luis had instilled the need for grooming into him and told him many a time that he was special to have human DNA. *Lucky to have it you are. Only the special ones could take it you know. It will benefit you one day, lad, it will. Mark my words, mark them well.* With a quick glance out the window, he grinned. It would be his time soon.

"I did not see you, Li. I was so taken by the view of the homeworld. Forgive me, I did not ignore you on purpose."

Li smiled again, her gaze flicking to the doorway and beyond before returning to him.

"I understand, Vo," patting his arm. "You have waited long for this. I should tell you though, and I'm not sure how this will affect you...I mean us...but the DNA profiles for visa classes have changed since we boarded."

Vo-nam shrugged and grunted. "I am part human that is enough to let me get a visa. I cannot see how they can change that fundamental right."

Li frowned. "Vo...they can deny you a visa or restrict the class of visa depending on their rules. They make the rules and can change them. I'm not saying it will affect us, only that I heard talk and wanted to warn you in case..."

Vo-nam found his mood had soured. "We should perhaps check which shuttle we are on and secure our luggage."

Li slid her hand down his forearm. "Yes, Vo. Let's do that. Immigration and customs are planet side so we'll find out then."

The entry hall at the London Customs Hall was full of milling people, voices churning and the occasional holler. Vo stood opposite the customs official, with his tail twitching and his hackles rising.

"What do you mean that I can only get a short stay tourist visa? I was advised not to apply for my visa before I left so that it would have more time on it. Now you are saying I can only enter if I agree to return in four weeks? That means I would have to leave on the ship I have just arrived on, which departs in two weeks or otherwise I'd be in breach."

Li stood beyond the barrier, her visa processed, and watched him as he listened with growing horror the effect of the DNA matrix assessment had on his right to land on the homeworld. The official had already explained things to him but Vo-nam couldn't believe it. His outrage drove all common sense from his mind. Anger was ripping through his blood. Only the quiet words from Li-pen penetrated long enough for him to calm down. He felt the need to reach out and squeeze with his clawed hands. He had waited so long for this moment. He had held the rage in check. All those times he had been excluded in the past. All those times where he was not welcomed and he could not show the hurt and the pain because he was Di-Nuk and to do so would betray his human heritage and would bring disrespect to all Di-Nuk and further shame. He remembered the whispered phrases from his childhood days. *Those hybrids are unstable. The human DNA makes them violent. Crazy even.* He remembered the shunning, the avoidance as if it was yesterday.

"I am sorry, Mr D'abela. The Colonial Statutes for mixed race species were amended six months ago and enacted three months ago, which means they are in force now. Your visa could not be processed at your point of origin because of the pending changes and you were advised to apply at the border accordingly. You can have a nice visit here for a couple of weeks. The tourist areas will provide ample opportunity to sample contemporary Earth life."

"Sample?" Vo-nam sucked in a breath fighting for calm. "But I want to live it, experience it. My wife's visa was processed without these problems. Why?"

The official turned to glance at Li-pen, his microbe shields glistening wetly in his nostrils. He faced Vo-nam again. "I am afraid that due to privacy concerns I cannot discuss your wife's status. You will have to apply to her for an explanation, although she is under no obligation to do so and her rights are protected under Earth law. However, you will deduce that there is some difference in the human DNA between you."

Li-pen drew closer and touched his arm, stroking the down near his wrist. "Vo, accept the visa so we can get to our hotel. We can try to sort things out later. We will lodge another application at the local office. Please, I am very tired now."

Turning, Li-pen nodded to the official, which was an action too subservient for Vo-nam's peace of mind. The official slid the visa card into Vo-nam's passport and passed it across the counter before calling out. "Next."

Vo-nam lowered his head, fighting for a dignity he felt had been stripped away. The feeling was more than disappointment but he could not articulate it to himself. With a glance at Li-pen's eager gaze as she took in the crowd and urged him into the transit queue, he felt he could not even begin to tell her either.

The transit to their Bath hotel was a blur. The visa issue loomed large in Vo-nam's mind and it soured the first scents of Earth's air. The green fields that surrounded Bath were a smear of treeless countryside that barely registered. The district's atmospheric shield shimmered in the sunlight. The Austen complex gleamed with freshly polished Georgian stone or so Li explained to him, reading from her guide book. There were only a few places on Earth that Vo-nam's restricted visa allowed him to go and the tourist area of Wiltshire was the most appealing and economical of them.

The relic of London city and its underground hotels held no appeal to someone from Nuk heritage. The trees and open skies were important and in the pre-flight education program, he had been warned that Nuk did not fare well in the dark, damp underground places. Stories of psychosis abounded and of the accidental execution of Nuks, who had lost control and stormed through the corridors. Vo-nam considered himself mostly human, but could not deny that there was a deep, inexplicable fear of being closed in and being held underground. Li often lectured him on his tendency to ignore that he had an equal Nuk DNA makeup. There were also the cultural imperatives from living on Dianur that could override any inherited human traits.

Li-pen drew her gaze from the guide book when the vehicle stopped. "Lo, cheer up, Vo. We will do some interesting things while we are here. You make too much of being part human you know."

Vo could only stare at her and nod dumbly. The bellbot delivered them and their luggage to a room on the top floor. Vo went to the windows and saw the views reaching out across lush green hills with puffed white sheep standing idle. While he stood there, Li-pen set about unpacking and arranging their things, talking to Vo-nam all the while and explaining where and why she was putting things. Vo-nam let her voice soothe him. Soon it would be time to eat.

Vo-nam gazed out of the window until sunset. When it was too dark to see he picked up the guide book and flipped through the pages idly. As the pages whisked by he wondered if it would tell him where he could get fresh killed game. Great grandfather Luis had told him that there was plenty of food on Earth and the people often ate fresh killed deer, or bears, or birds. Thinking about the landscape though, he could not think where the game would live. There were no trees, only pastures. Perhaps it was the sheep that were now hunted for food.

After breakfast the next morning, the hotel liaison recommended a day tour of the Bath region. Li-pen said yes before Vo-nam could speak.

"I thought we should go to the immigration office and see about changing my visa status," he whispered urgently in her ear.

"There's no hurry," she whispered back, while bowing her head to the hotel liaison. "Come on, I want to play tourist today. Think of me for a change."

She patted him on the arm and then scratched him under the chin. Vo-nam lowered his head and nodded. He would be patient.

The remains of the Roman baths were extremely ancient. The water still trickled up through the spring but the walls and the Roman statues were now replicas of the original remains. Vo-nam found it quite boring, despite Li-pen's obvious enthusiasm. She asked to tour guide to explain.

"A very good question," the tour guide replied. Li-pen grinned and nodded to Vo-nam. "By removing the originals and replacing them with the replicas we can best preserve the heritage of the area and still provide the look and feel of the times."

With a smile, Li-pen followed the guide onto the bus, leaving Vo-nam to make his own way. As they drove around, Vo-nam could see a few people dressed in period clothing. He thought that was strange, but Li-pen read from the guidebook, which stated that the re-enactment was to help visitors to picture Earth's past, the days when there was tranquillity and little or no technology.

As they drove along a road, past featureless pastures, Vo-nam thought that Dianur had such political sentiments. That was why the humans were ousted around one hundred Earth years previously. Nuk were rural. They lived close to nature, in clans. While some of the clans found human technology seductive, others found it pervasive and subversive. In school, Vo-nam had studied the re-establishment of home rule and the effects it had. It mattered not to him on an emotional level that the resentment of his mixed heritage was based on the political shenanigans of the time. Home rule did lead to a resurgence of historical backward looking and glorification of the past. Many clans purged themselves of human technology and reverted to pre-colonial methods of food production and manufacturing. In some cases the resentment went deep. So much so that his parents had been killed during a purge and he had been brought up in the human protectorate by his uncle.

Ah, Uncle Vin, thought Vo-nam, feeling his eyelids grow heavy as the bus ride lulled his senses. Long dead now was Uncle Vin but he remembered his voice. *Should have taken us all back to Earth. What's the point of maintaining the protectorate? Costs them loads and is so unwieldy. Must be some other reason, something they are not saying.* Vin often repeated this opinion after he had made his way home from one too many gin and tonics in the protectorate bar. After his uncle's death, Vo had to integrate into Nuk society as part of his transition program.

Once again at the hotel, Vo-nam stared out the window, looking across the city to the fields beyond. He felt himself frowning again and went to brush his pelt. He was not happy with the colour of his coat. It was dull grey in the Earth light and thinking about Uncle Vin reminded him that he could not imbibe alcohol at all. It had nearly killed him the only time he had tried. All pure Nuk could not metabolise alcohol. It was a sore point with him. Something that made him feel less human instead of more.

Again the next day, Li-pen insisted that they play tourist. Vo-nam held his peace. The tour guide stopped the bus in Wells so that they could view the cathedral, now preserved under a transparent dome. Clockwork knights came in and out of compartments located in the side of the building. Vo-nam yawned while drinking coffee and eating cucumber sandwiches.

"These are tasteless. Why do we not have a hamburger like him over there?" Vo pointed to another patron, who bit down on the meat and juices dripped down his clean shaven chin.

Li-pen nudged his arm. "Shush now. This is the most traditional of meals, you know. Royalty used to eat it every day. Come on, eat up. The bus will leave soon."

By the time they were returned to their hotel, Vo-nam's stomach was rumbling. As he had not seen fresh game on the hotel menu the previous night, he had decided that they should venture out on their own and prowl the streets of Bath for a suitable restaurant.

He thought it was odd that the concierge quizzed them about where they were going and how long they were going to be away. He asked for their visa tag numbers so that he could contact them in case of an emergency. Vo-nam was ready to make a curt response but Li-pen was there bowing her head and shuffling them out the door subserviently. Vo worried about Li's behaviour. Normally she would stand up for herself. Mentally shrugging, he realised that travelling to new places put a strain on people. His reactions were not normal for him so he supposed Li was allowed to be affected in some way too.

The night air was so moist that Vo-nam felt his spirits lift. His annoyance and Li-pen's insistence on a subservient attitude slid away. This was the homeworld that his great grandfather had spoken about, kindling Vo-nam's own desire to know his human heritage.

Again, the streets were rather bare of people. Tourists like themselves appeared to be the only ones around. Some of the tourists were human. They travelled in groups and often whispered when they neared any Di-Nuk.

"Surely they know we are part human and have native rights to visit and live on Earth," Vo-nam whispered to his wife. Well except for me, as I have a tourist visa, he thought sourly.

"Lo, don't let it up set you, Vo. Not everyone is as well-educated as you. And perhaps they don't see many Di-Nuks where they come from."

Outside one restaurant, Li-pen stopped him from entering. "Not that one. Let's find somewhere else," she suggested, tugging on his arm, her tail agitated. He resisted and went to step through the door. He was keen to try the restaurant because all the patrons appeared to be human.

Li-pen started to walk away and he was left holding the doorknob. He dropped his hand and followed after her. She had the credit cards after all.

"Why did you do that?" he asked as he trailed his wife down the street.

"Because I want a nice quiet dinner without you getting paranoid about humans and their reactions to us. You expect too much from them just like you do pure bloods at home."

"But...but..."

Li-pen walked faster and Vo had to hurry to keep up with her. The restaurants seemed to peter out after two intersections and Li-pen slowed down. There was an alleyway leading to a courtyard and another street beyond. Vo-nam thought he saw people walking there and headed off in that direction. Li-pen followed without complaint.

Vo-nam stood stock still and saw a number of rectangular vehicles with small windows cut into them. A quick glance and he could tell most of them were roboservers. However, in one of them a Di-Nuk handed out food to customers. Spices, sweet sauces and an array of food smells mingled in the courtyard. Immediately, Vo was drawn the cart manned by the Di-Nuk. As he neared, the tantalising scent of seared meat teased his nostrils. Beside him, Li-pen growled low in her throat, unable to deny her reaction to the closeness of the food. The Di-Nuk's eyes widened when he saw them.

"Not often we see Di-Nuks here in the back street. What can I get you?" His accent was rather strange. He spoke like his vowels had been flattened and his consonants sharpened. Vo-nam was not certain but he sensed that the food vendor was nervous.

Glancing at the price list, which was more than half what the hotel charged, Vo-nam licked his fangs with a wet tongue. "Meat for both of us. Rare if possible," he requested in his best Earth tongue.

"Sure. Coming right up." The vendor sliced off thick slaps of meat from a joint he had grilling and placed it between two large pieces of bread. "You want sauce?"

Looking at the vender sideways, Vo asked him in Nuk. "Do you have any Dinuda?"

The vendor frowned so Vo-nam spoke in the Earth tongue again.

The Di-Nuk nodded. "No, what about sweet chilli? It's good."

"Thank you, yes." Vo-nam glanced at his wife. Did that mean this Di-Nuk had never tasted Dinuda sauce? he thought. Ignoring his look, Li-pen paid for the food, and they stood to the side to eat it. Li-pen's gaze tracked the movements of the vendor as he served other customers. There was nowhere to sit and as Li-pen seemed as curious as he was to learn more of the strange speaking Di-Nuk, they loitered nearby, waiting for an opportunity to engage him in conversation again.

"So do you live around here?" Li-pen asked, when she caught the vendor's eye.

The vendor began cleaning the bench inside his window. "Not far from here."

"So you live in the tourist zone?" Vo asked, excited by the prospect.

"No, not really. No."

"So you have a work visa?" Vo asked.

The vendor's eyes arrowed around the courtyard and he began packing things away. "I have a visa but technically I'm not meant to sell produce here in the tourist zone. I don't usually but I heard there was a ship in and I thought I might attract some of the tourist crowd."

"So you are Di-Nuk like us but you speak differently. Why is that?"

The vendor looked uncomfortable. He leant out of the window saw there was no other customers and undid the lever that held the window shutter up. "Sorry. I've got to head off now. Nice meeting you."

Vo-nam stepped forward and held the shutter open. "Please talk to us. We really want to know and we won't tell anyone else if it bothers you."

"I can't say, truly. It's difficult."

Li-pen swallowed the last of her meat and bread. "You were brought up on Earth, weren't you? That is why you speak like that, why you can't speak Nuk well at all."

Vo-nam gaped at his wife and the vendor. "Is that true? How could that be? I thought none of the hybrids were brought to Earth."

The food vendor's hand was on the shutter ready to jerk in down. "I said I can't talk about it."

"So it is true? Will you be here tomorrow? Can we talk to you again?" Vo-Nam asked politely, bowing his head to show humility. His tail lowered and swept the ground from side to side with slow grace.

"Sure. I'll be here around sunset."

Vo-nam let his hand drop and the shutter closed with a clang. Soon after the vehicle powered up and lumbered out of the courtyard.

Vo walked with Li-pen to their hotel in the Austen complex. A group of people in Regency dress walked past them, laughing and chatting gaily. Vo frowned, finding he did not like the historic trappings of Bath. He wanted to see the real homeworld as it was now.

That night while he slept he thought up a plan. No more guided tours. He would sneak out and take a look at what they hide from the tourists. It was easy to exit the hotel before dawn without being noticed. There were nothing but cleaning bots and a sleepy receptionist in the foyer.

Vo-nam had left his wife asleep, hoping to be back before she woke up. It appeared she was able to survive on tea and toast. He found he needed much more meat than was on offer and wanted to make sure he got something more substantial to eat. Yet the hotel charged a lot of money for any kind of meat. It was either scarce or the owners were vegetarians and were eager to push their creed onto others.

The sun was not quite up and the street lights were still shining when he made it out onto the road. No people were about as far as he could see. He chose a street at random and walked down it. As the sky grew brighter, he thought that the edge of town might appeal. Perhaps he would find some trees, some wildlife (food) or least some real people going about their early morning business.

The empty streets and houses made him edgy. He supposed there were people in the houses and apartments but he was not convinced. Yet why would they be uninhabited? The air felt clean, the town was pleasant in an odd, historical kind of way. Why did he get the sense that he was alone? The scents too were stale, like people had passed this way once, long ago and never returned.

At the edge of town, a park called Hampton Down segued into pasture. There were a few sheep there, standing still on a slope. A small pond had ducks floating on it, an occasional quack audible. There was even a rabbit dashing in and out of a burrow, its cotton tail dancing tantalisingly. Soft undulating hills further on had sheep on them too.

Vo-nam found the scene quite pleasing until he heard voices. Suddenly he felt guilty, realising that perhaps he was where he should not be. Looking around for a place to hide, he found a stone monument and placed himself behind it. The monument commemorated something called Bath Golf Course, 1880 – 2050. His pelt matched the colour of the stone so he felt sure he blended in. While he watched, two humans came into view, males he thought they were, and each was holding an end of a sheep. Vo tried hear what they were saying but they were talking so fast, he found it hard to catch the words.

They positioned the sheep, opened the side of it up and tinkered with its insides before shutting what looked like a panel. Then one man went to the head and tilted it back as if it was connected by hinge. "Ahhh, here it is," the workman said in a slow, drawling way. "Short circuit." The other man's reply was muffled as he was bent over wiping the hooves of the sheep with a dusting cloth. Then the dialogue between them became incomprehensible again. They spoke in some kind of rhyme and half sentences. Some words he could catch but the meaning was lost on him. Closing up the sheep, the men walked away, still bantering with each other and laughing occasionally. Vo-nam ducked down to avoid being seen as the workmen walked away. As the sound of the conversation faded, Vo-nam put his head around the monument and peeked out.

The sheep bleated once and then moved slightly, giving the impression of life. Vo-nam felt suddenly ill. Next, he found himself gasping for breath, heart palpitating painfully. What did that mean? It couldn't be a live animal. His mind was working furiously, re-jigging all of his impressions and thoughts of Earth with those of his earlier expectations and beliefs. They did not marry up well at all. If the sheep were fake, what else? After the workmen disappeared from view, he crept over to the pasture and touched it. Going down on all fours, he sniffed it and then tasted it. Fake. It was some kind of resin, not real grass.

Still disbelieving he then padded up to the pond. The ducks did not react to his presence. He squatted down, watched them, listened for the quacks. There! The sound but no beaks moved. Sniffing, he found no scents. The pond smelt too fresh and chemical. The rabbit moved again, sprinting from its burrow. Vo-nam growled at it. The rabbit didn't even flinch. He watched it further and saw that it too, was following some predetermined routine.

This was beyond belief. He could understand the replica monuments and even the re-enactments with menus and period dress—but the animals and the vegetation? What had happened to the homeworld his great grandfather Luis had told him about and the books which backed up those tales?

He found his head swimming. Facts and fiction were stitched together like some sick tapestry. It was hard to take in. His homeworld was a fake. A replica. A façade. Lo, a tourist trap. Vo-nam sprawled in the grass, struggling to control his feelings, to compartmentalise his pain, his anger, his disappointment. The sun was well up by the time he decided to head back to the hotel.

Li-Pen was eating toast and jam when he entered the room. She looked up as he slammed the door behind him. "Lo, good morning, husband. I have ordered eggs for you. It was the best I could do on our budget. Where have you been?"

He nodded. "Out," he replied and sat down to stare at his plate. He did not know how to tell her how he felt about what he had seen. He did not know if she would understand. He had dragged her here to this fake homeworld. It was his fault, his responsibility.

"Are you going to eat that? If not, I am still hungry." Li-Pen said, fork poised to spear a mound of scrambled egg.

Coming out of his reverie, he growled low in his throat, which translated to "my food, back off."

Li-Pen laughed and reclined back on the bed. "Lo, that is more like it. So tell me what did see or do that upset your appetite?"

He tried to explain to Li-Pen what he saw. She nodded and scrunched up her nose, a Nuk characteristic for puzzlement. "So the sheep are fake? It is a tourist zone so I suppose none of it would be real."

"What about the grass? It is fake too. Why would anyone fake vegetation unless it is all gone."

Li-pen got up and began to brush her coat with vigorous, sharp strokes. "You are making a big deal out of nothing. I agree it is a puzzle but ...not...a conspiracy." She continued her grooming and after a few minutes asked brightly, "So what should we do today?" She looked in the mirror as she ruffled her coat with her fingers to make a random pattern.

"The immigration office opens at eight," he replied, grinning.

She turned to look at him and shook her head. "Not today, Vo. I cannot face arguing with bureaucracy. Maybe tomorrow. Mmmm?" She frowned and bared her teeth.

Vo-nam nodded. There was no point in arguing with her. He knew that look. At that moment too, he wondered if he really wanted to stay, now that he knew. But what choice did he have. He did not belong on Dianur. He was not one of them. So they readied themselves for more tourist adventures, with Li-Pen at least agreeing to see the Earth-raised Di-Nuk at sunset. After returning from viewing a dome with standing stones in it and the facade of Salisbury Cathedral, they snuck out of the hotel again, avoiding the questions from the concierge.

There were many people around the vending vans when they arrived. Vo-nam hung back waiting for the last of the customers to slip into the growing shadows. A few of the other vendors closed up shop and trundled out of the courtyard on noisy motors. Most of the customers were human tourists, getting a thrill from buying real meat at affordable prices. From overhearing the various conversations, these humans were from off world and enjoying visiting the homeworld too. Vo did his best not to envy their humanness.

The Di-Nuk lowered the shutter. Vo-Nam's ears pricked up. Was he leaving? But then he heard the whispered call from behind the van. Li-Pen and Vo-nam headed around the back of the vehicle to see him. The Di-Nuk was short and his tail was pushed into his human clothes. Through his open shirt, Vo could seen several surgical scars.

"What is your name?" Vo asked, completely mesmerised by what he was seeing. The Di-Nuk's gait was slightly off and his mannerisms were almost completely human. The Di-Nuk smiled like a human, his teeth square. Were they filed? thought Vo-nam.

"Round here they call me Petey."

"You have a human name?" Li-Pen asked. "What about your clan?"

Petey shrugged, using the human gesture. "Don't know who my clan are. Don't know who my kin are. I'm an orphan."

Vo-nam tried not to think of the possibilities that were denied him because he had a living uncle and had stayed on Dianur. He had been orphaned and could have been brought up on Earth like this Di-Nuk.

"So tell us then. What do robot sheep mean?" Vo-Nam asked, surprised he had taken on his wife's outspoken characteristics. Why had he not beaten around the forest to scare out the game, as the saying went on Dianur.

"You saw?" The Di-Nuk nodded and scratched his chin. Another human gesture. It made Vo's stomach turn and he shook himself, realising that this is what pure Nuk must feel when they looked at him. A parody of a Nuk. It was not a happy realisation. "It's all fake."

Li-Pen had been eying Petey with curiosity. "Where do you live, Petey?"

Petey looked around assuring himself that they were alone. "I live in the enclaves near here. Technically, I don't have a license to sell food in the zone but competition is tough for the likes of me."

"What do you mean? Are you discriminated against?" The fur on the back of Vo's neck bristled with indignation.

Petey jumped back, scenting Vo's anger, his own fur standing up.

"I never said that. Prices are tough. C...c...competition is intense. And tourists spend more money." His voice came out high-pitched.

Li-Pen put her hand on Petey's shoulder, meaning to comfort him. He jumped back as if she had hit him and cowered against the van. "Don't hurt me please."

Li-Pen's mouth dropped open and she gaped at Vo-Nam. "We mean you no harm, Petey. We offer only friendship. Forgive us if we offended you." Vo-nam said bowing, apologising for his wife's affront.

Petey peered out through his crossed elbows. "You want to be friends?"

"Yes, of course. You are like us. We know what it is like to be Di-Nuk."

Petey dropped his arms away from his head. "You do?" He stood there staring at them in turn, then shrugged human style and climbed into the van.

"Well, see you around then. I have to head home now."

Before Vo-nam or Li-Pen could speak, he fired up the van and drove away.

"Li?" Vo turned to his wife, wondering what she thought.

"Very odd behaviour. Let's go back to the hotel." She turned around and started walking away.

Vo-nam twitched his tail. "No. I will follow him."

Li-Pen paused. "What? Why?"

"Because I want to know what is going on. I want to see the real Earth, not this fabrication that has been foisted on me."

Li-Pen's tail curled around her left foot. "Vo, really...forget it."

Vo-Nam's tail twitched faster. "I cannot. You may accompany me or not."

Li-Pen watched him for a moment and then shifted her gaze to the retreating van. "Race you," she said with a smile. Then she bounded off after the van, on all fours like a Nuk cub.

Vo lost precious time gaping at her behaviour. On Dianur she would not have behaved so, not without shame. Vo trotted after her, using his human gait. She was fast but he would not stoop to grovelling along the ground like an unsophisticated child. After a few minutes, he switched to his native gait and then when it became clear that he would lose them, he dropped to the ground and bounded after them. After a few minutes, he got a stitch in his side and slowed down.

The van puttered along the deserted streets and then disappeared from view. Vo paused trying to see where his wife had gone. Then he inhaled deeply catching her scent. He caught up to her, as she was standing in the shadow of a street lamp. Vo-nam smoothed the hair on his head and scratched under his sweaty arm. "Gone?"

Li-Pen put her hand on his arm. "Wait. He is going there to that building. See?"

Vo peered into the dark, his night vision not as acute as his wife's. Then he saw it, a Di-Nuk-shaped patch of dark in front of the building. The door opened and Petey slipped inside.

Vo squinted. "Didn't he say he was living nearby but that building is in the zone."

Li-Pen loped away and Vo was hard pressed to keep up with her. As she opened the door, he arrived too. Behind it was another door with what looked like a visa card reader controlling it. A sign above listed the classes of visa permitted to enter.

Li-Pen ferreted about for her visa card, separating it from his. "Mine should work." It did. Vo-nam knew his visa card wouldn't operate the door. His was not one of the listed visa classes.

"Wait here. I'll go and see." She went to step through and, suddenly desperate, he flung himself through with her, tumbling them down a long flight of steps. An alarm sounded as he landed. Li-Pen pushed herself up and shook her head, dazed but unhurt.

"Run!" she said. "Now," she added when he did not move.

Vo-Nam wasted no time and sped off. He thought she was following him but when he checked over his shoulder she had not. Had she run in the other direction? It was too late to turn back. He would get caught by whoever came to investigate the alarm.

His pace slowed as his panic lessened. Vo tried to take in his surroundings. He had run mindlessly down a corridor and turned in random places. As he gathered his senses, the smell hit him—a thick, offal smell, mixed with sweat and filth. It staggered him.

Holding his arm over his face, he came out into a larger space lined with balconies. Here the voices and the sounds intruded and intertwined with the stench. He kept running, not feeling safe in these alien surroundings. There was no air, no natural light. He was underground. There were people in here, crammed in, flowing over the balconies, dropping their waste, their food scraps. Some hit him as he ran and he wiped at the detritus, desiring to stop and clean his pelt. How he hated to be dirty.

He found a corner and sunk into it, keeping his eyes to the thoroughfare. Breathing through his mouth, he panted, letting his heart slow its excited beat. He tried to groom his pelt but it was no use. Only a complete soak would restore it. Forgetting about his personal hygiene, he looked up and surveyed his position. There were creatures here all around him. They looked misshapen, inhuman and dirty. They talked, though, and he could understand them. Their clothes were rags and they carried bundles, shuffling to a conveyer belt to place them down. Vo's gaze assessed the space and the people. The smell took on a new dimension, overlayed with a sickly sweet smell. It made it easier to breathe but he wondered what it was. No one had noticed him yet. What would happen if they did, would they turn him in? What punishment awaited him? Would they send him home? Well they had already decided that his stay was short. What more could they do? That thought allowed him to relax.

After he caught his breath, he climbed to his feet and went up to one of the beings. "Excuse me, sir. Can you tell me where I am?"

The being ignored him and shouldered him out of the way. "Please speak to me," he pleaded to its back.

He turned to the next one and the next and all of them acted like he was not there. Then at last, a tall, rangy being came forward." Your kind is not welcome here. This space is for Laots."

Vo bowed his head. "Thank you for speaking to me. You are familiar with Di-Nuk?"

The Laot shook his head. "No, what I meant was that non-Laot are not welcome here. Find some other part of New London to inhabit."

He turned his back, and Vo saw the scales on his neck and the strange ears. "Are you part human, too?"

The Laot paused, hissed once as he turned around. Vo-nam's eyes widened as the creature puffed himself out, looming suddenly large. "I could kill you for that insult. No one speaks of the shame."

Vo-nam sucked in a breath. "Insult? Shame? Please explain what you mean. I am half human and proud of it."

The Laot stepped up to him and sniffed once or twice. "Maybe you are. Why would you own it? We are refuse, mistakes, fodder. Why would that make you proud?"

Again Vo-Nam struggled to make sense of the Laot. "I don't understand," he said, feeling close to panic. The walls seemed too shrink around him and he could not quite block out that these beings were working, and working in terrible conditions.

The Laot beckoned him over to a small alcove out of the way of the Laot working. He lowered himself to the ground and gestured for Vo-Nam to sit beside him. Gingerly, Vo lowered himself to the ground, trying not to inhale the pungent odours that assaulted his nostrils. "Not sure where you are from, Mister Di-Nuk. One of the many places humans went to find their answers, I would guess."

"Answers? Do you mean the colonial offspring?"

The Laot gaped at him and then grunted. "Offspring?" Then he laughed heartily. "You think you are offspring, natural born like? Hah. They created hybrids for a purpose. They wanted compatible tissue."

Vo-nam stroked his chin, his ears twitching. "You make it sound that you were created in a laboratory. In my case, I had parents and grew up with tales of Earth."

The Laot's eyes widened, showing red and blue around the vertically slit irises. "Rubbish. Complete rubbish. All were laboratory grown and the tales you were told are rubbish too."

"No. Not possible." Deep down the seeds of doubt were planted. "Why are you living here on Earth?"

The Laot put a cup on a small burner and heated it. "Too many questions. Time for you to leave."

Vo-nam stood, finding the being's manner difficult to interpret. "Forgive me. I meant no offense."

The Laot sniffed once and scratched the back of his neck. Vo caught sight of a brown bug slipping into his dirty shirt. "Suppose you don't, I guess. Find your way to the next enclave and you'll work it out. Fine educated specimen like yourself."

Vo frowned. "How many of us part humans are there?"

Laot sucked in a breath. "How am I supposed to know that?" Then he sunk back against the wall and appeared to sleep. Vo-nam waited for a moment and then crept away.

Throughout that day, he saw many different iterations of hybrids, felt his uniqueness slide away. There were humans, too, living in amongst the enclaves. They smelt and were thin and lifeless. Not what he imagined, not fat and happy like the off-world human tourists.

A small hunched over creature stopped to stare at him as he passed through a section of the enclaves. "What do you do here, stranger?" it asked boldly.

Vo-nam halted, surprise making his tail twitch. So far none of the various hybrids had bothered to talk to him or note his passing. "I am lost."

"Haha. Heard that before. Not seen the likes of you around here. You must be one of them newer hybrids, born and raised off world from the smell of you."

"Yes, I am a Di-Nuk from Dianura. I do not understand. What do you mean newer hybrids?" The creature had patches of grey fur on weepy pink skin. Vo found it quite repulsive and did his best to hide his distaste.

"I am an old reject. They used to bring us here and change us. But there were too many mistakes, too many rejects. Then the activists protested and the humans had to do their experiments off world. Only successfully compatible tissue was allowed to reside here."

Vo-nam shuddered. "Compatible tissue? I don't believe you." Vo-nam did his best to cling to the remains of his shattered dream and failed. The world he wanted to belong to did not exist.

The creature shrugged and walked off. "Nutter!" he called back before scampering up a ladder leading to a balcony. Vo-nam kept walking. He saw none of the fat, happy humans living in the enclaves. As he saw the decay, the despair, the twisted shapes of well over a hundred hybrid species, he began to believe. As he traversed the enclaves, he heard the chatter, pulled the threads of truth together.

The humans had filled this place with a multitude of hybrids, alien cultures, and fused them until they no longer resembled their original species or cultures. Then the humans went off world to make new homes, leaving their refuse behind them. Now on the surface, it was only the tourist resorts, sucking the money from the gullible and presenting a façade for the rest of the galaxy—pristine fakery, depicting a nostalgic past that probably never existed. But here, down here, this was where the real world existed—where the work was done, where the rejected hybrids eked out a pitiful existence. Vo-nam spluttered when he let those thoughts take root. He tried the stifle the sobs, but could not. Like the stench of the place, the truth could not be ignored. Staggering on, he found another enclave and then another, coming around in a large circle.

In a market, he thought found the source of meat that Petey had been selling. This type of animal was unrecognisable but Vo had his suspicions. When he allowed them to gel, he ducked into a corner and vomited. He suspected the malformed creatures were bred and slaughtered for food. How could he tell what the original species were and how different from the sentient hybrids around him?

The enclaves and the enclosed space started to overwhelm Vo-Nam. He wondered if it was best to hand himself in, best to end this putrid escapade within the bowels of the homeworld. Then he recollected that he had not seen anyone in uniform, not one human official at all. He wanted out but that would mean tracking his own scent and back tracking. It took a long time to return through the various enclaves, even though he bounded on all fours, disregarding the social niceties by ducking and weaving around the workers and those lingering in the passageways without so much as an apology. Yet necessity drove him. Too much, too fast, it threatened to corrode his sanity. He thought back to the pre-flight education program depicting Nuk being shot in the corridors of Old London, supposedly overwhelmed by the subterranean surroundings. His experience put a new gloss on that story. If they experienced what he did, then they were rational and appalled. Not insane or psychotic at all.

By the time he made the door, he was mired in fatigue. There did not appear to be any sign of Li-Pen. Nor was there anyone official there, ready to catch visa jumpers like him. He squatted for a while, trying to clear his head so he could detect Li-Pen's scent. At last he could smell her, he tracked her away from the door and then back again. The trails overlapped. Did that mean she had returned to the hotel? Was she there on the other side waiting to let him out? He shouted by the exit. No one came to investigate. Li-pen was not there.

Vo stood there gazing at the door, wondering how he could leave again. If he tried the door would that gain him anything except maybe setting off an alarm? He thought he had to risk it, even if they arrested him. What did it matter he had no more a place here than he did in Dianur. Vo-nam found that realisation quite shattering. All their money gone, all their goodbyes said and now this—a dead end.

Then he heard footsteps and quickly slunk away to the shadows. It was Petey, rucksack on his shoulder, using his visa card to open the door. Vo called out. Petey's head snapped around, his mouth agape. The door opened. Vo leaped forward, grabbed the visa card from Petey's hand and pushed past him to bound up the stairs. More alarms sounded but he kept on going. He heard the other Di-Nuk shout at him, yet did not understand the words. Vo-nam was breathing hard as he exited. Quickly looking around him, he threw the Di-Nuk's card back down the stairs. Petey grovelled for it. Vo loped away on all fours, glad to be clear of the stench and the crowding. He ran, and ran, through the pastures, dodging sheep and then he lay down and stared at the shimmering atmospheric dome above. Rolling in the grass, he rubbed the dirt and grime from his pelt. Then as he sat there grooming himself with his claws, he let his thought run. He was safe. He was free. He did not belong anywhere. No, he argued with himself. He had a wife and they would rebuild their lives, earn more money. Perhaps they could adopt a child. Li so wanted children, but their hybrid bodies could not produce compatible ova and sperm. They were effectively sterile as a couple. But there was a glimmer of a future there. What choice did he have?

After dark, he made his way back the hotel. No one challenged him or even appeared to take note of him. The authorities had not come to arrest him. That was a relief. He allowed himself to relax as he rode the elevator to his floor. Once inside their room he saw signs that Li had been back. The credit cards were on the bed and a message light was flashing on the side table. He stumbled over to it dumbly, realising that something must have happened. She should have been here.

Vo. There is no way to say this gently so I'll tell you straight. I am not coming back to Dianur with you. Earth has granted me citizenship and I want to stay. My uterus is useful here. I can breed babies for this company and they will pay me very well. And you know we could never.... I am sorry Earth is not what you thought it was. There are other places, better places. Don't look for me. Go back home, find a Nuk, and settle down. Sorry I've taken all our money to set myself up here. Had no choice. Sorry.

Vo-nam crouched by the bed and replayed the message he could not quite believe. A healthy female could carry four to five foetuses at a time. Technically, she could produce many litters of humans if her womb was compatible. Vo tried not to think about how Li-Pen had got her visa, maybe not because she had more human DNA at all. Then he recalled how she had been absent from the observation deck when they arrived. How she knew things like the new immigration rules. Perhaps that room with the humans and the catering.

It was her usefulness and compatibility that was the issue. He knew he had more human heritage than her, but he was not useful to them. He didn't matter. His humanness was a farce, created through lies and illusions. He was one of many colonial conquests, a residue of earlier policies, ones that Earth would like to forget about, like they had the hybrids in the enclaves.

The room's buzzer sounded, then the door opened before he could give permission to enter. Armed men in uniforms barged in, swinging the door open with a bang. Vo-nam's hackles raised and he growled, instinctively on alert. One of the men stepped forward, as the others kept their guns trained on him, a small card in his gloved hand. "Is this your visa card, Mr D'abela?"

Vo's tail swung from side to side. "Yes. I must have dropped it." Li-pen had held his visa card. She had had it when they entered the enclaves. His gaze slid to the bed, where the other cards were. His was missing.

"Yes, you did—in the enclaves—a place where you should not have been. Come with us now, Mr D'abela. I am afraid your visa has been revoked. Once your deportation has been processed you will be escorted to the next available ship."

"Deportation?"

"Yes, you will be ineligible to return to Earth or any of its colonies. Do you understand what I am saying?"

Vo nodded. He understood too well. The final link was broken. Vo-nam swallowed once.

"Yes. I understand. May I wash first? I am so dirty."

"No time for that. Come along now." The man placed cuffs on his hands and pulled him along. As they shuffled him out the door, he tried to resist. "But my wife has gone missing. Can you help me find her?"

"Come along quietly sir. We will see about your wife later."

Vo felt the sting of the needle in his arm as the relaxant poured in. For a moment, he thought he saw Li-Pen in the cubicle next to him but then the image faded. His last few days on Earth were torture. They had kept him locked up. No one would answer his inquiries about his wife. Vo had many hours to think about robot sheep. Although he reasoned that he was not like the Laot, an experiment gone wrong, he still felt the taint of being part human. It would take time to find out the truth and maybe he never would. There was too much layering in the bureaucracy, too much politics and hiding of history. More and more, he understood the Nuk attitude toward him and wished that he had never come to the homeworld. It was hard to find pride and superiority when your self worth had been expunged. On Dianur, he would finally understand his shame, his taint, his place.

Li-Pen had found a place on the homeworld but at what cost? She was useful, but would be treated as a person, granted the same rights as others? That was no longer his concern. The divorce notification had reached him two days ago. It was over. What would he do when he returned home? He chuckled to himself as the meds loosened his self-control. Run on all fours and chase tasty *hunin*. Yes, he laughed, thinking about the taste of fresh killed meat. As the stasis unit hummed to life sucking away his consciousness, he wondered what robot sheep tasted like.

This story took me years to write. The idea first came to me in 2005 while I was travelling around the UK. Green fields with sheep all looking so perfect. Then I got the idea of it all being fake and that workmen set it up every day for the tourists, you know trotting out the sheep and winding them up. Then I envisioned a future when descendants from Earth came back to see the mother country or, in this case, the homeworld. Having English grandparents gave me a view of the mother country, one that didn't live up to the hype when I got there. Green, green grass also discusses colonisation and transgenic manipulation, which fit in their nicely.

When Russell first put out the submission guidelines for Belong, *I thought fantastic I have an idea that might suit. I did think about it and maybe even wrote notes and then began a period of not writing for me. There were happenings like moving house and a relationship breakup and there were a number of other reasons, including questioning whether I should write at all. I believe many writers go through this. I came out the other side. Hopefully, you the reader is happy with the result.*

The deadline for Belong *had long since passed. I bumped into Russell in 2009 and said hey I still have that idea, sorry I didn't get round to writing it. He said I had time. Still more months passed and I queried again. I had a small window. So girding the loins, I sat down and wrote and wrote. Before long there was a first draft of the longest short I had ever written (technically the other long short I wrote became a novella but that's another story).*

I Belong to this Red Land

Edwina Harvey

I MAKE WATER for the few remaining plants struggling to survive in our courtyard, and sing the noon-day prayers to the sun perched high over head like a hunting bird.

The boom of another spacecraft launching from the evacuation station is a poor imitation of thunder, yet I watch as its artificial clouds fill the sky and it ascends into the stratosphere, becoming smaller and smaller to my eye until it disappears all together. Day and night, this artificial thunder roars its defiance to the elements, a useless parting gesture for those relinquishing their citizenship of this planet, heading to the planet next closest to the sun.

Those dreamers like my brother, who through their computers have already slipped away to another dimension where the air is still sweet and the plentiful water giggles as it flows through manicured gardens, claim the new world is a paradise. But this planet, our home, was a paradise once too, and look what we've made it. Where will we run to if we destroy that planet too?

I was the heretic who preached we should stay, pay for our sins, heal the hurt we have caused, nurse the planet back to health as we would our sick mothers, or at least ensure it had a dignified death. At first I had followers who believed me, but many have died in the plagues, while some lacked the courage of their convictions. A berth on the thunderships, the chance to start afresh on a new world too tempting for them. I am the only one left, it seems, prepared to see the end through.

"Are you coming or not?" my pale brother all but demands as he passes me in the cool, dim hallways of our house. Of late he's only been communing with the community that ignore our stark reality. He usually passes me wraith-like, neither seeing me or acknowledging my existence, so that I wonder if I am becoming the ghost, not he. We don't even lie with each other any more. Not even on holy days. Two minds that used to be intertwined have become polarised.

"I belong here," I answer him. "I am a High Priestess, consecrated to this red land, as you were. How could you even imagine I could leave?"

He's stopped wearing his robes of office, draped himself in despair and the dream of escape instead while I, clothed in heritage and hope, cling desperately to our old ways.

"Take your religion with you!" he snaps at me. "Isn't it better to be alive to practice it elsewhere than dead and left behind here? Who will bury you?"

The planet itself, I think, but do not speak my words, knowing they will anger him all the more. The winds that ravage the planet will mummify my corpse and cloak me in the red sands, and I will belong to the planet as I have always done.

I feel his eyes burning into me, as hot, as intense as the planet itself, but I cannot meet his eyes, cannot give him an answer he can accept.

He seizes my upper arms, squeezing them tightly, trying to get a response from me. "Don't you know I love you?" he almost pleads.

That makes me look at him. We connect, as we have not done for months, and all the bitterness that has flowed between us disappears for an instant.

"Let me book passage for you on one of the escape ships. Be reasonable. You know you can't stay here."

"I know you've already gone!" I reply defiantly, and the storm rages between us again.

"I cannot renounce my vows to this land! Not as easily as you did! You were consecrated too, my brother, yet you cast off the

mantle of office as if you were shedding dirty clothes for the wash!"
I scream the rage that's been twisting like a tornado inside me.

He turns his head from me and continues down the hallway, as if to say "The dead do not talk to the living." But which is which with us?

At sunset I travel to the Temple to light the massive candles, the little suns that will burn on through the night. The hot wind curls itself around me, pushes me along my way and sucks a little moisture from my body as it sucks a little life from my soul.

The Temple offers quietude, the comfort of repetition, the sanity of normality. While progress is thrust upon us outside these walls, here at least things haven't changed for thousands of years.

Except for the dead. Across the planet our other sacred monuments have been drowned in rising seas or fallen down fissures as the very ground opened up like a gaping wound beneath them. Too few of us are left now to construct monuments to our dead anymore so they flood into our last Temple like grain into a silo after the harvest. Wrapped in shrouds, their organs preserved in jars, their bodies come to us while their souls wander homeless on the other side. Those few of us still living have a surplus of homes in which to live.

I am prepared to wait out my end-days in this sanctuary, keeping the homeless dead company while we wait for this planet to die. Harvest cakes, wine, oil and water, sealed in amphora will sustain me, as I alone pursue our heritage.

The only one left, it seems, who will listen to her heart and also follow it.

As dusk lures the sky into night time the wind is stronger. It scours the tears from my face, pulls at the hem of my dress, drags at the folds of my cloak and tries to lure me back to the safe confines of the Temple as I trudge back to the house.

My brother has lit the oil lamps, and rows of candles dance brightly. How strange, I ponder as I wander from room to room, all joyously lit as if in celebration. He emerges from his room, his eyes heavily kohled, his head encased in the ceremonial headwear, gold on the stiff mantle worn over his robes reflecting colour onto his pale face for once. An imposing figure, as he has been in the past.

I question him with a raised eyebrow.

"I leave on the ship departing at dawn," he tells me, reading my mind from my upswept brow. "One last time I will ask you. *Will you come with me?*"

The hint of a smile at the corner of my lips, as if I don't have the strength to smile any more than that, tells him without words what my answer is: I belong to this red land, and nothing has changed.

He grabs my hand tightly, as if his strength, his will, is not to be questioned. I see the spark of the powerful man he was, before he succumbed to a fate worse than our planet's.

"Then go dress your eyes in kohl, and dress your body in the robes of office. Once more will we perform the ceremony of life overcoming death. My sister..."

And he breathes my name like a caress. I close my eyes and lean into his words, and let myself be carried away by this fantasy that we are still brother and sister sharing the same thoughts and dreams.

Bedecked in our finery we go through the ritual, making our lamentations, casting salt to the four corners, anointing the floor with oil, sweat and semen and drinking wine from our golden chalices.

I am one with this red land from which all life has sprung. I am one with the golden sun which hovers like a bird of prey, waiting to snatch away life. I am one...and when all the others leave, I will be one alone...

Exhaustion and contentment sweep over me in a hot wave. A personal darkness descends, kicking me behind the knees so I crumple to the floor.

When I come to, it is to a drumming in my temples that I know was not caused by the wine. My heavy eyelids open and I focus on my brother's face. Tears, or sweat or both have made the ceremonial kohl run down his cheeks in black stained rivulets. They remind me of those black king tides that used to swell the rivers until they burst their banks spreading their richness over the flood plains every spring, bringing life to our lands once more.

The drumming continues, outside my body but reverberating through it in a steady thrum like a motor...like an engine.

My head moves like lead upon my frozen neck as I look around, realise that I am no longer in my home.

"Steady, my sister. Steady." His hand upon me now is warm and gentle, caring, supportive as I come out of the haze.

I know where I am; in one of the thunderships far above the red land of my birth. How could I be tricked by he who I once knew better than I knew myself? How could I so trustingly drink the holy wine, not for a moment considering he could have tainted it with drugs?

"What have you done?" I accuse him, my head rolling back on the headrest of my seat.

"How could I leave you? You are my sister. You are our High Priestess, and you belong with your people."

"I belong to the red land of my birth," I tell him, though my words are still slurred.

He holds up a vial on a chain for me to see. Grains of red soil, malachite and copper sparkle enticingly within. "You take the old land with you as we head towards the new," he whispers in my ear as he fastens the chain's clasp around my neck.

"Help me stand," I ask him, my fingers gripping him like the claws of a bird grasping a perch. "Help me to a viewing port. I must look upon our planet one more time."

Consolatory in his actions, he does as I ask, and I stand leaning against him for support. Looking down on the red land where I belonged, I can see our last pyramid and the holy face of our Temple as our gods were meant to see them from high in the heavens. Life and Death stare back at me as I'm spirited away.

"She smiles at you," my brother assures me, knowing what has held my gaze. "She is happy that you are with your people."

But I see a sandstorm blow across her face in a scowl.

Who will sit with her now? Who will light the midnight candles for our homeless dead, and sing the noon-day lamentations to the sun?

"The same sun you sing lamentations to will still shine on us. We are only moving closer to its strength."

I belong to this red land! my mind cries silently, futilely, yet I know there's no turning back.

"We'll go back one day," my brother assures me quietly. "Many generations from now, our descendants will walk that red land again."

afterword

The Belong *anthology gave me the perfect opportunity to finally write a story about the pyramids and the face of Mars, two subjects I've been wanting to explore through my fiction for ages now.*
If you can't belong to a planet, where can you belong?

All Tales Must End

Michelle Muenzler

THE CITY IS dying. Children gather around my stall, half a plaza away from the cool shadows of the great cistern, and wait for tales. Their eyes are still bright despite the crust that grits their lids and the red dusty smears that stain where they last wiped the hollows of their cheeks. The line at the cistern snakes through the plaza, but its winding is more like a husk of skin than the snake itself. The people are deflated and drawn into themselves. But not the children. Not yet.

You would think life had always been like this, dust begetting more dust. Wind. Blue sky stretching into a purpled bruise horizon. The brittle salt-crust of the waste crackling beneath the city's sleep-curled claws. But every story has a beginning. And a middle. And yes, even an end.

I tell the children of when the city swam across the Great Waters and how the people wove nets of kelp and speared sharks with bone harpoons. I tell them of Kalessa who staked the first home atop the city's lacquered shell as it slumbered, her people's village crushed beneath its bulk.

I tell stories until dusk cools the air and the city lurches unsteadily to its feet and toward the first red glint of the Wayfarer's Star. By then, all the children are gone, gathered by parents done with bargaining for every drop of water, or simply wandering off on their own in search of lizards and hidden treasure.

I dismantle the small cloth frame that names me storyteller and shields me during the worst heat of the day. My cup is empty of coins, but money means little to me now.

The city is dying.

There's a tremble to its step, an uncertain tremor. Death shudders beneath its gargantuan feet and shivers in its bones. Everyone knows it. I can see it in their clouded marble eyes as they skirt each other warily in the market. Yes, the city is dying, and with it, us. Who can value a copper against that?

A coin falls into my cup.

"Tell me," says a young man. "Of Kalessa's first year atop the city." His lips are generous, though chapped and broken; his eyes are spare and gray. "Tell me of how she prostituted herself to the Wayfarer so he'd set a star for the city to follow and never crush another village beneath its feet. Tell me of the first family she tricked into the city by inviting them to stay the day and poisoning them with a month of sleep."

I shake the cup, let the coin scrape against the clay and break the sonorous rhythm of his voice. "It sounds as though you already know those stories well enough."

"Then tell me of the week it rained fire and ash. Tell me who lived and who died and who slipped away in the night never to be seen again."

The three children seated before me gaze in rapt attention at the young man.

I flip the coin to his feet. "Those are not the stories I tell."

"No," he says. "But they should be."

He turns and walks a dozen steps away, then pulls a cloth frame from his back and sets up his own storyteller's booth. One of my girls wavers, her eyes darting between the two of us. Then she snatches the fallen coin and scurries to the young man's booth where she settles in and drops the coin into his cup. He begins his story, but I shut out the words and focus on my remaining listeners.

There have been rivals before, but in the end, the children always return to me.

I am breaking my fast with a bit of stale bread along the low wall of the tail rim when the young man finds me again. The broken salt-crust of the waste flashes beneath the rising sun.

"The Watchers have spotted a city," he says, shielding his eyes.

"I know."

"Then shouldn't you be at the head with the others looking for its shadow on the horizon?"

I finish my bread and wipe the crumbs from my lips. "It will come whether I see it or not."

He nods as though I have said some great sage thing. A flush sparks unwilling in my cheeks; I do not want to please him.

"Besides, it is too crowded to see anything right now. I'll go later."

He laughs, a low rumble that chills the warmth from my bones. "Your stories will do well today, I think. But tomorrow will be mine."

"Tomorrow belongs to the Wayfarer alone."

I can feel his gaze on me, but I keep my eyes upon the rising sun and the glittering path leading from it to the tail of our city. He pulls away from the wall and the edge of my vision.

"Tomorrow," he says, the laughter gone from his voice.

By the lack of alternating chill and heat, I know then he is gone, but an uneasy splinter has lodged itself in my breast. He knows something I do not.

Perhaps the Wayfarer has spoken in his dreams.

The young man is right. Several coins find their way into my cup that day, and my booth is crowded with children begging for my tales. Even a few adults stop by and listen, swaying slightly beneath the sun with a faint smile on their lips. Some share their water with me when my voice turns dry.

I speak today of ancient encounters with foreign cities, of Jorubar and the Snakes of Imm, of Danyel who fought off a thousand soldiers of the Three-Fold Emperor in the hour before sunset. In the end of all the stories, our city rises to the Wayfarer's Star and moves on.

Twice, I break down my booth and visit the head wall, but I cannot push my way through the crowds, and they do not part for me. I hear broken words humming from their lips, though: The city will be great. The city will be poor. They will have water. They will take what water we have left. We are staying. We are going.

At dusk, I slide instead through the lesser crowds of the right rim and strain to see the new city. It is far. Too far to know anything until tomorrow. It stands as a dark shadow swallowed by the red of the setting sun. Several families have already gathered at the lifts, shuffling for the best spot in the morning and holding their children close against the night. Their lives are compressed in tight packets upon their backs.

I cannot sleep. Half the night, I watch the Wayfarer's Star and pray for our city to be saved. The other half, I wonder if perhaps it is time for even me to leave. I can count the years in the stories and know how long our city has lived, but nothing tells me how long it takes for a city to die.

I suppose the true answer is they are the same.

When sleep catches me at last, it drowns me. Voices clamber atop one another in my dreams, struggling to be heard, and above us all, the Wayfarer's Star watches. When I wake, dawn is well past and the Wayfarer's Star is gone. The cistern line shuffles like the dead, and whispers crawl through the dust.

Only one voice is bright and clear—the young man's. His booth is open and filled with shadow-eyed adults. The children are held tight against their parents' breasts, or strangers' where no parents are to be found. Their eyes are dull as stones.

The young man is telling of Izura who built a boat to take the people from the city when it seemed the Great Waters would never end. In my stories, he is Izura the Traitor for the children he lured onboard and stole away. The young man calls him Izura the Brave.

There is something wrong with the city we have found. I do not have to see it to know this. But my curiosity must wait. I pull out my cloth frame and raise it beneath the sun.

The young man has started a war, and I will not lose.

When the day is finished, I can count on both hands the number of people who stopped at my booth, and most simply shook their heads and slid into the young man's crowd. There were no children at all. I slip away from the market as the setting sun paints everything a violent shade of red. The right rim is abandoned. Even the houses bolted on the shell's slant have their shutters closed tight.

And now I see why.

The city we have found is dead. We will leave it behind us tonight, but I can see it clearly now, several shell-lengths away. Crumbling spires reach for the sky, their faded tops winking with the promised glint of gold. The walls are red, like the waste, and gleam from the salt-dust encrusted on their remains.

Yet all of this would not be enough to justify the emptiness snaking through my chest. I have seen dead cities before.

But the city also lies atop the half-buried wind-scoured remains of a great beast like our own. A bleached green, far quieter than the one beneath my feet, peeks between the buildings and bones. The remnants of a shell.

I cannot stop the tears that wash down my cheeks. A waste of water in these dry times. If I could gather my tears, I would have drink enough for a lifetime. When the sun falls beneath the horizon and our city rises, I turn away from the carcass of the other and dry my eyes.

How many cities like our own have died in this waste? And how many more are buried in our path?

The next morning, the young man's lips smile as he raises up his stall, but his eyes are hollow. A crowd gathers early for his tales, their backs turned to me. They belong to him now. I can picture collars buckled around their throats with leashes leading to the young man's swaying hands. He begins the story of Haiden the Mad who tossed those he deemed unworthy from the head of the shell so they might be trampled beneath the city's feet. He calls him Haiden the Just.

I can listen no more. This plaza no longer feels like home. There are no children to be seen. I wander to the tail of the sleeping city and watch the sun pass over our wake.

"You can still change your stories," the young man says three days later. "It is not too late."

We are like the moon and tide, he and I. Wherever I go for peace, he finds me, yet something unwilling colours his eyes when we meet. And how could I have thought them to be just gray? They are every colour of the rainbow in the dawn light. I could watch them forever, but close my own instead. Fine grains of dust blow across my closed lids and cling to my lips.

"You twist your stories," I say.

"And you do not?"

He is so close, I can hear him breathing. He sounds like the wind.

"There is no truth in stories," he says. "You know that. Just the lies handed from one generation to the next."

"If you don't believe, then why tell them at all?"

His silence lingers over the both of us, but I know he is not gone. Not yet. The tide knows when the moon is near. If he will not answer one question, though, then I will ask another.

"What is your name?" I should have asked a week ago. There is too much power in the unnamed.

I feel him pulling away from me, and I blindly reach out and grasp his arm.

"You should tell my stories," he says, his voice behind me now. He gently pulls his arm free, and when next I open my eyes, he is gone.

Three more days, and three more corpses of great cities, all buried beneath the weight of tumbling buildings on their backs. The third night, our city stumbles and falls to its knees. One home breaks loose and plummets to the waste below, taking a family of eight with it. I did not see it happen, but I heard the crack of its foundation in my dreams. I felt the children screaming.

In the morning, I do not set up my storyteller's booth, but watch the young man instead. The crowd around him today is all men. Who else could listen to his stories after such tragedy? Sometimes I find his gaze skirting across my own. His words are aimed at me, but I no longer hear them. As dusk gathers, he leaves his crowd. The men nod their heads to him and to each other as he passes, then leave in small groups. I try to sleep, but the city's steps, once comforting, now fill me with dread. Eventually, I rise and walk the streets, looking to the night sky for relief. As I near the tail wall, the city takes another step, and the sound of crunching stone joins the usual shudder. My heart stops, and I wait for the screams. Something crashes far below the city. It is quiet then except for a low scraping, the sound of stone grating against shell...and the voices of men.

I pad down the street, down the shell, down to where the voices are stronger. Down to the tail wall where everything is wrong. Where the wall once stood is now a gaping hole. Rubble is gathered along its edges. There are men at the wall and elsewhere, men whose faces I know from the market today. But I do not want to recognise their faces now. They are covered in dust, the pale gray dust of our homes, not the red of the waste. Several of them are pulling at the bolts holding down one of the tail rim homes. The bolts clatter and roll one by one through the wall breach. Other men are pushing an already freed home down the shell. Before long, the shell's slant takes over and the home screeches through the wall breach, leaving deep scores through the shell where it passed. I hear a shattering below. But no screams. Nothing but the murmurs of men and popping of bolts and low thud of the city's feet.

I cannot understand why nobody has come out, why I am alone. Somebody must stop this madness. I cling to the nearest house, slide around to the front door, and start to bang. The door falls open. It wasn't even fully closed. On the floor, bodies are piled atop one another, blood leaking from split skulls.

There is screaming now. It is my own, but I cannot stop it. I fall to my knees and take a child's still-warm hand in my own. A shadow falls over me from behind. The moonlight is gone.

"You shouldn't have done that," says a man's voice, coarse from too much dust.

There is a whistle, and a wet thud reverberates through my skull. The child slips away, the floor slips away. Darkness slides into their place. And all I can wonder is if this is how my story ends. I had hoped for a better tale.

I am dead. I expected silence or the soft voice of the Wayfarer, but the darkness is filled with screams and the thud of flesh. My skull throbs.

I should be dead, but I am not.

A crust has sealed my eyes. I scrape it free, and then open my eyes to more darkness. Only this darkness is pricked by starlight. And the stars are sliding, slowly sliding. And there is scraping. And the door hangs open, and through it are great gouges in the city's shell.

It is not the stars that are sliding. It is the house.

I drag myself frantically through the door as the house grates another foot downward. Outside, men struggle against other men. Several are sprawled near me, their eyes open but blank. There will be no more stars for them.

It is when the house begins to slide unstopping that I remember the hand I clasped before the darkness took me. The hand of a child. I spin back toward the house, but the world spins with me, and I fall to my knees. The house slips downward, then over the edge and shatters far below. The child is gone. They are all gone.

Only madness remains.

I do not know who will win the battle around me. Nor do I care. I drag myself foot by foot up the shell and away from the melee. If I watch it, I will be forced to remember each blow. I will be asked what I saw and what I heard and what it all means. But I do not think there are any answers. If there are, I do not want to find them. And watching will change nothing.

All stories have a beginning. A middle. And an end. Always an end. I was taught this by my mother when she passed on her art to me.

The young man is the end of this story. This truth aches in my bones with every inch I gain toward safety. The screams die behind me. Everything dies behind me. Ahead, the Wayfarer's Star watches and leads us onward.

The young man's stories must be stopped.

The knife is easy to find. Every street corner vendor sells them this morning. Nobody wants to die undefended. Nobody wants to be left bleeding in the waste. I have no coppers, but I weave a tale of helplessness until a passerby takes pity and purchases a knife for me.

The young man said there is no truth in stories, but that is a lie. The truth is in the ending. Always in the ending.

Dusk scrapes its early fingers across the horizon. The young man finishes his last story and packs away his cloth frame. The crowd parts, each nodding their heads when he passes.

I follow him from the market. My knife is not well-made—the tang too shallow, the blade too thin—but it should do. I hope it will snap in his heart so that he cannot pull it free. I want to hear him scream. For the child last night who could not.

He slips quietly through the streets, nodding at strangers and making his way closer to the head of the city. Soon it is just him and I. All others are barring their doors and tightening their shutters.

At the head, he steps to the wall and spreads his fingers across the stones. I creep up, the setting sun watching over us both. Behind him, I raise my knife and draw a deep breath. His stories leave me no choice.

With a jerk, I plunge the blade into his back. It snaps, and I drop the handle to the ground and wait for him to fall.

But he does not.

"The end is not that easy," he says, turning to face me.

I was wrong about his eyes. They are neither gray nor rainbowed, but red. Like the wasteland sand. Like blood.

I cannot speak. My tongue is lost.

"This is not one of your market tales to be spun in endless circles. You think you own this story, but it does not belong to you. It belongs to those who gave it birth."

I shield my eyes against the setting sun, against him.

"It will all be over soon. Tomorrow. Enough has been done. This daughter will make it home." He turns back to the sun. "When the time comes, you will tell your people to go north. The waste ends. Eventually. Some might survive to see it."

"I don't—" My throat catches. "I don't understand."

The sun's last edges dip against the horizon.

"Tomorrow," he says.

The sun slips away, and the young man flashes into a cloud of dust. Wind scatters him down the street. I reach out and touch the wall where his hands were a moment ago. Nothing. Nothing but a lie of flesh.

In the purpled sky above, the Wayfarer's Star flares, and the city rises.

At dawn, the city does not stop. Nor does the Wayfarer's Star fade. People mill restlessly in the market. They ask strangers for answers and give their own when asked. But all of them are wrong.

My booth is open, but nobody stops.

"Go north," I say. "The end is near."

They shy away and seek their answers elsewhere. The young man was right, so many days ago. I have been telling the wrong stories, and now the people will not listen to me. A heaviness settles on my shoulders. I bow my head and stare at the heaving shell beneath me. My words are nothing now.

The thin voice of a child interrupts my despair.

"What's north?" she asks.

I look up. It is the girl who first went to the young man's booth. She has aged much in such a short time, but something strong still glints in the stones of her eyes.

She is silent, and I realise she is waiting for me to speak.

"North," I say. I had not thought beyond the warning. I have no stories of north to tell.

She stares, and the weight of her patience draws her shoulders downward until they can give no more. And still I cannot find a story. She turns to leave.

"Wait," I say, and dig deep into my bones. "North. North is the land of the chosen. It is the hidden valley the Wayfarer has dug into the earth for those who have guarded his children on their long journey. North is—"

She sits at my feet and smiles, and I continue my lies of sweet-water streams and hillsides clustered with grapes. More children gather as the day lengthens. Some of them leave eventually, and I tell them to spread the tale, to make it their own. We all must be storytellers today. They smile and nod and rejoin their restless families. And on all their lips is a single word: North.

At noon, we see the coming of the end.

The Watchers cry out first. "The end of the world! The end of the world!"

People's screams are swallowed by the city's relentless footsteps.

"North," I say, one last time, and the children nod even as they scramble to their feet.

When the last one is gone, I take down my cloth frame and make my way to the right rim wall. Far ahead of the city is the end. It is not what I expected at all. A jagged edge of red rock glitters beneath the noon light, marking the world's edge, and then there is nothing but a star-filled void untouched by the sun. The Wayfarer's Star shines brighter than I have ever seen it. The city's step increases, and the buildings shudder at the pace.

The wall becomes crowded with families struggling to gain access to the lift. Some throw ropes over the side and clamber to the waste below. As the crowd at the wall grows, I force my way against them and go toward the head of the city, to the spot where I last saw the young man.

Across the waste, people scatter in the city's wake. Some north, some south, and some back to the endless east. I think more north than not, but I cannot be sure. There is nothing more for me to do, regardless.

The city is deserted by the end. I wait and watch as the last people turn to ants behind me, and then I turn my head back to the Wayfarer's Star. The moon and tide, I think. The young man is wrong. This is my story as much as anyone's. My beginning is here, and so shall be my end.

The edge of the world is three steps away. Now two. Now one. I pull in one last breath, heavy with dust.

And the city steps into the stars.

afterword

It is strange to watch a story evolve. The original tale was a simple one, a family struggling against those in power atop a great moving city. Yet somewhere during the third draft, a new voice interrupted.

The storyteller was born of a single line: "The city is dying." From that line, the Wayfarer became wrapped in flesh, and the great turtles found their purpose as his children, crawling persistently from the shores of their birth to the stars where he awaited them. In the midst of this broadening tale, the original family still struggled. Their house was one of many toppled from the shell in the night, and the patriarch's aging father still died, staring blankly at the stars, in the riots following the discovery of the atrocities along the rim.

But the story had become greater than one family. It became the story of an entire people, generations of immigrants bound together by one city's impending fate. And of course it was a story of the city as well, and of all the cities that never reached the stars, and of all the people they carried and lost to the red waste.

More than that, it became a story of stories, of the lies, the half-truths, and the myriad viewpoints which define us.

Yes, it is strange to watch a story evolve. But more than that, it is exhilarating.

Namug

Gustavo Bondoni

THE EVER-PRESENT weight dragged on her arms. Every movement, every keystroke seemed to require ten times the effort that Ruth was willing to supply. Epsilon Eridani II simply wasn't meant for human habitation; even those humans genetically modified for high-gravity environments found three times Earth-mass a bit of a stretch.

Living on this planet was torture—not the torture of agonizing pain, but the torture of continuous slight discomfort during every moment, waking or sleeping.

Colonel Ruth Khazak knew that the gravity wouldn't hurt her, and that it wouldn't hurt any of the other genetically modified colonists, but the pressure to find a solution was mounting: even people who volunteered to move to the most inhospitable regions in the galaxy needed some comfort. And it was her job to find a way, which wasn't helping her sleep any easier at night.

"Damn," she said, and turned to her lab assistant, whose flat, broad features and squat high-gee build had grown on her to the point in which their relationship had gone well past what was proper. She couldn't care less—no one among the colonists would complain, and none of those fragile one-gravity idiots from Earth could stand on the surface of the planet without more discomfort than they'd care to endure. "Any luck?"

It was a rhetorical question. She knew what he was working on and, though it might be a promising avenue, they wouldn't know whether it was actually viable for a few days at least. Kinney still thought about it before answering. "About the same as yesterday. We can graft heek legs to human nervous systems with no problems, but the arms are useless unless I can get human hands to work at the end of them—and the muscles just aren't there." The heeks were large, feathered primates, slow moving and strong, perfectly adapted to life on the surface—but had never developed opposable thumbs.

Ruth was working on trying to make the second colony on the planet a viable one. Her assignment was to find a way to adapt the human body to the environment without having to use prohibitively expensive imported bionics.

The first set of colonists had, logically enough, been aquatic. It was much easier to modify a human to breathe through gills than it was to make them comfortable in high gravity, and life in the sea was an immediate solution to gravity—natural buoyancy helped offset part of the extra weight from Newton's law.

The first colonists had ignored any kind of carbon-based unintelligent life, and overlooked the enormous squid-like creatures which prowled the depths of the oceans that covered ninety percent of the surface. They'd paid for this oversight with their lives when a huge phalanx of the creatures had come out of the depths and, despite high-tech resistance from the colonists, destroyed every structure in the colony. The colonists themselves, deprived of their metal walls, had quickly been picked off and, as far as anyone could tell, eaten.

The first thing Ruth's wave of colonists had done was capture one of the creatures and test it for intelligence. The only thing that even remotely resembled a brain, a structure in the central trunk of the squid-like being, was the size of an apple. No intelligence there. The attack had been written off as an instinctive reaction to the intrusion, not a coordinated action at all.

Namug felt the cool, caressing flow of the water on his surface. He could dimly sense the ripples that his neighbour was making nearby. Dwuugag could probably feel Namug's own happiness in the secretions he'd been leaving all this way. It was a good thing that his neighbour was a nice sort, or this open display of emotion would have been a cause for strife.

Even so, it would have been pointless for Namug to try to hide his emotion. He recognised this part of the sea by the temperature, the taste of the water. The colony was nearing the migration point where they always met Yunnin's colony. Sweet-scented Yunnin of the strong embrace. It would not be long until they were together again.

Namug was content.

Ruth's eyes opened suddenly. That's it, she thought. And then she agonised a little. She'd promised Kinney that, whenever a sudden inspiration struck at—she checked the glowing face of the status display—four fifteen in the morning, she would jot it down on a pad that he'd given her for precisely that purpose and go back to sleep. He argued that she was having these midnight flashes of brilliance often enough that her sleep cycles were shot to hell.

She smiled, glanced at the unused pad beside the display and got up carefully. It wasn't actually necessary to be silent, since Kinney could sleep through a meteor strike, but old habits died hard.

Five minutes later, she was in the lab, seated at one of the mainframe workstations. This wasn't the place where she preferred to work—the stylus tablets were much more comfortable for lab work—but she wanted to use the forty-inch screen on the workstation.

It took her less than a minute to find the recordings she needed, and she was soon watching the feed from one of the recorders salvaged from the wreckage of the original Epsilon Eridani settlement. The feed was 2D and a bit cloudy, but that couldn't be helped: all they'd been able to recover were a pair of recordings from security cameras that had been hastily converted to underwater use.

The resolution, such as it was, should be more than enough to show her what she wanted to see. The creatures, after all, were huge.

She sat back, coffee mug in hand, and studied the attack on the old colony. Despite what she herself had concluded after dissecting a number of the things, the attack definitely did look coordinated by some kind of intelligent agency. She watched as they first demolished the power cables and then systematically went about removing all the remaining heavy weaponry. The people, dressed in body armour and armed with various harpoon and projectile weapons, they left for last. They represented the smallest threat. Long before she could see what had happened to them, the camera was pushed away, facing into the depths of the ocean.

The second recording showed the flooded interior of one of the habitation spheres. A single tentacle entered the camera's sight through an aperture in the wall, attempting to capture one of the colonists, armed with a harpoon gun, who was huddled next to a wall. The amazing thing was that the tentacle wrapped itself around the gun, tore it out of the helpless colonist's grasp and, with a mighty wrench, tore it in two. Then, it withdrew, leaving her alive.

After forcing herself to watch the destruction of the underwater habitat a few times, she watched more footage of the monsters, taken with better quality equipment, filmed after the arrival of the land colonists. For some reason, the creatures didn't see the submersible film cameras as a threat—probably too small—and never attacked one.

Although they referred to the animals as squids, there were some significant differences with their earthly analogues. First, these creatures were organised radially, like giant starfish, and the central hub was just a small, flattish dome in the centre, as opposed to an elongated cone. This layout precluded quick movement, but, when not attacking large stationary targets, these starfish seemed to enjoy lolling horizontally about on the currents, submerged at immense depths like gigantic floating plates. There were air bladders on the tentacles so that they could be maintained at the same altitude as the rest of the body.

The tentacles themselves were the second major difference. Long and slim, they held no suction cups, being instead covered in long, strong cilia. They seemed much too thin to have caused the damage she'd seen on the tapes, but one had to remember that on this high-gravity world, the pressure in the ocean depths was incredible. The tentacles had to be extremely strong, just to be able to move effectively.

Once she'd re-familiarised herself in how the starfish looked, she activated the final set of recordings. These were the ones she was most interested in.

Namug had changed states. Before, he'd been content, now he was ecstatic. Yunnin had agreed to disengage, to join his colony. That she'd agreed to undergo such pain to be with him was a dream come true. That he'd have to wait until the next migratory round for her excision to be complete was torture. But the torture went well with the ecstasy—he'd have something to dream about as the colony drifted along the great circle it had established since times immemorial.

He could await the currents, could await the time. Fulfilment would be his, very, very soon.

Kinney entered the lab to find Ruth's head resting on one of the consoles. She was sound asleep, and, rolling his eyes, he almost left the lab in order to avoid disturbing her. Heaven knew she needed to rest.

But he'd left a correlation program running last night, and was anxious to see what results, if any, it had delivered. He was a scientist, too, after all. Maybe not as mad Ruth was, but mad enough to volunteer for the terraforming of an extremely uncomfortable place in the galaxy, a place which had killed off the first group of people to try it. He might be able to resist his nature better than she could, but ignoring it altogether was out of the question.

He initiated the active mode on his Stylus tablet, and heard the soft humming of the memory core as everything came back on line.

Ruth stirred, moved slightly, and finally displaced a light pen which rolled off the table and clacked onto the floor. She woke immediately and sat up with a start, looking around as if surprised to find herself in the lab. When her gaze settled on Kinney, she shrugged and gave him a sheepish smile. "I know, I know," she said. "I should get my sleep. But I think I've found a way to solve our little gravity problem."

Kinney tried to glare at her, but his heart just wasn't in it. Why bother? He knew that she'd never change, especially when dealing with a challenge. Anyhow, her hangdog expression was so completely inappropriate to such a forceful woman that it would have been impossible to stay mad at her. "Tell me," he said with a slight smile.

"We need to go aquatic again," she said, all business once more.

"What? That certainly wasn't what I expected. I assume you have a plan for dealing with the squid-things."

"I shouldn't even dignify that with an answer. Of course I have a plan. You should know me well enough by now not to ask such silly questions."

That was more like the Ruth he knew. He grinned. "Well, are you going to enlighten me or do I have to figure it out for myself?"

"No, I'll tell you. If we wait for you to figure it out by yourself, we'll be here until the end of time." Her smile belied the words. "Look here."

Ruth punched the replay command and the mainframe's screen lit up. It showed an underwater scene, which, though slightly murky, had to have been computer-enhanced; the light under the ocean was too slight to get the contrasts that they were seeing. And the scene must have been filmed at a considerable depth, since it showed not one, but two of the giant tentacled monsters. Kinney knew they never came together near the surface.

"The mating tape," he said. "I've seen it."

"Yes, you've seen it. But did you notice that the central section of the bodies never come together?" She pointed at the screen, in which the two creatures had fused into what looked like a bowl of spaghetti. How they managed to interact without becoming hopelessly tangled was a mystery.

Kinney immediately realised that she was right. Some of the tentacles wrapped around a tentacle from the other creature. They were perfectly paired up, always one from each creature in a group, and the distribution seemed to be random, as opposed to having adjacent tentacles pair off. Still other tentacles floated free, seemingly uninterested in the proceedings. But the central sections, where both the nervous system and the reproductive organs were presumed to be located, never came into contact with one another.

"I see it," he said. "But I still don't understand how it's going to solve our problems."

"Even with clues..." Ruth said in mock exasperation. She was in a great mood, which boded well for the success of the Colony. Colonel Ruth Khazak was very seldom wrong—if her gut told her she had the solution, Kinney would be willing to wager that she did.

"Look at the evidence. We know the squids will attack anything large that invades their territory, but don't attack each other. The only contact between them is tentacle to tentacle, right?"

"Yes."

"And we haven't seen eyes, right?"

"Nothing we can identify, anyway."

"Oh come on!" she exclaimed, as if lecturing a particularly slow student. "You know as well as I do that there's absolutely no reason for a species living in that lightless water to have developed eyes."

He held up his hands, palms out. "All right, all right! No eyes."

"So if they can't see each other, they must identify each other either through sound—and we haven't found much on them that would indicate a vibratory membrane of the type you'd use to project sound underwater—or through some kind of chemical fingerprinting."

"They taste each other?"

"The tentacles taste each other. The hairs—cilia—must have specialised taste organs. They must be able to sense the presence of one of their kind in the water around them. And I'm also willing to bet that the tentacles themselves secrete the telltales."

"So how does this help us?"

She rolled her eyes. "If we graft one of the tentacles onto a gilled human, we should be able to fool the squids into thinking that one of us is one of them."

"That's ridiculous! Those tentacles must be fifty feet long. They weigh two tons each!"

"So? They'll be in the water, remember? Buoyancy will help, and they've got their bladders for flotation—all we really have to work out is how to graft them to a human nervous system, and how to keep them secreting the right kind of chemicals."

Kinney had his reservations, but held his peace. Ruth had done this kind of thing often enough that he preferred to keep his mouth shut. It wasn't fun to be proven wrong.

Namug writhed in agony in the lukewarm water—impure, bathed in chemicals he couldn't identify. He tried to break free of the pain. But to no avail—he was being held immobile by giant metallic structures clamped painfully to his body.

The nightmare had started on the day the colony had first been taken. A huge artificial structure had enclosed them, so strong that the combined efforts of the entire colony had been unable to make even the smallest of dents in flat, dull surface.

And the pain. It was unbearable, as if some unknown agency was attempting an excision. But didn't they know that separation was the work of many days, that it should be an act of love, never an act of violence? He felt another wave of agony as his body shredded before the onslaught of something sharp. And then he felt a severance, a loss.

As he drifted into unconsciousness, he wondered if sweet Yunin would ever learn what had become of him.

The water in the tank had just subsided following her victory lap when Kinney walked up the steps to the causeway that circled the enclosure.

Ruth looked up at him, nearly exhausted, but not unhappy. She could see all the lab equipment arrayed around her: scanners, readouts, and even film equipment. Everything seemed to agree that things were getting better and better, that the discomfort of the operations and the hard work of the bio-integration had been worth it after all. "Watch this," she said.

She dived under the surface and pushed herself along with the tentacle. It was the latest in a series of movements she'd mastered and it wasn't yet second nature. She could still feel the skin of her back, just above her buttocks—where the tentacle had been attached, grafted onto her spinal chord—stretch with the movement. She also noted that breathing no longer presented any problems—her body had finally accepted the gills.

On resurfacing, Ruth found Kinney watching her with a slightly amused expression.

"What?" she demanded.

"You look like a giant tadpole," he said, chuckling.

She swung the tentacle—it was so tempting to call it a tail—around and showered him with water. "I've just managed the first successful melding of alien and human bodies in which the extraterrestrial component outweighs the terrestrial by such a large factor and all you can say is that I look like a tadpole? I ought to have you expelled from the colony for contempt of science."

"At least I wasn't the one who decided that all this equipment would work better wet than dry," he replied, shaking the water out of his hair. "Anyhow, how's it coming?"

How could she possibly describe the feeling of relief that came with no longer being subjected to the eternal crushing of the planet's gravity? But he knew how it felt. He'd spent a few nights in the tank with her. But the tentacle, now that she was finally mastering it, gave her a speed of movement she hadn't known since coming to Epsilon Eridani. "Better now," she said. "At least I don't feel like the damned thing is fighting me anymore. I'm the one controlling the motion."

"Well, I suppose you weren't expecting it to be easy."

"No, but I wasn't expecting it to be this tiring. It isn't fun trying to get two tons of alien muscle to bow to your will, let me tell you."

"I still can't believe it worked."

"You realise that this might be useful on other worlds as well—a great bit of defensive biology for aquatic colonists on high gee planets?"

"And another promotion for the great Ruth Khazak?"

She swished her tail—tentacle—contemplatively, coquettishly, she thought. "Probably not. You need to have commanded combat troops for them to make you a general."

"Pity. I can just imagine the name of the army: "Khazak's Tadpoles."" This earned him another sluice of water from the tank.

"Stop clowning and listen. I think I've got enough control over this thing so that I won't get pulled to the bottom of the ocean. Now we've got to get out there and test it, to make sure that it works as a way of communicating with the squids."

"I've been thinking about that. You've shown that it can be done. Why don't you let someone else do the testing. We've got a full complement of colony marines that were specifically assigned to us to take the risky jobs. Why can't you graft a tentacle on to one of them and let them test it?"

She shuddered inwardly. There was no way she was going to return to the hellish gravity of the surface, and if someone else was testing the squid's reaction, she'd have no excuse to keep the tentacle. "It would take too long. Think about it, a marine would take the same amount of time to get used to it as I have—those are weeks we simple don't have to spare. And I just need a few more day's practice.

No. I have to be the one to do it." She paused, making certain that he wouldn't voice any further protests. "Now get in this tank before I use this tentacle to pull you in. I feel like celebrating."

The next two weeks were a blur. Everything had to be coordinated. Her tank had to be transported to the ocean's edge, she had to undergo a period of acclimatization to the ocean's temperature and salinity. And there was another unexpected snag: as soon as the tentacle hit the ocean, it seemed to regain part of the independence that had characterised it in the days immediately following the graft. A frustrating few days were spent in the shallows getting her full command back.

But, soon enough, she was ready for the final test. Ready to go out into the open ocean to find one of these behemoths, to confront it and see whether her experiment would insure the continued survival of the colony.

Kinney made some noises about accompanying her with a squadron of helicopters—massive things that flew with difficulty in the high gravity. Knowing they would certainly frighten the squids into acting violently, she just smiled. Right after sunrise the following morning, set out without telling him. She'd make it up to him later.

She swam straight to the point where the continental shelf suddenly ended, and dived. She wanted to find one of the squids right now. And, somehow, she felt that her own eagerness was complemented by a sense of elation was actually coming from the tentacle itself.

This stopped her cold. If her tail acted up now, the weight would drag her to the bottom of the ocean. And she'd be crushed long before getting there.

But there didn't seem to be any problem, other than the feeling of well-being coming from the tail. She briefly wondered what it was: feedback from some instinctive reaction to temperature and salinity parameters? Something else? She quickly dismissed it and got back to the matter at hand, namely finding and... befriending?.. one of the giant aquatic monsters. Her tail pushed her on, further and further from the shore, deeper and deeper into the dark water until a shadow, large and tentacular, appeared in the distance.

She was nearly there.

Namug felt the cool water caressing his surface, something he thought was lost to him forever. He was back where he belonged, in the timeless expanse of the deep ocean. But this, he knew, was merely the illusion of freedom. He had no control over his own movements: no matter how hard he struggled against it, his body would not react to his commands. He was anchored to something unspeakably alien, sundered forever from the joyous interaction with his colony—were they even still alive?—and unable, even in the glorious deep water, to move freely.

He remembered the happiness that accompanied the endless wandering of the colony. He longed for just one more chance to meet one of his people, to feel once more the caress of another surface on his. He didn't even ask for Yunin; that would be too much. But he would give what remained of his life to be in the presence of any of his people once more.

And his wish, suddenly, unexpectedly, was granted. He sensed a that there was a colony in the water with them—he could taste it on the current. And the monstrosity he was attached to, instead of denying him this one last wish, swam straight towards the thickest concentration of colony-taste.

Soon, incredibly soon, his body was being ordered to extend towards the outstretched body of one of the colony's members. The approach, under alien control, was a clumsy thing, and it was a familiar approach inappropriate for greeting a stranger. But in the end, the stranger accepted it, and they intertwined in the accepted fashion.

"Greetings," the other said, by moving the hairs on her surface. "I am Guniod of the Carinaa colony."

"Greetings. I am Namug of the Woogen."

"You are alone. Are you the only member of the Woogen?"

"No. The Woogen are many."

"They are not here. Your hub has only one individual. How can this be?"

"My root is not a hub. It is a sentient creature, like one of us. But it is evil. It has taken my colony and excised me forcefully. It has damaged me beyond repair, and it controls my movements."

"But not your words."

"Not my words."

Guniod was still for a few moments. "Can you be transplanted to another colony?"

"No. I have been maimed."

"Do you wish to continue with your new hub?"

"No."

"What do you wish?"

"You are a strong colony. Destroy this atrocity."

"You will die."

"I am already gone. Do it quickly."

She signalled assent. "We will do it. Your name will echo in the ocean, Namug."

"May knowledge of this come to Yunin of the Raugee."

"It shall. Goodbye."

"Thank you. Please do it quickly."

The entire colony wrapped around the monstrous creature that had planted his base on its skin. Each individual applying his or her strength to the alien, crushing it and tearing it into tiny globules of flesh and droplets of blood.

And, as he sank to the bottom of the dark, murky ocean, Namug was at peace.

afterword

Namug is one of those typical SF tales that started with the question "What if?" This one actually started with two what ifs: What if human colonists arrived at a planet which already had an intelligent life form present? And what if neither side understood what was going on because they just had no common ground for communication?

It always seemed to me that any planet suitable for human consumption would not be empty, and terraforming would be unpleasant for anyone who already happened to be there, and this story takes the concept to the extreme.

Song of the Blackbird

Sarah Totton

"HOW ABOUT HER?" said confidence woman's apprentice.

"No," said the confidence woman.

They were sharing a bench in the concourse of Union Station, speaking without looking at each other, practicing the art of being inconspicuous. They made an odd pair. The confidence woman feigned absorption in a novel; her apprentice, somewhere in his twenties, but looking younger sat with his arm draped over a knapsack. The pack was a prop; there was nothing inside.

Not far from them, a white dial loomed above the departure board. Unsympathetic hands like the tops of wrought iron gates pointed the time: 8 p.m. A young woman—the woman they were debating the merits of—stood below the clock, gazing around the concourse.

"Why *not* her?" said the apprentice. He braced a boot on the edge of the bench and retied the laces. "She's well heeled for sure."

The girl looked a few years older than Eddie. Her coat, made of some supple, silvery material, brushed the filthy floor. Her face was striking, a kind of exotic-ugly that appealed to Eddie's contrary tastes. Her hair was black, short and uneven as though she'd been letting it grow out. Curls of it spilled over a blue bandeau that matched her eyes. She was studying everyone who came into the concourse. He could see it in the way her eyes flicked from one person to the next.

"She's looking for someone," he said. "*I* can be someone."

"Be someone else," said the confidence woman. "There's something off about her. She's not a typical tourist. She's got no luggage."

Eddie opened his pack and pretended to look for something in it. "I can handle myself fine. And as it happens she's got her eye on me right now."

"Ignore her."

"No way," said Eddie. "That's my cue. Let's see where this goes."

"Watch yourself," said the confidence woman.

Her apprentice winked at her and pulled himself up, drawing the straps of the pack over his shoulders. He ambled across the concourse in the exotic woman's direction. He affected an adolescent slouch and pocketed his hands. The confidence woman had taught him to exploit his young, clueless appearance. People tended to drop their guard when he did.

When he reached the woman, he stopped as though confused. "Excuse me," he said to her. "Do you happen to have the time?"

It was an idiotic thing to say; they were standing under a giant clock, but it was a clever little trick Eddie had learned. Most people, when asked the time, went into a state of momentary distraction, and in the moment of lifting their wrist to assess the time and reading it out, they were very susceptible to a subconscious suggestion. This woman wasn't most people.

"Would you like to get some coffee?" she asked him.

"Sure," he said, before realizing she'd wrong-footed him.

"Come on, then," she said.

She led him outside to the taxi stand. That was two rules he was breaking: never let the mark take control of the situation and never let them take you out of your territory. No way was he going to back out and face the confidence woman's I-told-you-so.

Before he got in, Eddie heard the woman give the cabby the name of a posh hotel. As they rode to the hotel, he rubber-necked like he'd never been in the city before, all the while keeping an eye on the woman who was keeping an eye on him. Her gaze was almost clinical in its intensity.

When they arrived, she took him straight to the hotel's café. At that hour, it was nearly empty. The lights were tastefully dim. He ordered a cold sandwich and hot coffee. When the waitress finally placed a steaming cup in front of him, he nudged it away and pushed himself back in his chair. The woman had removed her silver coat to reveal a green silk dress, the colour of early September trees. It was beautifully feminine—pointedly so. He could see what she was worth in the silk and in the gold bracelet circling her wrist. An eye-catching contraption it was: a red-eyed lizard straddling two thick bands of gold. Deep yellow. High quality, Eddie thought. But not particularly aesthetic—it looked too wide and heavy to be a woman's adornment. That she had money was obvious. That she'd always had it, that she was easy with it, was also obvious.

She rubbed the ball of her thumb back and forth over the crown of the lizard's head. "How did you know I was looking for someone?" She spoke with an accent he didn't recognise.

"You were in Union Station with no luggage. What else do you do there, but wait for people?" said Eddie.

"Are you married?" she asked.

He laughed. "Do I look that miserable? Do I look that *old*?"

"Yes," she said.

Shit, he thought. He straightened out of his slouch. "I'm not married, no."

"Attached?"

He'd picked up her tack now. "Not at the moment." He smiled coyly. The confidence woman might have other views on the extent of his freedom, but she wasn't here.

The girl nodded, as though approving. "What country are your parents from?"

He sipped his coffee to give himself time to think. "My mother's Canadian."

"And your father?"

He brushed the crumbs off his hands and took a yo-yo from his pocket. He began to play with it. It was a handy prop that often distracted the mark when distraction was needed.

"Your father?" she pressed.

He watched the yo-yo go up and down. It didn't pay to be sensitive. It took a lot to make him angry, but he was touchy on that particular point. *Foreign customs*, he reminded himself. *Don't take offense.* "Is it relevant?"

"You look as though you have the blood of the old country," she said. "That's why I ask."

"He's from the same old country as me."

"Do you have any sisters, brothers?" she said.

"Not that I know of."

"Did your mother miscarry any children?"

"Pardon?" He looked at her. "How should I know? That's not the kind of thing you'd tell your kid, is it?"

"Isn't it?"

He put the yo-yo away. "Did your mother tell you things like that?"

"My mother died when I was quite young."

Oh shit, he thought. "I'm sorry."

"Shall we go upstairs?"

The conversation was giving him whiplash. He heard the confidence woman's voice in his head, cautioning him. But she was always curbing him just when things got interesting. Well, she wasn't here now.

"Sure," he said.

In the elevator, the woman pressed the brass button for the twelfth floor. To Eddie's eyes, the button looked like a golden coin. *Jackpot,* he thought, trying not to smile. He unbuttoned his jacket.

The woman slipped her card into the hotel room door and flicked the lights.

She went to the window and put her hand on the curtains as though she were about to pull them closed, but instead, she just stood looking out. He went to her.

"It feels lonely without trees," she said.

"There's trees," he said. "All along the sidewalks."

"Have you ever seen real trees, Eddie?"

Eddie had a sudden memory of his father taking him out east to his home town, the forest there a hundred shades of green. He hadn't thought about that day for a long time. His father, thought Eddie, had had the same manner as this girl, a particular kind of sadness and distance, as though she weren't quite there with him.

"Have you ever seen real trees?" she pressed him.

Use it, Eddie. Use her pain. "Sure," said Eddie. "In your eyes."

A premonitory glistening welled on the lower lid of her left eye. The girl didn't speak, though her fingers clutched the curtains.

Eddie hadn't seen his father in almost twenty years. He'd walked out one day and never come back. Probably went home. Eddie tried to distract himself from his own personal pain.

"You miss home, don't you?" said Eddie.

She released the curtains and turned to him. Her eyes were spilling over, but she made no sound, only stepped toward him. He kissed her long, deeply, and her body began to lean into his. Her hands, relaxed, slipped inside his jacket and rested one on each hip. It was an innocent gesture, not calculated, and in a small, quiet way, though he didn't understand why, Eddie's heart began to break.

Partway into the proceedings, he produced a condom, but she took it away. "You have nothing to worry about from me," she said. "And I trust you." There was something innately trustworthy about her, or perhaps it was her obvious inexperience that put his mind at rest. This was not Eddie's first time by any means, but this woman had caught him off-guard, dredging up memories that left him saddened and dislocated. In the darkness, vivid and impossible sensations overcame him. He heard the roar of wind through heavy trees and saw a deep greenness all around him and was overwhelmed with the smell of open water, freedom. And he thought, *So this* is *how it feels....* And he was terrified and stunned as he hadn't been since he was a child. When he finally gave himself up in her, it was like having a tooth pulled; he felt the deep sensation of roots tearing free. A feeling of mortal emptiness followed.

As he lay next to her, paralysed with exhaustion, she smiled at him, and then laughed and kissed the back of his hand.

"My thanks," she said.

He had one last vivid memory of feeling hot, and of slipping the golden bracelet from her wrist, and holding it against his chest to cool himself. He fell asleep with it cradled in his hand.

When he woke the next morning, she was gone. He found nothing but a smear of blood on the sheet beside him. He checked his own body, but there were no cuts. He stripped the bed completely, and something spun to the carpet and rolled. Her golden bracelet.

He searched the room, but found no other personal effects. He raced down to the lobby, shoelaces flapping untied, shirt untucked. But she had checked out hours earlier. On inquiring, he found out that the room had been registered under the name, "Miss Romilly Burgess."

Feeling shell-shocked, Eddie slumped on the bench at the end of the concourse. He put his face in his splayed hands. He could still smell the girl on them. He peered between his fingers. Above him, the glassed-over archway gaped, full of dusty sunlight. A blue-gray feather, loosened from a wayward pigeon, drifted down through the dust. The ledge above was whitewashed with the leavings of birds. How many hours had he sat here, how many days, and he had never noticed that before, never properly seen it?

He wasn't left alone long.

"I did warn you," said the confidence woman.

Habit had brought him back here, and now he realised his mistake; he should have known that she would find him. He didn't want to talk to her, didn't want her near him.

"Look at the state of you," she said.

He seemed not to be able to take in enough air, there was such a want inside him. And a fullness in his mind that resented intrusion.

"Oh good Lord, Eddie," said the confidence woman. "Don't be so unoriginal."

Eddie said nothing.

"Pull yourself together," she said.

He shook his head. "We're done."

"We aren't finished," she said quietly. "You don't walk away from this without consequences. Where do you think you'd make a living without me? Not here."

Eddie looked at her. "There's a whole world out there," he said, thinking of open water and freedom. He left her on the bench at Union Station and went down to the harbor. He stared across the miles and miles of lakeshore. There was a lack of something here. A teasing, missing something. Salt, he thought. He had not seen the ocean since... He had a dim memory of his father taking him to a harbor bounded by black rocks. It was one of Eddie's only memories of him. He'd come to the city because this place had drawn him; now he knew why, and why it would never be enough for him.

The bracelet had been loose on her wrist. It fit snugly around his, as though it had been made for a man.

Eddie took the bracelet to a jeweller he knew. In his bright back room. He pored over it for some time, using a small handheld device to check the carat.

"Foreign, probably hand-made," said the jeweller. "It's eighteen-carat gold—unusual to find in jewellery here."

"What country?"

"I couldn't tell you. The lizard motif might be a cultural reference, though. It's a handsome piece. Did you want to sell it?"

"No," said Eddie.

The jeweller looked at him oddly. Eddie took the bracelet and left.

"Where did you get this?" said the biologist.

Eddie sat in the man's office, perched on the edge of a chair piled with folders. "My dad picked it up somewhere," he said. "He was in the navy. I'm doing a school project on it and I was wondering what kind of lizard it is."

"It's a not a lizard," said the biologist. "It's a crocodilian."

Eddie blinked. "Crocodile. So it's African?"

"Crocodiles are only one kind of crocodilian." The biologist squinted at the bracelet. "This resembles a caiman, but...the head's not quite right. The detail's taxonomic quality. Hmmm." The biologist stood and pored over the volumes on his shelf. He pulled one down and leafed through it, periodically glancing from the bracelet to the page. He set the open book in Eddie's lap.

It was a musty herpetological journal published ten years before Eddie was born, opened to a page displaying a colour plate. The shiny paper smelled damp. The plate was an illustration of the creature on Eddie's bracelet, only instead of being gold it was dark green, nearly black.

Eddie read.

Common name: *Lazarus dragon, river dragon.*
Length: *Fifteen to thirty feet (estimated from incomplete skeletal remains)*
Taxonomic Features: *This species is characterised by a bony ridge both cranial and caudal to the eyes and distinctive red feet.*
Habitat: *Coastal estuaries, inland waterways.*
Range: *Unknown. This specimen was captured near Auryhuan, Congaree.*
Status: *Believed extinct as of 1950.*

Libraries weren't Eddie's natural habitat, but he knew how to look the part of a student. He searched the Geography section in vain. Congaree wasn't in any atlas. It wasn't until his widening search reached the Mythology section of the library that he finally found a reference to it in a book published in 1943.

> *Congaree, meaning "Song of the Blackbird." Volcanic island reputed to lie off the Gwyntog Coast. An Oracle, or "Plague Man," has presided over the island for hundreds of years. There is mention of the first British settlers being greeted by a prophet dressed in black with hands dyed red. His costume's resemblance to the red-winged blackbird was thought to be the basis for the name "Congaree' given to the island by its settlers. The expression "to hear the blackbird sing' was often used to mean, "to seek the Oracle's wisdom."*
>
> *The post of Oracle is inherited, passed from father to son. The Oracle's powers are believed to be conferred on him by the mythical dragons purported to inhabit the island, though whether this link is totemic in nature or literal is unclear.*

Eddie had little money, but he was resourceful and determined. Two years after his encounter with Romilly, he arrived at the Gwyntog Coast. He had lost fifteen pounds he could hardly spare, and his face had shed its look of youth and taken on a haunted, hungry expression.

The Gwyntog Coast ran for over a hundred miles. The towns along the coast were serviced by a rudimentary railway. It was this that Eddie used, stopping at each station to make inquiries.

A few of the people he encountered understood English, and some were even willing to speak to him. However, without exception, as soon as Eddie mentioned Congaree, their willingness to help him disappeared, and they regarded him thereafter with wariness and pity. None of them would answer his questions. He couldn't twist or manipulate them, because, as a stranger, they wouldn't trust him. Eavesdropping was a fruitless pursuit as none of them spoke English to each other.

His journey along the coast took more out of him than the previous two years of searching for it. A month later he arrived, all but penniless, at the terminus of the coastal line, a village called *Gobaith*. He wandered along the coastal road. The air was thick with heat. Feeling a bone-itching discomfort, he pulled off his sweater and shucked it onto the ground at his feet. His t-shirt underneath rode up his back like sloughing skin.

Just to his left, a voice spoke sharply.

Eddie looked up and saw an ancient man, dark and shrivelled. He was leaning on a dirt-caked shovel on the other side of a stone wall, not ten feet from the road. The field around him was strewn with gravestones.

"What did you say?" said Eddie.

"Where did you get that?" The gravedigger nodded at Eddie's bracelet, exposed now that his sweater was off.

"A woman gave it to me," said Eddie.

"Then she stole it," said the gravedigger. "I had that made for the Oracle Alydar in payment for his services. Fifteen years ago now."

"The Oracle?" said Eddie. "On Congaree?"

"Where else?"

"If it *is* the Oracle's, I'd like to return it to him. Can you tell me where Congaree is?"

The man looked at him with cold suspicion.

"Look, if I'd stolen it, I wouldn't be walking around with it, would I?"

"If you seek the Oracle, find him yourself," said the gravedigger. "And God help you."

"Why do you say that?"

"The Truth is a hard thing to hear," said the old man. "Bad enough when it comes to you. Worse if you have to look for it." He picked up his shovel and moved off across the field.

Eddie scrambled over the wall. The old man neither turned, nor acknowledged him. When Eddie grabbed his arm and demanded that he tell him the way to Congaree, the man shook free of him and said, "Go back where you came from." Then he crossed himself and left.

"Thanks for nothing," Eddie called after him. He clambered back over the wall and made his way into town. No one would speak to him there either. *Gobaith* was the last village on the coastal line, the end of his search.

Some time between the interminable wait for the train at *Gobaith* and the beginning of his journey back along the coast, Eddie began to come to terms the fact that he'd failed. He sat in the railway carriage, squeezing the bracelet in his hand like he was trying to crush it. After a time, he was forced to acknowledge that what he had thought was merely depression was something physical. The illness that preys on those suffering prolonged hope and exhaustion had put its teeth into him.

When the train drew to a stop at the next station, Eddie got off and wobbled across the platform to the Men's. It was all he could do to keep his dinner inside long enough to get there. He had several experimental dry heaves, clutching the sink, before the remainder flooded his mouth, making his eyes tear as the illness milked his stomach.

He draped himself over the sink, pressed his forehead to the icy basin. A draft blew in from a hinged window above his head, and he heard the untidy flutter of wings. Fighting the seductive pull of gravity, he straightened up and cranked both taps. He cupped the water to his face, swiped his palms over the stubble on his cheeks. Brought another handful up and slicked it through his hair, pushing it out of his eyes.

He felt a strange invulnerability, as though the world was too disconnected to do him any harm. Staggering outside, he watched the train disappear into the heat haze. The platform was deserted. A sign in black letters on a rusting white background read, *Auryhuan*. And underneath, in gray, "Gold-of-the-Sun."

Eddie stood there regarding it for some time. This was the place where the dragon on his bracelet had been found. But Gold-of-the-Sun was in Congaree....

Behind the station, Eddie found a gravel lane wide enough for a vehicle. He followed it. From somewhere in the thick vegetation bordering the lane, a mourning dove's voice rippled. The smell of saltwater thickened the air. Eddie followed it up the lane. The slope, gentle though it was, tired him, and he had to rest several times before he reached the top. At its crest, he stopped again, for quite another reason.

He stood looking down at the harbor town of Gold-of-the-Sun. A dark headland of blue-black rock curved around the harbor. At the headland's base stood a forbidding-looking stone tower beside a white house. In the harbor, the ocean was calm. A few fishing boats, black in the distance, dotted the water. At the inlet of the harbor, a river mouth opened.

On either side of Eddie, the hillside was heavy with dark trees. Their leaves were like green sabres and they hissed and clacked as the wind blew through them.

Eddie felt his heart struggling madly in his chest. His body knew this place, had felt it on that night with Romilly more than two years ago.

He made his way down the lane. Close to the shore, he found a pub called Bindles. He went inside and out onto the patio behind it. It was early afternoon and the tide was going out in the harbor. Eddie sat at an empty table. Nearby, the only other customers, a middle-aged man in blue, deep in thought, looked out to sea. A younger woman sat at a separate table. A chain belt from which coins jingled held the woman's skirt around her hips.

Eddie flagged the proprietor and asked for a glass of something hard. The man understood English, much to Eddie's relief. He spoke with the same odd accent that Romilly had. The man returned a few moments later and set a glass down in front of Eddie. He stared at Eddie with undisguised curiosity.

"You've come to see the Oracle?" he asked.

Eddie took a swallow of his drink. The liquid hit his tender stomach like cold acid. He kept his braceletted wrist out of sight under the table.

"We don't often have guests like yourself here," the proprietor said.

"Yeah...?" said Eddie. "You mean in Congaree?"

"Where else?" said the proprietor. "Some people come quite a long way to see our Edenspar."

The woman with the coin-skirt snorted. "Not so many as formerly. Things have not been right in Congaree since our Alydar died last year. Edenspar's too young to wear his mantle."

"He's the same age as his uncle Alydar when *he* became Oracle," said the proprietor. "And Alydar named Edenspar his successor. Do you doubt Alydar's wisdom?"

"Blood ties bind and blood ties blind," said the woman.

"Some would call that blasphemy," said the proprietor. He glanced at the man in blue sitting nearby.

"Yet still, you serve me," said the woman.

"I don't bite the hand that butters my bread."

"Most of your bread," said the man in blue to the proprietor, "comes from Edenspar...through the people who come to see him. The supplicants only come to you," he addressed the woman, "when they are afraid to hear the Truth."

"Perception is not the province of men," said the woman.

"It is, here," said the man in blue.

As the proprietor reached over to take Eddie's glass, Eddie asked him softly. "What's their problem?"

"Don't mind our Dr Burgess here. The new Oracle is his son-in-law."

The proprietor leaned closer to Eddie and said, "Madam Alice there claims she has the Sight. But if you came here for the Truth, you ought to ask the Oracle."

Madam Alice waited until the proprietor had gone back inside then she stood and, coins clattering over her hips, crossed the patio, throwing an appraising glance at Eddie as she passed. Eddie watched her go. He turned the bracelet around his wrist, thinking. Maybe "Burgess" was a common name in Congaree. He mulled over the words, "son-in-law". The man in blue might be Romilly's father.

If Eddie was walking into a hornet's nest, he needed to know about it. He waited one minute by his watch before slipping out. He caught up with Alice near the fountain by the park.

"Can I talk to you?" said Eddie.

She stopped. "By all means, young man." She sat on the fountain's edge, and the coins of her skirt plinked into the water. She patted the stone beside her.

She's a charlatan, thought Eddie. *A charlatan with an ego.* He sat on the rim of the fountain.

"You don't like him do you?" said Eddie. "The Oracle."

"He's a false prophet," said Alice. "His uncle had the Sight, certainly. But not him."

"You don't think so?"

"I know he doesn't, and so does everyone, but they're too afraid to say."

"What do you think of his wife, Romilly?" said Eddie and watched her very carefully.

Alice shrugged, looked around them as though she thought they were being watched. "She's too good for him."

Eddie nodded, looked calm, didn't feel calm. Wanted to punch something. "How long have they been married?"

"They were betrothed as children. They wouldn't chance another Oracle dying without a son. They wed five years ago next month. Now, young man, let me give you a proper reading. What do you really want to ask me?"

"Do you predict they'll have a long and happy marriage together?" said Eddie.

"Together?" Madam Alice burst out laughing and her coins stirred in the murky water like a handful of spent wishes.

"Come on, will they?" said Eddie, smiling, though he wanted to throttle her.

Alice wiped the tears from her eyes. "The Oracle Edenspar practices out of the tower on Friar's Point, but he lives in the white house on the headland. Romilly lives at "The Venture' on the Avenue of the Sky."

"They don't live together," said Eddie. "How come?"

"No one can touch the Oracle and live. He carries the Lazarus Plague. Now enough about them. Let me read for you."

It was necessary to pretend that he cared about anything more she had to say. He left her in the park completely satisfied. She'd relieved him of the last of his coins, but that didn't matter. He knew how to get more. He strode off across the park towards the shore. He needed a cool head before he did anything else.

He whipped a great quantity of stones from the pebbled beach into the sea to take the edge off his anger, and when that didn't work, he ran the length of the coast, a mile of it, over the point and down the slipway in the harbor where the tide now lapped. He put his hands on his knees to catch his breath. He was still angry, but the need for physical release had gone.

Across the harbor, he saw the stone tower and the white house on the headland. Romilly's husband lived there. His anger resurfaced, strong. Two and a half years ago he had met Romilly, made love to her...and in a backhanded way, he'd fallen in love with her. And all the while she'd been married to this other man.

The temptation to confront him was immense, overpowering. But Eddie knew he was too tired, not sharp enough to go toe-to-toe with another man. He was feeling contrary, though, and hot for a confrontation. He'd come a long way for this.

He had to use what he knew, and use it the best way he could. With a few well-placed questions, playing the ignorant tourist, Eddie discovered that Romilly lived with her father, a local doctor, at "The Venture." She rarely made public appearances, so if he was to meet her, it would have to be on her home ground.

The Venture was a white villa overlooking the river. Eddie had guessed Romilly was wealthy, but never suspected she lived in a place so grand. He opened the brass gate and walked the path to the front door. He smacked the knocker against the wood. The door was opened by an imposing man in his forties, his black hair greying at the sides. There was something in his demeanour like those dogs that rich people used to guard their homes. Sleek and well-fed, but ready to kill you at the drop of a pin. This was not simply the doorman.

"The clinic is closed today," said the man.

"I want to speak to Romilly Burgess," said Eddie.

"Your name?" said the man, unmoved.

"She knows who I am."

"What's your business with her?"

"Hers and mine," said Eddie. "I don't think she'd thank me for sharing."

"I'd advise you to get off the property," said the man. "Before I call the authorities."

Bluff called. Eddie pulled the bracelet from his pocket, tossed it in the air and caught it.

This drew a reaction. The man inhaled sharply, looked at Eddie like he was trying to burn a hole through him. "Where did you get that?"

Touchy about Romilly's reputation, was he? *I've got some leverage,* thought Eddie, *but I'd better be careful.*

"I'd rather not say out here," said Eddie.

The man withdrew and opened the door to let Eddie in. He led Eddie through an opulent entrance hall to what looked like a doctor's waiting room and left him there. Though the velvet-upholstered chairs looked inviting, Eddie was too agitated to sit. He was about to see Romilly again. He paced the room restlessly. The clock on the mantelpiece, a heavy mahogany contraption, ticked once for every two beats of his heart. He noticed his reflection in the mirror above it and grimaced. He combed his fingers through his hair hastily. He realised he had not shaved for two days at least.

As he finished his perfunctory preening, he heard a muttering in the hall outside and a young child's shriek. Eddie tugged his shirt smooth as the door opened.

The man from Bindles—Burgess—came into the room and shut the door behind him. "Can I help you?" he said.

"It's Romilly I've come for."

"I understand you have some property that belongs to her."

"You understand correctly."

"May I see it?"

Eddie took out the bracelet, twirled it around his finger. The effect of his gesture was subtle but unmistakable.

Burgess went very still "How do I know you didn't steal this?" He sounded outraged, and nervous.

"A thief wouldn't know what I know."

"You haven't shown this to anyone other than myself and Malachi at the door, spoken to anyone about it?"

The tone of his voice reminded Eddie of the situation he was in, no back-up, alone and outnumbered in the company of people who had ample motivation to want him silenced. "If you want to know how discreet I am, ask Romilly."

And just then the door opened again, and he heard a woman's voice saying, "I don't see why I have to wait outside, Malachi. He's come to see me after all."

The woman came through the doorway. When she saw Eddie, she stopped, almost flinching away from him. She was tall with red hair falling to her waist. It was not dyed that colour; her eyebrows were pale copper and her skin freckled.

"Who are you?" she demanded.

Burgess turned on her. "Get out."

"I will not," she said. "He's come to see me, not you." She turned to address Eddie. "I'm Romilly. Why did you want to see me?"

There was a silence, then Eddie said, "You've got to be kidding me. You're not Romilly."

"I assure you I know who I am," said Romilly. "Who do you think you are?"

An angry laugh burst out of Eddie. "Nice try, but give me some credit. I'm not colour-blind."

"What do you mean?" said Romilly, and to Eddie's surprise, she sounded outraged. Maybe a good actress, he thought.

"Romilly Burgess has black hair and blue eyes. She doesn't look a thing like you. I've met her. I have her bracelet." He shook it in the girl's direction, "—and I—"

"Oh!" said the girl in surprise. "That's not mine. It's—"

"Quiet!" Burgess snapped.

Romilly flinched, and for several moments, no one spoke.

Then Burgess said, "This young man is obviously mistaken. He has not come to see you." He turned to Eddie. "I'm sorry," he said. "I think I know what has happened, and I'll explain. Please take a seat."

Warily, Eddie sat. Burgess waved Romilly out, but she ignored him and sat near the door. Malachi, the dark-haired man who had answered the door, appeared and stood watching Eddie.

Burgess paused and regarded the mantelpiece, as though considering what to say. "Some time ago that bracelet you hold, along with a great many other personal heirlooms of my daughter's were stolen from our house. The thief was never apprehended. The authorities suspected that he—or she—had left Congaree to sell the goods abroad. The thief could hardly hope to sell them here where everyone knew who the rightful owner was. The person you met was very likely the thief, using Romilly's name."

Eddie nodded. *She conned me,* he thought. *I can't believe she...*

"Wait a minute," said Eddie. "I met a man on the mainland who told me this bracelet belonged to someone named Alydar. The Oracle."

"It did, once," said Burgess. "Alydar died last year, and all of his possessions passed to his only surviving descendant, his nephew, Edenspar. Edenspar gave the bracelet to my daughter Romilly as a wedding gift."

Eddie rubbed his forehead. He needed time alone to assimilate this. He didn't need to pretend confusion now. "But... Could she have been...?"

"The woman you met lied to you about who she was," said Burgess. As though sensing Eddie's doubt, he added, "We will of course, pay you a handsome reward for returning the bracelet to us. And I would be happy to pay your passage home."

"And please stay here tonight as our guest," said Romilly. To her father's swift glance, she added, "It's too late in the day for a crossing to the mainland now."

A commotion sounded in the foyer, a high-pitched, gleeful shrieking. Then a toddler, a young child in blue tumbled through the door on a wooden-wheeled horse. Close on his heels, a woman rushed in. "I'm sorry, Ma'am," she said to Romilly. "He slipped past me."

"You should keep a better eye on him," said Burgess sharply.

"It doesn't matter," said Romilly. She stooped to lift the boy from the horse. She held him in her arms in such a way as to convey that the child was hers. Malachi looked as though he wanted to speak, but didn't. Romilly sat down and held the boy on her lap. He stared gormlessly at his wooden horse groping in its direction.

"Tell me, Mr..?" said Romilly, looking at Eddie expectantly.

"Edwards," said Eddie.

"Are you married, Mr Edwards?" said Romilly.

"No," said Eddie, and he wondered whether she would follow on with a lecture on the joys of parenting. He did not want to hear it. "Look, I've come a long way..."

"Yes," said Romilly. "You do look tired. I'll take you to your room."

Eddie followed her up the curving staircase, wide enough for them to walk abreast.

"Where are you from?" she asked.

"Different places," said Eddie. To change the subject, he nodded at the baby. "What's his name?"

"Aven," she said. "We were so glad he was a boy."

"Why?"

"Because the Oracle needed an heir," said Romilly, as though surprised he didn't know. "Only men of the Oracle's bloodline can take up the gift of prophecy. It is fatal for a woman to wield it."

"Oh?" said Eddie.

"It's the river dragon," said Romilly. "If it bites a man of the Oracle's bloodline, that man will gain the wisdom of the Oracle. If it bites any other man or if it bites a woman, even one descended from the Oracle's line, they die of Lazarus Plague."

They had just reached the next landing when Malachi ascended the stairs behind them. He took them three at a time, and when he reached the landing, not at all out of breath, he lifted the boy from Romilly's arms. Malachi held him with more tenderness, Eddie thought, than Romilly had. The boy clung to Malachi, and the gormless look was replaced with a smile. Seeing it, Eddie felt an unexpected pain. He could not remember his own father ever holding him like that. Malachi crossed the landing and continued up the next flight of stairs.

Romilly shrugged and led Eddie to a gold-painted door. Inside was a musty-smelling circular room with a panoramic view of the valley and the harbor. He sank down onto the embroidered bedspread, let his pack drop. *Stay awake,* he told himself. *Don't drop your guard.*

Romilly occupied herself with opening the windows. A cool breeze eased its way in. When she was finished, she turned to face him; there was something about her stance that spoke of readiness, anticipation. She opened her mouth to speak, and then Burgess opened the door. "Romilly," he said. "Leave our guest in peace."

Romilly sighed. "Yes, father. Goodnight, Mr Edwards."

Eddie heard the door shut and the latch click. He waited a few minutes before checking it, confirming that they'd locked him in. Hearing whispered conversation in the hallway outside, he pressed his ear to the door. He caught only a maddening few snatches of conversation.

"...keep him longer?" That sounded like Romilly.

"You want to ask him how he got it?" That was Burgess. "...you realise how dangerous he is to us? To Congaree..."

"...nothing we can do now...tomorrow..." Then footsteps ascending the stairs.

Eddie listened for a long time until he was sure they had gone. At last able to drop his guard, he felt the exhaustion hit him like a physical blow. He sat on the bed. He didn't want to fall asleep, didn't feel safe. But he needed rest. Part of him knew he should stay awake, plan. He had to think, concentrate. He wasn't safe here, he wasn't...

He woke with a start, feeling light-headed and strange. He sat up in the bed, looking through the windows, resting his trembling hands on the bedspread on either side of him. In the distance, the ocean glowed luminous against the deeper blue of the night sky. Looking at it, his mind cleared.

If what Burgess had told him was true, then the girl he'd met in Toronto had conned him...or had she? She'd given a false name to the people at the hotel, but not to him. It occurred to him as odd that neither Burgess nor Romilly had suggested that he give a description of the girl to the police. Burgess had seemed more interested in sending him on his way. Eddie was quite aware of the fact that he did not have a home to return to. He gazed at the bracelet in his hand. How many nights had he lain awake, staring at it, galvanizing his desire to find the girl who'd left it to him?

Just then, the latch on his door clicked, and he turned to see Romilly slip through, holding a candle in one hand and a set of keys in the other. She wore a dressing gown in rich-looking blue fabric. She shut the door behind her and started when she saw him watching her.

"You're awake," she said.

"Clearly," said Eddie. He remained sitting on the bed.

Romilly went to the window and looked out. With her back to him, she spoke. "People think it a privilege to be an Oracle's wife, but I wouldn't wish it on anyone. Most people choose their spouses. They marry for love."

"Overrated," he said.

Romilly turned and sat on the bed beside him. "What is? Love?"

"Whatever you want to call it."

She sighed. "All my life I've lived in Congaree. Because of my husband, I must remain here. I can't remarry, not while he lives, and I can never touch him. I've never been able to...not since he became the Oracle. He carries the Lazarus Plague. If he touched me, I would die."

"That's tough," said Eddie.

"No one here would ever think...it would be considered indecorous if I were to..." As she spoke, she put her hand on his arm.

He'd been expecting some such overture, but the anger he felt now was unexpected. The old Eddie would have welcomed the opportunity to use Romilly, get some pleasure from her. He hadn't been with a woman since that other Romilly, years ago. But he realised now that he didn't want to use to use this girl. He could put it down to exhaustion, a desire to avoid complications. But he knew it was more than that.

When Romilly kissed him, he stopped her, eased her away.

"Am I so ugly?"

"No," he said. "You're beautiful. I'm flattered. But you're married..."

"Why shouldn't I have some pleasure, a taste of freedom? Just once? I won't tell my husband."

"Your husband is the Oracle," said Eddie. "He would know. And I wouldn't sleep with a married woman in any case."

"Don't parrot propriety to me," she snapped. "I know damned well that it didn't stop you before." She went to the door, glared at him. "I find it hard to believe that you were the best that could be found." She left, shutting the door behind her, leaving Eddie to wonder what she meant about it not stopping him before. How had she known how many married women he'd been with? Or had she guessed? He rubbed at his stubble. He probably did look that sleazy.

He gave her a few moments to get clear of the door before he went to it. She had forgotten to lock it behind her. Well, he had no intention of waiting until morning for these people to escort him off the island. He'd had enough of their hospitality.

It was well after midnight by his watch and there was no sound outside his bedroom door. He opened the latch and slipped out, shutting the door behind him. He crept downstairs, pausing to listen for the noises of servants below, but no one was about. In moments, he was outside and off down the Avenue of the Sky.

Once he was clear of The Venture, he stopped to get his bearings. If he made his way to the coast, he could get a few hours of sleep on the beach. But when he reached it, all thoughts of sleep left him.

What are you doing, Eddie? he thought. He should have taken the Burgess' money, gone back home and maybe shown the confidence woman how wrong she was about him. Except... it wasn't enough.

There was a magical atmosphere about this place, a nobility. He had sensed it in the girl who had worn the bracelet. She was a native of this place, had lived here, assumed its mystery. That girl and Congaree, they were one and the same to him. And after their night together, it, and she, had become a part of him. He could *be* someone in a place like this. He didn't want to go back to that other harbor with its murky water in the shadow of industry with no future, no nothing. He'd travelled this far, and he wasn't going back. Never mind how untidy his presence made the lives of the Burgesses.

Across the harbor, he saw the white house at the foot of the headland. The window on the lower floor was lit. The Oracle was at home. This place was his, and Eddie had to define himself within it. That meant facing the truth.

He saw no one else until he was nearly there. When he reached the base of the headland, threading his way along a narrow footpath toward the white house, he heard footsteps approaching. He dove into the clutches of the wild bushes bracketing the path. The thorns caught him in a multitude of very bad places, but he didn't try to free himself, didn't even move. He kept as still as he could and peered through the bushes.

Someone was making his way down the path, walking slowly, as though troubled. Through the thorns, Eddie caught one glimpse of his face as he strode past. It was Malachi.

Eddie waited until long after Malachi had passed before extricating himself from the vindictive thorns. He hastened along the pathway to the house.

On the door of the white house, his fist thudded. When no one answered, he pounded on the door again. The point was deserted, the tide in with the wind blowing strong. Eddie contemplated circling the house to look in the window, when he heard the door open.

From the dimness inside, a tired voice spoke. "What do you want?"

"You're the Oracle?" Eddie asked.

"I am." The Oracle sounded a good deal younger than Eddie had expected, almost prepubescent. The Oracle let him in and led him, not to the well-lit front room, but along a dim hallway to a back room lit by a flickering candle.

Two chairs stood facing each other with a table between them in the middle of the room. The Oracle gestured to one of the chairs.

"I'll stand, thanks," said Eddie. He got his first good look at the Oracle and felt some of the wind drop out of his sails. He had been looking forward to a fight, a contest of wits, the moral outrage of the reformed charlatan for one still in the business. The Oracle surprised him. He wasn't slick, he wasn't pretty, wasn't any of the things one would expect in a professional charlatan. Eddie had imagined a lot of things. But not this.

Though the room was dim and Oracle was clad in black, Eddie could see enough to realise how slight the Oracle was, insubstantial almost. He was fifteen at most, thought Eddie. He stood not much taller than Eddie, all in black except for the red gloves on his hands. Eddie remembered what Madam Alice had told him about the Oracle's killing touch. That was the reason, perhaps, that the Oracle kept his distance from him now.

Eddie had been looking forward to a fight, but he hadn't prepared himself to be facing a kid. Let alone a kid with such a disarming presence.

"What do you want?" said the Oracle.

"How's your wife?" said Eddie.

"Very well, thank you," said the Oracle.

"I hear you've known each other since you were kids. Think you know her pretty well, do you?"

"Very well. I suggest you get to the point, Eddie."

Eddie started to speak then stopped cold. He hadn't given up his real name, not to anyone, not on Congaree, nor anywhere along the coast. He felt for his passport, but it was still there. "Okay," he said.

If the Oracle knew his name, it meant one of two things. Either someone—Malachi?—had discovered it and told the Oracle, or else this man *was* a prophet. In which case he already knew everything about Eddie that mattered, including what the real Romilly had tried to do with him.

Eddie took the bracelet out of his pocket and placed it on the table.

"I want you to see it," said Eddie. "I want you to think about how I got it."

The Oracle picked it up and regarded it for some time, rubbing the top of the gold dragon's head with the ball of his thumb. "You've come a long way to do this."

"I had a good reason."

"I can make you a wealthy man," said the Oracle. "If you'll leave the island. Never return."

Eddie felt back in control again. "You can't buy me. I won't leave Congaree. But you should know that already."

"I know that you don't want to die, Eddie. If you stay, you will."

"Why? Will you kill me?"

"Malachi would," said the Oracle, and his voice changed. Eddie saw that the Oracle was crying. And then he recognised the way the Oracle was rubbing the head of the dragon with his thumb.

"Right," said Eddie. He put his hands in his pockets, looking for he didn't know what, took them out again. "What the hell is going on?"

"Eddie—"

"It's you!" Eddie saw now that her hair was cut very short, and she must have padded her body somewhat to mimic a man's; she was not as slender as she had been when he had first met her. But her face was the same.

"Eddie, sit down."

"No," he said. "You..."

"Sit," she said. "I'll tell you everything."

Reluctantly he sat in the chair. "Who are you?"

"My name is Edenspar, but I am not the Oracle," she said. "There is no Oracle. My father died before I was born. I was his only child. My uncle, Alydar, the last Oracle, died young and childless, as he knew he would. I was the last of the Oracle's line. But a woman cannot become the Oracle. Alydar advised my mother when I was born to present me as a boy to the people of Congaree so that they would accept me as the next Oracle. A family friend betrothed his daughter to me as a wife. They keep my secret. But this...I am playing a part. You of all people should understand that."

"What part?" said Eddie.

"The Oracle is the lifeblood of Congaree. If my family line dies, this country dies."

"Your line isn't dead. You're still alive."

"I play the *part* of the Oracle," she said. "But I am not a true prophet. The Oracle's wisdom is passed through the bite of the Lazarus dragon. The bite confers the gift, but also a terminal sickness, and only a male descendent of the Oracle can survive it."

"I read about those dragons," said Eddie. "They're extinct."

Edenspar stood, took a woven basket from the window ledge and brought it to the table. She removed the lid of the basket. Inside, Eddie saw a flash of bright scarlet. The creature within was the twin of the one on her bracelet. "My uncle passed her to me before he died. We keep our secrets from the mainlanders."

"Then what were you doing in Canada?"

"Two years ago, my uncle told me he was dying. I knew that I would never have another opportunity to be myself. To be free. I chose a place where no one would recognise me."

"Well," said Eddie. "As one con artist to another, you sure got me."

"You have to leave here, Eddie."

"Why?" he said.

"If you stay, there will be suspicion, questions asked about your association with me. People would find out the truth. Your life would be in danger. Malachi—my godfather—came to see me before you arrived and told me about you. He and my father-in-law will not let you remain. They will do anything in their power to get rid of you. You must leave."

"I won't talk," he said. "I can keep a secret."

She picked the lid from the basket and drew out the river dragon. Its dark tail curled around her hand like a vine and its head cocked, red eyes gleaming in the candle light. "If you do not leave," she said. "I will poison myself. My uncle showed me how to make her bite. This way, I die with my secret intact. Your way, and the country's faith in me and my family collapses. I have no choice."

"You think I care?" said Eddie. "Go ahead, kill yourself. "

Her hand tightened around the dragon's dark body. She wasn't bluffing.

He lunged at her and grabbed her arm, twisting it hard She lurched, and he lost his grip on her. He felt a whisper like silk soaked in acid, across the back of his arm and then a shock, and when he straightened, the dragon was scuttling across the floor like a silken rope.

"Are you all right?" he asked. She pulled him through a dark hallway into a kitchen and held his arm under the tap. He watched as the water poured over him. After a time, she turned off the tap. Blood spider-webbed over his wet skin where the dragon's teeth had caught him. He sagged against the counter.

"You wanted too much," she said. "I couldn't risk getting pregnant again, now I am in the public eye."

Through the haze of shock, he fastened on one word. "Again...?"

A strange calmness came over Eddie, and with it, an eerie clarity. "That kid at The Venture. He's my son?"

She wouldn't answer him.

He put his hand on the counter to stop himself falling. "You weren't going to tell me." He stumbled through the hallway and into the front room. She followed him.

"How long have I got?" said Eddie.

"A day, at most. What are you going to do?" she said.

"See my kid."

"You've been infected. If you touch him, he will die."

"I'll do whatever I damn well want," said Eddie. "I'm his dad."

Eddie sprinted all the way back to The Venture. Each time his breathlessness sent him staggering, he forced himself onward. He found the door unlocked and went up past the landing with his own bedroom and upstairs. When he reached the second landing, he found one of the doors ajar. Inside the darkened bedroom stood a cot. Beside the cot, Malachi lay on a small bed, dozing. When Eddie opened the door, he stirred to alertness. Eddie went past him and before Malachi could stop him, he lifted his sleeping son, still wrapped in his blanket, from his cot. He held the boy tightly.

"Put him down," said Malachi quietly.

"He's my son, not yours," said Eddie. "Edenspar's dragon bit me tonight." He shook his arm in Malachi's direction. Droplets of blood struck the carpet. "If you don't get out of my way, I'll infect you."

Malachi stepped back, but he put himself between Eddie and the door. "For God's sake, don't touch him," said Malachi. "He's too young. It might kill him." There was genuine concern in his voice. It galvanised Eddie though he took care to ensure that the blanket protected Aven from his bare skin.

"Try to stop me, I'll touch him," said Eddie. "Understand?"

Malachi stood aside to let him pass, but followed him down the stairs. "You're going to die. What do you hope to do?"

When Eddie reached the first landing, he saw Burgess waiting for him.

"He knows," Malachi said to Burgess. "And he's infected with Plague."

"Now, boy," said Burgess. "I'm a doctor. I can help you."

"Don't bullshit me," said Eddie. He made his way past Burgess and down to the front door. Aven woke and began to cry. Eddie had to shift his grip so that he wouldn't accidentally touch the boy.

"Where are you taking him?" said Burgess.

Eddie didn't answer. They made an odd procession. Eddie in the gray light of dawn, walking backward down the Avenue of the Sky as Malachi and Burgess followed. The breakwater that protected the harbor was a thirty-foot high wall that curved across the bay. When Eddie at last reached the harbor, he found Edenspar standing at the point where it left the land.

"Don't hurt Aven," said Edenspar. She held out her gloved hands and Aven strained towards her. "Please, Eddie."

"You don't take a kid away from his dad," he said. "You don't know what that does to someone."

He turned away from her, walked along the top of the breakwater. Burgess and Malachi followed, but again, Eddie held his hand over Aven's head, threatening.

"For God's sake, give him space," said Edenspar. Both men stopped. Eddie reached the end of the breakwater. The tide was out, but the smell of the ocean was somehow stronger than it had been that afternoon. The smell of home. It started to choke him up, or something did.

"Edenspar risked her life and her honour for the Oracle's bloodline," Burgess shouted. "If you break it, you will destroy this country."

Eddie set Aven down on the wall but kept his good arm around him so that he wouldn't fall. The boy sat, still tangled in his blankets, no longer trying to escape.

Eddie looked across the harbor, back to the land, the trees, the place that had haunted him since that night with Edenspar. For the only time in his life, he'd felt like he belonged somewhere, and for the only time in his life, he had a family, a chance at a family that wasn't messed up.

Would Aven remember this night, the boats, the lights on the sea? What would they tell him about his father when he was gone? Eddie felt a terrible wrenching in his chest.

"You picked the wrong man, Edenspar," said Burgess. "Better you had let someone take you against your will than this madman."

"No," said Edenspar. "I chose rightly. Look at the fight in him, the love. Our son will be brave. He will not bow down to anyone, and he will love his country. He will live for it. He will die for it."

"Song of the Blackbird" is the second part of a triptych of novelettes about Congaree and its Oracles. Its prequel, *"Under the Bridge of Forgiven Sins"* was a semi-finalist in the Writers of the Future contest but is still looking for a home. Its sequel, *"A Sip from the Cup of Enlightenment"* will be appearing in my collection, Animythical Tales *to be published by Warren Lapine's Fantastic Books later this year. The thing I noticed with this series is how difficult it is to write a plot featuring a character who knows everything. He's incapable of making mistakes or of not seeing the consequences of every action. I got around the issue in this story by having a sham-Oracle, but I had to confront it head-on in the sequel.*

Edenspar's bracelet is based on one my Welsh grandfather made for my grandmother out of dental gold. It was supposed to have emerald chips for eyes, but they vaporized when he poured the liquid gold into the mold.

A Friendly Gesture

Chet Gottfried

SOMEWHAT LESS THAN twelve feet tall and weighing less than five hundred pounds, Georg Mlinkus was one of the smaller Antoids who had colonised Earth. Even though a lightweight—as far as other Antoids were concerned—he thought Earth's gravity was a bit much. He had to give up jogging, because his four kneecaps couldn't take the strain. That bothered him. Running was his favourite sport.

Naturally, Mlinkus applied for work on other planets. He'd even settle for Mars, a dusty and cold outpost of a planet, as long as he could start running again.

His applications were met with great interest. Many firms would have been delighted to hire him. Mlinkus was diligent, honest, efficient, and talented. But there was a rub. He had a great job on Earth, where he was Third Secretary of Import-Exports and had an office suite in the newly renovated Ministry building on Fifth Avenue opposite the Metropolitan Museum of Art. Equally comfortable was his duplex, situated farther down Fifth Avenue. Mlinkus was lucky in having not one but two prime Manhattan locations. Not that there was much left apart from Manhattan.

Queens, Brooklyn, Long Island, and New Jersey were bulldozed years ago. Buildings were flattened, bridges were removed, and roads were torn up. Newly planted trees, bushes, vines, and flowers transformed urban and suburban sprawl into lush forests and gardens, just one of the advantages of civilization that the Antoids brought to Earth. But it did make finding decent accommodations somewhat awkward for the average Antoid. Mlinkus shuddered to think what his life would have been like if he accepted a position in Housing. They were up to their eyeballs in that department.

Blessing his luck while cursing Earth's gravity, Mlinkus quietly worked on his department's budget. His spreadsheet was beginning to make sense when he noticed a motion by the open door to his office. Three tentacles decorated in blue and silver ribbon waved at him.

Mlinkus cleared his throat and rumbled, "Enter."

The tentacles were attached to a head, with three pairs of eyes, on a long neck followed by a huge body, upper and lower arms, and, finally, four spindly legs. The stranger wore a cotton shirt under a loose jacket, having numerous pockets, and brown canvas slacks. Mlinkus frowned in disapproval. Blue and silver tentacle wraps had gone out of fashion ages ago.

"Greetings, cousin," the visitor said.

Mlinkus frowned. "Have we met before?"

"We're cousins in the greater scheme—two Antoids alone on a distant planet."

Before Mlinkus could point out that there were thousands of Antoids in Manhattan alone, the stranger introduced himself.

"I'm Harst Arablooth. But everyone calls me Fingers." Fingers sat on a stool opposite the desk and smiled.

"How did you get past my assistants?"

"Do you have lookers in there or what? How do your mates stand for it?" "How did you get past my assistants?"

"I'll tell you a secret," Fingers said. "No one noticed me. They never notice me. We all have our little talents. That's one of mine, but you don't want to hear about that. You want to hear about the deal, and do I have a deal for you! Hold onto your tentacles because you're not going to believe it."

"I won't." People came to him with all types of offers—bonuses, vacations, and ready cash—to no avail. Money was not a crucial factor in Mlinkus' life. Antoids would throw up all eight of their arms in despair at budging Mlinkus into anything remotely illegal.

"First, you won't believe what I found."

"I won't."

"Two pairs of pureblood Irish humans. They're hot and ready to breed."

Six eyebrows did various dances around Mlinkus' face. "I don't believe you."

"That's the beauty of it. Because it doesn't matter whether you believe me or not. All you have to do is sign Export Form 422EZ."

"I can't sign that. Just because I don't believe you doesn't mean I don't believe you."

"Look at this," Fingers said. He withdrew item after item from his voluminous pockets. Mlinkus' desk was swiftly covered in what Mlinkus regarded as trash: a wristwatch with a leather strap, a box of cigars, a buffalo head nickel, a pair of gold earrings, a package of candy, a high school graduation ring, and a cat pendant. "Really something," Fingers said triumphantly. "I don't like to brag, but I've the finest Earth memorabilia collection. You wouldn't believe where I've been. I've fought through broken buildings and old tunnels across the planet for this stuff."

"Could you remove the junk from my desk?"

"Are you a hard sell! I'll say this for you: You're doing a wonderful job at hiding your enthusiasm. Yes, you're resisting. But you want one of them. I've a knack for that: knowing what people want."

"I don't want any of it."

"So you can't decide?"

"I have decided. Clean up this mess."

"This is what you do. Close your eyes."

Mlinkus was nothing if not polite. He sighed and followed Fingers' directions. He closed a few eyes.

"Close all of them. That's right. Now show me your favourite hand. That one? Fine. Circle your hand over the desk. Good, good, that's the way. Okay. Let your hand fall. There! You got it."

Mlinkus opened his eyes and saw he was holding the box of cigars. "Butera Vintage Maduro?"

"They're a classic. You were drawn to them."

"What am I going to do with a box of cigars?"

"Humans love them," Fingers said. "You got a pet human?"

Mlinkus nodded.

"Trust me. Your human won't be able to thank you enough."

"Don't I need matches or a lighter?"

"Shish! Look who's ready to bargain. Let me tell you a little secret. You don't have to give a lighter to a human. Your human will have one nearby. They're always smoking."

"I'd rather have the candy. Snickers?"

"You'll love them. They melt in your mouth."

"Thank you," Mlinkus said.

"You'll sign the form?"

"No. Do you want your Snickers back?"

Fingers crossed various hearts with various arms. "Fingers never goes back on a deal. Even if I get nothing in exchange. That's why everyone loves me, and why you see me in these rags. But maybe tell me why you won't sign the 422EZ. Do you know how much I can get for pure-blooded Irish? They're ready to breed. Why stand in the way of honest business?"

"Do you really expect me to let four breeding humans off this planet?"

"A blessing on your house. Yes."

"Do you know what this planet was like?"

"Hey! I can't be everywhere the same time. I was wrapping up business on Remus."

"Earth was infested. Billions and billions of humans everywhere. One year our astronomers saw mammoths, cave lions, and humans. The next time they checked, they saw no mammoths, no cave lions, but 8 billion humans. I tell you, 8 billion! Unbelievable. What do you call that?"

"Survival of the fittest?"

"A plague," Mlinkus said. "It's a lucky thing the planet didn't implode before we arrived.... All the same, it was a dirty business. I didn't enjoy being assigned to pest control, but it isn't as if I could turn down the job. I was an up and coming fledge at the office. What choice did I have?"

"You have a guilty conscience. Feelings. That's good. It shows how Antoid you are."

"I do not have a guilty conscience. I only regret how effective the humanicide was. One moment the humans were crawling over everything. The next and we were carpeted in carcasses."

Fingers clucked sympathetically. "One of life's hard choices. But they're not extinct. I mean, I found four pureblood Irish. They're ready to breed and worth a mint."

"Thousands of the humans were living in underground cities. After we dug them up, we restored harmony. We took away their worst toys and brought back other life forms to even out the planet. Mammoths were a tough act to introduce, but we revived a few frozen specimens."

"I'm happy for you. Now, what about my export form?"

"Haven't you been listening to me? You know how fast they breed. Oh sure, you have four. Only four. Before you know it, there will be thousands and then billions again. We'd have to run the humanicide again. And it won't be as easy as it was on Earth. It's a lot more difficult to apply a humanicide to a civilised planet."

"If they were going to be kept as pets, I agree with you. But these are going to be bred for game. For the Fritessicess. They're ready to shoot anything. No way that the Fritessicess would let the population get out of control."

"I've heard that one before. Remember what happened to the Huguna? They bred Dobinnas. A couple of generations later, all the native animals were extinct, and they had Dobinnas up to their orifices. It took a hundred years to bring the Dobinnas under control. And in the course of doing so, the Huguna were exterminated. Too bad, because the Huguna were a very productive race. They made all our ceramic vases. Who can buy a decent vase anywhere now that the Huguna are gone? And you want me to release four humans into the galaxy?"

"You have a guilty conscience."

"I don't have a guilty conscience."

"Sure you do," Fingers said cheerfully. "And I can prove it. Do you or don't you have your own pet human?"

"Well..."

Fingers laughed. "You already told me so."

"Okay, I have one. I take good care of him too. I suppose I do feel a little responsible. And he's very clever. He's learned our language."

"Marvellous. What do you call him?"

"I named him Jeb—a good human name—but you wouldn't believe how happy he becomes when I call him Mr President. He gets this special little quiver, which is so sweet."

"You're a tough customer, but I've the perfect trinket for you—and Mr President."

An hour later, Mlinkus unlocked the front door to his duplex. "I'm home!"

No one answered, but he expected that. His wives were out shopping, and his husband Dyna was away on a business trip. Antoid relationships were complicated at the best of times. It took five of them to have a single child. Afterward the general agreement was that it was hardly worth the effort. Fortunately, the average Antoid lived several thousand years, so they didn't need many babies to keep the species humming.

In English, he called, "Hey Jeb, I'm home early. Yo, Mr President!"

His human didn't come running.

Then he remembered that Jeb was always put in his cage if Dyna was going to be out a long time. Dyna was afraid that Jeb might dirty the apartment.

Mlinkus went upstairs and into the playroom. Sure enough, Mr President was sitting in his cage.

"How are you doing?" Mlinkus unlocked the cage and ruffled Jeb's hair.

"Stop that!" Jeb complained. "I'm not a kid."

"No, you're a full-grown man. You're forty-two years old." Mlinkus thought it amusing that anyone only forty-two years old could think of himself as full-grown.

"And don't forget it," Jeb growled. He was sitting on his chair and dressed in a white undershirt and briefs.

"I've a present for you. There was a crazy trader in the office today, and he kept trying to bargain with me. And he actually had something that I thought you'd enjoy."

"Really?" Jeb was somewhat on the plump side. He ate very well but neglected his Nordic treadmill. But his dark hair was very glossy and attractive. Mlinkus was very proud of his human.

"Put on some clothes. Your blue blazer and your striped shirt will do. And a pair of shoes. Maybe some trousers too. This is special. I'll be waiting for you downstairs."

They talked to each other in English, because Mlinkus had told a white lie. His human never managed to learn any Antoid except for "yes", "no", and "I'm hungry". That worked in the general household, but was lacking for general conversation.

Dressed as Mlinkus had requested, Jeb hopped down the oversize Antoid steps one at a time. After reaching the living room, he asked, "Is it something to eat? A chocolate bar?"

"Even better," Mlinkus said merrily. He was sitting in an easy chair and holding one end of a long length of twine that meandered into the hallway. "Here, take it."

Jeb took the end of the twine and yanked.

A young woman walked into the room. She wore a sequined crossover burgundy blouse and a patterned silk skirt. Her black hair was long, her green eyes large and round, and she was as thin as a rail. The cord was tied to a collar around her neck. Fingers had promised that Jeb couldn't resist the treat. Mlinkus was so captivated by the young woman that he immediately signed 422EZ.

Jeb cried. Tears gushed down his face.

"What's wrong, fellow?" Mlinkus asked.

"Why! Why! Why!"

"I'm Nancy Wegan," the woman said. "Would you mind removing the collar?"

"You know why. I thought you'd be happy to have one of your own kind. You have someone to share your cage with now. Not that you have to share the same cage, but I thought that you'd like to. I could buy another cage."

"But she's a woman, and I'm not a man."

"Don't be foolish," Mlinkus said. "Of course you're a man. I had you sexed before I brought you home. Do you want to see your papers?"

"About the collar?" Nancy Wegan said.

"You had me altered!" Jeb shouted. "I can't reproduce."

Mlinkus was taken aback. "Any Antoid would have his human neutered. It's the only responsible way. Do you know how many humans were on this planet before we came here?"

"Not me," Nancy Wegan said.

"That's not the correct number," Mlinkus said.

"I haven't been neutered."

"What!"

"Glory be," Jeb said.

"That miserable Fingers! How could he do this to me?" Mlinkus declared. "What if anyone finds out that I have a breeding female? It's all very well for Fingers to go traipsing across the galaxy and spreading humans around. But I'm supposed to be setting an example for all Antoids."

"So about the collar? It's not that I mind the fake rhinestones, but it's causing a rash to come up on my neck."

Jeb opened the buckle and slipped the collar over her head.

Mlinkus said, "The collar was for your own protection. Anyone coming across a feral human—one without a collar—would be allowed to eliminate her on sight. It's the only way we can keep your population under control."

"Feral humans will save us!" Jeb declared. "You aliens don't have any idea about how much freedom means to us." He turned to Nancy Wegan. "Would you like to see my cage? It's very comfortable."

"Do you have anything to eat?"

"You're awfully thin," Jeb said.

"That's me. Thin. I like to eat and eat and eat. Then I enjoy throwing up."

"Sounds kinky," Jeb said.

Nancy Wegan shrugged. "It's a life."

"Messy too."

"Messy?" Mlinkus asked.

"Messy? You got to be kidding," Nancy Wegan said. "You should see me when I get my period."

"That Fingers," Mlinkus swore. "I'm going to get him."

Jeb turned to him. "And we're going to get you! All of you. You think you wiped us out? Let me tell you, buddy. You have surprises coming. Don't you know that this has happened before. We understand alien invaders. You're not the first who's tried, and you won't be the last. Our movies, novels, and magazines show the whole history of slimy aliens invading Earth. But we're determined. We're steadfast. Earth will be free!"

"Didn't you say something about food?" Nancy Wegan asked.

"Yeah," Jeb said. "Follow me. The steps upstairs are murder, but you get used to them. Maybe I should carry you? You're so thin."

Mlinkus smiled and decided that Fingers knew what he was doing. "I haven't seen you this happy in a long time."

"Happy? Happy will be when I'm waltzing on your backside," Jeb said.

Mlinkus laughed.

"You think I'm funny. I'll tell you funny. Take a walk across Central Park. I've heard stories. Rumours. Lots of us humans running free in Central Park. That's right: feral humans. And you Antoids don't dare set foot in the place. First we reclaim the parks. Then the streets. You Antoids are going to be out of here on your butts before you know it!" Jeb took Nancy Wegan's hand. "But I want you to know most of all, you're going to be free. I love you. And I can't have any children. Not a single one. Do you know what that means to me? Not being able to have kids?"

"Yeah," Nancy Wegan said. "You want a blow job."

Mlinkus entered Central Park at the 72nd Street entrance on Fifth Avenue. There were no vehicles on the park roads, but he kept to the northern path, which curved slowly around trees. The gloomy afternoon shadows cast by the giant trees could have hidden a dozen humans, waiting with guns and knives.

He didn't take Jeb's remarks very seriously, but was curious as to whether he would be attacked. Mlinkus wondered what Jeb meant by the fact that the Earth had faced earlier invaders. As far as he was aware, no one had even visited Earth before. And if no one did, who could Jeb be referring to? Did he mean the mammoths and sabre-toothed tigers? Did humans view those as a threat?

Crossing the road, Mlinkus headed toward the Boat House. There was an active debate among Antoids whether the Boat House should be rebuilt to be suitable for their size or whether it should be left alone as an example of human architecture. The building wasn't particularly attractive, but he enjoyed its simplicity. It blended in so well.

Mlinkus continued walking past the Boat House and along a narrow path up a small hill. From the top of the hill, he looked across the lake. Very pretty. He was tempted to take the southern trail down to the footbridge across the lake, but that direction was out in the open. It was far too open to encounter any of the feral humans who preferred to hide in dark places. Besides, Mlinkus was feeling sentimental. He was heading toward the west side of the park and to the Museum of Natural History. He wanted to see the exhibits of animal and human life. The Antoids had constructed a new wing on the third floor of the museum, showing human life in its diversity—and number. Mlinkus felt somewhat guilty about the humanicide. He wanted to remind himself how terrible life was before the Antoids restored the balance of nature.

The narrow path wandered between oaks, elms, maples, and willows. Finches sang their little melodies, sparrows chirped, and woodpeckers went rat-a-tat-tat. It was a lovely evening. The autumn breeze tickled his face. Could he be in danger?

He realised that he wasn't alone. It wasn't that Mlinkus saw anything. He felt eyes looking at him. Something more than birds, rats, or cats. It had to be the feral humans.

Mlinkus walked slower. He didn't expect to be attacked. Or if he were, he'd give them every opportunity to prove Jeb either right or wrong. Would the humans rebel? Mlinkus didn't believe that. He liked humans. He always had. That's why he kept one as a pet. And now he had two. They would keep each other company, and they would be happy together.

No one jumped out at him. No one pointed a weapon at him. There weren't any traps. The trail was solid beneath his feet. If he kept up his pace, he'd be out of the park. So he stopped walking. He stood still and didn't move. Mlinkus had 360-degree vision and didn't have to turn his head to take in all the sights. He watched the leaves flutter in the breeze. Perhaps the feral humans were up in the trees? He didn't see any of them there. No, wait a minute. He saw one pair of eyes and then another.

Five feral humans were around him.

"Hello," he said in English.

No one answered. The five shifted positions and came a little closer. Mlinkus couldn't tell whether any of them had weapons. Their clothes, however, were torn and threadbare. They didn't look angry or afraid or vengeful. They looked curious. As curious about him and his intentions as he was about theirs.

"Can I do anything for you?"

None of them replied.

Then he knew. He wasn't the first Antoid to go looking for the feral humans. Other Antoids had come before him. The feral humans were waiting for something that had happened before.

Mlinkus could guess what they wanted. He reached inside a pocket. The motion caused two of them to bolt. But three remained. Those three stayed and watched him.

He took out the package of Snickers and slowly opened it. Mlinkus made quite a production out of tearing apart the cellophane bag. One of the two humans who had fled returned.

Mlinkus took out several candy bars. He tossed those toward the nearest human. The toss caused all five to disappear. He waited patiently. Their behaviour wasn't unexpected. Why should they trust him? They didn't know the wonderful care he gave to his own human. Nor could he tell them. Why would they believe him if he did? They had no reason to trust him. It could well be a trap.

One human—the alpha male, Mlinkus decided—reappeared by the candy bars on the leaves. The alpha slowly reached out his hand and took a Snickers. Then he took a second. Another human appeared next to the alpha. Mlinkus couldn't tell whether it was male or female. The alpha male pushed the newcomer away. So Mlinkus tossed a few more candy bars off to the right. While the alpha male claimed the original candy, the newcomer quickly recovered the others.

Mlinkus threw the remaining Snickers in every direction. Some of the candy bars remained in sight. Others had fallen behind roots or were partially covered by leaves.

For a brief moment he was surrounded by frantic activity. The next moment the feral humans were gone. None had said a single word, but Mlinkus was satisfied. He put the empty bag into a pocket and continued his stroll to the museum. He felt pleased. He had proved Jeb wrong. The feral humans weren't dangerous. They weren't killers. They were homeless. Perhaps one day they'd enjoy better lives in an Antoid home. The thought made Mlinkus happy. He liked humans.

afterword

Generally, in science fiction, most aliens coming to Earth have evil intentions, although in a few stories aliens are willing to help humanity reach toward the stars. So what if the aliens invade successfully, and they're neither particularly good nor evil? How would such aliens understand humans? How would they belong?

And what about the humans? Would the humans band together and defeat the technically advanced aliens, with odds of 99.9 percent success according to most stories. Being typical doesn't appeal to me, so I went my own way.

In my story I have benign aliens and humans who prefer creature comforts to rebellion. Neither truly understands the other, but I've a sense that it will all work out, that a sense of belonging, of fitting into a scheme in which each will profit perhaps not for the best but in a fun manner.

Initiation

Sonia Helbig

YOU COULD SAY I'm ungrateful, even insane. Most people on Australis envy chicks like me, but today I'm going to give it all away. My stomach goes into orbit at the thought.

Don't get me wrong; there are perks to being the daughter of the richest woman on Australis and the female lead in *The Man From Snowy River* musical. Take the penthouse and private beach for example. But touring a vast, black planet for thirteen out of fifteen months a year isn't all it's cracked up to be. Especially when the director is your mother who's hell-bent on resurrecting the Earthpast with all its capitalist inequalities.

If I'm gonna escape, it'll have be this week. Mum's off world and won't be able to sink her cultural claws into me to make me stay. I glance out of my bedroom window at the lavender sky. Will the Master get here before she returns? My palm tingles and I search the heavens for an entry streak to tell me it's time. Nothing. Just the twin, scarlet moons. Olga and Uluru. My eyes drift across the bay to the lush, black forest hugging the purple river-mouth. I should be over there in my cozzie like every other sane person. I should be swimming out across the warm lagoon or into the Indianis Ocean's violet cool. I could be tossing back some icy Earth dessert. But I can't. Today the Master's gift arrived and my palm is tingling in anticipation of initiation. Today I escape my bourgoisLife.

My eyes scour the sky for a moment longer and I finally admit I'm trying to do the impossible. No one ever sees a slider arrive. Glimpsing a nanosecond entry streak is as likely as winning Lotto. I touch the clear gel of the viscous window. It blurs the sea and the lava beach into a uniform teal and the window disappears into the wall. I grab the glare glasses that came with the gift, open my wardrobe and shut myself inside.

I feel a rush of excitement and then the same flush of guilt that I felt as a teenager, hiding in the wardrobe to masturbate or read the illegal *Merchant Bible*. It doesn't matter that I'm twenty-three and old enough to make my own decisions. That Mum's out for the day and I could be opening the gift downstairs. I just can't do it. I'm too used to colouring my life in between her lines.

"Light," I say and there it is, a silver plantport with a small florafeeder humming on its side, keeping the gift inside warm, fed and alive.

I wonder what it is, take a deep breath and press my hand to the palmpad on the securilid. The plantport scans my lifelines, chirps its recognition of me, then origamis itself away. There's a sudden blaze of UV and I can't see a thing. Fragrance floods the air and spins up my nose. My brain explodes with scent and my limbs go heavy. I feel giddy and grip the wall. This is what heaven would smell like if it existed. Sweet and thick.

I pull on the glare glasses and wait for my eyes to adjust. Then my breath catches. This isn't heaven. It's a slice of salvaged Earth. Not one of the million artificial scents that've riddled the Milky Way since the Exodus. This scent predates the comet that blew half of South America up into Earth's atmosphere. It survived the Greatfreeze. It's the fragrance of two Queen of Sheba sun orchids. A rare species, native to southern Western Australia.

Thelymitra variegata. Purple-spotted stars with yellow noses, lavender lips, red streaky petals with vibrant yellow tips and the shiny look of that twenty-first-century plastic you can't get anymore. I'd recognise them anywhere. There's a painting of them in Mum's study. Our ancestor Nan Jackson did it two years before the ice reached Australia and wiped every living thing out of existence. Truth be told, Nan probably held the germ of this very plant in the palm of her hand.

Nan became an Edenist after the comet hit. She spent the rest of her EarthLife gypsying around southern WA, collecting the seeds of rare orchids for the Eden Floracapsule. When Australia's turn for Exodus finally came, Nan's name was picked and she, along with three other botanists boarded the Australian Ark and set off for Gamma Crucis, some eighty-eight light years away. Nan died on that slowship and her seeds never made it to Australis. They were traded for a tank of fuel on Nippon. But now, one of those seeds has fulfilled its destiny, germinated, blossomed and made its way here.

These days, just one Queen of Sheba is worth a small Parisian moon. A fitting gift for a Merchant Initiate. A reminder to me that the League is about to place the Milky Way in the palm of my hand. I lean in and inhale again.

The external sensor chimes. Blood pulses in my ears. Is it time? I exit the wardrobe. A man in a deep-blue Merchant turban is flashed across the interactive. He looks up. It's Master Cojai, riding in on the surge his orchids have sent through my heart. I stare up at the screen, mesmerised. I'm an orchid drinking him in like sunlight. It's been at least two months since our last lesson. The buzzer sounds again.

"Coming," I say.

He nods. I walk downstairs to the door. My heart is thundering. I tap the viscous panel. It blurs and fades to clear. Master Cojai's pupils dilate as he stares through at me. I glance around the neighbourhood. Good. The street's empty and all the windows are solid. No neighbours to call Mother about the Merchant on her doorstep. I tap the viscous panel and it slides into the wall.

Master Cojai slips in. I'd forgotten how tall and dark he is. His hair is black and glossy, his nose is sharply angled and his skin is the colour of a creamy latte. His Greek DNA was what first drew me to him down at the lagoon. I knew he had to be an offworlder.

"Initiate Luna," he says.

"Master Cojai," I reply.

I take his hand, turn it over and kiss his palm. His skin is calloused from childhood days spent hoeing his father's farm on Olympus. He's a true proletarian, not a bourgeois convert like me.

"Knowledge is power," he says.

"Knowledge is power." I bow my head.

He takes my hand, turns it over and kisses my tingling palm. His nose brushes my wrist. Goose bumps roll up my arm. My eyelids flare.

"Did they make you giddy?" Master Cojai asks.

I blush, feeling like a naughty teenager again.

"Count every natural pleasure a gift." Master Cojai grins.

My diaphragm tightens. "Yes Master."

He nods and drops my hand. "I need energy," he says and heads straight to the swarthBank in the kitchen.

It's a blue metallic cube, perched on the kitchen bench. Master Cojai touches it and its front cover slides away to reveal a silver reception tray, complete with black delivery nozzles. He frowns for a moment at the intellipane on its top.

"Two Jerusalem vodkas. One bowl of Venutian peanuts," he says.

"Unauthorised command," the swarthBank replies in my mother's voice. "Please present your hand for imprinting and authorisation."

Master Cojai turns to me, frowning. Of course, he won't let it ID him.

"Obviously your mother has nothing better to do with her bourgoisLife than tinker with swarthBanks."

I nod. What he says is true. Mum has no idea about the suffering her lifestyle causes, no idea about the slave worlds, but she does have her good qualities. She taught me the history of Earthmusic and how it was performed up until the Greatfreeze. She taught me how to mix paint pigments to capture the shifting moods of light on landscape. She taught me how to love Earth's literary greats. Not that Master Cojai has time for such things. He's into Marx and Engels, Filbert and Milovich, philosophy and ethics. Ideology, not fiction.

"Please instruct the machine." Cojai moves away from the swarthBank to give me room.

"Of course," I say, noticing how his blue turban glitters in the fluoro light with tiny emeralds from the rings of Saturn. God, I think, he's been so close to Earth. My mind bursts with a million questions. None of them to do with the League's mines in the rings.

All to do with Earth's recovery. After all, I'm a refugee. Australia is my home whether I was born there or not. "How are the solar reflectors working?" I can't help asking. "Has the ice receded at all?"

Master Cojai scowls. Everyone knows that Merchants object to the artificial warming of Earth. But like most Australisians, my dearest hope is to someday help recolonise Australia.

"I am hungry," Master says with over-measured control. "The ice is not going anywhere; however, I may."

I blink at him. His teal robes rustle as he walks into the lounge.

Was that a threat? He wouldn't dare leave, would he? Not after all the training. Not after taking me off world for the wrist implant. I walk to the swarthBank and place my finger against the intellipane.

"Hello Luna," Mother's voice whispers.

"Two Jerusalem vodkas. A bowl of Venutian peanuts. One loaf of flatbread."

The swarthBank is silent.

"Please," I say. The machine pulses with light.

Mother can be so anal. She'll use anything to teach prehistoric English manners. She'd die if she knew there was a Merchant in her house, seducing me with his filthy ideology. She's never trusted the Merchant League, says its act of keeping the art of wormhole sliding secret is criminal. Lucky she's off world for the week, buying costumes at some interplanetary theatre fair. I smile. It feels good to have something over her.

"Did you paint this?" Master Cojai calls.

He's examining my impression of a solo scarlet moon above the purple Indianis. Mother paid a fortune to have it framed in eucalypt. I nod.

"Art is the luxury of the rich," he states.

"I see it more as expression of the soul," I dare to answer and take a deep breath.

"At whose expense?" he snaps.

Here we go. We are always arguing about what ideologies can coexist with socialism. "I don't accept that creativity has to die for socialism to be effective," I say. "Nor does feminism."

He glares from me to the painting. "The purple pigment was mined on Thelago, the red on Karst. This painting alone would have killed four slaves. Thousands more die each day so people like you can paint."

"Oh," I say. "I never—"

"Your culture's ignorance is not your fault." Master Cojai's face softens for a moment, then his jaw twitches and his eyes flash. "It suits the Refugee Alliance to keep slavery hidden, but the fact remains that no one has been able to find a source of non-Earth pigment that is not toxic when inhaled. In this day and age, the process of art kills."

I incline my head. "Forgive me Master, ignorance shames me."

He places his hand on my shoulder. "Don't fret. Your naivety and your painting skills will be of little consequence after initiation. Knowledge is power."

"Knowledge is power," I say.

Master Cojai flops on the black, leather couch opposite the kitchen. God, it's almost time. Soon there'll be no going back. My stomach cramps. I feel like spewing. I follow him, sit in my own recliner and drum my fingers on the chair. Master Cojai looks tired. He glances at me and smiles.

"It's normal to feel nervous," he says. "You're giving up all this." He waves his hand at the theatre-posters hanging on the walls.

"That makes me feel a whole lot better," I say.

He chuckles. It's a deep sound that normally relaxes me but today nothing will take away my nerves. Whether I pass initiation or not, there'll be no going back to Australislife.

"Glasses please Luna," the swarthBank says.

I jump up, grateful for the distraction, and place two glasses in its reception tray. The machine scans their volume and then measures swarth carbo-proteins into the construction chamber. The Hirgier beam hums and the swarths are melted down to the required consistency. The machine adds water, two standard serves of alcohol and a squirt of vodka flavour recreated from its library of a trillion tastes. Then it pours.

Master Cojai strips off his bronze jacket, exposing bare shoulders that glisten with sweat. His teal Merchant robes lie tangled about his long, tanned legs. My heart races like a slider through wormhole space.

"One vodka," I say softly and place it on the table beside him.

He rolls over and his eyes bore into me. Always measuring. I look away. His fingernails brush my knee.

"You've been away from us for too long," he says.

My breath catches. This is the beginning, the horrid first-stage of initiation. But it will fulfil its purpose, relax and ready my mind and body for stage two.

"Yes, too long." My lips tremble as I voice the formal reply.

He pulls me towards him. I despise him for it but I make no resistance. There's no point fighting this patriarchal Merchant ritual. It's the only ticket of here. And I'm not completely selling out. I'll be in a better position to change League laws once I'm initiated.

Master Cojai's body is harder and leaner than I expect for a star-slider. His kisses are sincere and my heart beats faster. His lips taste like spices. He fills my mouth with cinnamon and nutmeg. I peel back his toga and kiss his mottled shoulders, inspect the damage of the flares of Hades, Olympus' rogue sun. I run my tongue along two long scars that circumnavigate his torso.

"The Interrogator," he whispers and slips his tongue into my dry mouth.

I give myself to my Master who has suffered at the hands of the Alliance Interrogators and lived. My Master who frees slaves but exploits my femininity. I let him tug off my silky shirt and satin skirt. Let his slender fingers relax every part of me until all my fear disappears and we tumble turn onto the floor. We pant and thrust and merge. Melt into a single twist of legs and arms and necks. The first stage of initiation is complete.

"One unit of organic Venutian peanuts, ready for collection," my mother's voice barks from the machine.

Master Cojai puts his hands on my face and gently pushes me away. He slings his toga around him, collects the food and eyes it warily. Then, despite all his guilt about the masses, he places one peanut ball into his mouth and chews.

He grunts in surprise. "The blandness surprises me every time," he says, stuffing in a few more and swallowing. "It's silly. I should expect it. Swarth-based foods could never taste like the real thing."

I shrug. "It's better than rice."

"Better for who?" he whispers and cups my chin in his palm. "Sit."

He perches on the edge of the couch and I assume the pupil pose at his feet.

He sighs and closes his eyes. "Still so bourgeois, despite all your reading."

My cheeks burn. I don't want to be bourgeois, I've tried so hard not to be, but it's all I've ever known.

"Swarths are one of the Alliance's most powerful mechanisms of control," his eyes are open and his voice is patient again. "There's little point explaining why and how. You'll have full understanding after initiation is complete."

"Yes Master," I say.

If I make it through.

"Are you ready to take your oath?"

"Yes."

Master crosses his legs and slips onto the floor in front of me. He holds out his palm. I press my tingling palm against his and imagine the biochip deep within his palmflesh, full of knowledge, awakening to record my oath.

"Do you, Luna Jackson of Australis, swear to forsake the Refugee Alliance for the remainder of your life?" he says formally.

"I do."

"Do you pledge your body, mind and soul to the Merchant League and all its causes?"

"I do."

I already have, I think bitterly.

"Will you dedicate your life to the Revolution, to freeing humanity and the universe from the chains of capitalism, even if it costs you your life?"

"I will."

"Do you promise to develop and employ all your skills to undermine the Refugee Alliance and speed the Revolution?"

"I do."

"Will you protect the art of wormhole sliding and prevent it falling into capitalist hands?"

"I will."

"Do you forsake the expensive dream of rehabilitating Earth, in favour of preserving human lives on more economical planets, satellites and moons?"

"I..." My lips quaver. My stomach feels sick. This pledgepart hurts. Am I ready to give up that dream? Reject the hopes of my family and country?

"Well?" Master Cojai demands.

"I... I dream of a brighter future for every human in the Milky Way."

Master Cojai's eyes flicker with annoyance. His ethics can't encompass dreams. He sees them as a capitalist luxury but he knows League Law does not forbid them.

"Initiate Luna," he says after a moment. "Your oath to the League is recorded and accepted."

He drops his wrist away from mine, pulls his bronze datatube from his backstrap and twists its lid aside to reveal a palmeye. He imprints it, lets it flicker over his lifelines until it chimes.

"Is there anything you want to ask before we start stage three?"

I shake my head. Little bubbles of nervous air rise against the bottom of my lungs. Mum says that back in Australia, it was called "having butterflies".

"Search," Master Cojai says and his datatube turns translucent green. "File initiation." The datatube turns purple.

He places it in my hand. "Connect with Luna Jackson of Australis and upload."

The palmeye is warm. It scans my print and activates the biochip deep in my carpal nerve. My fingertips tingle. My palm stings. The datatube turns blue and sings its low note until my hand feels numb.

"Disconnect," Master Cojai says. The datatube chimes and he pulls it away, snaps its lid shut and slots it back into his backstrap. "Congratulations Initiate Luna, you now have the Milky Way in the palm of your hand."

I force a smile and turn my palm over. Now comes the real test. Stage four. Will I be one of the eight-in-ten that fails to safely upload the data into their brain? Will I be stranded in one Australis' satellite asylums by the end of today?

"Have you been practising?" Master Cojai asks.

"Three times a day, like you said."

"Good. Any anomalies?"

"No."

"Control of the cortex?"

"Yes."

Master Cojai pats the floor. "Time to infoplant."

My stomach turns to lead. We're finally going to do it. He pats the carpet beside him. I lie down, feeling like I'm sixteen and about to lose my virginity all over again.

"Begin when you're ready." Master Cojai places his hand on my abdomen. "Just remember to breathe."

I nod and begin to recite my mantra, move my mind towards a state of mindful dissociation so I can navigate my body and herd the electrical information through my nervous system. Not everyone can do it. Cojai says it's a genetically determined gift. On Earth, it used to be diagnosed as insanity. These days we understand the brain so much more. I recite my mantra until my mind stops circling and nothing but quiet awareness of brain waves exists. I gather my thoughts up like cotton threads and press them down into my brain stem. I work quickly. I bundle and press and pack my thoughts so tight they threaten to unravel. I grip them carefully and slowly relax the muscles of my upper neck until my spinal chord achieves optimal aperture. Then I send a probing thought slowly down my spinal chord, along my arm and into my palm. Now the real work can begin.

The biochip wakes with a single thoughtstroke. Its brightness sings at me, wants to spill three hundred years of data out immediately. I hold it tight, press my awareness against it, can't let it burn out my nerves and make me a useless tool. I breathe deep and loosen my thoughts allowing a small trickle of data to flow up my carpal nerve. The chip sings in electrical pulses all the way into my brain stem. I take a deeper breath and concentrate. Swaddle the file in thought energy and dam it into a fiery reservoir so it can't spill over, into my brain. This is the critical part.

The file leaps, dances and burns at me. Begs me to wade into its beauty and download it here and now. God knows I long to. I grit my teeth and repeat my mantra to stop myself downloading it immediately. Other Initiates have done it: exploded the file and fragmented their mind into a hundred voices that can't be recombined. I take deep abdominal breaths and knit my awareness down around the upcoming light.

"Flatbread awaiting collection," the swarthBank says.

Master's toga rustles. Tendrils of concentration slip backwards into my brain. File light flares and spills. Pain stabs through my eye. I struggle to refocus and slowly weave my concentration around it again. I sandbag it with my thoughts then slowly draw the data forward. Almost there. The last of the information sings into my brain and takes shape.

The file is Master Cojai. In robes and turban, pulsing white with dangerous light.

"You did well," he says. "But you can't have me yet. You have to lead me to the empty chamber."

I stiffen. Feel like I've been invaded. Master Cojai chuckles.

"I am not inside you," he says. "Concentrate! Every Initiate before you has felt the same protective urge you are feeling now. But there is no threat. I am simply an electronic icon, a guide if you like. I will disappear as soon as you download the file. Now, dissociate yourself into two parts. Let one take up the front, the other the rear. Shepherd me between your flanks and take me to your frontal lobe. Don't process any data along the way or it will permanently fragment you."

I take a deep breath and let my awareness split in two. It's not hard, just unsettling. I feel like the Red Sea and Moses all in one. I am the parter and the parted. Half of me plunges into the folds of my mind while the other ensures the file stays put. Between us, we prod the file and harry it towards the frontal lobe, swathing in our mantra. It's a painstaking process but we finally penetrate the temporal lobe. One of me pushes through the curtain of flesh concealing my frontal lobe. She locates the quietest fold and makes a funnel with her thoughts. The other nudges the file until it floods in.

Master Cojai dissolves and a pulsing rainbow of data courses into my frontal lobe. My brain spasms and a tingling wave floods my body. Flesh I never knew existed comes alive. I am full of magenta flashes. Then indigo and amber. Each new colour arcs through my body. Aqua and teal. Amethyst. Tangerine. The folds of my mind spasm and overflow with sapphire. I am awash with pulsating light. My whole body tenses in one long arc until I am the rainbow.

Then it's over and I'm back in my body, panting. I open my eyes and stare at the roof. My mind feels strangely cold, calculatingly aware. I know every detail of the Merchant League as though I've been schooled in it for years. The fourth stage of initiation is complete. I have survived and my bourgeoisLife is over. I'll never be the same. I look at the smiling man next to me, my master no longer. He is Cojai. He is nobody. Just a Merchant like me, one of many thousands, each full of information that is going to slowly change humanity.

"You're shivering," Cojai says.

He helps me up. My muscles cramp and I can hardly stand. He wraps me in a purple Merchant toga and places a glittering scarlet turban on my head. I sink into the couch. My eyes glaze over. I don't care that the sapphires on my turban come from the Sun system. I just want to go back to the transfer and do it all again.

"Are you okay?" Cojai says. "Did anything spill?"

"There is nothing..." I whisper. "Nothing like it."

"I told you," Cojai laughs. "Better than orgasm."

"More. I need more."

"Don't we all?"

"Where's the nearest infoport? Gotta have another download."

Cojai touches my chin, pulls my eyes to him. "No transfer will ever match this one. You've just had the biggest bang you'll ever get."

I pull away, refuse to believe him. "I'll find a way to match it," I promise.

He chuckles. "Until then, there's always this." He kisses me.

His tongue is salty. My mind fills with images of salt harvesters on the moon Eos. Men and women, even children, slowly freezing to death inside thin airsuits. My eyes widen in horror.

"What?" he says.

"Nothing," I say, hoping my mind hasn't been damaged.

Cojai pulls a second datatube from his belt. It's mauve. He twists the top and it opens. "Your datatube," he says.

I take it and press my hand to its palmeye, let it scan my lifelines.

"Hello Merchant Luna," my datatube speaks up my carpal nerve. "Welcome to your beginning and your end."

I blink. "My end?"

"The old is gone. The new has come. Now you must eat."

I raise an eyebrow. "Why do I have to eat?" I ask Cojai.

"To test the infoplant."

I close my datatube and slip it into my leather backstrap.

Cojai lifts the flatbread to my lips. "Take and eat. This is our body broken."

I open my mouth, bite in and chew. My brain feels like it's located in my tongue. The bread melts into swarths and flavours escape into my tongue pores and up my nasal passages. I close my eyes. My mind pulses with a infoplanted memory, the taste of real bread. Fluffy. Yeasty. Nutty. Fresh. Our body broken.

An image of Nippon flares. I'm on a warm, green planet, hovering over a yellow sea full of swarth fields that wrap around hydrothermal vents like golden crowns. Thousands of naked bodies, slaves, are diving off pontoons and plunging to the fields to harvest swarth pods. Fingers strip pods for swarth grass and bodies burst up from the sea, draped in bulging nets. They unload the pods into robotic harvesters for shelling and packaging for shipment across the Milky Way. Our body broken.

The ocean floor rumbles. A single bubble of yellow gas bubbles from a hydrothermal vent. Toxic sulphur mustard. Slaves thrash from the water, scramble onto the decks. Alliance police point tazers and press them into wet skin. Eyes widen and slaves swallow back fear and dive to the bottom again. The seabed rumbles again and a cloud of yellow cloud billows across the fields, fertilising them. Slaves shoot for the surface again but hundreds are too slow. They come up glistening with yellow, oily liquid. Their skin blisters as sulphur mustard burns through their epidermis. Groans fill the air and the death boats arrive. The police separate the yellow while the unscathed are ferried off to the next vent. Small mercies are doled out for the poisoned by a long zap in the head. Our body. Broken.

I dislocate from the images and focus on Cojai. Anger surges through me. I spit my mouthful of swarths onto Mum's floor. He laughs.

"We have to go to Nippon," I say. "Set things right."

"I thought you might see it that way." He grins. "Seems the infoplant's worked. Now you know why I detest bourgeois food."

"How soon until the slider can open another wormhole?" I stand up, detailed plans to destabilise the swarth economy filling my head.

"Four hours, but we can't just open a wormhole whenever we want," he says crossly. "They're delicate things and have to be officially sanctioned. Once you've assimilated the new data in your head, you won't have to ask me stupid questions like that."

I stare at him, my mind sliding in a thousand directions, trying to grasp the complexities of wormhole engineering.

"I've got cargo to offload," he says. "After that we can visit an infoport and get new mission directives."

My heart quickens at the thought of another download.

"Get your orchids," Cojai says. "They'll free a whole slave colony."

"Just a tick." I grab the orchids and a moviecard from my room.

"Forget your mother." Cojai sneers as soon I wake the moviecard. "You're better off without her."

"Maybe," I allow. "But she deserves an explanation."

"Women." He snorts.

"Women will change the way things are done in the League," I say in a low voice.

He laughs condescendingly. I ignore him and touch the card's recording panel. Let him think me a stupid sub-species. What he refuses to acknowledge, will be his undoing. Knowledge is power. A red light flickers on the card.

"Mum," I say and pat my scarlet turban. "Try to be happy for me. I've finally found my calling in life, just like you'll find a new lead." I grin. "This way we both get to follow our dreams." My finger wavers over the stop button. I think of Nan gathering orchids on Earth and make a snap decision. "These Queen of Sheba's are a parting gift to you. A thankyou from the League. Smell them before you sell them. They're heavenly."

I turn the moviecard off and put the orchids on the foyer table.

"Don't do it," Cojai says.

"Why not?" I gently position the moviecard between two shiny Queen of Shebas.

"But the slaves."

"I'm sure you've got more orchids where these ones came from."

He grunts and falls silent. I lean in and take one last sniff, drench myself in Earth fragrance. I imagine Mum doing the same after she's cried. But if I know her, the tears will evaporate into a smile the second she scans eMarket. She'll start an orchid auction and the motza will clink in. Within the month, she'll be buying a fleet of fusion rockets and touring her musicals offworld. Maybe we'll run into each other again someday.

Cojai follows me to the back door. I tap the viscous panel and it slides into the wall. It's dark outside. Stars wink all the way down to the inky sea. Sounds of a party waft over from the lagoon. Cojai trots and heads towards the beach. The panel slides shut behind me and my AustralisLife ends. There's a sudden hollow in the pit of my stomach, an emptiness I didn't expect. I glance at Mum's security camera and force a smile for her benefit. My purple robes ripple in the late sea breeze as I follow Cojai down to the lapping edge of the Indianis Ocean.

The kangaroo constellation rides high in the sky's west. Sun is the brightest star in the kangaroo. It marks the tip of its nose. I squint and imagine a white and blue Earth orbiting around it. Home, I still think. Home. At least initiation hasn't taken my dreams away from me. Or my femininity.

Cojai stops at the edge of the rough lava beach. "To me," he speaks into the sea.

The Indianis churns as an invisible object rises up from its depths.

"Unshroud," he says and an arrow-shaped slider materialises and unfolds its onramp.

"Time to slide," Cojai says and jogs up.

I follow him. My fingers trail briefly across the slider's smooth white shell as I go in. Vectrian metal: heat resistant and perfect for void sliding, mined on Californis by paid workers. The inside of the slider is panelled in leather and wood. I imprint the intellicontrol and sit down in the co-pilot seat, let it wrap its furry wings around me. Cojai speaks the slider up and we shoot through the atmosphere and out into the void. The overpowering scent of sun orchids fills the cockpit and suddenly I know exactly what's down in the hold. Orchids. Enough to buy a planet. Enough to buy Australis. Enough to bring on the revolution. I watch Australis shrink until it is a tiny black and violet ball, swathed in stars, until it disappears.

Cojai taps the intellicontrol and a map of the Milky Way unrolls across the console before me.

"Where to next?" the intellicontrol asks.

My eyes linger on the Sun and my palm tingles with excitement. I long to reach out and dig a wormhole home. Instead I tap a patch of void, five-light-years away, where Queen of Shebas are in high demand. My dreams will have to wait a little longer. The slideDrive hums awake and begins digging up the fabric of time-space in front of the slider. A small black-hole yawns into existence and begins expanding. I pull on my glare goggles, relax back into my seat, turn my hand over and smile.

I'm the first Australisian to hold the Milky Way in the palm of my hand and I won't be the last. I'll be Mistress Luna to hundreds of Australis women and I'll lead them through a new initiation liturgy. Maybe we'll be the secret ingredients the League needs to rally greater numbers to its cause. Who says a girl from Australis can't bring on the Revolution and cook up an ethical way to regenerate the Earth? Who says I can't have my swarthbread and eat it too? The slider begins to tip forward. The black hole roars and swallows us. We slide through a twisting tunnel of white light and I begin my MerchantLife.

afterword

When "Intiation" formed in my mental soup I was thinking about systems of power in society and the ways disempowered women try to create freedom and a sense of belonging in their lives. I set "Initiation" in the future, after a mass human exodus from Earth, and chose to explore the personal sacrifices and actions a single woman takes to escape familial, political, sexual, and economic control. Not all women would do the same.

In all human power systems, there are as many ways to dethrone top-dogs and crown under-dogs as there are personalities. Sometimes the stronger the system, the odder the sacrifices women make in the name of survival and freedom. Think guerrilla warfare, think the Geishas, think graffiti artists. Violence, sex, money, art, connections, communication, and even gender status are all weapons in power battles of freedom and belonging.

Then there is leaving. Leaving is a great weapon in the war of belonging. But leavers are usually loosers and winners. They lose a home and gain a new one. Most importantly they survive.

My own European ancestors were leavers; religious refugees; Huguenots and Australian Lutherans. They escaped death-hunts across France, Germany and Prussia and in the early 1800s, instead of converting to King Frederich's new state religion or fighting, they sailed on ships to the new English colony of South Australia to farm land in the Barossa Valley. They sacrificed culture and property in the name of freedom of belief. They fought for a new space to belong and feel safe in. I would not be an Aussie without their bravery. I wouldn't have written "Initiation".

"Initiation" is about people like them. People who are brave enough to hope, strong enough to leave, and persistent enough to find a space to belong in. They are my inspiration.

Slow Cookin'

Angela Rega

SO NONNA ELBA gets the shits big time and cracks a silent but deadly one at the kitchen table. She says that's it—if my sister Lilli and I are going to insist on eating all this rubbish and nothing else—then she's going to rip out the old slow cooking combustion stove in our kitchen and buy a new electric cooker.

"What do I need a stove that you need to still bloody chop wood for when you can just turn a switch on?" She says blowing minty smoke into our faces. "I spend hours preparing something good to eat and you come home and tell me you've eaten pizza that looks like it has been deep fried in fat that's three days old."

I eye the table and notice that she's been reading the White Goods junk mail. It's so thick; there's ten new cigarette stubs in the ashtray. She's on the page that says that all installations come with a free scratch lottery ticket. I suppose this is what happens when your Grandma trades in reading grimoires for junk mail catalogues. She's become quite hooked on the stuff. Nonna Elba reckons that reading junk mail makes her feel less guilty about smoking. She's reading so much junk mail, she's chaining a pack and a half of Alpines each day.

"Eden," she says to me. "What do we need this old slow cooking stove when you don't eat my home made pizza dough anymore?

Eh? I might as well buy an electric cooker. No chopping wood, just turn on a switch and hey, presto!"

I suppose Nonna Elba has a point. I look over at the old combustion stove. It has sat in the right hand corner of Nonna's kitchen from the first day she arrived here from Sicily in 1966. She carted the thing all the way over on one of the last ships to sail through the Suez Canal: *they wanted to buy it off me*, she always says to us when she's had too much to drink. *Could have swapped it for a camel and two sheep and some apple tobacco. But I said no. I love this thing.*

The slow cooker sits in that corner of the kitchen, a heap of dirty beige enamel with all the green knobs worn from use. It has a temperamental water boiler, crumbling fire bricks and a plate warming section that Nonna swears works better than any microwave the neighbours have.

How could she be ready to part with it?

"And another thing, you two," she says taking a slurp of her cold espresso. "I'm getting old, you know, how are you going to live when I'm gone? You've got the gifts and you're not developing them. This is your heritage! Don't cry to me if you don't pass your Clairvoyant test in two weeks time. Donna Lola is coming all the way from my Solichiatta near Etna to conduct your exams and she'll be jet lagged and very cranky if it is obvious you haven't prepared properly!"

I roll my eyes and pour a packet of pop rocks into my mouth.

Nonna Elba slams her coffee cup down on the table, spilling espresso on the glossy white goods brochure. "You eat that shit all the time; it's going to make you sick. Don't tell me if you get sick, okay? I can predict the future, remember? You keep eating that shit and not practicing your magic you're both going to end up married to guys like those two fat slobs down the street and working at McDonalds for the rest of your life."

There's a knock at the door.

"Who is it, Nonna?" I ask her. I hate it when she tells me my future.

"How the hell should I know?" She says exhaling a smoke ring.

Nonna points to the door and I point at Lilli. My sister goes to answer the door and returns with a parcel wrapped in an Ezy Buy Catalogue.

"Ah hah! Just what I've been waiting for!" Nonna Elba puts out the cigarette stub in the ashtray, pulls a cigarette out of the nearly empty packet and lights up. Cigarette in mouth, she rips open the parcel. "A toilet paper holder and magazine stand in one! Perfect for bathroom reading! And a toilet brush holder in the shape of a toilet!"

Lilli and I laugh, and I regurgitate some of the Pop Rocks onto the plastic tablecloth. Nonna Elba eyeballs her and Lilli grabs me a napkin to clean it up.

"We'll buy the stove this afternoon." Nonna Elba coughs up a half her breakfast and swallows it down again. "I really have to give up smoking. And you, Eden, you're growing a donut ring around your waist!"

The White Goods Warehouse is a sparse factory outlet with exposed pink bats hanging from the ceiling. Nonna's managed to get a $150 discount on the electric stove we've chosen because she made a scratch with a paper clip on one of the hotplates when no one was looking.

She grabs an acne ridden teenage guy with a name badge that states, 'Customer Service is my Specialty' and says, "So, with this free installation and scratchie, what time will you come?"

The guy clears his throat. "Well...we can't give you an exact time, Madam. It will be anytime on Friday between 7 am and 5 pm. Would you like your *free* scratchie you get with your *free* installation now?"

Nonna turns her back to him, bends over and lets out a huge fart. Lilli and I try to stifle our giggles. Nonna always tells us that sometimes the best magic is the magic you blow out of your arse.

"I'll take the booklet of ten you've got there, young man," Nonna says pulling the tickets out of his pocket. "Give me something to do while I'm waiting around at home instead of scratching my arse."

The stove arrives wrapped in really cool bubble wrap. Lilli and I spend an entire afternoon popping the bubbles. Nonna screams twice that we are supposed to be practising our summoning and banishing spells as that's 55 percent of the exam and twice we tell that we'll do it later. Popping plastic bubble wrap has to be the most satisfying way to procrastinate.

"Eden! Lilli! If I hear another plastic bubble pop—I'll pop your heads! Now try and move the slow cooker to make way for the new electric." Nonna means business.

It's really weird but when I look over at our old stove, it's like the poor thing knows its days are numbered and it seems sad. Maxi, our cat, has been sleeping wrapped around one of the legs all afternoon.

We squat on either side of the old cooker and give it a heave but it does not budge. Maxi hisses at us and skulks away, pissed off that we have disturbed him.

"It's too heavy! You'll have to wait for the installation guys to come!" We both scream out to Nonna.

"I won't hold my bloody breath!" She yells back at us. The toilet flushes and her footsteps get closer to the kitchen; we run away from the bubble wrap.

"And, what did I say to you?" She says biting the side of her hand at us.

"Summoning Practice?" I say.

"Don't forget to do it or else you are going to lose your skills! I've ruined you two!" She shoots the Medusa look at us and we both cross our hearts. She stays staring at us until I walk over to the drawer where the Summoning and Banishing Spells book is, pull it out it and drop it onto the kitchen table. We open it to Nonna's notes on page one and I read aloud to Lilli.

The first rule is: Practice Every Day.

Avoiding Practice in the developing years can be detrimental to the teenage witch's progress. From the ages of thirteen to sixteen, girls are prone to summon demons instead of elementals and elementals instead of the dead. This can prove disastrous for those working in the area of séance and channelling. Add the fact that due to migration, dissociated from their lands and beliefs, the arts of clairvoyancy are a part of our Sicilian culture that is rapidly disappearing. Practice must be maintained as must be the ability to banish the unwanted summoned—

"I'm hungry," Lilli interrupts.

I smile. Sometimes being a twin means you don't have to explain to the other what you are thinking. We hear *Days of Our Lives* on the television, Nonna's favourite soap and sneak out the back door, creeping down the drive until we reach the footpath and walk down to Pizza Hut on the Princess Highway. The vouchers we use are for a free soft serve ice cream with every Cabanossi Lovers Pizza.

When we get back home, Nonna hasn't bothered to cook anything for dinner and sits with a hunk of cheese, some green olives and a glass of wine for her dinner. She doesn't say anything about our little escapade either. We put the left over pizza in the fridge.

Reprieve.

The noise starts at 2.23 a.m. Lilli and I both almost jump out of our bunk beds at the clanging in the kitchen. Someone was banging a fry pan in the kitchen with a wooden spoon to a 4/4 rhythm.

"What the hell is that?" Lilli whispers to me.

"How the hell should I know? Ask Nonna, she's the psychic!"

"Maybe Maxi is chasing a mouse in the kitchen."

"Yeah to a marching beat! I left him outside tonight."

We link arms and I grab the hairspray from the dresser—it would make a good weapon if it is a burglar in the house. We tiptoe in the dark, down the corridor, until we reach the kitchen and switch on the light. Fry pans, saucepans, baking dishes, all of them lie strewn on the floor. On the kitchen table, written in salt are the words: *SLOW COOKIN*.

"Lilli!" I whisper and pinch my sister hard on the arm. "Have you been practising summoning without using the book? You know that is really, really stupid."

"I haven't been doing any summoning practice!"

"Me neither. I've been so slack that Nonna told me she's going to give up on me soon and I can go and work at McDonald's instead of the clairvoyant arts when I leave school!" She pinches my arm right back and I let go of hers.

"Well, there is definitely something that's been summoned here—something that doesn't like the idea of our new stove!"

I turn my head to look at the electric cooker, wrapped in half popped bubble wrap, it now lay on the floor, horizontal and smeared in the left over Cabanossi Lovers pizzas we had left in the fridge. "Well, let's clean this mess up and try not to wake Nonna. She's going to go off at us about our summoning practice again. She's going to say we've brought this on."

Nonna Elba's snoring could be heard from the kitchen.

"I can't believe she has managed to sleep through that racket," Lilli says.

"I can," I say, waving an empty bottle of Jameson's whiskey in my face.

We both jump at the sound of scratching at the back door. Lilli and I creep over towards the sound. Me, with the empty whiskey bottle in hand and Lilli with the can of hairspray, maybe whatever it was, was out near the laundry. We both exhale in relief. It's Maxi, wanting to be let in. The poor cat meows in surprise at all the loving attention, flicks his tail at us and runs down the corridor straight to Nonna Elba's room.

"Well, I think we both better get back to our books and work out what the hell was in our kitchen tonight before Nonna finds out!" I say to Lilli, licking the rim of the whiskey bottle.

"Tomorrow morning," Lilli answers.

"Okay, let's just have a bit more of that leftover KFC in the fridge, all we had was that Pizza Hut for dinner."

"That KFC is three days old," Lilli grimaces but she's already opening the fridge. "Whatever or whoever it is has covered our KFC with chook feathers and chicken feet."

I snatch the plate from Lilli's hands and throw the chicken bits, feathers, feet and plate into the bin. "Eehhew! That's gross! We should clean this up now, Nonna Elba's going to lose it if she sees all this mess in the kitchen tomorrow morning."

Lilli nods her head and walks towards the sink to grab the sponge. Nonna was going to have something to say about the fact that we had been avoiding Summoning and Banishing for the last three days. We would have a better chance to escape her wrath if we at least cleared the evidence of kitchen poltergeist activity before the morning.

It was too late. We could hear her already shuffling down the corridor in her fluffy slippers.

"Right! What's going on?" She says, hands on hips. She walks over the table, looks at the words SLOW COOKIN written in salt, dips her finger in it, tastes it and smacks her lips.

"You've bloody summoned a Mumacca! What did I say to you girls about summoning the elementals without consulting the right books—eh? I told you, you need to practice every day, you need to say the exact words in the book or else the wrong creatures can come. Ones you don't want around!"

"We were in bed! We didn't do any summoning —" I said.

"Exactly my point!" Nonna Elba banged on the table for maximum effect. "You haven't been doing any summoning or banishing spells lately. All the certified documents from the Etna Inherited Magic Board I had to organise in order for your school to approve your study leave and you have both done nothing!"

"But we've still got a week and half," I answered.

"I don't want to hear it! You and your sister—no summoning and banishing, no practice and no proper home cooking. You're going to lose our old magic and I'm not getting any younger and you both are making me lose it! What will you do when I'm gone? I think I've over- compensated for you two losing your mother. I've ruined you!"

"Well, Nonna. What about you reading all the junk mail? You're the one that got us hooked on the junk mail with the fast food in it."

"I'm an old lady and can do what I bloody well like! Why should I read the grimoires when I know them by heart?"

Something clanged inside the wall behind the cupboards.

"Well girls, he or she or it is not gone." Nonna Elba walked over to the drawer and pulled out the Summoning and Banishing Spells book; it was as thick as a telephone directory. She threw it at us. Lilli ducked just in time and it landed with a thud on the table.

"It's just like the yellow pages," Nonna says lighting up a cigarette. "I could have bashed you with it and have left no bruises. Now clean this kitchen up and get studying on how to get rid of whatever it is! You'll find Mumacca under "M'."

We clean up the kitchen and take the book with us to bed. We last five minutes before Lilli starts to drool a little and it drips onto the page. I turn out the light and decide to get some sleep. Banishing and how the heck this thing was summoned in the first place can wait until the morning.

So procrastinating has finally kicked us back in the butt. And we don't have anymore plastic bubbles to pop, either. Lilli's gone to do a tarot reading to earn money to support her Pizza Hut habit and I've just found the entry under "B' for "Brownies' in a book on folklore I borrowed from our local Library. After reading the first paragraph, I realise we don't have the friendly British variety. Those brownies like to clean things up. No. We've really got the Sicilian version—just like our Grandma.

It seems that Nonna Elba knew I would seek information from anything but the book she carted on the boat back in 1966 with the old slow cooker because at the end of the entry she's written in Sicilian, in very small print: *now that you've read through the fairy tale version please go back to THE BOOK and see "M" for Mumacca.*

Mumaccas are supposed to be Southern Italian brownies that wear cute red hats and like to hang out around wine cellars all day. This doesn't fit because we don't have a wine cellar but Nonna has plenty of grog around the house to drink. We know that he doesn't like KFC chicken and prefers slow cooking to fast food. But none of this makes sense.

Lilli walks in with a box of donuts. She's made enough to start her own franchise in a donut shop by reading Mrs Simoncetta's tarot cards every second day. The woman is as addicted to readings as we are to junk food. Lilli knows exactly what to say to women like her wanting answers about love and prospects. *There's an ending and a new beginning coming your way. And you're at a crossroads in your life, and you may not know it but you're very loved,* and Mrs Simoncetta thinks my sister is Madame Blavatsky or something. Me, I can't be bothered but then again, I'm not as hooked on Pizza Hut and Pop Rocks are much cheaper than pizza. But I am just a bit jealous. Nonna has never threatened Lilli with working at McDonald's until the end of her days as much as she does with me. I have found how to placate the little bastard but I'm not telling her. I just might win my own brownie points with Nonna if I keep this titbit of information to myself.

"Eden, have you found out how to send the Mumacca back?"
I shake my head.
"Holy Shit! Eden!" She screams as she opens the box and a putrid smell of rotten eggs fills the kitchen. "He's left a little turd in the hole of each donut!" Lilli throws the box onto the floor. "Did you find the banishing chapter? How do we banish him?" Lilli is frantic.

I shrug my shoulders. "Mumaccas are from Southern Italy, they're not from Australia. I thought we're supposed to have the friendly British variety here." I can't help but like him a bit for ruining Lilli's donuts.

"You mean he's probably like, from Sicily like Nonna?"

"Yep! And sorry to change the subject but we really have to get this old slow cooker out of the way. Council clean up is Saturday morning and the new electric stove is installed on Friday. It's Thursday today so we'd better get a move on. And the exam is next Friday!"

"Great!" Lilli yells. "Right! We so have to start studying. Let's start with this Banishing and then move onto the channelling of the dead. I heard there's no multiple choice in the exams—it's all *viva voce*. Let's have a chocolate reward two hours from now."

I pull out two Mars Bars from my pocket. "Let's have a motivating chocolate now!"

We sit at the kitchen table and open up the exercise books that Nonna has left out for us to take notes.

"It says here that Mumaccas are notoriously bad at arithmetic and can't count past twelve!" Lilli says.

I nod my head and keep the other bit of information to myself. Maybe Nonna has made the book that way so she can see who's done the study. If Lilli shines at the tarot readings at least I can earn some brownie points with banishing him.

We fall into a rare silence as we start taking notes when I feel a pulling on my left plait.

"Lilli, stop it!" I slap my sister on the arm.

"Stop what?"

"You just pulled my hair."

"No I didn't."

And then my sister's face goes white and she grabs at her own hair. "Run!"

Lilli jumps out of her chair and onto the table, I stumble out of my chair and see a little ruddy dirty face, a bulbous nose and nostril hairs protruding to his upper lip. It is the Mumacca and he's not happy. In his hand, he has the chicken scissors.

I scream and start running around the kitchen table. Lucky his stubby legs are a lot shorter than mine. I grab the kitchen stool to use as a mount to get to the top of the fridge. He catches my plait and pulls it really hard. There is the sound of a snip and a light feeling on the left side of my head as my plait falls to the floor. He's cut my plait off! I make it up to the top of the fridge but he has forgotten me and moves towards Lilli. He hoists himself up on the table and tries to reach her long hair but she has rolled it tight into a bun on top of her head. She grabs the book, jumps down and runs around the table.

I know I can't withhold my knowledge anymore. "Give him a gift, Lilli! One of the junk mail things. Anything!"

Lilli's hair starts to unravel out of the bun as she runs towards the boxes of Nonna Elba's unopened junk mail orders. She rips the nearest box open, while the little Mumacca is pulling at one of her long curls and snipping madly at the air. He opens the scissors to cut the long strands in his hand but Lilli has already handed him the bright orange colander still in plastic and says, "A gift just for you!"

The Mumacca drops the scissors and grabs at the colander. You can see from the delight in his eyes, the gurgle of snot coming out of his nose and the big toothy grin that he loves the gift, just like the manual says. He plops himself down with his back against the stove and sits cross-legged with the colander in his lap and starts to count the holes in it. He puts a stubby finger onto each hole and counts, "Water go, Spaghetti Stop. Water go, Spaghetti Stop. Water go, Spaghetti Stop."

"It's a colander," Lilli says as she twists her hair back into a bun and backs away from him. I want to laugh but don't want to distract the little man in case he decides to cut my other plait!

Lilli reads the bits that I had kept to myself about giving Mumaccas a gift to placate them. I've managed to leave my chocolate fingerprint there.

"Hey! So you already read the bit about the gift and decided to tell me only when he's about to stab me with the chicken scissors!"

"Well, I didn't know he was going to appear so soon! Anyway, we seem to have distracted him now. Look at him! Each time he gets to twelve the poor little thing has to start all over again."

"We can't get rid of the stove," Lilli says to me while watching him totally engrossed in counting the holes in the colander.

"Why not?" I ask. I'm pretty pissed that I have lost half a head of hair.

"If we do, he's going to be homeless. An elemental refugee so to speak. I can't let him be homeless!" Lilli sighs. I know that sigh. It's the same sigh she makes every time she walks past the pet shop when there are dachshund puppies for sale.

"He's probably been living behind the stove since 1966, helping Nonna with all cooking since then."

"I suppose that's why everyone loves her food. She's got a little helper. Every woman I've done a tarot reading for this week has said how lucky we are to have Nonna's slow cooking."

"Don't make me feel guilty now about eating junk!" I'm feeling a bit feral now and jump down off the top of the fridge and make my way to the bread tin and pull out a packet of salt and vinegar chips. The bag makes a popping sound and stops the Mumacca at number eleven. He lets out a screech, drops the colander and lunges towards me to seize the bag of chips.

"Hey! They're mine!" I yell at him but he isn't scared. He yanks the packet out of my hand, throws them on the floor and stamps on the packet until it is nothing but foil and sawdust. Picking up the colander, he runs inside the pantry cupboard next to the stove. We hear the sound of rummaging and he comes out looking pleased as punch with a colander full of potatoes, pulls out a small knife from his faded blue overalls and starts peeling the spuds cross legged on the floor.

"I think he's making us real chips," Lilli says. "I don't think we should try and banish him now. I'm hungry."

We creep backwards out of the kitchen and watch him from the doorway peel the potatoes, slicing them into thick wedges. He drags the old fry pan out of the cupboard, places it on the old slow cooker and lights up the kindling with a click of his fingers. He puts lashings of olive oil into the pan and when it is sizzling he tosses in the wedges, sprinkling big flakes of sea salt on top.

The aroma makes our stomachs rumble. He must have heard mine because he claps and jumps up and down with that toothy grin again and hands us the wedges on a plate.

As we sit around the old slow cooker crunching into home cooked chips, the Mumacca opens the empty Nescafe jar with our collected junk food vouchers and throws them in with the kindling. And we don't protest.

He doesn't do the same with Nonna's Ezy Life Home Shopping Catalogue.

We hear the front door open and Nonna's Cuban heeled sandals walk up the hallway.

"Aahh, so you've studied the manual, I see," she says as the Mumacca has gone back to sitting back against the stove counting colander holes.

"Do we have to banish him, Nonna?" Lilli asks.

"We do if we get rid of the old slow cooker," she says matter of factly. "I can't chop the wood for the fire on my own anymore; you girls have to chip in too." She opens her handbag and puts our exam registration forms on the table. "And if you keep eating all the junk, then there's no point keeping the stove or the Mumacca."

There's a knock at the door.

"Well, one of you go and get it!" Nonna rolls her eyes. "Such lazy granddaughters!"

I jump up and run down the corridor towards the door. I'm still pretty pissed at the Mumacca for chopping my hair but hey, it is the eighties and I just might get away with having half a head of long hair and a bob on the other. And he is pretty cute—in a dachshund puppy kind of a way.

I open the door. A courier has left a parcel behind our screen door. It's a vertical chicken roaster Nonna Elba must have ordered and a new roll of bubble wrap.

I run back down the corridor with the vertical chicken roaster and hand it to the Mumacca. "A gift for you," I say.

He blows me a kiss and starts to play with the metal contraption.

I suppose Nonna's junk mail addiction might come in handy after all.

That afternoon, Lilli and I re-wrap the electric stove in the fresh bubble wrap for the installation guys to take back on Friday. And Lilli swears she sees Nonna wink at the Mumacca and him wink back at her.

Now just to study for those exams....

afterword

As a first generation Sicilian, I didn't grew up on tales of sweet fairies, gnomes and Santa but was raised on stories of 'gnomi' that had brought bad luck to our family in Sicily three generations before we were born.

So strong was the belief—toys like smurfs were not allowed in our home and the discovery of my secret gnome stash occurring at the same time of my cat being run over meant that it was all the gnome's fault.

I was made to bury my secret gnome stash in the back yard to rid us of the bad luck.

I wrote this story at Clarion South after I read a snippet in a folklore book about gnomes having trouble counting. This story is me 'facing my gnomes' and having some fun with them. I've gone on to write several adventures with gnomes and think they're having a better time on paper than being buried in the garden.

And if you do ever have the chance to meet one, they make the best hot chips. Ever.

The Ballad of P'toresk

Simon Petrie

P'THURGLEBLUXL, A SIMPLE, trusting, and intrinsically brave young inhabitant of planet P'toresk, knew his world to be a place of heartrending beauty. He did not, however, suspect its hidden flaw: its location. For Planet P'toresk lay at the cartographic centre, the nexus, the cosmic crossroads if you will, of five ambitious and aggressively expanding space empires. This story tells the tale of P'thurglebluxl's involvement in the tempestuous events of a few short years, during which the Elysian setting of P'toresk was overrun by wave after wave of competing alien invaders before, ultimately, these aggressors were driven off.

First to pillage pristine P'toresk was the Vurtigon space army. The Vurtigonians met no resistance from the unsuspecting and peaceable P'toresquine inhabitants, and landed their majestic McGuffin Planet-Destroyer-class warships on the verdant fields of their new conquest. Overseeing the land that he now held in his thrall, the Vurtigonian high admiral could see that it was a place of unparalleled tranquillity, which had, in his eyes, only one minor defect.

Its days were too short.

Accordingly, the Vurtigonian cargo fleet shipped in a complement of massive McGuffin PEC MegaThruster orbital calibration units, which were anchored one by one to P'toresk's equator and fired up. Soon the booming roar of their exhaust became a part of the daily—and, more prominently, nightly—noises of the P'toresquine environment, and gradually the days grew longer.

P'thurglebluxl, who had been gathering his evening meal of berries, roots, and succulent sugar-grubs before the disturbance of the giant ships' first descent, hastily concealed himself in the long grass that surrounded the fleet's landing-ground. He watched in disgust and horror (incidentally both new emotions to him) as the Vurtigonians, unsightly blue creatures with too many eyes and with rubbery, ropy tentacles, slithered around and within their vessels, acting for all the world as if they owned the place. P'thurglebluxl's indignation at this behaviour knew no limit, and he vowed that, though it took him a score of years, he would find a way to repulse these vile creatures and to restore his homeland to its natural beauty.

It did not take a score of years. It hardly took one year, or indeed any coherent action on P'thurglebluxl's part. The Kallaginti warships, a fleet of new and deadly McGuffin Star-Pulveriser-class vessels which dove from the heavens in a lightning raid of unparalleled ferocity, decimated the outmoded hulks of the Vurtigonian space army and were able to claim the planet as their own, without the loss of a single ship. The Kallaginti commander-in-chief, surveying her new prize, perceived a wondrous land with only one failing.

Its nights were much too long.

Subsequently, the Kallaginti transport service was despatched to collect a complement of the new gargantuan McGuffin PEC HyperGigaThrusterDeluxe rotational re-adjustment modules, designated for emplacement on the planet's equator. Awaiting the shipment of these units, the military engineers of the Kallaginti Occupation Force busied themselves by dismantling and ransacking for parts the now-redundant MegaThruster installations which the defeated Vortigonians had misguidedly (and without any proper thought of aesthetic placement) foisted upon the pristine P'toresquine countryside. The brief respite from sonic assault which followed the dismemberment of the last of the ugly and obsolete MegaThrusters was, in truth, the prelude to a much more aggressive aural battering which began with the first ascending whine of the newly-installed HyperGigaThruster machines.

P'thurglebluxl peered, from his hiding-spot in the undergrowth, with a growing sense of dismay as this new band of ludicrous, copper-orange, crustaceoid invaders—who were all mandibles and long, jointed legs—now began to stamp their own foul mark on his beautiful homeland. He had fashioned for himself a rough yet sturdy dagger, but he could see that it would not prove useful in combat against these brutes. Nevertheless he vowed, for his heart and for his people's sake, that this despoliation would be redressed through his actions if it took him a dozen years to set things to rights.

It did not require a dozen years. It did not even need any involvement on P'thurglebluxl's part within the mere six-month occupation by the Kallaginti forces. The subversive assault by the Golgleglog infiltrators, which took advantage of a hidden weakness in the primitive defences of the Kallaginti fleet, was complete before the new McGuffin Nova-Blaster-class ships (the pride of the Golgleglog space navy) were even detected by the hapless Kallaginti army. On landing, the cognitive centre of the Golgleglog combat organism assessed its newly-conquered terrain. It found itself in possession of a bountiful world which had but one sole defect.

Its seas were too deep.

The Golgleglog engineering organism, when consulted, prescribed an appropriate correction to this problem, through the acquisition of several of the new monolithic McGuffin PEC TeraSquirter Ballistic Ejection dehydration plants. These were conveniently locatable on the ruins of the Kallaginti's now-worthless HyperGigaThruster machines, from which the noise, though deafening, had at least been *constant*. The TeraSquirters, essentially water cannons which were sufficiently powerful that their payload attained escape velocity, operated with a sporadic thump which was rumoured to be audible on the other side of the planet. That is, they could be heard from the planet's opposite face when this noise was not being drowned out by the nearer TeraSquirter installations.

The brave and patient native, P'thurglebluxl, gazed on with a deepening sense of foreboding as these new aliens, a tribe of ridiculously amoeboid quasi-transparent blobby giants, squelched their desecration across his once-proud land. His newly-fashioned spear, though a handy weapon in its own right, would not suffice to bring down these foes. He promised, however, that not five years would pass before he had avenged this hideous wrong against his homeland.

It was rather less time than that before the next wave of invasion smashed against the shore of once-beautiful P'toresk. only three months elapsed before the fearsome nuclear weaponry of the Terran star troopers was unleashed on the unsuspecting Golgleglog occupation force, who literally withered and died under the Terran assault. The Terran troopers, in their new McGuffin Quasar-Crusher-class warships, landed in force amidst the decrepit shards of the once-proud Golgleglog space navy, swept the area with radiation neutralisers, and took possession of the latest addition to their expanding empire. The Terran force's ranking five-star general took stock of her new planetary acquisition. It was, she decided, a nice enough place in its way, except for one thing.

There wasn't enough water on the planet.

To rectify this, the Terran engineering attaché placed an order for a prodigious quantity of the latest McGuffin PEC UltraMassive Comet Collectors, which would bring in unparalleled quantities of water ice from the star system's Oort cloud. The UltraMassive robot probes, guided by homing beacons to target the now-unwanted TeraSquirter plants as preferred impact sites on the planet (the better to celebrate P'toresk's liberation from its unfortunate but brief enthralment by the accursed Golgleglog), arrived only very sporadically but created an entirely unprecedented quantum of noise when they did impact.

From his hiding spot, P'thurglebluxl peered in anguish at the latest influx of usurpers, who were a brutish band of pinky-brown protosimians with ludicrously localised fur and a totally unwarranted air of self-importance. His newly-invented shortbow, slung across his back, seemed inadequate to the task of slaying these vermin. He still swore that he would, somehow, stamp out these transgressors, in some as-yet-unguessed manner and at some unspecified point in time within the next, say, two years.

The following week, the Blokkob military razed the Terran force in a hail of antimatter-fuelled annihilation. The Blokkobs, who as strategists were not in any way given to subtlety, prepared a landing strip with a few judicious gamma-ray laser blasts and rode their fleet of brand-new McGuffin Galaxy-Dominator-class spacecraft down to, in their eyes, a well-deserved and heroic victory. The Blokkob's chief dictator stared out at this new world that he and his underlings had subjugated. It would have to do, he supposed, but there was one aspect of the place that cried out for improvement.

The planet was the wrong shape.

To convert the newly-conquered world into the Blokkob planetary ideal of a perfect cube, the Blokkob engineers set up a network of six McGuffin PEC Neutronium WorldHammers—positioned, more often than not, on the ruins of the UltraMassive probe homing beacons—with which to pummel and crush this disturbingly round planet. To say the least, the WorldHammer was not a pleasant piece of equipment beside which to be standing.

P'thurglebluxl, once again hidden in the bushes, looked on aghast. His world could not take much more of this punishment. If he felt a greater degree of skill in wielding his new longbow, then he would have assailed these hideous creatures here and now; though he was not sure that an arrow would be of much use against the thick armoured carapace of the turtle-like Blokkobs. Just the same, he, himself, P'thurglebluxl, would do something about it, next month. That would give him time to develop a plan of attack.

As it transpired, this amount of time was not needed. The next day, the revamped and rejuvenated fleets of the Vurtigon, Kallaginti, Golgleglog and Terran space forces arrived and began aggressive negotiations for the return of their rightfully-acquired territory. When only a few vessels remained from each fleet, a truce was called and the representatives of all parties met on a forlorn patch of neutral ground. There they began arguing anew, each staking their claim in increasingly strident tones.

This was too much for P'thurglebluxl, who stood and revealed himself. He had bedecked himself in a suit made of the conjoined fragments of the battle-armours and exoskeletons of all of the planet's recent invaders, and he had equipped himself with a scimitar, a pikestaff, a crossbow, and a sturdy shield. He adopted a threatening pose and then strode out, fearing not for his life, to meet the despots of the several worlds which had brought ruination to his once-fair planet in the space of a scant couple of years.

His speech ran as follows: "You have no right to this place! You do not belong here! I say you must leave, and leave now! In the name of P'toresk, the place of unparalleled beauty and home to all that is true and just, I claim this land as belonging to my ancestors and my descendants, and those who share my form! Now—BEGONE!"

At least, that is what he would have told them, and what in his mind's eye he had seen himself telling them. In reality their translation devices could not cope with the grammatical complexities of the fair P'toresquine language; but a further obstacle to interspecies communication inserted itself even before he could deliver his edict.

His mind on the pressures of public speaking, he noticed not the spent piece of Vurtigonian artillery and tripped, his forehead impacting awkwardly upon the broken rifle-butt of a discarded Kallaginti photon blunderbuss. Of his diatribe, he managed only an enigmatic "Y—" as he fell.

The five warring factions were briefly startled by the sudden intrusion by this mysterious figure in badly-fitting armour, and directed a few lower-caste operatives to investigate the sad sprawled figure who had interrupted their ballistic dialogue. Then, judging that the ungainly interloper posed no significant threat, the assembled forces fell once again into the mode of negotiation with which they were all most comfortable and familiar, and the happy sounds of blasters and laser cannon ruptured the air all around them.

So preoccupied with their own concerns were the Vurtigon, Kallaginti, Golgleglog, Terran, and Blokkob forces, that they did not notice the arrival of the mercenary fleet which totally overpowered them in both numerical and technical superiority, and none of the soldiers, generals, or representatives of the five invaders survived for more than a minute. The new armada, a veritable swarm of McGuffin Universe-Annihilator-class warships, touched down, followed shortly by a small and entirely unprepossessing unmarked vehicle. The leader of the mercenary horde alighted from his mighty flagship and waited. Soon enough, a small froglike creature emerged from the unmarked vehicle and paid the mercenary leader the agreed prompt-completion bonus. Then the mercenary fleet once again took to the sky, leaving only the small froglike creature to survey his new world.

The Acquisitions Manager of the McGuffin Planetary Engineering Corporation looked around him, and liked what he saw. The new factories could go *there*, and *there*, and over *there*. The showroom would work best *there*, and the admin offices would make the most sense *there*. A security force, comprised of people like that unconscious fellow in the mishmashed suit of armour, could be stationed *there*. All in all, he felt, a very promising location from which to grow the business. There were, after all, five steady clients in easy reach of this planet, and it was plain that these five clients now had a great deal of unfinished business to discuss with each other. An excellent location, with just one slight problem.

The planet's sun was too close.

Not to worry. After all, they had a new model to fix *that*.

afterword

As a dual citizen (NZ and Oz), the issue of 'belonging' is one which resonates with me, though I can't claim that the above story illuminates my own serious perspective in any detailed sense, because that's not why I wrote it. I would hope, however, that some small sense of outrage does make itself apparent through the story's obvious absurdism. But I think my primary purpose in writing "P'toresk" was as an excuse to legitimately use the marvellous word 'despoliation' in a piece of text.

The Hollow Ones

Kylie Seluka

SALEESA SCANNED THE horizon of the world. The blue water glittered at her. *The Peril surrounds us so completely, so relentlessly,* she thought as she wrapped her thin arms around herself. A grey fin, prowling in the lagoon, broke the surface. Saleesa shivered and turned away. Yet her son stood firm beside her, watching it until the shrill calls of the seabirds distracted him and he looked skywards.

The blood heat prickled under her skin as the Peril taunted with its promised cool relief. Saleesa closed her eyes. Her stomach tightened, and she felt, once again, something pulling her towards the lagoon. She grabbed onto the coconut trunk next to her. Impossible, she thought.

"Tema," she said, snapping her eyes open. "I must go. The sun approaches the Maker, calling us to the meeting."

Her son nodded, his thick black hair lifting over his shoulders. "I'm coming too. I wish to speak to the Council."

She clicked her tongue. "I told you I can not sponsor you again."

"I know."

He glanced at her as he passed her by, a familiar rawness in his eyes. Saleesa winced, regret clawed at her heart, threatening to expose the truth. She bowed her head. She had buried the secret too deep for it to be released now.

The rich scent of coconut oil on her hair and skin ripened in the afternoon humidity. Smoke from the fire pit filtered across the thatched meeting space. Saleesa adjusted the fine mat wrapped round her waist before sitting cross-legged on the powdered white coral floor. The continuous beat of the wooden drum called the villagers and they gathered around the open Meeting House.

We are flourishing, she thought.

As befitting her status, Saleesa had an uninterrupted view of the Maker, its green bulk towering over them like a protective parent. She knew every part of it, from the patterns of pale stone and dense green patches to its distinctive outline. *Like a thumb*. The Maker's peak touched the sun and she joined in the song of praise.

Beautiful Savaku
Blessed by the Maker
Haven from the Peril
We are Savaku

She leant back against a wooden pole, motioning for a boy wielding an oversized fan to come to her. His efforts did no good. Sweat oozed from her skin and she felt like there was a stone oven fire inside her head. *Deep breaths, deep breaths*. She fixed her eyes on the Maker until the attack had passed.

Discussion of the next round of appropriate blood couplings faded away, leaving apprehension hovering in the air. Elder Lolo stood up, his mass of black-grey streaked curls drawing everyone's eye.

"I wish to sponsor Tema's request to speak. He has always done the right thing by Savaku." He turned to Tema. "Last time we granted you a permission. It was to travel beyond the lagoon, to the outer reef."

Tema wore his father's finest cloth. Its beaten fibres were now soft and supple with age, though the brown block patterns had faded. The memory of her man ached through Saleesa and she caught Tema's eye briefly. He looked away and her jaw tensed. *Surely he will not ask for more of the same? Surely he will not shame me again?*

Tema knelt before them. "I have not the clever words to persuade or fool you. I believe the Maker will take no offence at my request."

"It is not for you to say at what the Maker will take offence," said Elder Maniva, leaning forward over his significant stomach. "You are reminded yet again, it is the Maker's Supreme Law that we all must remain here on Savaku. Do not continue to waste our time asking for permission to break this law. Think of your family, Tema." He sent an exaggerated look of sympathy across to Saleesa.

"I will not break taboo by leaving Savaku to explore the Wild Peril beyond the reefs. You are resolved that it would displease the Maker. I have always obeyed the Council's directives. This time, I have a different request," said Tema.

Saleesa drew in a quiet breath, wrapping her dry fingers around each other.

"I want to build a new style of boat."

Her fingers squeezed together. The ever present roar of the waves crashed louder in her ears and her breath grew short as the heat enveloped her again.

"It will be larger, but lighter—made with bamboo and a trunk." His words rushed out. "I had an idea of using a mat to catch the wind and make the boat travel faster."

Elder Maniva banged his fist on the floor, making a large indentation. "Hah! For what purpose?" He sniffed loudly. "He's trying to trick us... sneaking closer and closer to the Wild Peril. First it was fishing past the lagoon. Then on to the reef at certain times, now it's a different boat. I say we put a stop to it. Tema is young and selfish. He doesn't understand what it is to be Savaku."

"He is our best fisherman and we have seen how his requests have benefited the people of Savaku. Yes?" Elder Lolo looked around at the other Elders, waiting for a few to nod. "Let us not be so quick to refuse, then."

"I have a model of the boat," said Tema, nodding to a young boy to bring it to him. "See, by adding the two bamboo side bars, the boat will be more stable." He held it up. "I have practiced with it... a little."

Saleesa refused to look at the ugly thing any more. The persistent tugging at her stomach continued like a warning drum. *No good will come of this.*

The Elders fired their questions at him.

"How fast do you think you could go... say to the reef and back?"

"What do you mean it is more stable than a canoe?"

"How will you protect yourself from a beast?"

"The wind is unpredictable. What if it does not like being caught? Do you really think you can tame it?"

These were not the sort of questions Saleesa expected. *This will not do.* Many of them seemed far too excited by the notion of a new boat design.

"The Maker gives us all we need," she interrupted, "He is our creator, our protector and provider. He asks for so little in return. Only that we worship him." She turned to Tema. "We live by his generosity."

Tema frowned, moistening his lower lip. "We get fish and other food from the lagoon," he said.

Saleesa smiled tightly. "Yes, that is true. But remember the lagoon is almost encircled by land—like the Maker's loving arms—keeping us safe."

"The reefs give us coral to help build our houses," Tema added.

"The reefs grow up from the land, like the Maker's hair that we trim. Even then he is protecting us. The Wild Peril throws itself against the reef again and again, wanting to devour us. It is full of monsters, dangers... death. It takes people who are p-precious to us." Her voice hardened. "All who fall into the Peril are lost. *All.*"

The villagers became quiet and still as Saleesa's words reached them. She breathed out her pain and relief.

"I know," he said, "I saw my own father fall and did nothing."

Saleesa's heart twitched as she looked at her son's face. "There was nothing you could do, Tema."

"That's just it!" Tema exploded, "We need to explore and understand the mysteries of the Peril so we can make it safe, so we don't lose anyone else."

"The Maker—" began Saleesa.

"And what if we have to leave? Or need to find more food?" Tema continued, "Or others come?"

Saleesa forced herself to smile and cast it around the room so they could see she was not disturbed by this talk. "The Maker has always provided for us. As long as we stay here, we will be protected. As for others? The Maker has made no others. There is only Savaku." She focused back on him. "Please Tema, stop this."

"What about the birds?" Tema's voice cracked slightly.

"Birds?"

"The seabirds. They come and go. Where do they rest?"

"You speak on things that you do not understand. Such thoughts are dangerous to our community," interrupted Elder Maniva.

"What if I had convinced an Elder to try out the boat, to see that it is sturdy and safe?"

"Is there an Elder willing to journey out onto the Peril?" Maniva looked around, eyes resting on Saleesa.

Heat spread up her neck and her heart squeezed its familiar dread. *Not me. It cannot be me.*

"Not only an Elder, but a spirit healer" Tema added.

Stupid boy! Why does he do this to me? There could be no question of her supporting his dangerous yearnings any more. She had a responsibility to the Maker. Saleesa pursed her mouth, reluctant to speak her denial, though seeing no other option.

"*I* support this," said Elder Lolo

"You?" She blurted out.

"Of course," he said, hair bouncing like a reef sponge as he nodded. "We all know you would never take part in such a journey."

"Of course," Saleesa frowned, looking at her son. He lifted his chin up at her, challenge in his dark brown eyes.

"I ask that we consent to a trial," said Elder Lolo. "Everyone we will be able to watch and see if there is any merit in Tema's claims."

How dare Tema put me in this position! She fumed as she and Maniva were eventually forced to consensus.

Saleesa paced along the side of her hut, the brown earth cool under her feet. Shaded in by hibiscus bushes and the Maker, she was sheltered here, away from the other huts circling the lagoon. Far away from the Peril.

The heat returned, spreading like liquid fire to every part of her body. She could barely breathe. It was all Tema's fault. *He treats my position with contempt. My only child... and he continues to humiliate me. I am done with him!*

A young man approached the hut.

"Greetings, Spirit Mother." He carried a basket of green fruit. "Papaya is your favourite?"

"Oh yes, thank you." So thoughtful and considerate, she mused. Not like Tema who never brought her papaya, only smelly fish.

Perhaps she needed to have another child, quick, before it was too late and the heat burned up her mother blood. Saleesa shivered as a breeze cooled across her sweat-soaked skin.

"Please, put it down here," she said, watching his chest muscles dance as he unloaded the basket. Her hands became clammy.

"In return, I will give you some healing energy." She knelt, swallowing thickly as she rubbed his leg.

"Please Spirit Mother—"

Her hand cramped as she moved it to his inner thigh. She could see her fingers—bony and creased with age—on his firm skin. *What am I doing?* She was being ridiculous. She pulled her hand away. "You seem f-fine." She cleared her throat.

"It is my sister," he blurted out, "Ever since she went up the Maker, she does not thrive. My mother asks you to visit."

The hut was very close to the lagoon. The Peril surged towards her, winking malevolent in the sunlight. The unwelcome pull in her stomach returned. *Why did we allow people to build here? It is asking for... accidents.*

"Thank you for coming Spirit Mother," said the woman, "My daughter, Peni, she cries, does not eat, does not want to leave the hut. She has come down from the Maker, but she won't tell us about her vision."

The girl lay on a mat, all bones stretched over skin, her black hair lank and knotted. Fear flashed in her eyes. Saleesa frowned as a memory stirred but remained concealed.

She sat down next to Peni, speaking softly. "It can be a difficult thing, the vision. When I went up to the Maker, he sent me a Spirit vision so terrible and painful... I thought I would never recover." She clenched her face, clamping down the memories and forced the lie out yet again.

"The Maker shook and shook, rocks tumbled down, smashing against me. My legs lay ruined in front of me in an agony of splintered bones and blood. My hands were pulped like the over-ripe papaya. Then a tree crashed across my back, shattering me into pieces. The Maker sent the animals to me—the bitter bug, the jumping greenstick, the striped beetle, and the black eye birds.

They used their cruel, sharp tools to devour and rip at my flesh. I felt it all—every tiny piece of me—being torn away. Then the spiky lizards came and took my bones.

"I suffered there, unable to move, cry, scream out my pain until all that was left was my wounded spirit and a memory of who I once was. I knew I had to rebuild myself. The rocks and the wood and the leaves and the earth became my new body, all gifts from the Maker." Saleesa gave Peni a forced smile as her heart flinched. "It is as every spirit healer has experienced before."

Peni lay still and stiff, while her eyes crinkled with a strange anguish.

"Let us begin," said Saleesa, "Do you wish to receive the Maker's healing?"

The girl nodded. Tears slid out from the corner of her eyes onto the mat.

Saleesa called out. "Maker, let your healing energy flow from me to where it is needed in Peni."

She closed her eyes, drawing energy from the earth, visualising it moving up through her legs, stomach and into her hands. She held her hands over the girl's chest. Normally different things would come to her; sometimes a word formed in her mind—'anxiety' or 'sadness', sometimes it was a colour—red for trapped anger, yellow indicated a fear. She would then put her hands and let the energy in to heal. Sometimes she would draw out the sickness, flinging it away.

But this time she saw nothing. No colours, shapes, words—just a void. The light energy curled out from her hands but it didn't fill up the girl, didn't affect her. Saleesa couldn't sense what was wrong. The fire built up inside her again and she wiped the sweat from her face.

"You must relax. Allow the Maker to flow through you," she said sternly.

Saleesa's body tensed as she tried sending in more energy. *Still nothing.* She was supposed to become stronger as the mother blood dried up. Her back cramped as she held her position. *Why can't I see anything?*

"You are not cooperating!" she yelled at the girl, "You are refusing to accept the Maker's power," She stood up. "I can not tolerate such resistance."

Legs and heart trembling, she left. Nothing was making any sense anymore.

The boat rested half in the lagoon and half on the shore. Tema and a few people stood close to it, feet in the Peril. They glowed with an unhealthy bluish energy. Saleesa frowned. *They are far too familiar with the Peril.* It was all wrong. They should be like the others who hung back with the fear. She scratched heavily at her arm, skin crawling with unseen irritations.

Elder Lolo nudged Tema who then glanced across at her. Tema continued directing people as they manoeuvred the strangely flattened out canoe with its bamboo attachments down the beach. *When did he become so confident?* Saleesa wondered.

She continued to watch them, all eager, all admiring. Her blood drummed up the heat inside. Elder Lolo ran his hands along the bamboo as if he saw something else than the ugly and crude boat. *Elder Lolo is too involved, too keen for it to be successful,* she thought. He shouldn't have taken this role. It was her right. How dare they assume they could predict what she would do and say! Her stomach twisted around. They were all being so unreasonable. This sort of discord was why she couldn't heal. She stepped forward.

"I shall go."

Everyone turned to stare.

"What did you say?" said Elder Lolo.

"You should not be doing this. Obviously you support this... this activity. Some one neutral, with a clear mind, is needed."

"But you are not neutral, mother," Tema said, "You support the Maker over everything, over *all* others."

"That is my duty for the well being of all Savaku. It is why I must go with you."

"No," Tema said, "Please...mother, don't do this."

They carried her to the boat and she perched on a wooden stool, feet lightly touching the damp mat underneath. She clenched her tingling hands, wondering how she could change her mind. Everything moved and she could not centre herself. Ignoring the crowd and the accompanying canoes, she focused her eyes on the Maker. Its constancy calmed her. *Breathe. Breathe.* She shuddered as spray of salty water tingled against her skin.

Tema raised his eyebrows, asking if she was all right. She nodded slightly, not daring to move. Above her, the woven mat bulged with the wind and the boat increased speed, as if it too was flying over the water. The Peril's waves smashed its white anger against the reef. *They are so much louder out here*, she thought, *like they are crashing right inside my head.*

She wanted to curl up, hide from it, but she knew people were watching her from the shore. Tema was beaming. He dipped the paddle into the water, curving to the left and the boat moved in response. *He knows what he's doing*, she realised, *like he has done it many times before.* She wanted to question him but she feared the answer.

Saleesa turned back to the Maker, blinking as it looked like a giant thumb ready to squash them all. Her home suddenly seemed so small. Panic gripped her, catching in her throat, making it hard to breathe. *What have I done?* She had vowed never to get so close. She tottered on top of the seat, heart thundering.

"How long will it take? Where are we going?" She looked back to across the village, but it had disappeared into insignificance.

"Just around the lagoon—to Lonely Place and back."

Lonely Place! Saleesa struggled to think of which was a worse place to be. This shouldn't be happening to her. *The blood heat has made me mad.* She half-closed her eyes, not wanting to see, but as they drew closer she couldn't help but stretch herself up to take in a better view. Truly a forsaken place, she thought, distracted.

It was a piece of land, abandoned by the Maker. The Wild Peril clamoured almost all around it, trying to swallow the rocks and trees up. Saleesa could hear it roaring its claim. She held her nose. There was a reek about the place, like rotten eggs.

The boat slowed and rocked awkwardly as Tema fiddled with the mat. Saleesa panted, struggling for control. It was one thing to be travelling over the Peril but to be sitting right in the middle... *It's too close. It will get me.*

"Go back!" She yelled at Tema.

"The wind has escaped," he said, "I just need to move the mat so it can catch it again."

"Hurry," she said, "I can't be out here any more. Take me back. Now!" Her nails cut deep into her palms.

Two grey fins appeared.

"Beasts!" she yelled

"Don't worry. I have been out here many times. We are safe."

"Safe!" Saleesa grabbed him, "The fin demons are a sign. The Maker doesn't like this."

Tema scowled, pulling his hand away. "Why do you ruin everything? Why can't you let me be?"

Her heart squeezed as the lie fought for its freedom. "I'm sorry, Tema," she said holding it back, "I can't do this."

He jerked the ropes and the wooden stick. "Hold on."

The boat rocked sharply as Tema spun it around. A wave broke over the side and the Peril landed on her in a great splash. She shrieked and something reached inside her stomach and filled it with an intense yearning. The pull was too strong. She couldn't help it, Saleesa went into the Peril.

The grey beasts came, brushing by her. She screamed and the Peril poured inside her. She sank to the bottom.

Everything was strange—sounds were muffled—but the Peril was alive. Tiny fish flittered like flashes of sunlight, the sand wriggled with strange shapes. Shadows lurked at the edge of her vision. She had closed her mouth to stop the Peril, but now her chest began to burn. The light filtering through the heavy water began to fade and she was so tired of struggling, of keeping things inside. She closed her eyes.

Silver light glowed fiercely around her. Her hands sank into the white sand. As she pulled them out they became enormous, the tips of her fingers rising through the sand like huge stones, like mountains. A storm-swirl erupted from the vivid blue water cupped in her palms. Giant waves crashed against Saleesa's fingers.

A blue woman leapt out from it, hair like furious seaweed. She looked right at Saleesa with blue-black eyes, as her face twisted with contempt. *Liar,* she mouthed at Saleesa, *Liar... Liar.*

A grey beast broke through the woman's image, coming at Saleesa. It changed, darkening, teeth sharpening, ready to tear her apart. To tear her lie apart. Then she saw... not the face of a beast, but the face of her son.

Saleesa's throat burned as she coughed. She turned over and vomited again, a foul salty taste clung inside her mouth. Some one pressed wet ti leaves on her forehead. She jerked awake.

"What happened?"

"You fell into the Peril," said her friend, Lenka.

"But how did I get here?"

Lenka looked away. "Tema jumped in."

"Into the Peril!"

"Yes, but... but the Peril didn't harm him." Lenka frowned, lowering her voice. "He was like a *beast* moving, He pulled you to a nearby canoe."

"No," Saleesa whispered. "Where is he? I have to see him."

"He is fine. Do not worry about him. He will be dealt with at the meeting tomorrow."

"Dealt with?"

Lenka shrugged and Saleesa's world spun.

The lagoon's shore was littered with pieces of charred bamboo and ash. Strange emotions tumbled about inside her. Saleesa looked down at a bluish light now glowing above her stomach. Nausea burned her throat as her hand passed right through it. Her eyes kept flicking to people as she passed them. *Can anyone else see it?* No one spoke to her.

She turned away from the lagoon to stare up at the Maker, hoping for the familiar calm. *The Maker will help me. He will tell me what to do.* The blood heat simmered through her as she staggered up the path.

It was her special spot. She looked down from the ledge, onto the sprawling crowd of huts—brown dots invading the green. Leaning against the rock face, she closed her eyes. The Maker pressed cold on her back. All that came to her was the image of fingers and thumbs rising from the sand with the blue woman—liquid and restless in her hands.

No! She wouldn't think of that. Of what that might mean. And yet her eyes were drawn to the Wild Peril. Even up here she could hear it, booming out its accusation. *Liar... Liar... Liar.*

She watched, transfixed by its relentless movement, finding it unpredictable. She had thought that the Wild Peril was trying to reach out and seize Savaku, take her, but now she could see it also pulled away, moving off to... *Where?*

Saleesa's thoughts stilled and a truth came. Her hand gripped the hard ground next to her. She leapt up and screamed. The wind snatched up her rage and regret, whipping it around her. Then she turned and beat the rock with her fists.

The Meeting House loomed before her and she took her usual spot, turning slightly so she did not have to look at the Maker. She felt ill, panic twisting through her. *Liar... liar... liar* roared the Wild Peril as it continued to crash itself on the reef. Shut up, she cried. *I know I know.*

The solemn crowd parted briefly as Tema shuffled up to the Council. Saleesa stared at him, trying to catch his attention, but his eyes remained downcast. Elder Maniva, standing sure, presented his formidable bulk to the council. "It is a heavy day for Savaku. One of our own must be reckoned with. We all have seen Tema's blatant and continual disregard for the Maker's Law. In good faith we allowed him concessions. But no more. He almost killed his own mother, our elder and one of our spirit healers. He put us all in danger. Such behaviour is unacceptable. It is not the Savaku way." Elder Maniva shook his head, "As for him being able to survive inside the Peril... who knows what that has done to him, what dangers that will bring us. Tema must be made an example to any of those who harbour such subversive and disloyal ideas." His voice boomed out the last four words. "Tema must be banished."

Several people cried out. Saleesa closed her eyes. It was worse than she imagined. *Banished!* The crush on her chest exploded in agony.

"Tema," said another Elder, "Do you have anything to say in defence of yourself?"

"No," he said quietly, "All Elder Maniva has said is true. I... I almost killed my mother. I have shown little respect for the Maker. The mysteries of the Peril tempt me. Maybe it is true and I have been possessed. It is fitting that you make this decision."

Saleesa watched as her son's head bowed low. Her hands went to her stomach, passing through the light still swirling above it. She remembered how he glowed while on the boat. Now she could sense a gaping blackness inside him. Something inside her broke and suddenly she understood. *No, he is hollow!* Her head jolted over the crowd as realization struck. *There are others! The girl, Peni! Sickly Sami! Not black but hollow.* And she knew why. The knowledge struck deep inside her like a sharp stick. She rubbed her chest, crying out—the pain, vicious, as the truth began to tear its way free.

"Is something wrong Elder Saleesa? You wish to speak?" Elder Lolo asked her.

Saleesa pushed herself up to stand in front of them, her body fighting her intentions.

"Tema is not to blame. I am." She straightened her back, eyes fixed out towards the Wild Peril. "If you banish any one, it must be me."

The truth burst free, rushing out of her mouth like a steam spurt of fire and water.

"When I went up the Maker and received my Spirit vision, it was not he who claimed me. It was not the stones and trees that shattered me. I did not rebuild myself with the gifts of the Maker."

Saleesa paused, glancing across to Tema's fierce stare. Silence settled heavily through the crowd. She continued to force the words from her heart.

"For me, it was different. She claimed me, the Peril. The grey beasts came and ripped me apart—and I had to remake myself into a spirit healer with the seaweed, shells and coral. I did not want to be claimed by her. I hid from her and opened myself up to the Maker. But he could not see me."

"You lie!" Elder Lolo burst out, "You are the Maker's most faithful!"

"The Peril has damaged you somehow, filled you up with nonsense," said Elder Maniva.

"The Peril is a god too." Saleesa eyes bulged at what she had said out loud and yet she had more to tell them. "When I fell into the Peril, I was sent a vision. The Maker is but a thumb in a great hand. There are more lands, like fingers, coming out from the Peril."

Hisses and outraged gasps exploded across the space.

"That is not all," Saleesa's mouth was so dry the words seemed to tear themselves from her throat. "You should know that there are others here, who have also been claimed by the Peril. They walk lightly on the earth for they are hollow. They do not thrive here. Their spirits need to be filled by the energy of the Peril. This I say as a Spirit Elder."

Finally her words were finished. Her stomach heaved slightly, her head spun and she felt so light she thought she could float away. No one spoke but Saleesa could sense the dark red energy sparking through the Elders. *Almost finished*, she added to herself.

She faced her son before her courage faded. Tema turned from her, his expression cold like stone. She tried to steady herself as the grief of it sliced through her. It hurt beyond measure... more than the lie ever had.

"She defies the Maker!" spluttered Elder Maniva, "Banish her!"

"She fills the council, the people of Savaku... her own son with destructive lies," yelled another, "Banish her!"

Saleesa held her head high. Now she had stepped on this path, she would walk it to the end. She would not take the words back.

"For Savaku, I carried a lie within my heart. For Savaku I sacrificed all. Beware," she said, "The mysteries of the Peril will not be denied now you have been told. She will come for you."

The canoe arrived, carrying the few things Saleesa would be allowed to take—mats, some tools, a few clay vessels and the fire pot. A smile stuttered across her face. Of course, the most skilful person to take her to the place of banishment was Tema. *One last chance to make some amends, make him understand*, she hoped. Elder Lolo accompanied them to make sure she was dispatched properly.

Tema would not meet her eyes. He paddled the canoe with deep angry strokes. She waited. *It must come from him.* They neared the Lonely Place. Grey stones greeted her, uncompromising and bleak in their own expulsion from the Maker. Saleesa's resolve wavered. They were going to leave her in this terrible place. She would be left to die here alone and unloved. *I can't do it*, she thought, *I can't bear to be alone in this place... not without his understanding.*

"Tema," she pleaded.

He still would not look at her as he pulled up the oar. "All my life I have struggled with this feeling of being wrong, of wanting to help people and solve the mysteries of the Peril," he spat out, his voice low and hoarse. "All my life you have chastised me for not looking to the Maker."

"You are right to be angry with me. But you must understand why. Please. It has always been that Savaku follow the Maker. They do not understand the pull of the Peril. I did not understand it. I hid the truth to do my duty as spirit healer, as Elder. Discontent, division—it is not the Savaku way."

"Yes, your *duty*." he nodded, his body rigid. "I know all about that. So what of your duty now... spirit elder?"

"Aah," she said softly, "This time I did my duty as a mother."

He looked at her then, hurt tearing across his eyes, his face. "But you are banished now!"

Saleesa's heart clenched at his pain. "I deserve such a punishment," she said, "You do not. You are needed by those that... think like you."

"What can *I* do?" Tema's voice grew rough, "No one will listen to me. The Elders won't let me try anything again. I might as well be banished too."

Saleesa glanced at Elder Lolo who was looking away from them, pretending not to listen. "Those with the yearning for the Peril will come to you now. Help them. Your boat is very *important*." She wanted to tell him so much more. "*Teach them*," she mouthed.

"That's enough," said Elder Lolo. "Time to leave."

"But we can't just leave her here... look at this place!"

"You must," said Saleesa, "The Peril will send you help. The day will arrive when things may change. Then we shall see." A look of understanding crossed between mother and son.

The unnatural storm blew fierce for days, blasting Saleesa as she huddled in the small cave, nurturing the fire coals they had given her with coconut husks. What had she done? How could she live like this? She sobbed at all that she had lost while outside the Wild Peril, danced and cavorted with the wind.

Finally a day dawned clear. The stone Saleesa sat on was sun warm and smooth. Her feet dangled over, occasionally wet by spray as the waves splashed against the rocks. Solitude, not loneliness sat with her.

She was thankful. The wind had spared the few coconut trees in the small cove. The birds returned to their nests. And she was thankful for more. Truth hung in the air—fine but gritty. It settled. Cheeks became smooth as it grated against the skin like a layer of sand. Black dust. *Not from Savaku*. She felt it rasp between her fingers and wondered what a place with soil like that would look like.

She jumped from the rock, into the Peril, feet sinking into the soft sand. A flush came to burn away the last of her mother blood. *Signs of the change.* Saleesa's heart raced as she considered... *and not just for her.*

Saleesa sat down allowing the Peril to against swirl around her stomach. The blue light above her stomach shimmered and stretched into a light tether that extended from her, deep into the Peril. She gasped as a rush of energy tingled through her body.

Knowingly she looked up at the Maker and summoned the vision. Holding her hand out in imitation she cupped the water— her thumb and fingers breaking through. This time she watched the shadows formed by the late morning sun run across her hand and fingers, impressing it into her heart and memory.

afterword

This story began with the image of gritty, dry skin as part of the beginning symptoms of menopause. I think this is a time when some women revisit who they have become and reflect on who they want to be. They remember aspects of themselves they might have hidden away or discarded. Sometimes people put themselves into boxes that don't fit. Or are put into them.

Trassi Udang

Patty Jansen

LIKE ANY FIFTEEN-year old boy, Ari Suleiman Rudiyanto thought he knew everything: how to fool a food dispenser into spitting out double rations, where to get alcohol when under-age and how to get into the docks.

The latter was easy, really. He'd stood at a techno's back while the man punched the code into the door's keypad and he remembered the sequence for later use. Of course Ari told no one else; that would be stupid, giving away secrets without a trade, and no one had offered him a trade valuable enough.

That was why he always came here alone, to this dingy and oil-stained part of Ring 2, Section C. Not smart, and with smugglers and filchers about, not safe at all, and something his grandma would sure clobber him over the head for, if she knew, which she didn't.

One quick look over his shoulder—no one in the grey metal corridor—and he keyed in the numbers.

Click—hiss. The door slid aside in a silent whisper and Ari slipped into the large space beyond. The air bit into his face, empty and cold, sterile with white efficiency, whining tools and snaking hoses and the controlled shouts of techno-crew at work. So unlike the warren that was his home.

He peered at the dockside walkways, past the grey shapes of several transport vessels, past the bundles of feeder cables leading from dockside to the ships, to the openings of offices and storage rooms. Even there, the organised purpose of unloading crew and the meetings between pilots and dockside technos spelled order. And order meant orders, funnily enough, and that meant some Tier 1 person giving them, an Enforcer perhaps.

Ari already had more run-ins with Enforcers than there were stamps on his education report, been sent to scrub the recycling station floor for more times than he cared to remember. Today, he didn't see any green uniforms, so he crossed the floor between two ships and clambered up the walkway.

The *New Moon* was in dock number four, hooked up to feeder leads, grey, worn with scratches, the Pilot's Association's emblem on the nose. A line of brown-skinned Tier 2 workers shuffled up and down the gangplank, one after the other, empty-handed on the way up, carrying blue plastic-wrapped boxes on the way down. They moved across the docks like orange-clad ghosts, padding feet on the metal floor, disappearing in the gravity-curve of the outer ring. Just look at them go. Did they ever want to do anything else, or had boredom sucked their wishes dry?

Ari schooled his face into a sullen look and slipped into the shuffling line, up the *New Moon*'s gangplank, just one more orange-clad drone joining the pack.

He was about halfway up when he noticed the ship in the next dock, much larger than the *New Moon*. Servicemen in blue uniforms lined the gangplank, guns slung over their shoulders. Everything about the ship spoke in thinly-veiled threats, its white surface, its batteries of arms, its gold-and-blue emblem, which Ari had never seen.

He shuffled closer to the man in front of him. "Who are they?"

"Hush—don't look. They're International Space Force."

International Space Force? A war unit? This was a mining station, far away from the front line of a war Ari didn't understand. The only military vessels that came here were supply ships. "What are they doing here?"

The man shrugged. "Just don't look. They like young boys."

Ari didn't need to have that warning explained, but he looked anyway. The servicemen followed him with their hard, blue gazes, their faces eerily similar, much more so than the station's Tier 1.

Constructs, artificial people. Clones. White, tall, god-like creatures with names like Robertson, Kessler and Landau. These men had been made for war.

Lee Jin was standing at the entrance to the cargo hold watching the line of workers unload his ship. He wore his usual sleeveless vest in defiance of station rules which said that everyone in dock must cover bare skin. He spent most of his days of space-bound loneliness in his on-board gym, and had muscles to show for it, bulging at the dragon tattoos on his upper arms. Ari liked the tattoos, but when he said to grandma he wanted one, she had clobbered him on the ear. Apparently good men should like tattoos just as little as they should like boys.

As soon as Lee Jin's eyes met Ari's, he flicked a glance into the passage behind him, a familiar gesture that said *I got it*. Ari slipped after him into his office, where the air smelled of things alive, of soil and flowers and real food, of the Earth he would never know.

"Not much time to talk today." Lee Jin pulled the package from the drawer, thudded it onto the table with a slap of its plastic-wrapped exterior. His hazel eyes were full of unspoken words, words that would clash with his Pilot's Association uniform.

Ari groped for the card in his pocket, passed it across the table. Lee Jin slid it into the reader, punched ten thousand credits, gave it back to Ari without a flick of his eyebrows.

Ari slipped the package under his overalls, where it sat, warm and comfortable.

"The ship out there, International Space Force, do you know what they're doing here?"

Lee Jin gave him a sharp glance, an oh-so-brief stiffening of his muscles. "No."

"Really? I don't believe that. You can tell me. I'm not going to tell anyone. You know me."

"I know you too well, Ari. You're too curious. These are war troops. You can't play with them like you do with Enforcers."

Heat crept into Ari's cheeks. "I don't play with Enforcers."

"No. You run rings around them. Come on, Ari. It's a game, for both of you. Just to keep everyone busy talking about something else while ISF weeds out the last of the independence rebellion."

"What independence rebellion?"

"Forget I said that." Lee Jin shook his head. "See it like this: if your Enforcers are annoying bees, these men are angry hornets. Leave them alone, Ari."

Ari didn't like Lee Jin's tone and was sure there were things he wasn't saying, things left out, things Lee Jin didn't think appropriate for a fifteen-year-old Tier 2 worker's son, but Ari let it be. After all, when Tier 1 was involved, ignorance was as good a weapon as any of the illegal knives he kept under his clothes. And what should he care, really? War, independence, whatever, it had nothing to do with him. Whoever ruled, Tier 2 were slaves. End of story.

He snuck out of Lee Jin's office into the cargo hold—deserted. The gangplank was empty, too. Yet there were still some boxes left, stacked against the far wall. Where was everyone? Why hadn't they finished unloading?

In the middle of the floor lay a comm unit such as dockside workers used. They would hold these devices over the labels on the freight, and then Tier 1 would know that the worker had done the right job. Ari picked it up and shoved it in his pocket. Dockside workers lost at least a thousand credits when their units went missing. He'd ask in the nightclub who the owner was. Tier 2 people stuck up for each other.

The sound of voices drifted into the open door of the cargo hold.

There was a disturbance on the dockside, right outside the ship. Two ISF soldiers had one of the station crew pushed against the wall, his arms pulled behind his back. A third soldier poked the end of a gun into the side of the man's neck. He jerked and shouted, his eyes wide with fear. A green uniform: an Enforcer.

Ari met the man's sky-blue eyes, brief and intense, gaunt and frightened. He wasn't all that old, perhaps only a few years older than Ari. His lip had split and an ugly bruise grew on his cheekbone.

Ari ducked back into the cargo hold, his heart thudding.

Enforcers would treat him like that if he was caught in a place where he shouldn't be. There was something satisfactory, weird, perverted about this. But it gave him no pleasure.

Three men against a boy—the cowards. And then their faces— hard and without emotion. Even when the Enforcers caught him and told him off, and sent him to clean the floor, their faces were stern, not mean. They never pointed guns at him.

"Boy, come out!"

Ari gasped. They'd seen him. What to do? Grandma always told him, *If the boss wants something, you give it to him, if you want to live.*

He hated that. He wasn't going to crawl on his knees for Tier 1 clones, but there was nowhere to hide. He could run into the corridor, but the soldiers might shoot and damage the ship that was Lee Jin's livelihood.

There *was* no option.

Ari shuffled forward, meeting an ISF soldier who came bounding up the gangplank, his hand on his gun. "Why are you still here? Don't you understand orders?"

Orders. Drones. All the others had been told to leave.

He stammered, "I... I was talking to the pilot. I didn't hear..." Lame excuses. Drones did not talk to pilots.

"I said: everyone out. Off with you." The voice quivered with threats.

As fast as he dared, Ari scuttled down the gangplank, trying not to run, trying not to think of the package in his pocket. If they'd discover that he'd really be in for it.

On the dockside walkway, the young Enforcer sat on the floor among four ISF soldiers, wiping blood from his face. He met Ari's eyes with his clear blue ones, his jaw set. Ari squirmed inside. The young man's lips moved, but Ari didn't catch what he said. His name patch said Tash. There was blood on his uniform. Ari wanted to do something, anything, but he didn't know what. And doing something would be really stupid, besides, no matter how the young Enforcer's eyes pleaded. An Enforcer, for crying out loud. A Tier 2 boy did *not* help Enforcers.

But it was unfair. But he was only young. But he looked so... helpless.

His legs shaking, Ari walked to the end of the dockside walkway, jumped off onto the floor and ran to the dock maintenance exit.

Out of here.

He keyed the numbers with a sweat-slicked hand. The door opened; he slipped through, into the grey corridor, but where the air was warm and stank of people. Back in the embrace of the chaos, the smells and noise of the residential section. He slipped into the crowd, the network of curved tunnels, thoroughfares once wide but now narrow with makeshift furniture, barber stalls, fortune tellers, food stalls and laundry. There was talk and laughter and the soothing gamelan music drifting from somewhere in the network of corridors. Here, all the people were small, lithe and brown and apart from that orange uniform, for which he was too young, he didn't stand out.

Still, it was hard, trying to dispel the fear; it was hard to forget those guns, the blood and the look in those frightened eyes.

Tash.

Live, Tash. Beat them. Don't give them what they want.

No. It was better if he forgot. It was none of his business. None at all. He had what he had come for. Enforcers could look after themselves.

First he went home to ditch the overalls, because he couldn't let his grandma see him in those.

The unit he shared with his grandma, parents and sister was lifeless except for the projection screen. Sunlight blazed on the outer skin of the station. Slightly smaller and a handful of millions of years younger than Earth's sun, the star went by the code LS-3856. Tier 2 people called it Saravati, after the Javan goddess of the sky.

Similarly, the official name of the station that orbited its sole gas giant planet was Aurora, but everyone in Tier 2 knew it as New Jakarta. Every couple of days it would spew forth a flotilla of harvesting craft, which attacked the planet's outer ring without making a visible impression on it, the station's workers harvesting ice to be picked up by carriers. There were a few more stations like that, circling the gas giant like moons—New Hyderabad, New Mumbai and New Calcutta.

One day, a long and boring six years of his life away, he would be old enough to board a harvester and go out there to those blue rings, and then he would stuff himself into a vacuum suit and would float out there, attached to the ship only by a few hoses, armed with a cutter and grappling hooks, and he would taste freedom, until someone reminded him that he needed to harvest his daily quota.

He was a drone after all.

Then he would do that for the rest of his life, and there would be no more time for sneaking onto the docks and meeting Lee Jin.

As Ari peeled off the overalls, something fell out and bounced over the floor—the comm unit, which he had forgotten. He picked it up, sat down on his bed and turned it on.

It beeped. A message came up on the screen.

Where are you? There was no sender.

Strange—this was not the same type of unit the dockside workers used.

Ari flicked through the screens. No ID number, just messages about meetings with people he didn't know and groups he didn't know. *Independence Party* came up several times. There were messages about rooms in the station and what was in them, weapon stores, and a map of the entire station, including the service tunnels. Ari could definitely see some good use for that. He could sell the maps to the boys who skimmed the central kitchens.

He put the unit in his drawer, flung the overalls in the cupboard and put on his regular clothes—shirt, sarong and sandals, and a jacket with pockets. His plastic-wrapped package went in there.

The tiny restaurant run by his uncle took up all of a standard family room and fitted a mere six tables. Customers sat back-to-back, with barely enough space to squeeze between them. During night-shift, his uncle moved those tables into the thoroughfare outside the door, and piled up the chairs, so the family had room to sleep.

Right now, his uncle was in the tiny kitchen, cubing proteinall, a meat-replacement from Station Supply. A gro-lamp strung up with wires and tape on the ceiling shone down on a couple of hanging pots. Snaking wires—tapped electricity—coiled from a jagged hole in the ceiling to power the—illegal—stove.

Grandma sat at the table peeling eggs. Where his uncle kept the chickens, Ari never asked, but he was guessing someone had stolen them from Station Supplies and that they lived in the maintenance tunnels.

Uncle and grandma were talking, but fell silent when Ari came in the doorway. Both looked at him in an expectant sort of way.

"I got it," Ari said, to no one in particular.

His uncle grinned. "Good boy."

Ari warmed at that compliment. Sometimes he wished his uncle and his father would swap places. Whenever his father came home, he was always tired.

Ari shimmied past his uncle into the pantry, where he took the skin-warmed parcel from under his jacket and cut the wrapping with one of his uncle's huge knives.

About two dozen wrapped packets cascaded onto the shelf. The pungent fishy scent wafted into the pantry. Trassi udang, shrimp paste.

He couldn't say it smelled nice, but it carried a hint of the fragrant dishes grandma would call *home*. When she said this, she would stare into the distance, her unseeing eyes registering images of a world far away, the real Jakarta, the capital of a country called Indonesia, on Earth. As sixteen-year old, it had been her job to look after ten babies during the long flight, babies sold by their parents into the space colonisation program. She had no choice in going; her parents had been too poor to keep her, let alone marry her off well. A man on the space program would take her for free. She had been ripped from her world.

Every day, she carried the wounds with her. Ari couldn't see them, but they bled when she didn't speak and when her eyes went misty like this. Ari never knew what to say, because he had never known anything other than these corridors of metal, but he understood that home was a place to long for. A place to which they were not free to return.

He set aside two silver-wrapped packets, his uncle's share, and slipped them between the packs of shredded coconut and plastic bags of krupuk, hard, pink and translucent. Both those items bore blue quarantine stickers. His little treasures, of course, did not. They were raw materials, not dried, cooked or fried to death. Notifiable to Station Control. Punishable under Quarantine Law. Not allowed on-station.

He tucked the rest of the contraband back in his jacket and shut the door to the bathroom-turned-pantry.

With his carrot-juice-stained hand—carrots also came from the maintenance tunnels—his uncle swiped two thousand credits onto Ari's card while two little boys, Ari's cousins both, looked on with wide eyes.

"Wow, Ari has enough credits to get himself a real good girl," the oldest said, aquiver with importance.

"Hush with your nonsense." Grandma held up a half-peeled egg as if she was going to throw it. "Wherever do you hear such talk? Good girls don't cost nothing."

"Then why don't Ari have one already?"

"You ask him that question."

A sideways glance, an accusing look. No, he had no girlfriends to report. Girls made him nervous. Why couldn't she talk about something else?

"Uncle." Ari wished grandma would stop looking at him as if there was something *wrong* with him. He leaned against the doorpost, knowing he should go and sell the rest of the trassi, but his young mind churned.

"Yes, Ari, what is it?" His uncle's voice had that and-now-we-talk-about-the-facts-of-life tone. He wasn't going to follow grandma's lead and bother him about the lack of girlfriends, was he? Tell him about What To Do and other stuff?

"Uncle—what's the Independence Party?"

"Independence of what?" Too quick, too sharp.

Ari shrugged, feigning carelessness. Politics passed him by. He didn't really want to tell his uncle of the comm unit he'd found. "Is there an Independence Party?"

His uncle came to stand close, with a waft of sweat. His black eyes were intense. "The day we're free to run our own station would be the day of independence."

Ari retreated from his uncle's garlic-breath, backing into the table; his grandma muttered to watch where he put his big feet, but Ari stared at his uncle. This was not the answer he had expected. "You mean..." His uncle was part of this independence party?

"What I mean is that if Earth thinks it can control who visits and who lives where, and send in ISF soldiers to keep us under control, they're in for a surprise."

"So..."

Ari had always considered the station's Tier 1 as his enemy. Enforcers. What had Lee Jin said? *Just to keep everyone busy talking about something else while ISF weeds out the last of the independence rebellion.* "Who are these people in the Independence Party?"

His uncle shook his head. "I'm not going to say more. You're too young to get involved. It's dangerous. Your father would kill me."

And his uncle returned to his cooking.

When Ari left through the smoky main room, his uncle was shouting at his cousins to put on the board that gado gado was back on the menu tonight. Customers cheered. It must have been that sort of week, when contraband ran out, when controls tightened and people were forced to eat the stuff from the Station Supply kitchens.

He fended off the old woman who always sat outside his uncle's restaurant wanting to read fortunes. Ari already knew what path his future would take. He was Tier 2, a drone. His path was mapped out, wasn't it?

He was about to step into the next tiny restaurant when someone whistled hard ahead in the corridor. It was the signal. Enforcers coming.

He froze. Enforcers didn't come unless they were looking for something—and that something was usually contraband goods. Already, he could see a knot of people in green on the upward horizon.

Ari bolted into the nearest door, the recycling station, yanked the package from under his jacket and slipped it in the clothes chute. He would come back later. Tonight, before the chute was emptied. Unfortunately, he was all-too-familiar with recycling procedures.

On the night-shift many of the lights in the main thoroughfare were turned off. To save power, they said. To mimic day and night like on Earth, they said. Whatever, it suited him.

Ari slipped through the semidarkness, a lone figure in a world of shadows. Close to the recycling station, the air smelled of refuse. It wasn't meant to be that way, but the machines often broke down, or ran poorly.

He pushed open the door... noticed movement, and just managed to stop.

Someone was already in the room. Soft voices drifted from the entrance to the compacting room. He ducked behind one of the machines just in time, as one of the figures, a woman, came out of the compartment. A green uniform. Enforcers.

She asked, "Are you sure he went in here?"

"Yes. I saw him."

Ari's heart thudded in his throat. Did he hear that right—were they looking for him? For the smuggled wares?

The woman went back into the compacter room; there was a clang of a panel being opened, the hiss of an avalanche of cut-up rubbish sliding out. The man swore.

Good. They were looking in the wrong place.

As quietly as he could, Ari crawled behind the first bank of machines, slipped his hand into the clothing chute, grabbed the package and ran.

Out of the room, into the corridor... into a wall of armour. ISF soldiers.

He reeled back with the force of the collision, too stunned to react, or run away. Four of them, all at least a head taller than Ari, and twice the width. Three men and a woman. They laughed, and spoke to each other in Universal Standard.

The closest soldier grabbed Ari's shoulders, and said in halting Bahasa Indonesian, "I think you like to have chat with us." It sounded strange coming from the mouth of a white man.

Ari said nothing. He didn't want to chat with them. The package burned in his pocket and now he wished he'd left it in its hiding place.

The men dragged him through the deserted corridors. He could protest of course, but knowing the Tier 2 ring as he did, he knew that no one would come out at his shouts. Tier 2 people might stick up for each other, but they knew a hopeless situation when they saw one and right now his situation was pretty hopeless.

The men sat Ari down on a chair in an empty office. There was only a table in the room, and the woman sat on it, giving him a penetrating look with those blue eyes.

"Why were you with the pilot of the *New Moon*?"

"I... he's a friend of mine."

Golden eyebrows flicked. Tier 2 people didn't make friends with pilots. They stayed neatly in their quarters and did as they were told.

There was really nothing for it. He would be searched anyway and they would find the trassi. Better to give it up voluntarily and escape the worst punishment.

He gasped for breath. "I can explain." Slowly, he took out the package out of his pocket and put it on the table.

The officer in charge frowned, picked it up, unwrapped the plastic, recoiled. "Urgh, what's this? It stinks."

"It's..." Ari's throat seized up, as he realised how dull and boring his life would be. No more money, no more visits to the docks.

"Something dead?"

"It's..." Ari tried again.

"I don't care what it is. What I'm interested in is this: back there, on the docks, you picked up something that wasn't yours."

Ari opened his mouth to protest that he hadn't picked up anything and he didn't steal, least of all from ISF soldiers, but remembered: the comm unit. And now he realised: it belonged to the young Enforcer who had dropped it or flung it—he had been sending around messages of rebellion. And that brought another shock—Enforcers, planning a rebellion? Against whom? The man staring him in the face? Oh, this was way over his head.

He swallowed hard. "I... sold it."

Tash. What would they do to him when they found the unit? The maps, *weapons* stores.

The man repeated blankly, "You sold it."

"Yes. That's what we do with those things." It grated to say that. Ari had never sold anything he knew belonged to anyone except the station. He pilfered Station Stores, but he didn't steal personal possessions.

"And who has it now?"

He shrugged, trying to look careless. "A man bought it in the nightclub. I don't know who it was." Then he got bolder and added, "Why is it so important? It's only a machine."

"It's not the machine that's important."

"Oh." He feigned a frown. "I cleaned it up of course."

"You—what?" The woman grabbed Ari by the front of his jacket.

"I could hardly sell it with all the previous owner's stuff on it."

The woman glanced at her fellows; they exchanged some words in Standard, which Ari didn't get. The she said, "You know that we can track the unit, wherever it is?"

She let go of Ari's jacket so that Ari slumped in the chair, smelling his own sweat. At least he was glad he had taken the unit out of his pocket. At the same time, he worried about Grandma. She would be asleep in the room where he had hidden the unit.

The woman's blue eyes met his squarely. "Look boy—I don't know what you've done that's against station rules, but it stinks and I don't care about things that smell like that. Get out of my sight."

She flung the package back into Ari's lap.

Clutching his treasure, he bolted out the door.

The lights in the nightclub danced over the young man's face and his hair, turning it alternately red, green or blue. His cheek was still bruised, but he looked better. Not wearing his green uniform, he didn't look like an Enforcer either.

"So... your name is Tash?"

He nodded. "You're Ari?"

Ari felt all-important and self-conscious. That most awful of feelings—a blush—crept into his cheeks. "Ari Suleiman Rudiyanto."

"That's a pretty big name for someone your size."

They both laughed, awkwardly. A girl danced past, wriggling her hips at Tash, soliciting business. Tash only looked at Ari, intense, piercing. Ari couldn't bear to meet his gaze any longer. He averted his eyes to the comm unit on the table.

"Anyway, here it is. Just make sure they don't find it again. She said they can track it."

Tash snorted. "They wish. You know they bluff. I know that you know. I can see it in your eyes."

Ari smiled, but looked down again. What was he thinking? That somehow this strange act of kindness towards an Enforcer would make his life exciting? That this man would really tell him about the Independence Party? He made to get up. "Look, I better—"

"No." Tash's hand closed on his. Warm, comforting, *not right*, but altogether not *wrong* either. His heart jumped. "You're not going anywhere."

"But my grandma—"

"Your grandma will be happy when she's allowed to visit Indonesia. That's what we're fighting for. Freedom."

"Freedom." *Visit Indonesia.* The words tasted strange on his tongue.

Another wordless look. Tash's thumb caressed the skin on the back of Ari's hand.

"It's alright, Ari."

Confused now. "My grandma says..."

But what grandma said wasn't really important. Get a good girl, get her pregnant as quickly and often as possible and raise more Tier 2 drones? What for?

"Really, Ari, it's alright. There are a lot of us in the Independence Party. Nobody cares."

Us, meaning boy-lovers. "Really?"

"Yes. You know you're such a dead give-away?"

"I am?" Wasn't there anything *wrong* with him after all?

"Yes. I saw it first time I laid eyes on you."

"Oh. I thought you were asking for help."

Tash laughed, a comforting sound. "I did. And you did help. Thank you."

The blush went all the way to Ari's ears. It was as if his heart had been unchained. The relief, the revelation. Now, it was up to him—what did his uncle tell him to do next on a date? "Uhm—do you want to go for dinner?"

"Good. Where? I'm guessing you don't eat at Station canteen."

"Have you tried their food?"

Tash grimaced. "Any other suggestions?"

"My uncle makes a mean gado gado."

"Would that be with or without illegal trassi?"

"Hey, what are you accusing my uncle of? Bad cooking?"

Tash rose and pulled up Ari by the hand he was still holding. "The gado gado sounds perfect."

afterword

Traditional SF tends to be western-oriented. People of non-western origin are slowly finding their way into SF, but only if they play by western rules. Traditionally the domain of high-tech, space-based SF has little room for the poor and disenfranchised of the third world.

In the future portrayed in this story, western governments have sought to deal with overcrowding and poverty in third world cities by 'offering' the poor places as space colonists.

Like the Greek and Italian migrants arriving in Australia after World War II, these people have brought their culture and their conflicts, both of which are poorly-understood by the artificial humans appointed to look after them.

"Trassi Udang" is the first story I wrote in this universe. Other stories in this world deal with tension between natural and artificial humans ("Luminescence", to be published in Martian Wave*) and the ethics of creating artificial soldiers ("Charlotte's Army" — novella, to be published in* Distant Worlds *anthology).*

Deeper than Flesh and Closer

Carol Ryles

THE SHUTTLE HAD come down hard, burning a hole in the Rhizome. Although the ground was scorched and smoking, regenerated vines were already snaking their way into the fuselage. Another day and the craft would be eaten. Untraceable.

Bevan had not been this close to the enemy since the war. He skirted the shuttle's perimeter, checking for weapons. When he was sure there were none, he smashed its surveillance nodes and climbed into the cockpit.

The pilot was a woman. Alive.

She was strapped in the flight seat and out cold. Blood from a gash in her forehead dripped languidly over her flight suit, puddled at her feet. Without checking to see if she was armed, Bevan pressed his fingers over her carotid. Her skin felt cool, unresponsive. He moved his fingers to her scalp and tried to commune.

Not a hint of emotion. Only a pulse, beating faintly.

Years ago, Bevan would have saved life first, asked questions later. That's all they had time for during the war. Even that hadn't been enough...

But the woman wasn't a Glyr defending Glyrrish territory. She was an Oldener trying to take it.

He turned away. She wasn't his responsibility. She should have bailed out when she had the chance.

Remembering what had brought him here, he knelt down and rummaged under the seat. The medical kit was right where it should be. He pulled it out, tipped it upside down.

Bandages, slings, dressings, skinstats, haemostats, pills and lotions clattered to the floor. "No needles? Damn."

He picked up the haemostats. They were good quality—Olden manufacture. During the war, he'd seen Glyrren dying from the lack of a haemostat...

...dying like the Oldener beside him.

He swallowed. Was he a healer? Or a judge?

Of course, not all Oldeners were enemies, he reminded himself. This one wasn't even carrying a gun.

He eased a haemostat into the gash at her forehead. A fragment of bone shifted beneath his fingers. Wincing, he pulled away.

Up close, he could see she was around his age: early to mid twenties, maybe? Shattered glass and rubble covered her legs. Carefully, he brushed it away. He hissed through his teeth. Her right leg was jammed between the seat and the console. Splintered bone jutted out through a tear in her trouser leg. If he wanted to save her, he'd have to commit fully.

Then what? Tell her she couldn't go back?

Glyrren had been shot for doing less. Even so, he couldn't watch her die.

He covered the fracture with a clean dressing, making sure the skinstat congealed firmly at the edges. Then he rifled through her pockets.

Her ID confirmed her as Elena Jacques, but nothing else. A good sign. In her chest pocket, he found a camera, flipped it open. The air in front of it lit up with a miniature holopic of a woman standing in an Oldener city.

It was her. The pilot. He could tell by the slant of her eyebrows, her bobbed, black hair and the sharp angle of her nose. Quickly he scrolled through the rest of the pics. Jacques standing beside a shuttle with Glyrrish villagers, Jacques talking to Oldeners, Jacques standing in a wooded patch of Rhizome drinking sap from a bubwood tree...

Confused, Bevan frowned. Oldeners hated the Rhizome, so why would she stoop to drink from it? He flipped the camera closed, pocketed it.

Outside, a horse nickered, followed by the squeak and rattle of an approaching cart.

Wilder.

Although Wilder was not fond of pulling rank, he nevertheless had limits. Bevan braced himself for trouble. Those limits, he knew, were about to be tested.

Wilder climbed into the cockpit and paused. He flicked his gaze to the dying pilot and over to Bevan again. He shrugged. "Not our fault."

"We can't just leave her," Bevan said.

"We can and we will."

Bevan held up the camera. "She drinks from the Rhizome."

"That doesn't mean she can't hurt us. Anyway, how are you going to heal her without a hospital?"

Bevan waited for Wilder to work it out for himself.

Wilder whistled incredulously. "Oh no. We're talking about an Oldener here."

"She's still human."

"That's debatable. She's a pilot, for hell's sake. I doubt she's innocent."

"Innocent until proven guilty."

Wilder spat into the blood at the pilot's feet. "You suppose an Oldener is going to thank you?"

"She drinks from the Rhizome," Bevan reminded him .

Wilder gave a grunt of disgust. He turned around, climbed out of the cockpit.

"Wait!" Bevan loped down after him. When he caught up, Wilder was already reaching into the cart.

He spun around to face Bevan, metal cutters in hand. "If we don't hurry, the Rhizome will eat our salvage."

"Wait," Bevan repeated.

Wilder glared.

Bevan lifted his fingers to Wilder's forehead, expecting him to flinch, but he didn't. Gradually, as Bevan communed, he felt his guardian's muscles relax. Wilder's emotions flooded into him: fear, anger, resentment, grief...

Bevan knew that Wilder would be thinking about the war and the first wave of Oldeners—how they'd destroyed entire villages to make way for their cities. The Rhizome they'd cleared had never recovered.

"Remember Udo?" Bevan asked.

Wilder managed a wry smile. "Udo is no longer an Oldener. He's one of us."

"He was an Oldener when he taught us how to heal."

"But this is protected territory," Wilder insisted. "Pilots trespass at their own risk."

"She crashed."

"Five hundred kilometres from the border?" Wilder's anger surged into Bevan's fingers, sharp and prickly. Bevan snatched up Wilder's hand, lifted it to his own forehead. He reminded Wilder how it used to feel during the war, when they watched Glyrren die for the want of treatment.

Wilder pulled away. "Fine," he snapped, "But if she causes trouble, I'll make it your duty to shove her back into the Rhizome and bury her till she chokes."

Bevan refused to flinch. "Gladly."

He returned to the cockpit. The woman would most likely die if he tried to move her. Better to leave her strapped in her seat, so he unbolted its base from the decking. Then he used metal cutters to open the fuselage. By the time the hole was large enough for the seat and its occupant to be lifted through, the Rhizome had sent dozens of vines questing into it. Bevan stroked them, whispering encouragement. Obligingly, they lengthened and followed his hands as he knotted them into a sling.

He severed the sling from its mother-branch and stroked it until it stopped twitching from shock. The Rhizome wouldn't miss it, so long as his destruction didn't continue.

When the sling was ready, he anchored it around Jacques's flight seat. Then he lowered it directly into the cart.

"We need to get her home...now," he said to Wilder.

Wilder grunted. "Salvage doesn't come this easily." He kept working on the fuselage, cutting out long, narrow strips. "Take a look behind. The Rhizome's eaten the tail already."

The back end of the shuttle where it had snapped in two was already a tangle of leafy green. "If you get off your arse and help," Wilder suggested. "We'll leave for home earlier."

Bevan cursed to himself, but helped anyway.

At sunset, when the cart was almost full, the woman seemed even closer to death. Bevan flung his metal cutters into the back of the cart. "She won't last the night. Not without treatment."

Wilder shrugged. "That's assuming there's treatment available for her."

"You know there is."

"Ha," Wilder spat. "You're not using yours."

"That's for me to decide."

Wilder threw down his metal cutters. "Whatever."

They sat next to each other at the front of the cart, travelling through the Rhizome in silence. The cart jittered and lurched as the horse picked its way over the rutted track. Now and then, when they passed beneath a break in the tree canopy, Bevan glanced upwards for signs of Oldener shuttles searching for Jacques. The sky remained silent above the thrum of the Rhizome, the stars unmoving.

They arrived at Bevan's cottage just as the village bell rang for first supper. They carried Jacques and her seat inside, where they unstrapped her and shifted her onto the spare mattress. Wilder stood back. "I'm supposing she won't be dangerous until at least tomorrow night, but I'll call a watcher if you like."

Bevan hefted the flight seat towards him. "I'll be fine."

Wilder carried the seat outside. "Are you coming for supper then?" "Later."

When Wilder was gone, Bevan knelt beside the pilot, pressed his fingers against her carotid, hoping for a sign that maybe she'd recover without a transfusion. Her pulse felt even weaker than before.

He went to the cupboard, pulled out a coil of tubing. His fluid bottle was full, donated to him only that morning by Wilder. He connected it up, hung it from its stand, selected a needle—one of his last sharp ones—and plugged it into Jacques's jugular vein. "Even an Oldener would prefer life over premature death," he muttered.

Working slowly, he set about cutting away her flight suit. He left her underwear in place and sponged her down as best he could, removing only the worst of the blood because her skin was pallid and cold. He covered her with a blanket and watched her breathe.

Her face was pretty, but fragile-looking within its frame of black hair. That was the trouble with Oldeners: they weren't strong. The transfusion would deal with that, its complement of nants replicating inside her, keeping her alive. By morning they would be well on the way to healing her, atom by atom, from the inside out.

He went to his bedroom, cleaned himself up and changed his clothes. Outside, a soft rain had started up, bringing with it the fertile smell of wet Rhizome. Bevan took a deep breath, trying to draw on its comfort, but with the Oldener present, it felt wrong. Shivering, he wrapped himself in a blanket and settled into a chair between the mattress and the front door. "Even if she doesn't thank me," he told himself. "At least she'll live."

Elena's head throbbed. She lifted a hand to her forehead and explored the wound. It was sore but not as sore as it should have been. She smiled. Luck had been on her side for once.

The air smelled wrong. Not burned up like the interior of her shuttle, but moist like compacted soil. She opened her eyes, winced at daylight slanting through a narrow, open window.

She was lying on a bed.

No...she was lying on a straw mattress on the floor, covered in one of those greasy blankets the Glyrren made out of their own hair. Beneath it, she was dressed in her underwear.

She levered herself up onto her elbows. The room was poky, Neolithic. She glanced around, taking in the rammed-earth walls, rush floor, crude fireplace.

Not far away, a Glyrrish man sat sprawled in a wooden armchair, sleeping.

"You!" she called out. "What space am I in?" Her Glyrrish was probably clumsy and arrogant, but it couldn't be helped. Most of what she knew was self-taught.

The Glyr ran a sleepy hand through tangled, russet hair.

"You. Stir up." she called.

Startled, he opened his eyes. They were glittery around the irises, the same russet brown as his hair.

"I'm in Glyrrish space, am I now?" she asked.

The Glyr seemed young, though it was difficult to tell with Glyrren. They all looked thirty or less, except for the dying. He unfolded himself from his chair and stepped cautiously towards her.

Lord he was tall! Lucky he seemed friendly.

"Your capacity to heal is astonishing," he said in Olden. "I would never have thought..."

Surprised by his fluency, Elena switched to Olden, keeping her voice soft, partly out of politeness and partly because the effort made her head throb all the more. "Am I in Glyrrish territory?"

"Yes. Five hundred kilometres past the border."

Five hundred kilometres? So far off course? She studied the Glyr. He looked concerned, afraid almost. "Your accent is perfect," she said.

He shrugged. "I grew up with Oldeners."

"What village is this?"

The Glyr eyed her up and down. "That would be like exposing a prized possession to a thief, wouldn't it?"

Elena sighed. Standard reply. "Is your name a secret as well?"

"Bevan," he said. "Bevan Shastara.

She held out her hand. "Elena Jacques."

He came forward hesitantly and placed his palm against hers. His skin felt hot and sweaty. He pulled away, stepped backwards.

"Relax," she said. "I'm not a soldier. I work for an anthropology team. I was returning to base for supplies when the stabilisers failed."

Bevan's lips tightened. "Why the surveillance nodes?"

"Oh those." She grimaced. "Second hand shuttle. I meant to get rid of them, but was hard pushed for time. For the record though, we were using the nodes to map village patterns. The anthros were looking at demographics and trying to connect them with local myths and legends."

"I see," he said.

Abashed, she looked away. She shouldn't have used the word *myth*. The anthros had told her that Glyrren got upset about that, which was fair enough. From what she'd heard, their collective memories were more accurate than anything Oldeners had written.

It occurred to her that, if she'd lain unconscious for days, the anthro guys would have probably organised a search party by now. Though she wasn't sure how they'd locate her. The Rhizome would have eaten the shuttle already. Her too, she supposed, if Bevan hadn't found her.

"Has anyone been looking for me?" she asked.

"No."

"You haven't heard anyone flying around?"

"No."

"Do you have a radio?"

"No." He seemed pleased about it.

Elena fought back a wave of irritation. "I need to get home."

"If the council decides you're worthy, then you'll be free to go."

"When?" She tried to sit up, then sagged back again as pain shot down her leg. She lifted the blanket, just enough to expose a dressing on her thigh. She peeled it away. Her stomach lurched at the sight of bone jutting above partially healed skin.

"You were dying when I found you," Bevan said. "I had to choose between leaving you and bringing you back."

"When was this?"

He hesitated. "Yesterday."

Shocked, she lifted her hand to her forehead and explored the scar more thoroughly. The bone beneath it felt tender, as if she'd smashed her head against a brick wall.

Her skin prickled. No wonder she was so damned alert. "You've infected me with nants, haven't you?"

"You were dying."

Sickened, she lay back on the mattress. She imagined the nants replicating inside her like bacteria, repairing her neurones even as she spoke. God almighty, they'd be rearranging her brain as if it were some out-of-date computer. Before she knew it, she'd be Glyrrish.

Bevan gave her a flat, measuring look. "It's only for a few weeks. Donated nants are dependent on the DNA of their donor. They'll work on a recipient's body for a week or two, then your immune system will take over and they'll degrade. When you've finished pissing them out, your body will return to what you call normal... unless of course I top you up with a new batch."

"Tell me," Elena said. "How many Oldeners have you transfused with nants?"

Bevan's cheeks reddened. "None."

"I thought so." This time she could not hold her temper. "Do you know that Olden immune systems don't see nants? We don't piss them out. That once given them, we're stuck with them."

His jaw dropped. "No...I didn't. No one told us." He sounded indignant. "I've only ever transfused Glyrren."

"You should have asked," she said.

He met her gaze, his face impassive. "I'm asking you now."

"What do you mean?"

"If it's death you want, it can still be arranged." He gestured to the door. "I can name at least one Glyr who'll willingly oblige."

She looked away. "I'm sorry."

"You could always get cleansed," he offered.

She rolled her eyes. "Yeah. Cleansed of nants and cleansed of my savings to pay the fines." Her head was pounding now, like it probably should be. She felt a perverse satisfaction that at least part of her was acting as God intended. Why the hell did it matter anyway? It was not as if she was *losing* control. She was merely riding it.

He stared at her, eyes narrowed.

She wanted to apologise, but could not stop herself from babbling. "Whose nants did you give me? Yours?" Her words felt detached, spilling out of their own accord. Nant talk, she decided. Part of her brain was probably still blacked out and the nants had found a connection to her long-term memory.

Her eyes felt waterlogged, sparked. "This is going to cost me my job, you realise. Bad enough that I lost a shuttle, but turning up full of nants... They'll crucify me." Nauseous now, she closed her eyes, willing herself to shut the hell up.

"So, your fate is worse than death. I should have left you to the Rhizome." Bevan's voice was at once gentle and uncompromising.

She sighed and opened her eyes again. He was standing with his arms folded, frowning. His eyes glittered darkly.

"Nants are against God's will," she said.

"They're not. There are *ten* commandments, not eleven."

Elena sighed. "For what it's worth, I voted against the forced cleansing programs. If it were up to me, I'd leave every last one of you alone, but not to the extent that I'd..." She paused, searching for the right words.

"You mean you wouldn't stoop to turning Glyr."

Elena winced. "I'm sorry. I'm having trouble thinking straight." No, that wasn't right. The problem was, she was thinking too straight and too quickly. Her head felt like it had been pulped, scrambled and poured back into her skull.

She closed her eyes.

"You're sweating," Bevan said. "It happened like that for me, when I first transfused."

"You transfuse yourself?"

"A legacy from being cleansed."

She took a deep breath, feeling guilty as if she were the one responsible. Bevan's fingers brushed her forehead. The sensation felt pleasant, like tasting him through the pores of his skin. She imagined his fingers coated in nectar.

Bevan pulled away.

Damn nants, Elena thought. What are they turning me into?

"Try to sleep," Bevan said.

Elena's mind raced. He said he'd been cleansed. Which meant he was an escapee—maybe a criminal. Surely not. His voice was pure, rolling over her consciousness like an ocean, soothing. She could no longer make out his words, but she didn't care. Her mind was too willingly adrift.

Bevan slipped off his shoes and left them on the landing. He stepped through the arched, stone doorway and into the council hall where the scent of moss, humus and candle wax enveloped him. Any other time, it would have made him feel welcome, but not today.

"Let's not be formal," a woman's voice said. It came from the end of the long, narrow hallway. Bevan forced himself to step towards it, over an earthen floor edged by flickering candles. It took him to a chamber with a squat altar. Beside it, an ancient dreamwood sent offshoots up and along the walls. Wiry roots hung down from the ceiling, a trailing curtain.

"Come," said another voice. It sounded like Merrid Taronil's. "We won't keep you long."

The counsellors sat cross-legged on a low pedestal in an alcove lined with moss. Both were draped in the deep-red robes of communion. Bevan knelt in front of them, head bowed.

"Relax healer." Merrid proffered his hand.

Bevan lifted his face, accepted Merrid's hand and held his own against it. Merrid's palm was strong, unwavering, his emotions an exquisite balance of opposites. He drew away from Bevan and nodded towards the woman. "Let me introduce you to Raikin Immera."

Bevan inclined his head respectfully. He'd not met Raikin before, but knew she was at least five hundred years old. Her pale eyes barely glittered. Motioning for Bevan to sit, she said, "Tell me, how is your Oldener?"

Bevan blinked and sat on the floor at the councillors' feet. He had expected reprimand, not interest. "She's healing remarkably well. It appears that nants work faster in Oldener bodies."

Raikin nodded. "Oldener bodies are like ours used to be five thousand years ago. They're empty vessels waiting to be filled." She paused. "It was a noble thing you did for the Oldener. Is she grateful?"

"She's grateful for being saved, but she despises the nants. She tells me they will not degrade. If she wants to be free of them, she'll have to be cleansed."

"A small inconvenience," Merrid observed.

Bevan sat with his hands resting on his knees, waiting for the councillors to continue. The musty scent of the dreamwood curled around him.

Silence spread out between them. Bevan wondered if this was a cue for him to leave. He was about to stand up when Raikin said, "You never speak of your past. And neither does your guardian, Wilder."

Bevan swallowed dryly. Don't ask, he thought. Not today.

"Start at the beginning," Raikin pursued. "Where were you born?"

"I was never told." Bevan looked at Merrid, willing him to ask Raikin to stop, but Merrid gestured for him to continue. Bevan swallowed again. "I was adopted as an infant by Oldeners and raised in New Hobart. They told me my real parents had died on the street." He paused, looked up. "I'm not so sure."

Raikin raised an eyebrow. "How so?"

"I used to believe everything my foster-parents told me. But when I look back, I realise their loyalties were with their cause, not with me."

Raikin gestured for him to continue.

"I liked the city. I wanted to be a perfect Oldener. At the same time, I was proud of being Glyrrish. My nants protected me from everything." His throat tightened. "Everything except Oldeners."

"Go on," Raikin prompted.

"At fourteen, they sent me away to be cleansed."

"How did it feel?"

"Every scratch, every discomfort, every hour, day, year reminded me that my life would be over in less than a century."

"Not time enough to understand your purpose even," Raikin acknowledged.

"After that, I left home. My foster sister, Georgia, kept in touch but, after I learned to make a living on the streets, she couldn't bring herself to see me. So I left the city and made my way into the Rhizome. Soldiers came after me, but Wilder found me first."

Bevan shuddered. He wanted to stop there, but Raikin nodded for him to continue. "I thought Wilder was a traitor. He aimed a gun at my head and held me down. I stared at the barrel, imploring it to shoot cleanly. The soldiers were closing in behind us, hacking through the Rhizome with knives."

Bevan forced himself to continue. "Wilder lowered his gun. *Sweet Rhizome*, he whispered. *You were stumbling through the undergrowth as if it were your enemy. I thought you were one of them.*

"I was nantless, as weak as an Oldener. So he carried me on his back, up to the canopy where we wove our way through the treetops, back to his camp. There, Udo Jeffries taught me how to look after myself, how to transfuse. When the war started, I worked with Wilder and Udo, transfusing cleansed Glyrren who'd been injured." A lump caught in his throat. Dreamwood clouded his senses. "There were too many of them, mostly women and children. So many we couldn't save...burned up by lasers...torn up by grenades and gunfire..."

Sinewy hands gripped his shoulders. "Bevan look at me," Raikin said.

Bevan felt as if he were being lifted out of a cold and unending horror. He looked up and saw Raikin and Merrid kneeling in front of him, their faces up close. They smelled of rain and Rhizome. Merrid's hands tightened on Bevan's shoulders. "Why did you save the Oldener?"

"Because...because I couldn't walk away. Because she made me remember the injured Glyrren. The ones who died.

"Is that all?"

Bevan nodded.

"Are you sure?

Of course he was sure. He closed his eyes, but it wasn't a Glyrrish face he imagined. It was the face of an Oldener.

"Who else did you remember?" Raikin demanded.

Bevan opened his eyes. "My foster sister, Georgia. She reminded me of Georgia."

"This is good," Merrid said. "You understand what it's like to be torn between two."

Bevan slumped as the councillors' calm acceptance flooded into him. He sat in silence, breathing deep and slow, forcing his memories of Oldeners back into the past where they belonged.

Merrid let go of Bevan's shoulders. "Are you interested in this Oldener?"

"Interested?"

"Do you miss your Oldener conversations? When you were young, it must have been hard not being able to commune. Even so, Oldener minds are intellectually fascinating. Do you miss that?"

Bevan nodded. "Their art is a means of communion for them. Looking at it is like touching a face that's no longer there. I miss it. And their poetry as well. It speaks differently than Glyrrish thought."

"Yes," Raikin agreed. "You belong to two peoples, yet you're forced to choose between them."

Raikin's words felt truer than Bevan cared to admit. He missed Olden writings. He'd enjoyed their songs too, especially the ones from Old Earth. He understood the Olden need to transform Earth into the world they remembered. Yet at the same time, he despised that need.

If only he could discard the horrors and retain the joys, but the two were as deeply entwined as hair and fleece in a Glyrrish blanket. One could not be pulled free without destroying the other.

"Tell me," Raikin said. "Apart from Oldeners' uncompromising ideals, what is their biggest failing?"

"They're lonely, but they like it that way."

Raikin drew her robes around her. "What would happen if they tried to commune?"

"They would hate us all the more."

Merrid put his hand on Bevan's shoulder. "You're as lonely as they are. Even Wilder doesn't understand how deeply you're connected to them. Remember: our childhoods are precious. We cannot discard them fully."

"I can't commune with her. I—"

"You can," Raikin interrupted. "If you're to reclaim your past, you'll need to share it with an Oldener."

Merrid let go of Bevan's shoulders. "I want you to show the Oldener your mind. Teach her to commune."

Bevan stood up, his stomach churning. "It's different for them. She won't understand."

"For both your sakes, she must."

"And if she doesn't?"

"She will not be permitted to leave. And you will not be permitted to stay."

The councillors lifted their ancient faces. Their eyes glittered.

Elena's stomach growled. She opened her eyes to daylight, sat up.

"Welcome back," Bevan said. He was sitting in his chair, looking like an overgrown street urchin. He tossed her a pile of clothes and turned around to face the window. "You can't stay under your blanket all day."

From the outside, Elena's leg appeared fully healed. She wriggled her toes. Everything felt as it should. Carefully, she slipped on a pair of trousers and then a fitted, woollen shirt. Both fastened at the front with tiny, wooden toggles.

Bevan turned back to her. "How are you feeling?"

"Better." She eased herself onto the edge of the mattress. When she tried to stand up, her muscles overreacted. She almost toppled over.

"Not so fast," Bevan said. "You need to take into account that the nants have made you stronger."

She tried again, this time not putting in so much effort. Her leg bore her weight easily. Testing it, she shifted from side to side. Her hips felt out of kilter.

"Your femur's still misaligned," Bevan said. "The nants have built up a callus around the fracture, but they're still working on straightening it up.

The thought made her squeamish. She felt like some kind of reptile growing a new limb. She took a few slow steps. Her leg began to ache as if she'd pulled a muscle, but not enough to stop her. "Sometimes even the devil works miracles," she muttered.

Bevan glared.

She cleared her throat. "Okay, I take it back. Your nants are a Godsend." She offered him a smile.

He watched her, his glittering eyes unfathomable.

She ran her hands down her shirt. Its weave was coarse, but exquisite like a complex sculpture. "Everything smells, feels and sounds...different." She'd heard about nants improving the senses, but hadn't realised it would feel so disgustingly pleasant.

"Nants are our connection to the Rhizome," Bevan offered.

Elena suppressed a shiver. The things were turning her Glyrrish. Thank God there were no mirrors here. She wasn't sure how she'd react to seeing her eyes speckled with glitter.

She took another turn of the room, testing her leg. When she reached the window, she looked out. Bevan's hut appeared to be on the village outskirts. Ahead of it, rammed-earth buildings sprawled along both sides of a narrow, cobbled street. The beginnings of the Rhizome proper rose up greenly behind them.

From this distance, its trees looked the same as real trees in Olden plantations around cities. But unlike real trees, its leaves and branches did not merely sway in the breeze, they thrummed to a pulse of their own. She wanted to run outside and immerse herself in the thick of it.

She gripped the windowsill, forced herself to think clearly. As Bevan had said, the nants must be connecting her to the Rhizome. Damn them. They were playing with her mind.

Bevan came over and stood beside her. Although he was head and shoulders above her, he didn't seem quite as intimidating as yesterday. "I can take you there, if you want," he said.

"Maybe later". The way these people worshipped the Rhizome frightened her. It was, after all, nothing but a construct—a world-wide weed.

Bevan handed her a plate of biscuits and a cup of tea. She ate and drank while still standing at the window. Food had never tasted so good.

The front door burst open. A Glyr—a man even taller than Bevan—strode into the room, his eyes fierce and glittering. Elena took a step backwards, but the Glyr ignored her and went straight to Bevan. He hugged him for much longer than politeness demanded.

Elena looked away, embarrassed. She knew that communion was not at all sexual, but it still confused her to see them pawing each other. She couldn't tell if they were friends or lovers.

When at last they were done, Bevan said, "Wilder, this is Elena. Elena, Wilder."

Wilder gave a curt nod. He settled himself into Bevan's armchair and rolled up his sleeve. His biceps were smooth and brown, pumped up like a wrestler's. He twitched his chin derisively towards Elena. "I'm supposing that, last night, you gave your nants to her." His Olden was halting, badly pronounced.

Bevan flushed. "I can wait for my next dose. I feel—"

Wilder cut him off. "It's been two weeks. You'll sicken." He glared at Elena, then back at Bevan.

"You can't bleed yourself two days in a row," Bevan said.

Wilder grunted. "That's for me to decide."

Face tense, Bevan went to a cupboard, pulled out a coil of tubing, unwound it onto Wilder's lap and connected it to a needle. He wrapped a tourniquet around Wilder's upper arm. "Thank you," he said.

Ignoring him, Wilder turned his glittering, amber eyes towards Elena. "I'm glad to see you're whole again. Tell me, how does it feel to flex your muscles?"

Elena managed a grin. She wondered if Wilder was here to test her. "It'll take some getting used to."

Bevan pushed a needle into the crook of Wilder's arm. Blood dribbled from the end of the tube into a jug wedged between Wilder's thighs.

As the jug filled, Bevan and Wilder chatted in Glyrrish. When Bevan pulled out the needle, Wilder stood up and poured himself a cup of tea.

Bevan decanted the blood into a series of metal cups. He sealed them and attached them to a primitive centrifuge. Carefully, he turned the handle. The cups spun out, whirring. "I'm harvesting nants," he said. "They weigh very little, so when the haemoglobin is separated from the plasma, they float to the top. Then I mix them with dreamwood sap so they won't switch off when I transfuse them into myself."

"Are there others like you who transfuse?" Elena asked.

"Not this close to the border."

Bevan scooped out layers of silver sludge from the centrifuge. He dropped it into a bottle of yellow fluid, capped it and connected it to the tube.

"So how do you sterilise your equipment?" Elena asked.

He regarded her with amused patience. "No need. Nants clean up for themselves."

"What I don't understand," Wilder interrupted. "Is why Oldeners are so against them. Why do they care?"

Not sure how to begin, Elena fiddled with the toggles on her shirtfront. "We've seen nants malfunction. My grandparents saw them swallow entire cities whole. If they did the same to Glyrren villages, *you'd* want to eliminate them, wouldn't you?"

Wilder eyed her askance. "But that was a long time ago. You'd think that, if nants were going to go bad, they would have by now."

"That's the problem with nanotech. It's unpredictable. And worse still, your people have forgotten how to control it."

"Is that so?" Wilder said testily. He finished his drink and went to Bevan. He swept the back of his hand down the side of Bevan's face. "Don't trust her." Then he took hold of Bevan's fingers, and pressed them to his own face.

Disturbed, Elena looked away. It wasn't so much the thought of seeing two men display affection for each other, even if that affection was sexual. Lord, her people weren't that backward. But Wilder was so much more dominant than Bevan. She wondered how much was choice on Bevan's part and how much was merely obligation.

Wilder must have noticed Elena's reaction, because he let go of Bevan and stood over her, his face menacing. "People who are afraid to commune cannot understand what it is like to be people," he said.

Elena wasn't sure what Wilder meant and was even less sure if now was the right time to ask. She looked up at him, not willing to look him in the eye, but not wanting to turn away either.

"I once tried to explain it to an Oldener," Wilder said. "A good man. A friend. But it was useless. He refused to feel."

Bevan spoke to Wilder sharply in Glyrrish. Then Wilder hugged him again, curling his hand around the back of Bevan's neck. When at last Wilder left, Bevan said, "You'll have to forgive him. He's my senior guardian. He worries."

"Your guardian? I thought..."

Bevan threw her a twisted smiled. His eyes seemed amused and annoyed all at once. "It's all right. I know what you thought."

Flustered, Elena looked away.

"You need to rest," Bevan said. "You won't feel a hundred percent for at least a week."

Elena settled onto her mattress while Bevan set up his transfusion equipment. He sat in the armchair and held her gaze, keeping his face emotionless even as he pushed the needle into the crook of his arm. Disturbed, Elena wanted to say something by way of apology, but was afraid it would sound like a platitude. She looked away.

When the transfusion was over, Bevin soaked the tubing in a bucket of water. "I'm going to the dining hall to fetch some food," he said.

When he was gone, Elena looked out the window to where Glyrrish women pushed a cart laden with vegetables. The Rhizome made an idyllic backdrop against their flawless, brown skins. It all looked healthy yet, beneath it, lay a technology so dangerous that only a fool would dare embrace it.

She curled up on the mattress, pulled the blanket over her head. Where before, its mixture of human and animal hair repulsed her, today if felt oddly calming.

When Bevan returned, she said, "Tell me, why do you weave human hair into your blankets?"

Bevan smiled. "You treat me like an equal, then ruin it with an insult."

"I don't understand."

"You acknowledge we're human. Most Oldeners don't. Yet our habits repulse you."

"I didn't mean to be rude." She sat up. Bevan handed her a plate of fruit. She took a bite of what looked to be pear, then almost dropped it in surprise. Lord, it wasn't just fruit. It was a three-course meal.

"The blankets," Bevan began. "Well, it's like this. Everyone owns at least one. Each blanket contains strands of hair from every villager, tufts of fleece from every goat that grazes the surrounding Rhizome. Our blankets remind us we're one."

Elena took another bite of pear. "Interesting."

"Is that all?"

"I'll tell you when I meet the other villagers. If I feel connected, I'll admit that the blanket works."

Bevan laughed. A lock of hair fell over his eyes, making them glitter all the more. "It's not just the blanket." He smiled. "It's the Rhizome as well. If only Oldeners would stop thinking of it as a disease."

Elena suppressed a sigh. "Look at it from my grandparents' point of view. They left Old Earth when they were children. They still remember it as it used to be, before it was tainted."

Bevan gave a harsh laugh. "Earth untainted? Oh please...it had been dying for centuries."

"Dying from nanotech, remember? Look, they knew Earth would turn into something like this. That's why they headed for the stars. Just their luck something went wrong. They didn't plan to go near-superluminal. They didn't ask to end up back at Earth, either. Imagine being thrust five thousand years forward through time and no going back." She was clenching her fists. She unclenched them, folded her arms. "Bevan, nanotech was a mistake. The Rhizome was an experiment gone wrong."

Bevan's mouth tightened.

"Look, I'm sorry," Elena said. "The nants...they've loosened my tongue."

Bevan shushed her. "Don't worry. I've heard it all before. I was brought up by Oldeners, remember?" He leaned forward over the windowsill. Light played across his russet hair where it fell to his shoulders. Elena wanted to go to him, reach out and touch it. She wondered if her nants were responsible for that too.

"I thought you were different," Bevan said accusingly.

"How so?"

"You drink from the Rhizome."

"How do you know that?"

"I found your camera."

She was about to ask for it back, but changed her mind.

"Did bubwood sap taint you?" Bevan pursued. "Did it turn you into a monster?"

"I only drank from it once. On a survival course."

"So, your camera lied."

"What?"

"In the holopic, you seemed happy." He looked over his shoulder, gave her that curious twisted smile of his. "Tell me. How much time did you spend with your anthro friends?"

Sheepishly, Elena smiled back. "A little less than two weeks." She squirmed, huddled into the blanket, surprised that its greasy smell comforted her.

When Elena slept, Bevan would go out, but never for long because he could not be sure who would call in. Hours became days. When the meal bell rang, he would walk down to the dining hall and pick up a platter. Usually, a village watcher would walk home with him, more out of curiosity than duty. It was not so much the oddity of seeing an Oldener, but the sheer delight of looking at the holopics in her camera.

Even Wilder couldn't keep away but, in typical Wilder fashion, he waited for a genuine excuse. "Here," he said, handing Bevan a small package. "Traders passed through this morning, on their way to Murless. I had to give them an entire strip of fuselage for this."

Bevan grinned. He guessed what was in the package before he opened it: needles. They were still in their original wrapping. "Unused? How?"

Wilder shrugged. "Who cares how? They probably fell out of the sky like your pilot."

"Thank you." Bevan tucked them into the cupboard with the tubing. They'd last him at least a year.

"How's it going, by the way?" Wilder asked. "Have you two communed yet?"

Bevan rolled his eyes. To prevent Wilder from following up with something equally blunt, he tossed him the camera. "Take a look at New Hobart. Before she wakes."

Wilder flicked through the holopics. "Is this where she lives?"

"Pretty much."

"You could have been neighbours."

"No, we're from different parts. My foster parents were administrators. Hers were underlings—historians."

"Historians? What need do Oldeners have for them? Everything they see is stored in one of these?" Wilder held up the camera, his finger on the tab. The holopics flashed past in a blur.

"It's more complicated than that."

"How so?"

"It just is."

Wilder frowned. "You should sleep more. Let the Oldener look after herself." He didn't wait for an answer, but instead enfolded Bevan in a bear hug. This time, the emotion Bevan sensed from him was different. There was less anger and more concern, submerged in a swirl of confusion. Wilder stood back. "The councillors had no right to force you into this."

"I forced myself when I brought her here."

Wilder hugged him again, this time pressing his forehead against Bevan's, sending him waves of spiky regret. "I'm sorry," he said. "I should have stopped you."

"You tried, remember?"

"If they send you away, they'll have to send me too."

Elena stirred, gave a little cough. Bevan pulled away from Wilder. His face grew hot.

"You're ashamed of me now?" Wilder asked, brusquely. "That's why you don't bring her into the dining hall, isn't it?"

"Of course not. She's worried that people won't want her there." Bevan reached out to commune, to show Wilder that he meant it, but Wilder stepped away.

Wilder looked at Elena sternly. "Your camera is not the only way to see things." He tossed it onto the mattress. Then slowly, with more pride than he had cause for, he made his way to the door and let himself out.

"What was that about?" Elena said. She sat up, her eyes puffy with sleep.

"He's worried. It's a long story."

"Not for my ears, I suppose?"

"Um...no."

Elena bit her lip and looked even more fragile than she had when she'd first woken up after the accident. If she were Glyrren, he would offer to commune so she could understand how Wilder felt. But that was a boundary he dare not cross with an Oldener, male or female. It would be like asking her to strip naked.

To stop himself from even thinking about communion, he answered her question. "Wilder is over a hundred years old. His birth-village was destroyed to make way for New Hobart. His family were herded into a cleansing depot and stripped of their nants. They died decades before they should have. Wilder survived because, before the cleansing, he escaped to find help. But he was only a child, and help was nowhere."

Elena huddled deeper into the blanket. She stared out the window, towards the Rhizome.

"But that was in the past," Bevan added. "We need to look to the future now. That's partly why I couldn't leave you in the shuttle."

Elena nodded with what Bevan hoped was understanding. "I heard what Wilder said about the dining hall," she said. "He's right. I should go."

Bevan smiled. "Good, we both need to get out for a change."

In the hours before supper, Elena sat quietly flicking through her holopics. Bevan kept out of her way and tidied up. Strands of her short, black hair had fallen everywhere, easily distinguishable from his. Instead of throwing them out, he hoarded them in his pocket. Then he took out a handful of goat's hair left over from the bales he'd sorted to sell to the spinners. He spent the rest of the afternoon plaiting it into a bracelet, threading it with Elena's hair and strands of his own. He slipped it onto his wrist and decided that, with the addition of a few wooden beads, it might look half decent.

He took Elena to the dining hall. She looked around, awestruck. "The furniture," she said. "The stonework looks centuries old, but beautiful. It will last for centuries more, won't it?"

"At least as long as the Rhizome. It was fashioned from it."

She ran a hand over a smooth-backed chair. "But it's stone."

"It looks like stone, because the furniture makers encouraged the Rhizome to grow that way."

"They cultivated it?"

"They talked to its nants using their hands. It takes years, for something like this, but with the right touch, you can get the Rhizome to make whatever you want."

Elena fell silent. She ate even less than usual. When people tried to speak to her in polite yet halting Olden, she answered them uneasily. The villagers sensed her reluctance so, in the end, they left her alone.

"Do you recognise anyone?" Bevan asked. He kept his voice light, teasing. When she didn't answer, he added, "From the colour of their hair, perhaps?"

She looked at him quizzically, guilty almost. "Why?" She blinked. "Oh...the hair in the blanket." She gave a shaky laugh. "No...they feel like strangers."

Bevan reached for her hand, thinking it might help. At the last moment, he stopped himself, remembering that boundary again.

"Can we leave now?" Elena asked softly. "I need to get outside. It's been days since..."

"Sure. Let's go."

Bevan led her past the chattering, communing, laughing diners, and out onto the street. They started towards home. "Can we go a different way?" Elena asked. "I need to walk."

"Well, there's only here or the Rhizome."

"The Rhizome will be fine."

This surprised Bevan as the forest could be intimidating at night, but surely she'd know that. "We could see the firebuds if you want," he suggested. "They're pretty."

Elena smiled for the first time in days. "Firebuds?"

Confused by what seemed like ridicule in her tone, Bevan said, "I suppose they originally had a scientific name. Their bioluminescence is derived from firefly DNA. Can you imagine the creators of the Rhizome deciding that Glyrren might want to travel at night? Firebuds burn with heat as well as light. In winter, you can harvest them and use them for warmth."

"I'm not criticizing." Elena looked ahead, took a long deep breath. The Rhizome smelled clean, fresh, more alive than any Olden forest. "I'm even starting to like it here."

They entered the forest along one of the well-marked tracks. "I'm wondering," she said. "Are your councillors planning to keep me here forever?"

Before he could stop himself, Bevan grimaced. "They'll let you go home, but there's a catch."

"What is it?"

Bevan picked up his pace. An owl swooped in front of him, screeched and darted away. "It's difficult. I'm not sure if you're ready to know."

"Shouldn't I be the judge of that?"

"Seriously, you're not ready."

"So in the meantime, I'm meant to stay here and rot until you decide."

He stopped walking. Shushed her. "Look."

"What?"

"There."

The path ahead began to glow faintly. Above them, the treetops sizzled with firebuds.

Elena lifted her face to them. "They're beautiful. Like the Milky Way, only warmer. You know, I've never climbed a tree before, but right now, I want to go up there and find out how warm those firebuds really are."

"Why don't you? You'll be strong enough."

She swivelled to face him, her black hair swishing at her nape. "It's not something I'd normally do."

"Maybe because you haven't had good enough reason. What's in the canopy of an Olden tree anyway? Bugs? A view? But no real prizes...not unless you were hungry and the only fruits were out of reach."

"I wouldn't climb a tree for the last apple. Even if I were starving."

"But you're a pilot. I thought you'd be used to heights."

She laughed. "Heights have nothing to do with it." She stood rocking backwards and forwards on her heels. "It's crazy. I really want to see one up close, but I don't know if it's because I'm curious or because I'm simply compelled by some rogue programme written into me by nants."

Bevan shrugged out of his pullover. "Well, if you want one that badly, wait here and I'll get it."

"No," Elena said. "This is something I need to do. I want to know how it feels."

Bevan pointed out a conifer with well-spaced branches, strong enough to support them both if needed. At first, she pulled herself up hesitantly, but soon gained confidence and climbed like a Glyr.

She reached the buds. "Come on," she called down. "It's beautiful." She hooted, pushed past them and continued up. "It's full of birds up here." She flapped her hands around her head. "You should have warned me about the moths."

Bevan laughed, both with her and at her. He scaled the tree, reaching her near the top where the main trunk fanned out and swayed to a pulse of its own. The firebuds simmered beneath him, strung through the trees like the silvered threads of a tapestry. Above them, the sky glittered with stars.

"You forgot to pick a firebud," Bevan said.

She laughed. "No need. Up here I can feel them through the pores of my skin."

Bevan leaned against the trunk with his eyes closed, drinking in the sounds and smells of the Rhizome, swaying as they surged through him. Vines curled gently around his wrists. He flicked them with his fingers, and they flicked him back. "Hey Rhizome," he muttered. "It's been too many days."

"Argh!" Elena screamed.

She was sitting on the branch above him, her legs straddled either side. She plucked frantically at a vine circling her ankles. "Get it off me. Argh!" The more she struggled, the faster it wrapped around her.

"Hold still," Bevan called up. "It's only playing."

"It's wet."

"It's tasting your nants."

"What do you mean, it's tasting my nants? Wasn't my shuttle enough for it?"

"It won't hurt. It's curious."

Elena tore the vine away, but several more took its place.

"Don't move," Bevan said. "Or else you'll encourage them." He pulled himself up onto the branch beside her, took her hand. "Just sit still. I'm guessing the Rhizome's confused. You probably taste like Wilder because of his nants. And it knows you're an Oldener because only an Oldener would act so damned cowardly."

Elena held still. Bevan felt her fear oozing through the pores of her skin. He dared not send her reassurance. Even scared witless, she'd think he was trying to come on to her.

"It's hideous," she said. A new vine curled along her arm, worked its way inside her sleeve. "It looks like a vegetable, but feels like a warm-blooded fish."

Bevan forced himself not to laugh. "It's not that bad."

"Why isn't it leaving me alone?"

"It will. You're like a new toy."

She wriggled, coughed, squirmed. "The damn thing's crawling down my back. If it doesn't stop soon—" She shuddered. "It's wet. Are you sure it's not trying to digest me?"

"If the Rhizome was capable of that, it would have eaten your cities up decades ago. It doesn't eat living or useful things. Only the dead and discarded."

She tried to stand up. The vines had pinned her to the branch, weaving around her like a net. She gasped, lurched forward. Bevan put his arm around her shoulders and steadied her. If she fell, the vines would keep her from hitting the ground, but they wouldn't stop her from cracking her skull on the way down. Even if her nants did repair her, it wouldn't be pleasant.

Her fear arced through him, so strongly he almost fell himself. "Elena."

She stared at him, eyes wide.

Tentatively he pressed the back of his hand against her cheek. "It won't hurt you."

Her fear would not stop. The Rhizome was feeding on it, he realised. He could either sit and watch her frighten herself nantless, or show her exactly what the Rhizome was trying to do.

Praying that it was the right thing, he sent her a wave of reassurance. "It wants to protect you." Gently, he showed her how it felt to be nurtured as a Glyr.

Her fear dissolved into contentment. Slowly, the vines retracted.

Elena's relief surged through him. He could barely tell where her feelings ended and his began: loneliness layered over trust, curiosity, acceptance, joy. When, one by one, he separated them, he realised that her feelings matched his own in a way that no one had matched him before. He felt Glyrren and Olden all at once.

He felt right.

Before he could stop himself, he reflected her emotions back to her. She shivered with the pleasure of them.

Then she pulled away.

"What in God's name was that?" she said. Her eyes were wide again, shocked.

If Bevan could shrink and scamper into the undergrowth unnoticed, he would have. He hadn't meant to commune with her so deeply, yet when she'd responded to him, he'd forgotten to hold back. "I'm sorry," he said. "I didn't mean..."

She shook her head. "No, don't touch me. I'm not Glyrrish."

He sat on the branch, not daring to move. When she shimmied to the ground, he made no effort to stop her.

Elena stood on the track, catching her breath. So, that's what communing was all about: a closeness—closer than anything she'd ever thought possible. Not so much a sharing of ideas, but a sharing of feelings—a reflection of them—building up like some never-ending wave that could strip her bare if she let it.

No, it wasn't like that at all. It was more like he'd understood her in a way that no one else had ever come close to. It wasn't quite love or even sex, but it was just as beautiful. Even so, it was the sort of thing meant only for people who knew each other. Bevan was a stranger.

She wasn't sure what to do next. Go back to the village? Or run as far away as she could possibly get?

"I'm sorry," Bevan said. He stood nearby with his arms dangling awkwardly at his sides. "For what it's worth, it had to happen. The councillors wouldn't have let you go otherwise. They would have sent me away."

Elena looked at him, agape. "You're telling me this was planned? This was the catch?" If she wasn't so disgusted, she would have laughed. "You should have asked."

"As if I had a choice." He, too, sounded disgusted.

"So what happens if I go now?" she asked. "Will the Rhizome keep wanting to taste me?"

"No. Not unless—"

"Not unless I'm dying?"

"That's how it works."

"Well, that's reassuring." When he did nothing but stare at her, she said, "I know the way back to New Hobart. I've seen it from the sky often enough."

"I..." Bevan looked away. He slipped something from his wrist and proffered it. It was a bracelet plaited out of fleece. "I made this for you."

He looked genuinely distraught. She couldn't bring herself to refuse. She slipped it over her wrist, adjusted the fit by pulling an ingenious, little knot. "Thank you," she said. "Thank you for everything."

He turned to leave, then turned back. "Your camera..."

"Don't worry. Keep it."

He stood looking at her, his hair falling over his eyes making them look both shadowy and vulnerable. "I was hoping we could be friends. I love the Rhizome, but I miss Oldeners." His features softened. "If I hadn't been brought up by them, I would have never understood why you're leaving."

She looked away, determined.

Bevan remained silent. She closed her eyes. The thought of traversing the Rhizome both terrified and intimidated her. The air thrummed with its presence, wrapping her in a tight layer of sound. Beneath it, deeper than flesh and closer, she could sense Bevan's footsteps treading silently away from her, east towards the village.

It took two days to notice that the bracelet Bevan had given her was threaded with hair. Elena held it up in a shaft of light that angled down from the Rhizome canopy. Russet strands were entwined with black.

His hair combined with hers.

It should have annoyed her, but it didn't.

Since leaving the village, the Rhizome had left her alone, just as Bevan said it would. She'd followed a well-used track heading west, slept in hollows, drank sap from bubwood trees and picked fruit she recognised from the meals Bevan had given her from the dining hall. By the end of the third day, she couldn't help but concede that the Rhizome was as comfortable as any Olden city. Even nature wouldn't have cared for her as such.

Normally, a five hundred-kilometre walk would have daunted her but, with her nant-given strength, she guessed she was managing at least forty a day. If the weather held, she'd be home in a little under two weeks. She'd submit herself to a cleansing depot. And then what? Start over?

On her fifth day out, she heard a group of travellers some distance ahead. They were talking loudly in Glyrrish, heading towards the city. Elena was in no mood to explain herself, so she climbed up into the canopy and bypassed them, unnoticed. That night, she heard them from her hollow, talking and laughing. She couldn't understand a word of what they were saying but, curled up in the undergrowth, she felt safe. With growing respect, she realised that the Rhizome had accepted her, despite her not wanting to accept it. She regretted not being able to tell Bevan.

The following evening, the rain started. Water from the canopy gushed down in a frenzy, making the overhead firebuds flicker. She sheltered beneath a thatch of vines and ate a pear.

A rustle came from the canopy ahead. "What have we here?" a woman's voice asked. "An Oldener turned Glyrrish?"

The woman was dressed in Oldener clothes, but her glittering irises and halting Olden marked her as a Glyr. "Are you lost? Or running from something?" she added.

Elena sprang up and faced the woman. "Neither." She tried to think of an excuse that would attract the least number of questions. "I'm an anthropology student," she said. "On a field trip. Survival skills." She held out her hand.

The woman pressed her palm against it. Swiftly, she caught hold of Elena's wrist and studied the bracelet. "Not quite standard issue is it?"

"I found it," Elena said. "On my first day out."

The woman ran her fingers over the fleece. "I suppose you pulled out all that pretty, brown Glyrrish hair, mixed it with your own and wove it back again. Nice try."

Elena shrugged. "What am I supposed to do? Explain a prized possession to a stranger?"

The woman grinned. "Well said." She let go of Elena's wrist. "My name's Maudi. And your nants are looking unusually healthy for an Oldener's." She gestured to her own glittering eyes. "What are you doing out here?"

"To be honest. I don't really know."

"Well at least you don't talk like an Oldener. In fact, I'm guessing you're a pilot."

Elena kept her voice even. "How do you know?"

"Well...it kind of all fits. My friends back there..." She pointed with her thumb to the track behind them. "They're not the most honest of traders. They stopped at a village a few days ago, traded some needles for a strip of salvage. Well, you know yourself how Oldeners get all upset about having their property interfered with.

The bet's on, that when my friends get the salvage to the city, they'll be selling it to the highest bidder. And it won't be just salvage they'll be bartering with, but information as to which village sold it to them." She held Elena's gaze. "You get what I'm saying? A Glyr could lose his nants over it."

"Why are you telling me this?"

"Well, the truth is, my friends aren't really my friends any more." Maudi spat into the Rhizome. "They're Oldener scum."

"They're not Glyrrish?"

Maudi gave a cynical chuckle. "Oh they're Glyrrish alright. Dirty, nantless back-stabbers. If anyone deserved their cleansing, it was them." In the forest light, her face looked haggard. She lifted her hand to Elena's cheek, assailing Elena with an immense sadness and a longing for peace.

It surprised Elena that the intimacy of it did not repulse her. Instead, it reassured her that Maudi could be trusted.

"Look after yourself," Maudi said. "You're one of us." She pulled her hand away, tossed her head, sending out a shower of raindrops. "Well, I'm off. My ex-friends can make their own way back to the city. If I were you, I'd get moving too. You really don't want to meet them." She shimmied up a tree, disappeared in a flurry of wet foliage.

The hollow Elena had chosen for the night no longer felt safe. She climbed the nearest trunk, finding easy purchase in its wetness. Halfway up, she made her way north, neither closer to home nor further from it. When she was sure the travellers wouldn't hear her, she huddled in a dry patch and waited. Firebuds lit the canopy above her, steeping her with warmth.

The rain eased. A vine wriggled towards her. Bevan had said that struggling would only encourage it, so she dared not move, even when it curled itself tentatively around her wrist. She closed her eyes, took long, deep breaths, focussing instead on the patter of raindrops.

As much as she wanted to focus on getting home, she couldn't. Wilder did not deserve a cleansing.

The vine held on to her until sunrise. When it let go, she was glad to be free of it. Yet, at the same time, she felt suddenly deserted. She ran her finger over the bracelet, trying to sense Bevan's presence in the russet hair that circled hers. But that was just myth, she reminded herself. It wasn't his hair that connected them, it was the

Rhizome. The thrum of it thudded in her ears, as much a part of her as her own heartbeat.

She wondered if the rhizome had claimed her. Or maybe, she had claimed it.

She heard the travellers break camp and head west towards New Hobart. She picked a firebud and tucked it in her shirt, where it warmed her skin like a piece of summer. Then, eager to get moving, she made her way to the ground.

It rained the entire eight days it took to retrace her steps to the village. When she arrived at dusk, clutching a firebud that had long since cooled to a pulp, she was drenched to the bone. Bevan's house flickered with candlelight. She stood looking at it, wanting to go in, but not sure how.

She decided to go the dining hall instead and find Wilder. On her way past Bevan's open window, she saw Bevan standing in the living room with a Glyrrish woman. They were communing, not deeply, but enough for Elena to sense that they were more than friends. The woman pressed her forehead against Bevan's. When she lifted her arms to embrace him, her long, blonde hair, fell over his shoulders. Elena stopped walking and tried to make sense of the past weeks, not sure why Bevan had kept the woman's presence a secret. Even though she wanted to, she could not look away.

The communing didn't look like it was ever going to stop. Bevan seemed sad and, at the same time, deeply moved.

Elena wrapped her arms around her chest. Now that she'd cooled down from scrambling through the Rhizome, she was keenly aware of every scrape and bump she'd collected since morning. Tomorrow, her nants would have healed them, but right now she needed only to curl up and forget about everything.

A hand grabbed her shoulder from behind. "What are you doing here?" It was Wilder.

Elena spun around. "The people who gave you the needles," she blurted. "They're traitors."

There. It was said. Now what? Turn back and head for the city? There was nothing else for her here. Nothing and no one.

She pulled away from him, started back towards the Rhizome. She tripped, dropped the firebud and fell. Wilder caught her, steadied her. "Hey, you're not getting away that easily. What's this about traitors?"

Her legs shook. It occurred to her that even nants had their limits. "I'm tired. I can't—"

"You're wet through."

Although she could see no point in going to Bevan's cottage, she did not protest when Wilder led her there. He sat her in an armchair and handed her a mug of warm tea. When the shivering finally stopped, she told him everything. The woman who'd been communing with Bevan watched in attentive silence. She went to Wilder and put her arms around his neck. "Let's feed the salvage to the Rhizome now. It's not worth it."

Wilder nodded grudgingly.

The woman put her forehead to his and the two communed more deeply than Elena had ever seen anyone commune before. Bevan looked flustered, "You'll have to forgive them," he said, "They're worse than teenagers."

Elena blinked. "Wilder and..."

"...Alki. They've been together for years. She's like a guardian to me."

Elena threw back her head and made a poor effort of trying not to laugh. Her cheeks stung. "I thought—"

"I know what you thought." Bevan smiled. His eyes glittered teasingly.

Someone threw a blanket over Elena's shoulders. Alki knelt down in front of her. She touched Elena's cheek and sent her a surge of gratitude, genuine and unmistakeable. Elena settled back into her chair. She closed her eyes and gave into the pure pleasure of it. The blanket smelled of wool, hair and Rhizome. She took Alki's hand and showed her how good it felt to be home again with an entire village wrapped around her.

She no longer cared whether or not the nants made her feel that way. She had already walked away from the village once. If she wanted to, she would do it again.

If she wanted to.

When the soldiers came, Bevan and Elena hid in the tree canopy with Bevan's transfusion equipment coiled up in a hessian bag. The salvage from the shuttle was gone, all trace of it eaten by the Rhizome.

The soldiers searched, found nothing and departed, red faced and apologetic. When the village returned to normal again, Bevan could not shake a deep, uneasy restlessness. The more time he spent with Elena, the more she reminded him of his sister, Georgia.

"Not everyone wants to cleanse Glyrren," Elena said. "Olden loyalties are changing every year. When the city's ready for us, we can go back."

Bevan did not need to commune with Elena to believe that she meant it. But she put her forehead to his and communed with him anyway.

afterword

In 1960, when I arrived in Australia at the age of five, my family's home was built on cleared land west of Sydney. I quickly forgot England's picture book greenness. The nearby bushland seemed no longer mysterious and dangerous, but comforting and familiar. When several years later, it was bulldozed to make way for new houses, I worried about the loss of birds and bandicoots. I listened as the thrum of cicadas became the hiss of overhead power lines. It felt like H.G Wells's War of the Worlds all over. Except, instead of Earth's vegetation being replaced with red weed, bushland was replaced with bricks, mortar and fibro. All for the benefit of people like me.

Forty-something years later, "Deeper than Flesh and Closer" began as part of my honours dissertation, which focussed on postcolonial science fiction. I wanted to write a story from the point of view of a migrant like myself, whose Britishness was sustained by the memories of my parents, and whose Australianness was shaped by everything I experienced elsewhere. As an adult, I consider myself belonging to both cultures. My Australianness, however, came with the realisation that my home was not gifted to me, but taken from people whose culture had long since been decimated.

I started "Deeper than Flesh" while sitting in the shade of eucalypts. It began with this thought: five thousand years ago, Australians had never seen bulldozers or power lines. What might they see five thousand years from now?

I would like to thank Professor Van Ikin, whose advice and encouragement kept me going with this story. And also the Katherine Susannah Prichard SF Writer's group, who willingly critique my stories, even when they exceed 11,000 words.

About the contributors

KURT BACHARD lives in South London, UK, where he was raised as a feral child by stray dogs. His fiction (which has been nominated for the Pushcart Prize) and non-fiction has appeared in numerous publications online and in print, notably in multiple issues of the Black Quill nominated *Shroud* Magazine. He also writes under several pseudonyms.

GUSTAVO BONDONI was born in Argentina, which, he believes, makes him one of the few — if not the only — Argentinean fiction writers writing primarily in English. He moved to the US at the age of three because his father worked for a multinational company that bounced him around the world every three years. Miami, Zurich, Cincinnati. He only made it back to Buenos Aires at the age of twelve, by which time he was not quite an American kid, not quite a European kid, and definitely not Argentinean! His fiction spans the range from science fiction to mainstream stories, passing through sword & sorcery and magic realism along the way, and it has been published in five countries and two languages to date. You can find him online at www.gustavobondoni.com.ar .

STEPHANIE BURGIS's family emigrated to America from various countries across Europe, including Croatia. She lives in Wales now with her husband, son, and border collie, and is a dual American-British citizen. Her historical fantasy trilogy for 10- to 15-year-olds, The Unladylike Adventures of Kat Stephenson, is being published in the US and UK, starting with *A Most Improper Magick* in

2010. Her short fiction has appeared in several magazines and anthologies. To find out more, or to read more of her published stories, please visit her website: www.stephanieburgis.com.

LINDA L. DONAHUE, an Air Force brat, spent her childhood traveling. Having a pilot's certification and a SCUBA certification, she has been, at one time or another, a threat by land, air or sea. For 18 years she taught computer science and mathematics. Currently, she teaches tai chi and belly dance. Linda has published some twenty stories in anthologies, including *Sword & Sorceress* 23 and *Strip Mauled*, edited by Esther Freisner. Her novel, *Jaguar Moon* is available from Yard Dog Press. Linda and her husband live in Texas and keep rabbits, sugar gliders and cats for pets. www.lindaldonahue.com

ZDRAVKA EVTIMOVA was born in Bulgaria, where she works as a literary translator. Her short story collection *Bitter Sky* was published in 2003 in UK by Skrev Press. Her collection "Somebody Else" was published by MAG Press, San Diego, USA in 2004. Her novel *God of Traitors* was published in USA by Books for a Buck Publishers in 2006. Her collection *Miss Daniella* was published by Skrev Press, UK, in 2007. Her collection *Pale* was published by Vox Humana publishers in Israel and Canada 2010. Her short stories have appeared in the USA, UK, Canada, Australia, France, Germany, Turkey, Poland, Japan, Spain, Argentina and in some other countries of the European Union. Three of her short stories were broadcast on Radio 4 BBC. Zdravka has won awards in the Radio BBC world short story competition in 2005, in the Utopia worldwide short story competition Nantes 2005, France, and in the Lege Artis short story competition in Leipzig, Germany, 2000 with her short story "200 000".

With his wife and cats, CHET GOTTFRIED lives in a townhouse at Cooper's Pond (State College, Pennsylvania, USA), directly opposite a game land, which means easy access for hiking and photography (while dodging bullets). Chet is an active member of SFWA, and his publications range from JBU to Read Before Dawn, a mix of science fiction, fantasy, and horror. He also has one novel, *The Steel Eye*, published by Space & Time.

EDWINA HARVEY is a writer and editor, silk painter and ceramic artist. She regularly edits the Australian Science Fiction *Bullsheet*, and is a member of the *Andromeda Spaceways Inflight Magazine* publishing co-operative. Her first YA SF novel, *The Whale's Tale*, was published late last year by Peggy Bright Books. Her silk and ceramic art can be viewed and purchased at www.celestialcobbler. com Edwina claims a severe allergy to housework gives her time to pursue her creative endeavours.

DONNA MAREE HANSON resides in Queanbeyan, NSW. Her short fiction appears in various places including anthologies: *Machinations*, *Elsewhere* and *Masques* by CSFG Publishing; magazines: *Redsine* and *Potato Monkey*; and ezines. Donna co-edited the CSFG anthology *Encounters* (2005) and edited *The Grinding House* (CSFG 2005) by Kaaron Warren. Under her own imprint, Donna produced *Australian Speculative Fiction-A Genre Overview* (ASF 2005) and *Johnny Phillips-Werewolf Detective* (ASF 2008) by Robbie Matthews, which was short listed for best collection in the 2009 Aurealis Awards. Donna usually concentrates her efforts on novel length manuscripts, one of which gained her a fellowship at Varuna Writers House.

SONIA HELBIG was born in Queensland, has lived in Melbourne, Adelaide and outback New South Wales, but she belongs in Perth, Western Australia. She feels connected to Perth and its people. She wouldn't give up the woodlands and swamplands, the Indian Ocean with its kilometres of white beaches, nor the relaxed lifestyle she shares with friends, family, and children for anything. Sonia's fiction, poetry and articles have appeared in places like *Island* literary magazine, *The School Magazine, The West Australian,* and the *Writers of the Future* XXIV anthology. She's currently working on a children's environmental fantasy series.

GEORGE IVANOFF in an author and stay-at-home Dad residing in Melbourne. He makes a meager (but happy) living out of writing books for kids and teenagers. He occasionally decides to earn even less money by writing for grown-ups. His latest novel is the teen science fiction adventure, *Gamers' Quest* (Ford Street Publishing). Check out the official website: www.gamersquestbook.com And

while you're web-surfing, check out George's website: www.
georgeivanoff.com.au

PATTY JANSEN lives Sydney with her husband and three teenage
children. After having worked in science, having written non-
fiction and edited non-fiction magazines, she decided to embark on
a new challenge and life-long interest: to write science fiction and
fantasy. Her stories will appear in *Andromeda Spaceways Inflight
Magazine* #46 and *Midnight Echo* #4.

PENELOPE LOVE works in university administration and lives in
Melbourne, Australia, with her partner and no zombies.

MARY E. LOWD lives in the Pacific Northwest of the United States
with her husband Daniel, daughter Elaine, and a plethora of pets.
Her house is populated with dogs and cats; her yard is populated
with dogwoods and pussy willows. These populations are where
she finds much of her inspiration. Mary's time is unevenly divided
between raising her two-year-old daughter and writing. You can
find links to more of her stories at: www.marylowd.com.

JENNIFER MOORE's writing has appeared in a number of publications
in both the UK and the US, including *The Guardian*, *Mslexia*,
The First Line and *Short Fiction*. "United" is the first piece to be
published in Australia. She was the winner of the Commonwealth
Short Story Competition 2009 and lives in Devon, England.

MICHELLE MUENZLER was born in the broken pines of East Texas
where she fought boys with her concrete-sharpened pine spears
and mastered squeezing through rabbit trails for quick escapes
in the games of childhood war. Her short fiction can be found
in magazines such as *Electric Velocipede*, *Shroud Magazine*, and
Coyote Wild.

SIMON PETRIE is a researcher at an Australian university. His fiction
has sprouted in various outlets, including *Andromeda Spaceways
Inflight Magazine*, *Aurealis*, *ticon4*, *Kaleidotrope*, *Semaphore
Magazine*, and *Sybil's Garage*. His first short-fiction collection,
Rare Unsigned Copy: tales of Rocketry, Ineptitude, and Giant

Mutant Vegetables (its cover illustration depicts a scene from "The Ballad of P'toresk") is out now from Peggy Bright Books.

ANGIE REGA's fiction has appeared or is forthcoming in Drollerie Press, *Cezanne's Carrot*, *Mytholog* and Twelfth Planet Press. She is a lover of folklore, fairy tales and furry creatures and currently works as a school librarian. She is a graduate of the Clarion South workshop and is currently working on a YA novel.

BARBARA ROBSON wrote a few stories several years ago, took a long break, and then wrote two stories for anthologies with themes that inspired her. The first of these was "Mrs Estahazi". The second, "Neighbourhood Watch" will appear in *Sprawl*, a Twelfth Planet Press anthology edited by Alisa Krasnostein.

BARRY ROSENBERG was born in London in 1943. Completing a Ph.D. in Artificial Intelligence, in 1970 he joined CSIRO in Canberra. Left in 1974 to practise meditation and tai chi. In 1986, joined the Australian Public Service but resigned in 1992 to do craftwork. In 2009, Barry's sculptures won places in two local competitions. He has been involved with creative writing since 1974. Since 2008, Barry has been very active in submitting stories and have had quite a few successes. He lives with his wife, Judith, in Nambour on the Sunshine Coast, Queensland.

CAROL RYLES has spent twelve years trying to think of a suitable pen name. Meanwhile, she has published eleven short stories in various small press magazines, including *Eidolon* 1 Anthology. She has worked for fifteen years as a registered nurse, including a three-year stint in China. She now has a BA in English with first class honours and is a graduate of Clarion West 2008. When not hiking in wild places, or keeping house as a stay-at-home mum, she is writing her first novel as part of her PhD, focusing on steampunk. Carol blogs at egoboo-wa.blogspot.com/

KYLIE SELUKA has had some short stories published such as in the anthologies: *Fantastic Wonder Stories*, *Daikaiju* 2 and *The Outcast*. She is now living in New Zealand and hopes to get back into some serious writing after a year of significant changes.

SARAH TOTTON is a wildlife biologist who developed an allergy to intermittent unemployment and so became a veterinarian. She has worked in England as a zookeeper and in India with stray dogs as part of a spay/neuter/anti-rabies program. She also spent a year radio-tracking raccoons in the hinterlands of eastern Ontario. Her short fiction has appeared in *Andromeda Spaceways Inflight Magazine* #33, *Dog Versus Sandwich*, *Writers of the Future* XXII and the UK's *Black Static*. She was the Regional Winner (for Canada & the Caribbean) in the 2007 Commonwealth Short Story Competition.

GWEN VEAZEY lives in the foothills of the Blue Ridge Mountains in North Carolina, USA. Her stories and articles have appeared in *The Charlotte Observer*, *Charlotte's Creative Loafing*, and the 2008 anthology, *Killers*. Her poetry has appeared in *Aoife's Kiss*. She writes regular columns for her local newspaper.

Acknowledgements

"Border Crossing" copyright © 2010 Penelope Love.
"Mrs Estahazi" copyright © 2010 Barbara Robson.
"Norumbega" copyright © 2010 Linda L. Donahue.
"Ice" copyright © 2010 Zdravka Evtimova.
"United" copyright © 2010 Jennifer Moore.
"Rekindle the Sun" copyright © 2010 Mary E. Lowd.
"The Gift" copyright © 2010 Barry Rosenberg.
"Prisoner of the Faceless" copyright © 2010 Kurt Bachard.
"Merpeople" copyright © 2010 Gwen Veazey.
"Feather-light" copyright © 2010 George Ivanoff.
"Speaking English" copyright © 2010 Stephanie Burgis.
"Green, Green Grass of Homeworld" copyright © 2010 Donna
    Maree Hanson.
"I Belong to this Red Land" copyright © 2010 Edwina Harvey.
"All Tales Must End" copyright © 2010 Michelle Muenzler.
"Namug" copyright © 2010 Gustavo Bondoni.
"Song of the Blackbird" copyright © 2010 Sarah Totton.
"A Friendly Gesture" copyright © 2010 Chet Gottfried.
"Initiation" copyright © 2010 Sonia Helbig.
"Slow Cookin'" copyright © 2010 Angela Rega.
"The Ballad of P'toresk" copyright © 2010 Simon Petrie. Appears
    simultaneously here and in *Rare Unsigned Copy: tales of Rocketry,
    Ineptitude, and Giant Mutant Vegetables*, Peggy Bright Books.
"The Hollow Ones" copyright © 2010 Kylie Seluka.
"Trassi Udang" copyright © 2010 Patty Jansen.
"Deeper than Flesh and Closer" copyright © 2010 Carol Ryles.

*All stories appear here for the first time, except as otherwise
noted. All rights reserved. Story afterwords copyright © 2010
their respective authors.*

ACKNOWLEDGEMENTS

The editor would like to thank Elizabeth Grzyb,
Kurt Bachard, Gustavo Bondoni, Stephanie
Burgis, Linda Donahue, Zdravka Evtimova,
Chet Gottfried, Donna Maree Hanson,
Edwina Harvey, Sonia Helbig, George Ivanoff,
Patty Jansen, Penelope Love, Mary E. Lowd,
Jennifer Moore, Michelle Muenzler, Simon Petrie,
Angela Rega, Barbara Robson, Barry Rosenberg,
Carol Ryles, Kylie Seluka, Sarah Totton, Gwen
Veazey, Terry Dowling, Simon Brown, Jonathan
Strahan, Peter McNamara, Ellen Datlow,
Grant Stone, Jeremy G. Byrne, Sean Williams,
Garth Nix, David Cake, Simon Oxwell,
Grant Watson, Sue Manning, Steven Utley,
Bill Congreve, Jack Dann, Stephen Dedman,
the Mt Lawley Mafia, the Nedlands Yakuza,
Shane Jiraiya Cummings, Angela Challis,
Donna Maree Hanson, Kate Williams, Kathryn
Linge, Andrew Williams, Al Chan, Alisa
Krasnostein, everyone I've missed ...

... and *you*.